Dedicated to Raphael,
both my father and my son,
and to my lovely wife, Julia,
who bridged the gap.

CONTENTS

FOREWORD

Having caught the bug of writing (and it *is* a kind of illness) and seen Murder In Absentia receive a modicum of success, there was nothing left for me to do but write a new Felix adventure.

The idea for this novel (and for several others) came to me while I was still editing and publishing MIA. It took me some time to do the research, write drafts, edit – and then go through more rounds of feedback and professional editing, but I got there in the end.

My thanks go to my wife, Julia (who can only read my stories during daylight, but doesn't let it stop her from urging me to keep writing), and to my editor, Nikki B Williams (who whipped the manuscript — and me — into much better shape). Special thanks also go to my sister and her husband, Ramit Mehr and Eric Klein, for their support and input to the world of Felix. Last but not least, my thanks to Ruth Downie, for letting me borrow Gaius Petreius Ruso when Felix needed a healer.

I would also like to thank my beta readers, who took the time to read and comment on early drafts of the novel: Bonnie Milani, Brent Harris, Stephanie Barr, Rebecca Norman, Kelly Philips, Kayla Matt, Judy L Mohr, Jane Jago, Jacqueline Patterson, India Emerald, Erin Michelle Sky, CC Dowling, Brandi Trimm, Bethany Dickens, Stacie Tyson, Nick Bagrationi, Chesnaye Long, Fuchsia (Aurelia) Carter, and Anaïs Chartschenko. Thank you all for suffering through my early drafts and helping me improve my writing.

Thank you also to all he dedicated fans of Felix, who kept encouraging me with demands for his next adventure. I hope you enjoy reading this novel as much as I did writing it.

Videas lumen!

Assaph Mehr
July 2018
Sydney, Australia

MAPS

High-resolution maps — as well as an expanded glossary, short stories, and more — can be found at **www.egretia.com**.

EGRETIA

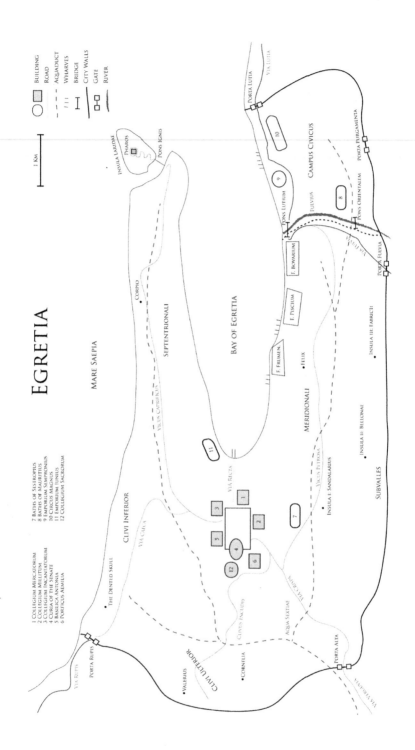

Legend:
- ○ □ BUILDING
- – – – ROAD
- AQUADUCT
- ┬┬┬ WHARVES
- ╫ BRIDGE
- ▫▫ CITY WALLS
- ▫ GATE
- ～～ RIVER

1 KM

1 COLLEGIUM MERCATORUM
2 COLLEGIUM MILITUM
3 COLLEGIUM INCANTATORUM
4 CURIA OF THE SENATE
5 BASILICA ANTONIA
6 PORTICUS AEMILIA

7 BATHS OF SESTROPIUS
8 BATHS OF MAURITHIUS
9 EMPORIUM SAMPIONALIS
10 CIRCUS MAGNUS
11 EMPORIUM IUNIUS
12 COLLEGIUM SACRORUM

MARE SAEPIA

BAY OF EGRETIA

SEPTENTRIONALI

MERIDIONALI

SUBVALLES

CAMPUS CIVICUS

CLIVI INFERIOR

CLIVI ULTERIOR

THE DENTED SKULL

INSULA LARIDAE
PHAROS
PONS IGNIS

CORPIO

FULVIUS

PONS LUTIUM
PONS ORIENTALEM
PONS FULVIA

F. BOVARIUM
F. PISCIUM
F. FRUMEN
FELIX

INSULA III: FABRICI
INSULA II: BELLONAE
INSULA I: SANDALARIUS

VICUS PATRONA

VIA RECTA
VIA GLICA
VIA LATA

AQUA SEXTIAE
CLIVUS INCLITUS
CORNELIA
VALERIUS

VIA RUBIUS
PORTA RUFIS

PORTA ALTA
MATERA VIA

PORTA LUTIA
VIA LUTIA

PORTA PERGAMENTA
PORTA FULVIA

ASSAPH MEHR

IN NUMINA

PURPLE TOGA PUBLICATIONS

Published by Purple Toga Publications, Sydney, Australia.

ISBN 978-0-9944493-4-4

3nd printing

A catalogue record for this book is available from the National Library of Australia

EGRETIA – COUNTRYSIDE

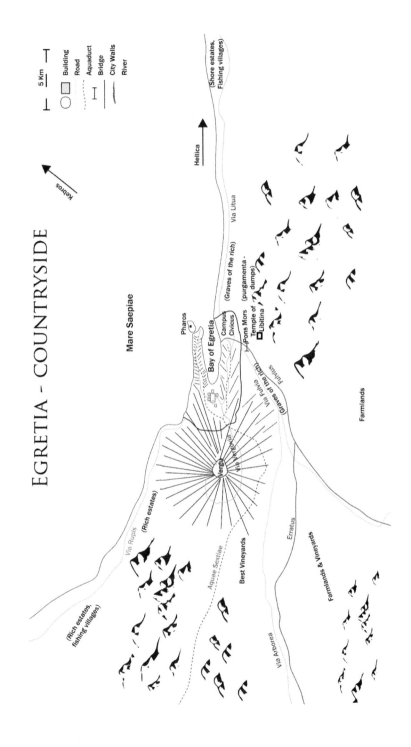

Mare Saepiae

Bay of Egretia

Pharos

Campus Civicus

Pons Mors

Temple of Libitina

(purgamenta – dumps)

(Graves of the rich)

Via Litua

Hellica

(Shore estates, Fishing villages)

Farmlands

Verge

Via Vectiana

Via Fulvia

(Graves of the rich)

Futilus

Aquae Sextiae

Best Vineyards

Via Rupis

(Rich estates)

(Rich estates, fishing villages)

Via Arborea

Erratus

Farmlands & Vineyards

Kebros

5 Km

Building
Road
Aqueduct
Bridge
City Walls
River

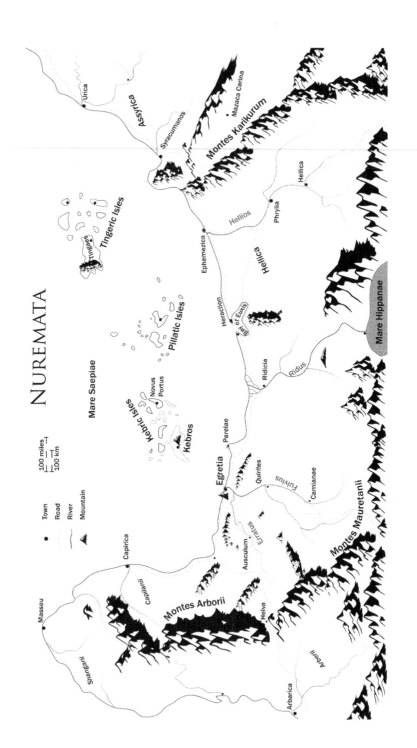

NUREMATA

Town
Road
River
Mountain

100 miles
100 km

Mare Saepiae

Massau

Shangarii

Capirica

Capilanii

Montes Arborii

Ausculum

Egretus

Helva

Arborii

Arbarica

Egretia

Parelae

Quirites

Fulvius

Camianae

Montes Mauretanii

Ridicia

Ridus

Kebric Isles

Novus Portus

Kebros

Pillatic Isles

Heraclion

Bay of Eutis

Ephemezica

Hellios

Heraclion

Hellica

Phrylia

Hellica

Helica

Mare Hippanae

Tingeric Isles

Tingaes

Assyrica

Urica

Syracumanos

Montes Karikurum

Mazaca Carina

SCROLL I - INSULAE

CHAPTER I

Summer's heat was inescapable, though not for lack of trying. I was lying in my loincloth in my garden fountain, letting the madly leering faun spray the waters from his erect member on me. These waters came from the Aqua Sextiae, the aqueduct that brought a fresh supply to Egretia from the six sacred springs in far-off mountains. The waters were fresh and cool at their source but travelled many miles to reach our city. After flowing all that distance under the brutal Sextilis sun and soaking its heat, the stream from the faun's prodigious member felt truly authentic.

Somewhere out on the Vicus Petrosa, the main thoroughfare that ran along the ridge of the hill where my house sat, I heard a religious procession. Priests played the double flutes and banged on cymbals and drums. A bull was lowing, being led from outside the city to be sacrificed in front of some temple. My hazy mind recalled this must be the annual sacrifice to Sol Indiges. I hoped that the sacrifice would propitiate the god and that he would take his orb of fire under control and stop baking our city in its merciless heat.

I had given up all pretence of doing anything useful during the long summer days. The last bit of work I had done was to put up a sailcloth above the garden to block the sun, since there was no breeze to speak of. This was almost five weeks ago. I had not done a single day of honest work — or a night of dishonest work, for that matter — since. Business had evaporated, as all prospective employers had taken their money with them somewhere cooler. I planned to spend the last of my cash on drinks with my friend Crassitius that night and see whether he had any jobs for a desperate man. I just hoped he wouldn't send me down the sewers to chase monsters again.

Dascha came shuffling into the courtyard. "Young *domine*," she said, using the title reserved for disapproving of my actions, "there's someone here for you."

"Show him to my study — and bring us some water and wine while I get dressed."

A few minutes later, still damp but dressed in a light tunic, I entered my study to find a messenger boy, who silently handed me a sealed wax tablet. So much for my excuse for wine.

"Who sent you?" I asked as I inspected the seal, which bore the emblem of a aurochs.

The boy answered promptly. "My master is Lucius Valerius Flaccus."

That was promising. The Valerii are one of the richest and most powerful families in Egretia. Of course, it meant I would have to wear a toga, which in this weather meant I might not survive the walk to his house. Better read the message.

I broke the seal.

To Spurius Vulpius Felix from Lucius Valerius Flaccus, greetings.

I find myself in need of special services, and your name has been brought to my attention by my cousin Cornelia Rufina and her daughter Aemilia. I wish to discuss a matter in confidence, and therefore invite you to my house for a private interview tomorrow afternoon in the tenth hour of the day.

Please erase this message after you have read it and indicate your acceptance in reply.

Well, *that* was unexpected.

Aemilia was a young shrew who tried to upstage my investigation of her cousin's murder, got tangled with the wrong crowd, and almost died. She was intelligent, if rather snooty, and not particularly wise.

Pretty, though. Occupied a few of my naughty dreams, but then so did her mother with whom I did have an affair. While we all parted on good terms, I did not expect to hear from either again, and I certainly did not expect a recommendation. This could only mean one thing, I thought as I smoothed out the wax with my palm and wrote my acceptance of the invitation. Someone had run afoul of something smelling of bad *magia* and wished to keep it away from the authorities.

***

I was waiting in the vestibule of Valerius Flaccus' *domus*, high up on the Clivi Ulterior. This was the richest part of the city, where only the elite of the *nobilitas* — those families with old money going back centuries — could afford a house. And the Valerii were just such a family, with consuls, censors, and *rhones* going back to the founding of our city.

It had taken me a long summer hour of climbing from where I live on the Meridionali. Considering the day's heat, I had elected to forgo a toga for the trek up the hill. Instead I wore my best tunic — the one least patched and stained. I had stopped on the way to refresh myself at a public fountain, and thus had managed to arrive in something resembling dignity.

While waiting in Valerius' atrium, I gazed at the impeccable decor. In one corner, a marble-panelled alcove housed the statues of the *lares* and *di penates* of the Valerii. The altar before them was discoloured by old wine, and a few crumbs remained from the morning's offering of a salt cake. As my gaze wandered up, I noted the *imagines* of Valerius' forefathers mounted on all four walls. Being an illustrious family with roots reaching further than the establishment of our city, there was a great number of those beeswax masks. Those austere countenances of Valerius Flaccus' ancestors peered gravely at waiting visitors, reminding them of the greatness of the house they were about to enter.

Eventually, a slave arrived to guide me through the

domus. It was more of a mansion than a house, spread on the steep inclines of Vergu. We passed through several atria and impressively large peristyle gardens, with many corridors and rooms branching off into the private areas of the mansion.

We reached a loggia that stretched around a corner, offering spectacular views down to the Bay of Egretia. From this high vantage point I saw, as if in miniature, the impressive public buildings around the Forum, the many terracotta roofs and small gardens on the two hills on the sides of the bay, and, far off, the Insula Laridae with the ever-shining Pharos lighthouse.

We neared the corner of the colonnade and soft voices drifted on the sultry air. The view shifted to the open seas, dazzling as the westering sun reflected on far-off white-capped waves. Against this backdrop, a man and two women chatted around an exquisite chryselephantine table.

The women were more dazzling than the view, and even more beautiful than I remembered them. Cornelia and her daughter Aemilia, both dark-haired, grey-eyed, fair-skinned, and as beautiful as twin Hellican statues of Aphrodite. The man, whom I presumed to be Valerius Flaccus, was in his forties and bore the characteristic fine features of that noble family — light brown hair arranged in locks around a high-cheekboned face with a slightly bumpy nose set above thin lips.

"Felix, good of you to come," said Flaccus. "I believe you know Cornelia and Aemilia." The women smiled at me as I sat, and I happily returned the smiles. Both women were wearing light *stolas* that left their arms bare, accentuating their enticing figures.

"Wine?" offered Flaccus. "It's from my private estates on the foothills of Vergu." He poured the dark purple liquid into a glass goblet and added water from a silver pitcher.

I picked the glass up and flinched — it was ice cold. Flaccus chuckled. "I have my kitchen supplied with ice blocks all summer. There is an *incantator* in town that specialises in it. Makes life in the Egretian heat much more civilised."

We continued to discuss the weather and ways to combat it for a short while. Valerius Flaccus was a politician from a noble family — small talk with charm and grace on any subject came naturally to him. I didn't mind. I was sure he would get to my commission in time. Meanwhile, I got to enjoy the view, the wine, and the company.

Especially the company. What happened between us on the boat trip back from Kebros two months ago must have met with Cornelia's approval, for her leg brushed against mine under the table a bit too often to be merely accidental.

Sadly, I didn't get to enjoy it for long. "Cousins Cornelia and Aemilia have told me about your work following the death of young Caeso Quinctius," said Flaccus. "It seems I am now facing a situation that may benefit from the skills of someone with your background. This matter could turn out to be mundane — or not. I need someone who can handle either." He paused, and I savoured my wine while I waited for him to organise his thoughts and continue.

"Am I correct in assuming you are aware of the business restrictions on senators? I cannot actively participate in businesses except those involving land ownership. I own interests in several enterprises, but always as a silent partner — a mere shareholder. My main business is property — from *latifundia* farms to the far south and east, to *insulae* here in Egretia. And it's here in the *insulae* where the problem lies." He paused, sipping his wine thoughtfully.

"As any landlord will tell you," Flaccus continued, "tenants come and go. There is nothing unusual about it. Properties are never fully occupied. But recently, it seems, more residents in my *insulae* are leaving rather than staying. At first, it was dismissed as a bad season. But over the days and weeks — and it has been going on since spring, I should say — it has become a real issue. My agent now reports he cannot get new tenants, even for disastrously low rents."

"Is this the situation with all your *insulae*?" I asked.

"It started with the low-class tenements," replied Flaccus. "The ones in the Subvales. Those are usually always full, even the ten-storey buildings. Our city never seems to run out of the poor and miserable who need housing. But, it turns out, those tenements were just the first to be affected. I have other *insulae* scattered all around town, varying in elegance in relation to their location and size. Some of my better holdings are here on the upper slopes — sumptuous apartments for discerning clientele." He leaned toward me conspiratorially, "You would be surprised at how many of the rich still require a discreet and private place away from their main home." He sat back, a grave expression on his face. "My fear is that this problem is starting to spread out of the Subvales."

I doubted Valerius could tell me anything about housing arrangements of the rich that would surprise me, but I've always held myself a cynic. "And why me, then?" I asked instead.

"I need this issue resolved while it only affects my lower-class holdings, before it reaches the ears of the people who matter. I have made some enquiries, you see, quizzed my agent and had him ask the residents. It seems the reason I can't find new tenants, why the old ones are leaving, is, well… word on the street is that my properties are haunted!"

That sounded like my kind of business. It also explained why Cornelia and Aemilia recommended my services. The experiences we shared over the death of Aemilia's cousin Caeso Quinctius were the best calling card I had — and indeed it seemed I was beginning to attract a better class of employers than was my usual wont.

As for the matter at hand, although I have dealt with a few real shades of the dead in the past — never a pleasant encounter — I fully expected this to be some kind of elaborate hoax. These things often are.

Out loud, I said, "I would be happy to assist you in this matter. I have a modicum of experience with such, and I'm sure I can find the root cause of your troubles to your satisfaction. To do so, I will need a list of the affected properties, the name of your agent who deals with them, and letters of introduction to ensure I get his and the tenants' cooperation. I will get started right away."

Aemilia coughed lightly, and Valerius Flaccus shifted in his chair. "Oh, do go on," said Cornelia. "We discussed this, and you know I have given my consent."

"It seems…," he began. "It seems cousin Aemilia has some reservations regarding her recommendation of you." I glanced at her, and she flashed me the sweetest smile — which I trusted not at all.

"The last time you worked together," Flaccus continued, "there was some business of hoodwinking the governor of the Kebric Isles. Now, I understand there was an issue with national security," he added hastily, "and that you never betrayed your employer's trust. However, Aemilia has had very fine education in her youth, and…"

"And she would be verifying my reports?" I said. "Don't worry, I am sure —"

"Not quite," Flaccus cut me off. "She'll be accompanying you during your investigations."

I was dumbstruck. Aemilia was still smiling sweetly, although there was a mischievous twinkle in her eyes. The corner of Cornelia's lips turned up, and she could barely contain her giggles.

As soon as I found my tongue, I protested. "This is most unusual, not to mention quite risky! I will not be able to speak freely to informants, my work often starts at dawn and carries through the night, I may have to chase leads to very unseemly places — even downright unwholesome one — and we all know that danger and violence can spring at any moment. We've seen it with Caeso's death. I mean, Aemilia was kidnapped and almost sacrificed! And what about prospective husbands? Should word of this leak, the young lady will never be able to find a suitable match."

"Come now," interjected Cornelia, still smiling. "Your concern for her is touching, but why don't you leave it to me to worry about her matrimonial future? We could supply you with bodyguards if necessary, and I am sure that you could think of a dozen ways to work her into your investigation without raising suspicion. I will, of course, expect you to personally return her safe and sound to our house every night." That last pronouncement was accompanied by a definite brush of her foot against my leg.

"Well," I said weakly, "if you insist. It seems I am left with no choice in the matter."

CHAPTER II

Night gave up the ghost under the onslaught of the rising sun. I rose before first light and by the time the sun was over the horizon the water in my garden fountain was already getting warm. Lighting a stick of incense and performing the morning placation of my ancestors came first, even before a hasty breakfast of bread dipped in wine. I donned my lightest tunic and a broad hat and coated the straps of my sandals with some olive oil to minimise the inevitable chafing of a long day of walking under the merciless sun.

Our plan for the day was simple.

Aemilia would take me to meet Flaccus' agent, and then we'd visit the *insulae*. Cornelia realised any attempt to constrain her daughter was likely to fail, so they reached a compromise together with Flaccus. Aemilia would take part in the investigation under me but would defer to my judgement if I deemed a task too dangerous for a young lady. I was to update Cornelia as well as Valerius Flaccus with daily progress and plans. Thus, Valerius would be assured an honest and speedy service, Aemilia was to enjoy a safe taste of a side of life normally forbidden her, and Cornelia would remain involved in the matter to satisfy both her curiosity and need to feel relevant.

Of course, they reached this agreement without asking me for my opinion.

I met Aemilia on the Via Crispa under the shade of the Aqua Sextiae aqueduct. For me, this meant a walk across the length of the Meridionali on the avenue that runs on the ridge

10

of that southern arm of the bay. For Aemilia, it was an easy stroll from the heights of Vergu, where her family had their *domus*. We trod the same mountain yet came from very different neighbourhoods and lifestyles.

Even so, as I lifted my gaze from the fountain where I was refreshing myself and caught sight of her, my misgivings were mollified. Of average height and a youthful slender build, dark hair pinned up both fashionably and sensibly, she was wearing a fetching aquamarine *stola*. Her smile widened and reached her large, luminous grey eyes.

"*Ave*, Aemilia," I said. Behind her were her slave girl and a burly type, no doubt a competent bodyguard assigned by her mother.

"*Salve*, Felix. We don't have far to go to meet Decimus Aburius. His offices are just on the other side of the ridge."

The part of the city where we met, around the Via Crispa between the Forum and the Porta Alta, is the temple district of Egretia. Many edifices, some old and humble, others new and magnificent, cluster along the road that leads from the heart of the city to the sacred heights of Mount Vergu, and forms part of the triumphal procession route. As we walked eastward, the scenery changed into residences and local businesses. On the ridge and the north side, leading down towards the waters of the Bay of Egretia, the houses were modest but respectable. Down the south side, however, once one is no longer benefiting from the fresh sea breezes, are the Subvales — cheap, crowded, smelly, and over-populated with the less fortunate. Valerius Flaccus' affected properties were there, and his agent Aburius kept offices close by.

We chatted idly as we walked. She told me of her life in those past few weeks; of how the experience we shared last had changed her, intensifying her resolve to be her own person rather than submit to the cultural expectations of women. I was mildly surprised, as I expected near death to scare her into good behaviour rather than encourage rebellion. Yet, at the same time, I was glad to hear it — to know that the spark of her personality was not extinguished despite the harrowing experience.

In turn, I regaled her with the story of the philosopher Athenodorus. When he found a house for sale at a suspiciously low price, he enquired and was told the house was haunted. He bought it anyway, as he wished to see the ghost. To keep himself up at night so he could observe any apparitions, he dragged a table outside and worked on his philosophical treatise. He was so engrossed in his work, that when the ghost first came and rattled its chains at him, he shushed it so he could keep working.

Aemilia laughed at this, but the walk was short and I didn't get to tell her the end. A lot more than that was left unsaid — things I wished to know about her, stories I wanted to tell her — leaving a strong desire to keep talking.

*** *

Aburius' offices were on the ground floor of one of Flac- cus' *insulae* that was still fully occupied, seemingly unaffected by whatever troubled the other properties. His suite was composed of two rooms, the front one arranged as a large open space with tables for scribes and clerks on the right and couches for loiter- ing ex-gladiator-types on the left. This dual set of employees let Decimus Aburius know who owed what rent and to collect it efficiently.

We met the man himself in his private office at the back. He was of average height, with good teeth and good hair, yet somehow smarmy and oily in demeanour — a classic landlord's agent. Flashing us a shiny smile, he urged us to sit, saying, "Look- ing for a new place? I have everything a nice young couple like you will need — from an affordable private *domus* fit for raising a family to a quiet apartment for discreet meetings. Just tell Deci- mus what you need and he will guarantee your satisfaction!"

"Why, yes," I said, on a spur-of-the-moment decision, "that is exactly what we are after. We need a discreet apartment, as you put it."

"Preferably in an *insula* not fully occupied," added Aemil- ia. "We would appreciate as few neighbours as possible." The girl was sharp, I'll give her that.

Aburius quickly gauged our ability to pay and said, "Oh, I think I know just the place. A nice place, not too many floors, half-way from here to the Forum, yet the entry is located on a side street with little traffic. Just the thing for a prudent couple."

As this wasn't one of the properties on the list Flaccus gave us, I said, "My darling and I passed an *insula* we liked the other day and were told you were the agent. It's on the Vicus Sandalarius, in the upper Subvales. Appears to be practically empty."

His face barely registered a pause. "Why, yes, I know the building you are referring to. Would you like to sign a lease? It has a choice of available apartments at the moment, from ground floor with a garden, to first floor suites, to upper level cosy units but with good airs and views. Just tell me what you are after and I can have the rental contract ready while you wait."

"Oh, *meum mel*, I'd really like to see it before I settle. You know me," Aemilia said to me.

I tried hard not to look into her eyes lest I break out in laughter at the way she called me 'honey'. "Of course, *cara*, of course." I turned to Aburius. "As the lady says, perhaps we could go right now? It's not far."

"Oh, but I thought you already saw the property? I can vouchsafe that everything is in perfect order."

"We only saw it from the outside. We wish to see the various offerings there. If all is well, we could sign today — but we really would prefer to take a peek inside."

The agent tried his best to get us to sign first — on that or any other *insula* — but we persevered. A quarter of an hour later we compromised on going there and signing on the spot if we liked it. He called for one of his scribes and two guards, and we set out to view the haunted apartment blocks.

***

Of Flaccus' list of affected *insulae*, two were at the slopes of the Subvales. These weren't quite the worst parts next to the walls, but that was nary a redeemable quality. Both had been completely deserted by then. The third was a reasonably upmarket establishment, close to the Baths of Sestropius, where tenants were only now starting to leave in unusual numbers. This last — the one we indicated for Aburius — was just a bit down from the Vicus Petrosa on the wrong side of the hill and was the one that triggered Flaccus' worries.

As we walked to the building, Aburius in the lead and servants and bodyguards in train, he kept talking and flashing his shiny smile at us, assuring us that all was in order, the property well cared for, the current tenants all charming and polite, and so on and so forth. Having lived all my life in my family's *domus*, I was glad I never had to deal with landlords' agents and their silent gladiator friends. No amount of charm on Aburius' part could mask the garlic breath of the two brutes who followed closely.

We were in sight of the Vicus Petrosa when Aburius turned to a side-street. Of the five ground-level shops facing the street, four had their shutters down. The tavern at the intersection with the side alley was closed as well — highly unusual at any time of day.

At the main entry to building's stairwell stood a guard — a freedman, given his conical *pileus* cap — who gave Aburius a smart salute, and got a nod in return. I always pay attention to how people treat those whom they deem lesser than themselves and the looks they get in return when they turn their backs; I could detect no resentment from the guard.

"Over here," said Aburius, "we have the central light-well and only two apartments off it at ground level, sharing the garden. Both are currently unoccupied, and you can have your choice. There is a well in the centre of the courtyard, and latrines on the side alley." He walked us through one of the apartments, a reasonably-sized affair with all the important rooms a residence requires to support a family with their slaves.

"It seems a bit too large for our current needs," I said. "Perhaps we can see one of the first-floor apartments?"

Aburius nodded and led us outside and up the main stairs. The stairwell opened to a long internal corridor, with sunlight streaming in from the half-wall open to the central courtyard. "On this level are four apartments. The whole building is aligned to the north, to ensure the favour of the gods. Facilities are below, but it's not a hard climb as you've just seen. These apartments are smaller, but each has ample rooms for a young couple and their slaves. The ones on the upper levels I fear will be too compact, just one or two sleeping cubicles and a shared room at the most."

"And are all four apartments on this floor unoccupied as well?" I asked.

"You are in luck indeed. The owner has recently renovated," he lied through his teeth, "and only one is occupied. You can have your choice of the others."

"Oh, but *corculum*," said Aemilia, nearly making me snort at her portrayal of a loving wife, "I hope it's not one of those cursed *insulae* we heard about."

"Of course, *deliciae meae*, of course." I could see her eyes sparkle and her mouth twitch. She was enjoying this game just as much as I was.

I turned to Aburius. "We have heard distressing rumours. It seems certain apartment buildings in the area are haunted! Would you believe that? I need to be certain the place I choose for my family is absolutely wholesome."

To his credit, Aburius barely blinked. "I assure you that is not the case here. This *insula* is owned by a prominent senator, a man dedicated to our great city and its inhabitants. I think I mentioned he took the opportunity to renovate the building rather than lease with new tenants immediately. There is none of the shoddy maintenance you might find in less reputable residences. He takes the health and safety of his renters seriously and uses the utmost care."

"Oh, that is comforting," I said. "But perhaps, just to ease my *amasiuncula's* mind, could we perhaps talk to some of the other occupants?"

"I doubt they would be at home at this time." He replied

blandly, continuing without pause, "Why don't we go back to my offices? You seem like a perfect young couple, the kind my employer likes. I'd be happy to even offer you discounted rents, to entice such esteemed clients as yourselves into this upmarket *insula*. The apartments are going fast, but I like you and I want only the best tenants here. I think you'll find no other property of this quality with similarly reasonable prices."

"That is quite convincing, Aburius," I said and, before Aemilia could think of another epithet for 'darling,' added, "However, we have not been entirely honest with you. My name is Felix, known as Felix the Fox, and I have been employed by Lucius Valerius Flaccus to find out why his *insulae* are in such low demand recently. You will be happy to know that his niece Aemilia, here, and I will report to him tonight that the reason is definitely not with his trusted agent."

I let that sink in for a moment, then presented him with the letter of introduction bearing Flaccus' seal. After some more formalities and further reassurances from us that we had nothing but praise for him, Aburius was keen to talk. This matter has been preying on him as well, both financially and on his professional pride.

"It started two months ago, late in spring. The first *insula* where this happened was at the Vicus Bellonae. In the beginning, I thought it was nothing but squatters or the superstitious grumbling of cheap foreigners and drunks, as is often the case with reports of weird noises in the night or whispers heard from empty rooms. Then, items were found away from where their owners swear they left them, or they disappeared for a time only to reappear later. Nothing alarming, just the carping of malcontents. I put an extra bodyguard on duty, to deter any pranksters. Then tenants complained of nightmares, cats and dogs being restless, and young children having disturbing visions. Still nothing that could not be explained by wine-induced prattling." As he talked, Aburius led us back down to the central courtyard.

"During *Quinctilis*, affairs became more serious. Strange lights moved about, sometimes even by daytime; the whispers were replaced by blood-curdling screams at odd hours; people woke with curious marks on their skin. Then a child died, her body covered with bloody lesions that appeared overnight. Her skin became all wrinkly. I saw her myself, when I came to pay the master's respects," he shuddered at the memory, and rubbed his arms as if suddenly cold.

"It was becoming hard to find replacement tenants. Those who left spread the stories, and only the truly desperate would take up the vacated residences. I installed another guardian — one of my rent-collection assistants — in addition to the caretaker. Not a bright fellow, Crito. I fear his time in the arena has left his brain somewhat rattled in his skull. Still, dependable. He was to patrol at night and sleep during the day in one of the vacated apartments. His instructions were to deal with any untoward activities swiftly and violently. I wanted an end to this, still believing it was some neighbourhood pranksters. I made a big show to the tenants about it, how master Flaccus was looking after them at his own expense." His tone rose a bit, as if he was still addressing the tenants and trying to convince them.

"At first this seemed to work. No reports of strange happenings came during the first three nights and days. I felt confirmed that the whole thing was nothing but pranks and that my man had scared off the perpetrators. But on the fourth morning Crito showed up in my office, confused and babbling. He wasn't an orator, but I've never seen him incoherent like that either. And his hair... He used to have thick, dark hair, cut short. When he showed up that day, it was completely white. I got him to calm down eventually, with enough wine. He fell asleep on my couch, and never woke up." Aburius paused at the memory, before collecting his thoughts and continuing with his report.

"After that it was almost impossible to get any of my other guards to stay the night. The tenants started to leave in droves. The same type of rumours started in another *insula*, the one on Vicus Fabricii. I offered prizes to my men to entice them to take the guard's job. I told them if they caught the perpetrator of these pranks or brought me solid evidence, they'd get their freedom and a large purse. A couple took me up on it. Stayed together all night. I found them huddled on my office doorstep in the morning, saying I can whip them to death but they will not be going there ever again. Told tales of the floors shifting, of murals coming alive. That was the last of the tenants, too. The remaining residents soon left and now the two buildings stand empty. Even squatters will not occupy them."

CHAPTER III

We were standing alone in the garden at the centre of the light-well after Aburius and his goons went back to his office. Aemilia peered curiously around. "So, what do you think is the cause — a shade of the dead? Are we going to trap it with a ritual?"

"Slow down, we're not at the chariot races. You'll soon find out that this job is not as glamorous as you think. It's not all dark *magia* and ancient incantations. It's far more likely to be something mundane, like a rival landlord paying a gang of goons to frighten the residents. You'll be lucky if you get to witness some minor country *incantator* casting a few cantrips to cause the noises. Instead of rushing, we need to start by talking to current and past tenants."

"What about the dead white-haired gladiator?"

"Unless you want to summon the dead, I suggest we first speak with his cronies who survived."

***

Most of the previous residents of the Subvales *insulae* would be nigh impossible to track down. The people who normally occupy such apartments, particularly the top floors, are the dregs of society. Nobody cares much for them, least of all their landlords. As long as rents are paid, they can stay — if not, they go. Where to, no one cares.

I still intended to locate some past residents, of course — look for ground-floor shop owners who might have stayed in the area and such. I just didn't have much hope for success. The situation with this particular *insula* was different. It was a better address, which meant less of the invisible, transient people and more of those that had regular paying jobs.

It also had some remaining tenants. Aburius had kindly provided us with a list. A very short list, as only three apartments remained occupied.

We had a chat with the guardian on the way up, but he only recently came to Aburius' employ and was new to this post. The first apartment door was answered by an ageing steward. Once we spoke loudly enough for him to understand, he admitted us and fetched his mistress, a woman in her eighties. For her, we had to speak even louder than with her manservant.

This was one interview made easier by the presence of Aemilia. The old woman took a shine to her, claiming she reminded her of a great-granddaughter she hadn't seen in years. In fact, I think she just saw me as a bodyguard. Aemilia carried the interview through with charm and grace.

There was nothing that Minucia, the old woman, could tell us. Having lost her husband many years ago, she lived alone with her steward and a cook in that apartment. All were too old and too set in their ways to notice anything. All noises were either missed or attributed to rowdy neighbours. She hadn't noticed any other supernatural events, and when asked, maintained that her devout worship of the Bona Dea would protect her from anything.

By the time we left, Aemilia was calling Minucia *avia* and promising to visit again. If she was disappointed at not uncovering a horror story of ghosts and shades, she hid it well.

***

We trudged up the steps to the third floor, the second being completely unoccupied. The top two floors each had ten apartments, built as suites of two rooms.

A female slave named Elpis occupied the first apartment. She accepted our explanations without pause. Her master, she said, was away on business. He was an officer on a trading ship and had sailed in spring at the opening of the shipping season. He spent his winters at the apartment and his summers on voyages, only stopping for a couple of nights at a time whenever trade carried him back to Egretia.

She was in a talkative mood, but I got impatient when she got to ruminating about a Hellican friend and their plans to buy her freedom and a start a small business. When I interrupted her and explained the full reason for our visit, Elpis paled, and the stories gushed out.

First there were noises. Scratching sounds in the dead of night, like rats in the walls. Baited traps were set, but no rodent was ever captured. The scratching noises were then accompanied by chittering — high-pitched sounds, like a plague of locusts, making the skin of anyone who heard them crawl.

The tenants banded together to put pressure on Aburius, who — considering this was the third *insula* to be hit — hired a *veneficitor* to place traps for all types of pests, from rats and roaches to things less mundane. The *veneficitor* came in with his bundles of herbs and poisons, buried them in the garden and in holes in the walls, chanted as needed, and left.

At first it seemed his charms worked. No noises were heard for several nights and the occupants slept with ease.

Then the screaming began. Piercing, horrifying screeches, as those of a man being torn apart by harpies. These happened in the dead of night and went on for several minutes. All the tenants had awakened and gone around carrying lamps and torches searching for the source of the disturbance. Yet no cause had been found and all residents had been accounted for and unharmed. After the second night of screams, tenants began looking for alternative accommodations.

Stories of Valerius' other affected *insulae* began to percolate through the neighbourhood. Amplified by gossip, these tales were enough to scare tenants at his other properties. Though nothing extreme had happened in that *insula*, no one wanted to wait around till it escalated. Potential renters were scared away too, and only those without options remained behind.

As we made our way to the last apartment, I asked Aemilia, "What do you make of her story?"

"What do you mean? I thought you were after first-hand accounts of events."

"But did we get that? You'll note she told us about her Hellican lover, the freedman. Put aside all the tales of buying her freedom and opening a bakery. I'll bet you coins to acorns that she has not been sleeping in the apartment for weeks. As soon as her master leaves on his voyages, she's bound to spend her nights with her lover at his place. It won't be possible for him to stay here, but she can account for a night's absence when her master returns. She must only come here in the morning to care for her *dominus'* residence. This will make the majority of her stories hearsay based on retellings by the other tenants in the mornings — before they all left, that is. Not the most reliable of sources."

***

One can always tell how classy an *insula* is by the floor on which they stop installing doors and hang cloth screens instead. This one was a decent affair, with only four floors and all apartments — even at the top — fitted with solid wooden doors.

We knocked at the last occupied apartment in the building, located at the furthest end of the corridor on the top floor. There was a shuffling inside, and a bleary-eyed woman opened the door.

"Yes?"

"Good morning, neighbour. Are you Memmia, the washerwoman?"

"Who wants to know?"

"My name is Felix, known as Felix the Fox. This is my — *eh* — associate, Aemilia. We are working for the owner of the *insula* and his agent Aburius."

"I paid my rent for the whole month in advance!" she proclaimed indignantly.

"Oh, no, that isn't why we came. We were hired by the

landlord to resolve some disturbing events that have been happening of late. We wondered whether we might talk with you for a moment about them?"

"I haven't lived here long." said Memmia.

"How long is not long?"

"Two *nundinae*."

"And in this time, have you heard any strange tales? Witnessed unexplained events?"

"I don't pay much attention to gossip," she said, with curt efficiency.

"No strange sounds at night? No unexplained sights?" asked Aemilia.

"I saw something," piped a tiny voice from behind her.

"Marcus! Go right back inside! I told you never to come to the door!" A boy of around six years shrank back into the room. "I don't have time for this," she muttered over her shoulder at us, and slammed the door shut.

***

"Does anything strike you as odd?" I asked Aemilia as we made our way down.

She thought for a moment. "I find it really strange that she dismissed gossip of the strange events here. People of her ilk are usually superstitious. That's why Aburius couldn't get more tenants for my uncle — the rumours running wild have driven away the simple folk."

"Superstitious or not," I said, "there is something more fundamental. None of the washerwomen I know could afford this place, and none would be at home during the day. Everyone has secrets, Aemilia. It's our job to separate the ones related to our case from the noise."

"Oh! Ooohhh — do you think she's involved with what's been happening? Is she related to the cause? Somehow working illegal and *nefas magia* here?" My attempts at curing her naïveté were failing.

"No, my dear. Adopt a cynic's outlook. That she has

something to hide is plain but jumping from there to *nefas magia* is a leap that defies logic. Have you seen how she got flustered when the boy showed his face? Perhaps she really used to be a washerwoman. Perhaps she got involved in something shady and is now hiding from someone. It is far likelier that her secrets have more to do with money and the boy's father than anything nefarious."

At Aemilia's crestfallen expression, I added, "This is not life in the Clivi Ulterior. It's not the place for hatching covert schemes and backroom deals for the fate of our city. This is the neighbourhood of simple people, from lowly craftsmen and traders to pimps and thieves. If we chased everyone shifty, we would see the new year without any results. Time to learn to focus on what matters, which requires developing a gut instinct, which — in turn — involves much time spent in insalubrious environs."

"So, what did we find here today?" she asked, eager to learn.

"A senile old woman who wouldn't hear the house crashing around her, gossip from a slave that doesn't sleep here, and a door closed in our faces by a desperate woman hiding with her boy. Prepare yourself for many such disappointments."

Chapter IV

We decided to visit one of the completely abandoned *insulae* for which Aburius had given us directions. With several hours of daylight left — and with Aemilia's bodyguard in tow — I thought it quite safe. I wanted to uncover any traces of the unsavoury events, follow up on the claim that even squatters abandoned the buildings, interview potential witnesses or at least build a list of such — all while we still had good light. I could always return Aemilia home before dark and investigate more at night if needed.

As we made our way down the southern slope of the Meridionali into the warren of alleys that make up the stews of Egretia, I stopped at a stall I knew which sold decent street food and bought us all squid-on-a-stick. Her slaves — Na'ama and Titus — thought nothing of the snack, but Aemilia approached it with a mix of excitement, curiosity, and trepidation. She was clearly not accustomed to eating on the go and held the skewer awkwardly lest the fish sauce drip on her clothes. Her behaviour again reminded me of the sheltered life she had led. Women of her class seldom roam the streets, and certainly not on this side of town.

We reached the tenement building, located not far from the intersection of the Vicus Bellonae and the Clivus Amulae. All *insulae* are separated from adjacent buildings by streets and alleys, which is how they got to be named 'islands.' The side of this building facing the Vicus Bellonae had shops at ground level — all closed and locked. Above the shops rose tiers of shuttered windows hiding, I imagined, increasingly cramped dwellings as the number of stairs to reach them increased. I counted nine floors — a place for the wretched.

The entryway into the building was dark and quiet. Piles of leaves swirled under stairs, windows and doors were shuttered, and neither the light of a torch nor the sounds of life escaped from inside. I suggested to Aemilia that she should wait outside with her girl and guardian, but she remained obdurate, insisting she would be safer with me. It was a fair point, so I loosened my dagger in its scabbard and told her bodyguard to remain alert.

As we stepped inside, the sounds of the surrounding streets dimmed along with the light, the cries of vendors and noise of traffic becoming distant and surreal. The place was derelict, a stark contrast to the teeming neighbourhood. Smells of rot and decay hung in the air like the miasma that accompanies marshes, making it hard to breathe at first. Aemilia gagged and covered her face with a fold of her *stola*, but when I suggested she wait outside she just waved me onwards.

The vestibule opened to the inner courtyard. Upper-class *insulae* usually divide this space between the ground-floor apartments for use as garden-beds, but in the Subvales it was common to have a fountain or well and other shared facilities for the tenants.

The scene that greeted us was grim. The fire-pits were filled with rainwater, the alcove housing the shrine to the *insula*'s household gods piled with leaves. Everywhere were closed windows, abandoned sundries, and discarded clothes.

And silence. Not even cooing pigeons or scurrying rats.

I shut my eyes and breathed in deeply, ignoring Aemilia, who was clutching at my arm. I concentrated on the scents of the place and the sensations of my skin. Proper *incantatores*, graduates of the Collegium Incantatorum, have the *visus verum*, the true sight. If they concentrate, they can see the flow of *magia*. I, however, never graduated. I developed some sensitivity, though, and can feel when I am close enough to the presence of a source of *magia*.

The more I concentrated, the more goosebumps dappled my skin, and the acrid smell of bad *magia* suffused every corner of my imagination. But that was probably just my mind playing tricks on me, amplifying the background noise of Egretia, with its flows of *magia* from things as large as the Pharos lighthouse to thousands of trivial superstitious charms. Nothing conclusive.

***

"Before we go digging here," I said to Aemilia, "We should interview the neighbours from the shops and buildings across the road." The divination I had in mind for this place was best done after dark — and without putting Aemilia's pretty nose in danger.

We crossed the street to a basket-weaver's shop, where a bent-backed, grey-haired woman in her fifties hunched on a low stool. Her fingers flew as they worked threading wicker, but her eyes and ears were trained on the street. She was just what I was looking for — a perfect gossip.

After pretending to be interested in a hanger for potted plants, I asked about business.

"Business is well, praise Minerva. Me baskets are respected, and them people come in from all over the Subvales for 'em."

"That is good to hear. The streets are a bit empty, what with that *insula* there looking completely abandoned," I said.

The woman spat on the ground and muttered a formula for protection. "A nasty business. A curse! By gods or men, it's a curse."

"That sounds ominous! What happened?" Aemilia asked.

"It started with noises," told the woman with apparent glee, eager to impress her new audience. "Strange ones first, then others that were downright disturbin'. From voices gibberin' in hallways to screeches in the dead of night." The old gossip modulated her voice to match the horrifying sequence of events. "We thought gangs at first, playing *cacat* pranks. Them tenants banded together and made the crossroad college sacrifice to the *lares* and *penates*. That di'n't help. That night came unnatural howls, and in the morning," she paused, her eyes gleaming with anticipation, "they found out why. The grocer owned a cat to keep mice from his wares. They found the poor thing, flayed and gutted, spread in a 'orrible mockery of a mural on the ceiling of his shop."

"Oh, my!" cried Aemilia.

"That was only the beginning," said the basket weaver with an evil smirk. She went on to tell of the increasingly gruesome events which followed — of bleeding statues, animated homicidal furniture, missing children. "The worst was the night of the *Kalends* of *Quinctilis*," said the woman. "There was a scream like Proserpina being dragged to the underworld. The next mornin' a young couple was found tangled in bed. Them what cried out — their bodies was all dried up, squeezed of all juices. Like those pickled dead the Mitzrani worship. The embalmers, they tried to separate the bodies, but those dead ones snapped and broke like dry twigs. Wasn't much to cremate, just dust and ashes."

"Is that when the tenants all left?" I asked.

"No amount of propiti'ory sacrifices, of cleansin' ceremonies, of blessings and chants by half a hundred fancy priests and wise-women helped. Petitions to the landlord di'n't help either, not at first. His agent just posted an ex-gladiator whose brains were a-stirred from too much fightin'. Man was too drunk at nights to notice if his own nose was cut off. But one night he seen something and ran away, sayin' he won't come back even if they crucify him." Her fingers never paused from weaving, but the woman spat on the ground to accentuate her point.

"Finally, that agent paid for a proper *incantator*, and even them renters chipped in. The man showed up, sniffed around, chanted some incantations — which were, I have on good authority from a wise-woman who delivers babies what saw him work — absolutely worthless. Then he left, none of his business no more. That night...," she paused, as if considering. "Well, after *that* night, the tenants left. Whatever that *verpa* of a *veneficitor* did, angered whoever — or whatever — cursed the *insula*. The walls shook and oozed stinkin' pus. People tried to run but was flung about as if by an invisible god. One man fell from an eighth-floor corridor screaming and flailing straight into the well — which then spewed some foul black liquid, like old blood."

She made a protective sign with her fingers to ward off evil spirits before continuing. "From that day on, the building stood quiet — except for once when a family of squatters came." She lowered her voice to a whisper. "If you go to the ground floor apartment on the western side, you'll likely find what's left of 'em. After the noises what came from there that night, no one ever to set foot inside again."

We thanked the woman, who swore to us that at the first sign of any strange voices in her *insula* she would be moving to her sister in Parelae. I bought Aemilia a wicker hanging flower pot, and we stepped back into the sunny street, our eyes squinting as the glare of hot sunshine burned the shadows away.

***

We canvassed a while longer and heard similar stories. Some of the shop owners in the vicinity had already moved. Those who remained had a variety of charms hanging about their person and premises. All had bolt-holes ready to run to on the first sign of trouble spilling beyond the afflicted tenement. But, so far, it seemed that only the *insula* was affected, and other buildings in the area hadn't experienced anything even remotely similar.

It was the eighth hour of the day, and I decided it was time I escorted Aemilia back. We faced a long climb from the base of the Meridionali to the highest reaches of the Clivi Ulterior where Cornelia had her ancestral residence.

While we walked, we chatted about the day's findings. My hope that exposing her to the rough life of the Subvales would scare her off the case was soundly dashed. Not even the horror stories of witnesses fazed her for long. I would have to keep an eye on her, which meant an eye less to spare for the investigation.

At home, her guard disappeared to the slave quarters

when we were safely inside, and her girl went to arrange a bath. I hesitated for a moment, but when Aemilia bade me goodbye I wished her a good evening, adding, "Give my regards to your mother," over my shoulder as I stepped back out to the street.

I don't know what I had expected. The last time I had seen Cornelia she treated me as a play-thing, having her fun with me on a sea voyage. Her behaviour remained a mystery. Though I keep myself fit, my looks are nondescript — dark curls framing dark eyes, bumpy nose, and a clean-shaven chin. It must have been my dubious charms. She made it clear I was merely a diversion for her and nothing could continue in Egretia. Aemilia, on the other hand, seemed always to dislike me, right up until I rescued her from being sacrificed to Vulcanus.

I didn't know what to make of them. They had both recommended me to Flaccus — but then saddled me with Aemilia. That meant less freedom to act and more trudging up and down the volcanic slopes upon which our city nestles as I provided her an entertaining glimpse at the plebeian world before she settled into the life of an elite socialite. It certainly didn't mean that I became a sought-after guest for high-society dinner parties.

By the time I returned home, I was too tired to follow through with my plans for night-time investigation of the insula. Instead, I resolved to leave Aemilia to do the trudging tomorrow and preserve my energy for some of the less savoury aspects of my investigations the following night, without her watchful eye.

CHAPTER V

The next morning began the same way as the previous had — by meeting Aemilia under the arches of the Aqua Sexitae. I had some ideas about how to proceed with the *magia* side of the investigations, but I wanted to wear Aemilia out before we got to the exciting parts — to make the eventual resolution appear more satisfying and bonus-worthy.

We began with the third *insula*, the one on the Vicus Fabricii. Like the *insula* we'd visited yesterday, we discovered an abandoned building, a faint acrid smell of *magia* I could not place, and the now-familiar second-hand tales of gibbering voices, homicidal statues, and living murals. A fun way to spend a sunny morning, hearing stories of suffering and loss.

One particularly gruesome incident was told by the laundress from around the corner, and she swore it was the one that caused most of the tenants to leave. A young family had rented the eastern apartment of the first floor. The man had been a new *quaestor* in the treasury, at the start of a promising public career. He, his wife, and their six-month-old son had lived there with a couple of slaves. In the nursery, they had hung a picture done in encaustic of the baby Hercules fighting off the snakes in his crib. A charm perhaps, or just an inspiration for the young boy.

That night there were no unnatural screams. Instead, the tenants had been awakened by altogether human wailing that began when the mother checked on her son in the middle of the night and found that the snakes in the picture had come alive and were devouring her child.

The laundress' vivid description of the two serpents entwined in the crib, each gulping one of the torn halves of the baby's corpse had shaken Aemilia to the core. We stood in the sunny street, myself and the bodyguard to one side as Aemilia sought solace with her handmaiden, Na'ama. I felt sorry for her, of course, pretty little flower that she was. But it was her idea to accompany me on this case. The quicker she was exposed to the harsh realities of Egretian life, the quicker she would make her choice — to grow up or go back to her sheltered life.

I led us away from that place, walking in the sunlight to help ease Aemilia's distress until I found a friendly tavern. We sipped spiced wine in silence till our meal arrived. Aemilia poked the poached gull eggs in anchovy sauce, probably wondering if using her hands might be safer than the dirty spoon. Once she finally tried an egg, her eyes widened, first in surprise and then pleasure. While the decor may have been the Subvales standard of decrepitude, the food was top-notch.

"How do you make sense of today's crop of paranormal occurrences and desiccated corpses?"

"According to the philosophers," she said, over a piece of bread dipped in olive oil, "one should be able to use pure logic to separate truth from exaggerations and lies. Since we interviewed second-hand witnesses, we cannot discount the possibility that their recounting of events is flawed. So, we shall assume there is a grain of truth to it and strive by reason to extract it from the spun yarns." She put the bread aside as she warmed to her topic.

"First, all accounts mention chittering voices in the dark of night. We could conclude this was a common start to the affairs, as witnesses across all the buildings are unlikely to have known each other. As for dead babies and desiccated husbands, I think we are safe ascribing it to exaggerations in the retelling. Yes, I'll grant you people have died. People die every day in this city, for myriad reasons. So, night noises of burrowing insects followed by a death, and perhaps a shifting of Vergu which leads to statues falling, or a leaky roof that causes paint on murals to run and resemble blood all become fuel for wild claims." The more she talked, the more animated she became. "A wild snake somehow making its way into the city or escaping its handler is more plausible than a repeat of old legends. Tie a natural event to people's propensity for exaggeration, and let the gossips retell the stories. With repetition comes elaboration and embellishment. Now a shoddily held statue becomes a moving one that creaks and speaks and causes the death of a man — who might have already been sick with the ague. No mystical horrors here, just the superstitious reading in events what they wish to find there."

I was impressed, both at her analysis and at her recovered emotions. "You present the sceptic viewpoint," I said, "but what if you are wrong? What would you consider the gamut of possibilities?"

"Pure superstition on one end, as noted. A random shift in the flow of *magia* comes second. Don't look at me like that! I may not be trained, but I am educated — I read the treatises of the Arval Brethren. The *magia* flows throughout the city, till a random shift coupled with a focal point in one of the *insulae* causes these phenomena. As before, this is a natural phenomenon that lends itself to superstitious misinterpretation. A third explanation is directed occurrences. This theory is supported by the fact that the strange events seem to afflict only my uncle's properties, and nothing around them. Perhaps a curse, by a dissatisfied tenant."

"Fourth," I added, "events directed, but not by a human hand. Has your uncle been diligent in maintaining the colleges of the *lares* and *di penates* of his buildings? A dissatisfied spirit might cause these events."

"Pchah! Spirits! According to Plinius, there are no intelligent *numina*. These are the uneducated irrational explanations for natural *magia*." She tore into her bread again with gusto.

"And if you're wrong?" I asked. "On any point, from the inflated accounts of events to the presence of intelligent gods?"

"I go by the best scholars," she replied, "I can't see where they would all be wrong."

"Let's go back to the case, then," I said, as this wasn't the time for a philosophical discussion and I was loath to admit to her that her reasoning was actually sound and similar to my own. "How would you proceed in determining the exact root cause — whether an exaggerated natural phenomenon or a directed event?"

She chewed thoughtfully on a pickled cabbage leaf stuffed with barley and prunes, recovered enough to continue eating while discussing dead people. She wiped the fish sauce from her fingers and said, "We only spoke with the agent and tenants. My mother told me she has seen you perform a location incantation when..." She paused, giving me a sidelong glance, "You know when. Do you know any incantations that can locate the source of the trouble?"

"It doesn't quite work like that. The rituals I know ask a specific question, expecting a particular type of answer. They are also not always reliable. But you are right, that is probably our next step. I use old-fashioned investigation and interviews to narrow down the options. Running through every possible incantation is too time consuming, costly, and draining. But once I get a clear picture of what is happening, I can find the right ritual to ascertain the answer. We'll start with your sceptic view, stating this was directed by a human hand. Not," I added, "because I agree with your view about the *numina*, but because given that the strange events have been happening only in your uncle's *insulae*, it smacks too much of a directing hand to be a coincidence."

***

We stood again in the inner courtyard of yesterday's abandoned *insula*, the one on the Vicus Bellonae. "We've decided to start with the human angle," I said to Aemilia. "So, we need to explore what might a man do to achieve these effects."

We climbed up floors to inspect the apartments and identify those where the atrocities happened. We heard tales from the neighbours we interviewed, but I wanted to examine the evidence for myself.

A few apartments did not have any discernible signs of the nightmares that took place there, but most did. There was a mural on a wall depicting a pastoral scene in a green meadow, where the colours ran and smeared to the point that the sheep were deformed and covered with blood. A room where all the furniture was smashed, and five long lines ripped the paint on the walls resembling scratches made by inhuman claws. Bloody footprints and hoof-prints, tracing the steps of an intricate, macabre dance.

In each of those places I stopped, closed my eyes, listened, concentrating on the tingling of my skin, sniffing to see if I could find traces of the particular odours of *magia*.

Aemilia has dismissed her girl for making too much fuss. Then she sent her bodyguard to guard the girl, since a lone girl on the street would be a juicy target for mischief. While I was concentrating, she poked at the gruesome evidence with a stick.

"Can you really sense it?" she asked.

"Sometimes."

"How does it work? I know the *incantatores* have the *visus verum*, the true sight. They can see the flow of *magia*. Is that what you are doing? Following *magia* flows?"

"I don't have the *visus verum*. It's why I need quiet to concentrate."

"But how does it feel? Is it like seeing the wind blow?"

I sighed and opened my eyes. "Yes, the *incantatores* can 'see' the flows, when they focus on them. No, I have no idea how it actually looks beyond the same descriptions you probably read yourself. Acquiring the true sight is a lengthy process, and students start out with basic senses first — touch and smell mostly. The graduates tend to forget it, though, and rely too much on their eyes. But just like the blind will tell you, sometimes the other senses can show you things you can't see. Smells linger longer. Textures carry information not visible to the eye alone. Now, please, let me concentrate!"

I made Aemilia go to the *insula*'s latrines, sniff about, poke her head down dirty holes, and tell me if she could spot anything that did not belong in the sewers. Not that I was expecting results, but I needed a few minutes of quiet concentration without constant questions and chatter. I drew a deep breath, shut my eyes, placed my hand on the wall to match a bloody handprint, and tried to sense its original owner's unfortunate demise.

She came back and announced, "Nothing there. I even dropped a burning torch down one, but all I could see was the flow of water in the shunt to the nearest *cloaca* line. I didn't see any bloody marks on the seats, or anything unexpected floating down there."

"Good. I think we should return you to your mother now," I said.

"Oh," she sounded disappointed, "I thought you might have seen enough to try an incantation."

"I need to do research first — a task we'll tackle tomorrow," I answered. Privately, I planned to come back to the *insula* that night, unobserved by any except the shades of those who died there.

On our way out, I froze when I absentmindedly turned a corner, stumbling across something unexpected. The old basket-weaver told us of poor people who tried to squat after all the occupants left and were never seen again. Four human figures — presumably an actual family, by the apparent sexes and ages — were huddled in the corner. Stretched entrails extended from their little clump of limbs and bodies, clinging to the floor, walls, ceiling. I could not comprehend what manner of being would eviscerate each one in turn and arrange their guts in geometric designs that twisted and turned upon themselves. It made my mind reel.

A strangled cry restored my wits. I turned and scooped Aemilia in my arms, shuffling her out. But she had glimpsed enough. She was trembling as her spirit tried to come to terms with something not meant for civilised minds.

She clutched my tunic, burying her head in my shoulder. I could not ignore the scent of her hair or the warmth of her against me as my own spirit recovered from the sight. After a brief moment she stiffened slightly, withdrew from me, and turned away to compose herself.

"Go outside," I instructed her. "I'll join you in a minute."

This allowed her to resume her proper dignity and gave me a moment alone. I stepped back inside that room, forced myself to examine the atrocities in detail. I extended a hand gingerly, brushing my fingertips against the nearest end of the pattern of viscera on the wall. It was as if I scuffed my feet on a carpet and touched a metal rod. A spark flew up my arm, making my hairs rise and my skin break out in goosebumps. My senses flooded; a vision too brief to understand flashed like lightning in my mind. *Magia* has flavours. This was not one I cared for.

***

I decided we'd had enough. I'd gathered several hints from spending time in the apartments — snatches of sounds, words and inhuman utterances, acrid smells, the occasional fleeting vision. I was sure the patterns of viscera on the wall had meaning, but my mind and stomach baulked at sketching the dead squatters. The image was indelibly lodged in my memory, enough for me to recognise or recreate later. What we had learnt was enough to give me something to start research on so that I could glean an understanding of how the forces were manipulated, and thus seek out and locate their sources.

I joined the others outside. "Time to go home, I think."

"That... that was..." Aemilia stammered.

"Yes," I said. "That was no prank of some hoodlum gang or a small-time magician. That was far more sinister. Your uncle was right to employ me."

I kept breaking the promises I made to myself. I ended up walking Aemilia all the way up back to her *domus*. Our conversation veered away from the supernatural horrors to those of human origins as the topic changed to politics. We became engrossed in a discussion about why the wine-growers' lobby in the Senate was trying to limit wind manipulation in the harbour due to its flow-on effects on rainfall on the other side of Vergu where their vineyards lay.

I was about to leave, having said my goodbyes to her as she crossed the doorstep into her house, when the family's steward shuffled into the vestibule. "Your mother is waiting for you, *domina*," he said in a wheezy voice. "She wishes master Felix to dine with her as well."

A free dinner and a chance to see Cornelia were more than enough reason to accept. I was given the opportunity to refresh myself on the way and took time to admire the tasteful décor of the mansion on the way to the dining room. The many rooms and corridors, the internal gardens with fountains, and a glimpsed loggia with views to the bay, were all exquisitely done. I do not often get the chance to visit the private residences of the ultra-rich, but I learnt enough from my father's antique business to discern the good taste of the decor.

Gilded pilasters were kept to a minimum, columns were modestly ionic, and the furnishings were not extravagant. The choice of artwork, though, was the sign of a real connoisseur. The paintings above the dados depicted varied scenes, each room maintaining its theme in both subject and colour scheme. All were expertly executed, as were the many statues hiding in niches and amongst bushes in the gardens. One in particular, of a boxer resting in between fights, caught my eye. A bearded, muscular, naked figure, sitting with hands on his knees and head turned to look over his right shoulder. His face showed complex emotions, frozen in time. It was done in bronze, with inlaid copper to simulate blood on its cut lips, broken nose, and droplets along his shoulder, arm, and thighs.

I reached the *triclinium* together with Aemilia, ahead of the *domus'* mistress. Aemilia took the couch on the right, while I reclined on the one to the left.

A slave took my sandals off and washed my feet while I gazed around the room. The murals on the walls matched the kingdoms of food: a seascape, with frolicking fish and nymphs; a pastoral glade, with grazing sheep and cows; hills with fields of golden wheat; blue sky with white clouds, with flocks of ducks and geese crossing them. The floor mosaic held elaborate depictions of tables laden with dishes of fruit and meat interspersed with bright flowers, while on the ceiling were pictures of gods and goddesses dining on ambrosia and nectar, done in the Hellican style. I settled more comfortably on the couch and chatted with Aemilia about the statue of the boxer in the garden.

Before long, Cornelia arrived. I was struck again by the resemblance between mother and daughter. The same dark hair, milky skin, grey eyes. Cornelia's voluptuous curves were accentuated by a moss-green tunic, which, despite its modest cut, still clung closely to her. She was accompanied by a friend, whom she presented as Icilia.

"Felix, how lovely to meet you again," Icilia smiled at me, as she slid onto the middle couch with Cornelia, placing herself close to me.

"The pleasure is all mine," I replied politely.

"Tell me, what brings you here tonight?"

The case was Valerius' business, and so I said, "Merely an old acquaintance of the Cornelia."

The Icilii were an old family, well respected for their contribution to our society in times of strife. Two minutes of conversation with Icilia, however, convinced me that this latest scion was not likely to rise to the same standards. A dumpy, frumpy woman, with too many pins in her hair and folds in her chin, whose incessant giggling was only marginally better than her outright braying laughter.

She seemed overly keen to learn about my ancestry and position in life until Cornelia said, "Felix works for cousin Lucius Valerius. We've recommended him, as he has knowledge of arcane matters."

"Oh?" said Icilia. "How exciting! Were you a *rhone*, then? I confess I do not follow their yearly elections and am not intimate with the politics of the *Collegium Incantatorum*. But I think I remember you were mentioned in the senate —"

"I'm afraid you must have me mistaken with someone else," I interrupted.

"But you are just the right age! Will you be running to the office of *rhone* soon? I'm sure you'll be brilliant at it." She twirled a stray strand of hair around her finger.

"Felix is a great expert," said Cornelia, "but isn't quite from senatorial background."

A disappointed 'Oh' was all I got from Icilia, who mercifully spared me further attentions.

When the meal's courses changed, we moved to discussing the events of the day. Cornelia seemed more disturbed than her daughter by what we found. I don't believe Aemilia gave her mother a full account of our investigations the day before, which might have explained some of Cornelia's distress. Aemilia, meanwhile, had recovered and remained detached when we touched on the subject of human remains. Cornelia paled at the more graphic descriptions, and Icilia nearly fainted.

Cornelia quickly steered the conversation away. "So, what's next, Felix?" she asked. "Can you resolve this matter for Lucius Valerius?"

"Next is determining the exact cause, for which I'll need to do some research. Once we do that, we shall see how to go about restoring the *insulae* to liveable conditions. Having worn our feet out, it is now time to wear out our eyes on ancient scrolls — a task I suspect Aemilia will be happy to take on."

The meal we were served consisted of classic, simple dishes, done expertly. Lettuce with raw egg yolks and anchovy dressing, whole fish crusted in almonds and fried, and honeyed sesame cakes. The food and sauces were fresh and exquisite, proving once more that skill and elegance beats exotic extravagance.

At dinner's end Aemilia retired, citing tiredness from walking. I rose too, and bade goodbye to my hostess while Icilia fussed with some loose hair and her many pins. With her coif secure, Icilia said, "I should be going too. I'm afraid the conversation about the unwholesome mess at Valerius' *insula* has given me quite a fright, and I'd rather be home before night sets in."

Cornelia walked us to the door, embracing Icilia as she departed, but stopping me before I could move beyond the threshold. "Are you in a rush to get somewhere?" asked Cornelia. "I thought you said your next move will be to spend time in libraries, not nocturnal skulking."

It was, in fact, my plan to return to the *insula* that night and investigate the remains of the squatters. "I'd like to prepare for tomorrow," I answered. "Refresh my knowledge with my scrolls, perhaps."

"She won't forgive you if you start without her, you know. Why don't you spend the night here, instead of walking home so late, only to meet Aemilia half way up again tomorrow? It will leave you fresher for the day."

Her smile was innocence itself, belied only by my memories of our shared past in circumstances that bridged our very different strata of society. Yet here she was, acting contrarily to what I understood when she ended our affair. She hooked her arm through mine and led me to a sleeping cubicle deep inside her mansion.

Her servants, I presumed, were well-trained and well-paid not to gossip, because what happened between us that night was certainly inappropriate for a woman of her social circle.

Chapter VI

Aemilia was only mildly surprised at my presence during breakfast, and she accepted her mother's explanation about saving valuable research time without comment.

Due to the previous evening's welcome diversion, I did not accomplish what I had planned — for the second night in a row. That meant I would have to tackle it during the day, with Aemilia at my side.

There were two things I had to do — locate my old acquaintance Araxus hoping he was in one of his lucid states and test some theories about the *insulae* in ways that are best done under moonlight. Sometimes the bright, warm, yellow light of the sun makes the faint silver traceries of *magia* fade away. This is especially true in matters of life and death, as the underworld is a world of shadows whose traces are easily banished by the sun. Since all the testimonies we heard attested to paranormal occurrences happening past midnight, I thought it prudent to spend the night there. Well, perhaps not prudent. Or even advisable. But educational, certainly.

Since any night-time activities would now have to wait, that left finding Araxus. He was an old acquaintance, one whom I once called a friend until some bad blood ran between us. I avoided him for most of a decade, until two months back when a complicated case — the one where I met Aemilia and Cornelia — forced me to seek him out.

Araxus and I studied together at the Collegium Incantatorum. Unlike me, he did graduate, after which he dabbled in things he shouldn't have. He paid the price for it, his mind no longer his to command. But in the process, he had learnt a lot about the darker aspects of *magia*, including curses and the underworlds. If I got lucky, I'd find him lucid and agreeable. Less lucky but more likely, he'd be lucid but disagreeable. Even likelier, he'd be in a mental state that'd render him about as useful as a barnacle to a blacksmith.

Due to his dementia, he lived on the outskirts of normal society and was usually found out in the *purgamenta* — the dumps in the hills outside the walls. I warned Aemilia about the location and implored her to stay behind, as we would be traversing areas not fit for young women of her class, yet she insisted on accompanying me. I guess she was curious to meet Araxus, having only seen him once before and under extreme circumstances.

I tried a different tack and appealed to Cornelia. "Remember when we agreed that if I deem a task too dangerous, Aemilia would stay behind? There is no benefit to your daughter — nor any to Valerius, for that matter — by having Aemilia tramp through one seedy tavern after another, or by galumphing through back alleys in the Campus Civicus, thick with thieves and cut-throats."

"Don't even think about it, mother," Aemilia spoke before her mother could respond. "This was to be my chance to see life across Egretia. To experience everything about it, as well as *magia*."

"I'll report back as soon as I find anything," I said, "and we'll take it on from there."

"But I also want to learn how you find out things. That is a big part of the investigation," Aemilia countered.

Cornelia vacillated at first, but then, worn down by Aemilia's pleading, she gave in. She did send an entourage of bodyguards with us, but they were more hindrance than help. At that point, I was almost ready to walk off the case. I didn't want to take a young woman to meet the man implicated in the death of my first love. But Cornelia reassured me, and, I reasoned, the circumstances were different. It had been a decade since Helena, and, to be fair, Araxus was at fault by negligence rather than malice. If I did quit the case, Aemilia would try to continue it herself. She'd done that before, the idiot girl. While I could not be faulted for anything that might happen to her, I doubted my conscience would let me sleep at night.

And so we set out, taking the quickest route possible — down from her house, angling south of the Forum to the Vicus Petrosa, traversing the length of the Meridionali, crossing the Fulvius at the the Pons Orientalem, then going across the Campus Civicus, and out the Porta Purgamenta. It took more than an hour of brisk walking.

From there we walked to the dumps proper, where I had seen Araxus last. We saw the temple of Libitina with its sacred grove on top of a hill to the south and west, where the undertakers set up their shops. Further eastward, we found the debris and refuse of a city of a million people. From broken furniture to a veritable hill made of shards of discarded *amphorae* and from discarded clothing to the discarded bodies of those who once wore them and could not afford a funeral. If something was unwanted — and if no one was found who could be forced to claim it — the city's slave-gangs carted it out here.

My luck held, and the fifth derelict misfit we saw sifting through the rubbish was Araxus.

***

"You're welcome. Well, it was nice seeing you again," said Araxus when he saw us. I thought he was about to scamper away, but he approached us instead. Araxus was my age, though so unkempt and stooped that he appeared twice that. A face, once fair, was ravaged by the elements. Dank hair hung down around his face and his scraggly beard. He leaned on his crutch, his green right eye was looking at us curiously, while his black left eye never stopped roving about.

"Araxus, I need your help again. I want to ask you some

questions," I said.

"You'll find the lead merchants you seek right there on the Campus Civicus, in that cluster of buildings across the road from the Emporium Sempronicus." He waved his hand in the direction we came from.

"What? Why would we be after lead merchants?" asked Aemilia.

"I haven't even told you what it's about!" I exclaimed.

"Surely, you remember our training," Araxus said. "It was one of the fairly basic lessons in cults."

"Oh, wait, I think I see where you're going with this," I said.

"Well, maybe you can tell me," interjected Aemilia, "because I certainly don't follow anything you two are talking about."

"I'm sorry, that was crass of me," Araxus straightened up. "Of course I'd be glad to help, if you'd just tell me what's it all about."

"Huh? But I thought you already knew."

"Is this the same young woman as last time?" Araxus leered at Aemilia. "We've barely been introduced when we met two months ago. It was night when we did, but I bet Felix here was taking all the credit by morning's light. He still blames me for his love life."

"Araxus, you *fellator asini!* How dare you bring up Helena!" I shouted.

"Felix! What brings you here again, my friend?" Araxus asked with a smile of surprise. He then turned and walked away without a word, leaving us gaping at his back.

"What was that all about?" Aemilia asked as we made our way back to the city walls.

"His mind is no longer all there," I replied. "It's the effect of a curse he brought upon himself years ago. You can see it in his one black eye. He is not the man he used to be, either in body or in mind."

"But he was just babbling — and so rude!"

"He wasn't babbling. He was having the same conversation we did — only he was holding it back to front. As for rude — well, some things don't change, even with curses."

"What do you mean, back-to-front conversation?" Aemilia looked at me, puzzled.

"His speciality was the *magia inanitas*, those forces that lie between things. It's the hardest, most esoteric branch of incantation. Few people take it up, and fewer still retain their sanity attempting to master it. He was brilliant, but when he brought that curse upon himself his mind became unstuck and permanently buffeted by the flows of *magia*. Today he experienced the conversation in reverse to how we did. Instead of starting with *ave* and ending with *vale*, he just went the other way." I paused for breath. "Anyway, he answered my question, which is all we came here for."

"But you never asked any questions, Felix! You never even told him why we came. I don't understand any of this."

"We came to ask about a possible cause for the strange occurrences. I thought it might be a curse of some sort, and Araxus agrees. There are several ways to effect curses and using lead sheets inscribed with the right formulae is one of the oldest. It's not much in use anymore — more of an old wives' technique with dubious results."

"So that is why he mentioned lead merchants?"

"Correct. The *rhones* cracked down decades ago on the real practitioners and eventually made the practice illegal. The Collegium locked the knowledge behind thick doors and wards. They turn a blind eye towards the charlatans though, so you'll see mock curse tablets show up occasionally. The *rhones* round up the foreign wizards and witches when they need something to distract the public's opinion. But it would seem someone managed to uncover the lost knowledge and craft a real *tabula defixionis*." I stopped my lecture to catch my breath under the shade of a tree.

"And the lead merchants would be able to tell us who bought lead tablets?" Aemilia asked.

"Regular lead tablets are available for sale all over town,

for less nefarious reasons. But I imagine whoever made a tablet for a real curse would need specific, high quality alloy, the kind available only from an artisan metallurgist. These wouldn't be the vendors supplying large volumes of lead to the city's aqueducts, but a retailer specialising in refined materials and supplies to the *incantatores* and other knowledgeable persons. Before we try to find the right one, however, I want to consult someone else — even though it means walking back to the Forum then coming back here to the Emporium on the Campus Civicus."

"Ah, I see," she said. "Only one more question, if you please."

"What is it?"

"Who was the girl he mentioned — Helena?"

I blinked. "No one you should concern yourself with." I resumed our walk at a quickened pace.

"Felix, you're hiding something. I can tell. Is she relevant to this case? Does she know anything of such curses?"

I stopped, looked her dead in the eye and said through gritted teeth, "She was someone I loved. She was your age when she poked her nose into the affairs of dark *magia*, just like you are now. The next time I saw her she was floating down a well, dead and rotting, her arms and legs hacked off. So, shut up and listen when I say things are too dangerous for you, or you'll end up the same."

We trudged the rest of the way in silence.

I cooled down after a while but kept a gruff expression and a quick pace. Aemilia stayed a respectful step behind me, and her bodyguards brought up the rear. She didn't deserve my outburst — it wasn't her fault Araxus had dredged up awful memories. Still, she was on the same track as Helena had been. I told myself this rough treatment was for her own good, that I needed to beat some sense into her. But just like with my Helena, I knew she wouldn't let go easily.

***

I led us back to the shop of my acquaintance Quintus

47

Sosius, a renowned trader of scrolls. "While he also deals with the usual plays and memoirs, his expertise is in works of an occult nature. He has agents roaming far and wide, locating rare manuscripts for him. He employs teams of scribes to copy them and sells the copies to discerning customers at a hefty profit. He knew my father and has had a soft spot for me since my father passed away," I explained as we neared his offices in the Basilica Antonia.

"Why can't we go to the great library of the Collegium Incantatorum?" asked Aemilia as we stepped under the porticos of the basilica.

"Because they won't let us in. You need special permission to access those sections, or at least a bribe so high even your uncle Valerius would baulk at it. Besides, you have to be a graduate to use the master index. Without the *visus verum*, it's practically useless."

Sosius' private study was an airy space, dominated by the large glazed windows. Tables and pigeon-hole shelves for scrolls occupied corners and spaces between columns, while his main massive desk sat right under the windows for the best light. Sosius' appearance was as impeccable as always, grey hair cut short in a classic style and toga draped meticulously. We exchanged greetings, and I introduced Aemilia.

"Ah, yes, I remember," he said. "The young woman who came looking for the non-existent first edition of Liberalis."

I saw her blush and intervened, lest we get distracted by how I originally set her on that wild goose chase. "This time we're after some known manuscripts, of which I was hoping you might have copies. All to do with curses, unfortunately." I gave him a few names of authors and works relevant to the case.

He didn't even blink. "You do realise that over half those scrolls are contraband? Anyone caught with an unauthorised copy will have to answer to the *rhones* of the Collegium Incantatorum."

Crestfallen, Aemilia asked, "Then how are we to proceed with the investigation?"

Sosius and I smiled. "You'll note that dear Quintus Sosius was just making an observation. An opening statement for negotiations, to set the background for an atrocious price."

"You wound me," Sosius said, placing his right hand on his heart and feigning insult. But the gesture lost something with the twitch of his mouth. "But Felix is correct, of course. While I only deal with legal manuscripts and transcripts, I might be able to put you in touch with those less upright citizens who take a dimmer view of the sanctity of law. Let's start with what I have in stock, though, and we can take it from there should you need more information."

We spent the rest of the afternoon in a side cubicle at his offices, but the scrolls in his possession proved useless to us. The knowledge they contained was restricted to describing some of the curses and their effects but did not provide the technical details I needed to be able to devise a method of divination.

Sosius ended up writing us a letter of introduction to a man he was certain would have the required works. "I wouldn't dream of charging the son of Spurius Vulpius money for any of this," he said, "but I might have a service I would require from you later. Call it a favour for now."

CHAPTER VII

The address of the man to whom we had the introduction was on the Clivi Inferior. It suited us to go
there after we left Sosius, as it was on the way back to Aemilia's
residence, and at a time when the occupant was likely to be home.

We walked first from the Basilica Antonia across the
Forum and down the Via Recta, where my banker held his shop.
Navigating the Forum is always a challenge, it being the stage to
anything worth watching in Egretian public life.

We passed a senator recently elected as one of next year's
aediles standing on a stool, proclaiming his manifesto for his term
in office. Behind him, his slaves washed the chalked-on slogan of
one of his opponents from a basilica wall. Further down, a tutor
lectured a dozen children in the basics of grammar, making them
chant verses of the Aeneid. Hawkers and peddlers of anything
from food to trinkets for tourists accosted passersby, only lowering their voices next to a trial in progress held under the shade
of a portico. The trial was not a grand affair, and a few people
stopped to watch. The judge kept an impassive face, though his
eyes darted to a dark corner where a prostitute wriggled inside
her toga to flash her breasts at potential customers. Life in our
city is carried out in the open, as a form of spectator sport.

"I doubt anyone dealing with the kind of information we
want would let us peruse his collection out of the kindness of his
heart," I said to Aemilia.

"So, you would buy the scrolls from him?" she asked.

"Doubtful — more like buy a few short hours to review

them. Be ready to take quick notes."

"Ah, Felix!" cried Barbatus, my banker, when we entered his office. "Haven't seen you in a while. Been away? Depositing some commission?"

"Taking a loan, rather."

He peered at Aemilia and said, "My dear, you are far too good to be the kind he normally affords. I hope he promised you a proper marriage."

"Oh, shut up, Barbatus," I retorted as Aemilia blushed. "I'm here on business for the lady's uncle, and just need a quick advance."

"Keep a close eye on him." Barbatus smiled, while we waited for his clerk to get us the coins. "I employ a special scribe just to keep up with dear Felix's creative accounting."

From there we walked through the alleys behind the Collegium Incantatorum and up the Via Caeca a short way. This area was populated by Egretia's middle class citizenry, its streets mostly clean and devoid of beggars.

We found the house of Titus Fonteius Capito by the mark of the owl Sosius described to us. When the little slit in the door opened at our knock, I told the door-slave we had business with his master.

"What's your name?" he asked gruffly. "The master only sees the people on this list."

I pushed the letter from Sosius through the narrow slit, whereupon the slave closed it. We waited under a tall cypress tree, and got the chance to examine our surroundings — a stretch of private domiciles in between low *insulae*. Not the best street, but neither the worst. The area was notorious for the rapidly shifting environments, where one end of a street could be quite decent while the other was a veritable slum, riddled with dens of thieves. My inner cynic observed that it must make it easier for those seemingly respectable citizens to find their whorehouses.

The door opened. "The master will see you now," said the burly slave.

We were shown to the *tablinum*, through a house that

had seen better days, or, at least, better housekeepers. Titus Fonteius was seated at his desk, a grey man in his late fifties — grey hair, grey eyes, grey skin, grey expression.

"I don't normally see visitors," he said as he indicated the guest chairs, "But Quintus Sosius wrote it will be worth my while."

"If you have the right information for us, I am sure I would be able to compensate you fairly for it. We are after a specific kind of knowledge, which Sosius indicated you would have. We are researching old practices that have fallen out of fashion amongst educated people but are still remembered and used amongst the more superstitious. I understand you might be in possession of scrolls detailing the ancient custom of inscribing charms on lead sheets."

"Charms? Curses you mean! There is only one thing you can inscribe on lead tablets — and that thing is very much frowned upon."

"You are, of course, correct. You're most astute and observant — I see Sosius was right to speak so highly of you. We are trying to track down some weird occurrences surrounding this young lady's uncle. Things no one can explain, putting the poor girl and her family at their wits' end." I gave Aemilia a gentle nudge with my foot, and she started to sniffle convincingly. "We are purely trying to research ways of breaking such enchantments to give a poor man some peace in his old age."

"And how would I know you are not after creating such 'enchantments', as you put it, yourself?"

I took a fat purse of coins from the sinus of my toga and put it on his desk. "Perhaps this will convince you of our good intentions."

"I am still not convinced," Titus Fonteius said. "I have heard that in recent times the *rhones* of the Collegium are cracking down on folk practitioners and paying well for information about them."

"Not in gold," I said, and undid the purse's strings. "And, besides, no one needs to hear about it."

The lustre of gold coins did the trick. "You are a fool, but it's your money. As far as I know, all that remains today are mere charlatans, earning dishonest commissions from the superstitious. The true art, *ahem*, practice of *tabulae defixiones* died centuries ago. It is no business of mine if you want to chase wild geese."

Thus, establishing that all of us were merely scholars and not law breakers, Aemilia and I were soon sitting together in Capito's library, poring over scrolls describing the less savoury folk practices in details beyond the ken of charlatans. As is often the case with any metaphysical knowledge, the language was oblique and overly flowery. Words and terms had been appropriated, given symbolical meaning, and used in a way that each line had several possible subtexts.

In a way, having Aemilia there with her constant questions helped me. Being forced to take the role of pedagogue, introducing her to the art of interpretation of arcane writings, had also forced me to sharpen my own wits. Talking through things out loud with her helped me recall lessons from my past. Plus, her note-taking was far above my own, in a clear and neat hand.

At last, in an obscure scroll by Iamblichus, I found what I was searching for. As with everything in life, and *magia* is no exception, there are several ways to achieve the same effect. Curses take many shapes. The lead tablets that Araxus' hinted about are only one such mechanism. They involve calling on a god or *numen* and asking it to bring its wrath down upon the victim. The target can be named ("my sleazy neighbour, Gaius Appius, pox be on his head"), or just generally described ("whomever stole my mother's horn comb from the baths"). A result is petitioned, ("may their food turn in their stomach, their bile rising and not giving them rest"), in exchange for a service by the petitioner for the god ("and for this I shall donate a silver *denarius* every week at the temple").

In essence, a contract.

There were always rumours of ways to bind real *magia* to

such tablets to achieve the effect, but they were never as precise as incantation. Graduates of the Collegium Incantatorum are usually more direct in their way of effecting desired results, and scoff at the idea that the *numina* have intelligence and will of their own. For the *incantatores*, the forces that shape our world are merely flowing energies. Whether to curb competition or from a desire to be on the safe side in case they're wrong, the *rhones* ruling the Collegium routinely run any folk or foreign practitioners of *magia* — including the craftsmen who produce curse tablets — out of town, claiming foul magic and sacrilege. For the common people, though, these tablets are ways to get manifestations of divine direction, and some semblance of justice.

The *tabulae defixiones* are therefore to be found dealing with humdrum matters. A lawyer, requesting that his opponent's tongue seize, his step falter, and his prosecution fail. Or bathers at the public baths, cursing the unknown person who stole their tunics while they were getting clean. There are even love charms for any occasion, from unrequited love to ensuring a partner's willing participation in certain erotic practices. The majority, perhaps due to the dark and heavy aspect of lead itself, are chthonic in nature. In other words, curses.

All the gods can be petitioned, but those of the underworld are more often so. Men would call upon Dis Pater or Orcus and women upon Proserpina or Trivia. Sometimes, the god or goddess invoked depended on the target or the particular effect desired. Tablets could be folded, or nailed, or interred in a grave, or thrown down a deep source of water, or buried in a particular location dedicated to the god. Often, the magic would involve several of these at once, especially in case of lead tablets. When the tablets were made from clay, they might be smashed and mixed in cement, or disposed of in any of the many and varied ways people could think of, with the hopes that it would reach the right *numen*, but lead had proved the most efficacious and became the standard material.

Almost invariably, these supplications were empty of

power. Sometimes, simple folk would imitate the *incantatores* and would utter what they thought to be words of power. Without understanding the rules of *voces mysticae*, however, they would just end up speaking nonsensical gibberish. No wonder the simpletons could never reliably get power into the tablets, and supplications to strike the guilty party with ague and dysentery resulted in nothing worse than diarrhoea, cramps, or nothing at all.

Finally, it was in the writing of Iamblichus that I found mentions of the exact way to construct a functional *tabula defixionis*. He detailed with mathematical precision the ratio of lead to tin and other metals in the base alloy, the way to stretch and create the blank sheet, how to inscribe the curse-words, the various ceremonies and manipulations needed afterwards, and in general how to channel the *magia* into the *tabulae* and achieve desired effects. I explained all this to Aemilia, even as we were translating together Iamblichus' scroll from its original language. Her Hellican was better than mine, though she got lost with the more esoteric and technical terms. No matter, our spheres of knowledge complemented one another's perfectly.

Armed with a firmer understanding of how the curse-tablets affect the flow of *magia*, I could devise a ritual to detect them more clearly in the affected *insula*, and — should Araxus prove right — contain the curses.

***

By the time we left Titus Fonteius' house it was after sundown.

"There was a point I meant to ask you about," Aemilia said. "In his writing, Iamblichus detailed quite explicitly the ceremonies one must perform over a tablet, and yet you said nothing would happen if I recite them out loud."

"That's because his scroll is written in hexameter to conform to the rest of his text, but the chants have to be recited along different rules."

"But even Phaenias describes everything in hexameter,

and he's very specific about the performance of chants."

"No amount of reading will — or even could — give one an understanding of *magia*. The reason it takes so long to learn is that besides the theoretical understanding of the philosophical underpinnings of *magia*, one simply has to feel it. Awakening this kind of sensitivity can only be done under the guidance of a master. It has to be built up slowly over time."

I recounted for Aemilia some of my experiences with the tutors at the Collegium. The greatest achievement of the Collegium Incantatorum is setting up a standard learning path for aspirants. By carefully controlling the education process, we Egretians are able to both repeat it and ensure no one gets too much power too quickly. The results of that are all too often disastrous. In other nations and cultures, the training was more haphazard, with contents and scope controlled by the master himself. The Hellicans, with all their love for teaching and debates, were held back by the constant in-fighting and striving for personal glory. We Egretians managed to turn it to a kind of engineering, like bridge building and road laying. Well, almost like that.

And Aemilia, with her sharp mind and quick grasp, picked up the ideas and concepts I was talking about easily. That's how she understood where I was heading, even before I realised it myself.

"So, to detect the *magia* you work off of the traces, but it's always easier to witness the actual flow?"

"That's right," I said, thinking about the right kind of animal for the blood sacrifice I would have to make.

"And you can then devise a ceremony to enhance your acquired sensitivity and follow the flows to their source?"

"Correct again," I answered, trying to recall where else I'd seen some of the sigils in Fonteius' scrolls, and what hints that might give me.

"I hope mother is at home," she said, "because you will be staying for dinner."

"Ah, what? Thank you kindly for the invitation, but I wouldn't want to impose."

"Rubbish! First, I hardly think either you or my mother will find it an imposition. But more importantly," she smirked at me, "you should know better than to expect I will let you go tonight. You've pretty much admitted that you need to carry out a ceremony in the presence of the *magia*, which means spending the night in one of my uncle's cursed *insulae*. If you imagine for one minute I will let you send me to bed like a child while you have all the fun, you are crazier than a spinster with twenty cats! The agreement was that I get to watch and report to my uncle."

"The agreement, young lady, was that you may observe and that I would warn your mother if there was anything I deemed too dangerous. And if you think spending the night in an abandoned building waiting to observe what form of atrocities the curse will try and visit upon us is not dangerous, then you are more delusional than a galley-slave dreaming of being elected to the senate!"

She opened her mouth to speak but I cut her off. "Anyway, that is not relevant for tonight. We have to make preparations ahead of time and I need to design the ceremony. You, my dear, will get to watch the preparations. But no more."

"You forget who's paying whom. My uncle —"

"Has hired *me*, for *my* knowledge."

"I will tell him you cheat him!" Aemilia snapped.

"I will tell your mother that you are trying to learn incantation for yourself!" I snapped back.

"Will the two of you shut up already? You are embarrassing me in front of my neighbours." We were standing at the entrance to Aemilia's house, and without our notice Cornelia had come to the door. She was glaring, clutching a shawl around her shoulders as her door-slave cringed behind her, trying to meld with the wall.

"Now come inside," Cornelia said, "and we can talk about this over dinner like civilised people."

***

I hardly noticed the food that evening. Aemilia and I

glared at each other while Cornelia found the whole thing amus-ing. Icilia was there too, making incessant small-talk that grated on my nerves. It seemed like every time Aemilia or I would start to speak, we'd do so at the same moment. As soon as voices start-ed to rise, Cornelia would clap her hands, shut us up, and order the next course or more wine. Icilia took the following silences as a challenge, filling them with inane gossip.

Aemilia left right after the fruit baked in milk with can-died nuts and black pepper was served. As she walked out, she said over her shoulder, "Make sure you keep him here tonight, mother."

Icilia did a poor job at concealing a snigger at that remark. After a last sip of wine, Icilia rose to leave, forgoing further enter-tainment. I got to my feet as well, but Cornelia stopped me from leaving. "I'd rather avoid another argument with Aemilia. You might as well stay the night and start together in the morning."

"You have to see my point, though. It is far too dangerous for her. You have heard the stories about mutilated corpses and dead children. We will stand right in the middle of the worst of it! And what if I'm wrong and this isn't a curse? We may be completely unprepared to deal with whatever causes this."

Cornelia sighed. "All true, of course. I can't let her go. It will be a hard day tomorrow when I tell her. There's one way you can make it easy for me — find some research she can do, a scroll she can read — to keep her feeling like she's still involved." She paused, adding with half-lidded eyes, "Well, two ways you can make it easy for me. I need a good night's sleep, and Icilia will have already spread the gossip."

CHAPTER VIII

The next morning reaffirmed my life's choice of not sharing my home with a woman. Even before leaving my sleeping cubicle, I could hear Cornelia and Aemilia arguing. I followed the yelling around the corner to the peristyle garden. A few of the house-slaves were pointedly keeping themselves busy with chores, away from the raging storm.

As I got closer, I could make out the words.

"I am not a child anymore! I will be married soon and —"

"And I'd like you to live long enough to see that wedding! We agreed that we'll let you indulge in a little fun this summer and in return you agreed to cooperate with marriage."

"Exactly! This will be a long life of boring duties as a senator's wife. I wanted to experience real *magia*, the kind forbidden to women. You didn't think for a moment I'd settle for a couple of third-hand stories to frighten children and a visit to some seedy scrolls dealer?"

"But a haunted house? It is far too dangerous. These aren't merely stories to frighten children, as you put it. You described to me the gruesome blood and gore you saw in those apartments. I can't possibly agree to let you place yourself in such a risk."

"I will have Felix there to protect me. You certainly appreciate his 'services,' don't you?"

"Don't get smart with me, young lady!"

While I was curious about how an argument regarding yours truly might turn out, I decided it was best to interject at that moment. I coughed, and said, "May I make a suggestion

59

that might satisfy you both?"

They both turned to me, glaring fiercely. I had to rethink the wisdom of my recent action and my past record with women in general. Out loud I said, "Aemilia, you want to experience some real *magia*, of the kind not normally allowed to women, at least inside our city's sacred boundary, right?"

She nodded, and I continued. "I have something to offer you, then. Your mother and I agree that coming at night to witness the curse in action is too perilous. We know that there might be some wild and dangerous manifestations and I will be far too busy dealing with them to protect you properly. But I can arrange a taste of what I will be experiencing. Your argument gave me the idea for how to trace the origins of the curse. It will be quite safe, and so long as you are not near the source you'll be fine. I'll give you this taste away from the haunted houses and any danger and afterwards you'll return here."

Aemilia didn't appear entirely convinced and this was a deviation from the purely academic activity Cornelia had in mind, so before either of them could speak I added, "I will still need help in devising a ritual to contain the curses as we discussed, in dealing with the source. You can assist me with the research, and, if I deem it safe enough, I will arrange for you to watch me perform the curse's undoing from a distance."

Neither of them looked particularly pleased, but they agreed nonetheless.

***

I decided to postpone finding the lead merchant.

Our investigations down that avenue would be more productive if we found a sample of the metal sheets used. Instead, we headed to the Street of the Embalmers to visit my acquaintance and master herbalist, Akhirabus. As my discerning readers may tell by his name, he comes from far off Mitzrana. They have a bit of an embalming fetish there, preserving the corpses of their dead for centuries. They believe that when the *animus* leaves the body, it still needs that physical earthly manifestation in order to function in the afterlife. Or, at least, that's how I understood it. All sounding a bit exotic to most Egretians, who prefer cremation to inhumation. Still, in a city as large as ours there was always a need for people with special skills in handling corpses.

Although Akhirabus' profession was embalming, his passion was herbalism. His mind retained information as comprehensive as you'd likely find in any library and he had enough scrolls and codices to complement his knowledge and rival the best collections. The *veneficitores* of the Collegium Incantatorum might have taken a dim view of someone like that, except that he was doing brisk business in supplying them with ingredients of the finest quality for their potions and poultices. For every *rhone* that rose and wanted to rid our city of 'unnatural foreign influences,' there were ten members of the college who owed Akhirabus favours. And so, his shop remained open through the years, its modest facade hiding a most unusual collection.

As we entered, our noses were assaulted by the plethora of smells and scents competing for attention. I had been there on many occasions and was overwhelmed anew each time. I stood awhile, letting my eyes adjust to the gloom and my mind adjust to the urgent messages of my nose. I peered sidelong at Aemilia as the expression on her face changed with every waft of air that brought new smells to her attention. Her eyes narrowed, her brows furrowed then shot up, her expression lightened, and a quizzical look crossed her face — a succession of curiosity, surprise, disgust, and pleasure in each heartbeat.

Akhirabus' assistant came to greet us and soon we were seated in his study at the back, amidst his most treasured scrolls and samples.

Akhirabus did not let me jump straight to business. "Please, you must first tell me how you met this charming young lady."

"Aemilia is the niece of my current employer. In fact, it was upon her recommendation that he hired me," I said.

"But to what do I owe the pleasure of her visit today? You are always running your errands in a solitary fashion, never accompanied by the clients you service."

"I am here to keep him honest," Aemilia responded. And before I could respond, Akhirabus erupted in such good-natured, hearty laughter that I could do naught but join him.

Akhirabus wiped the tears from his eyes and said, "You will have your hands full then, though I can't tell if this is a bad thing or a most enjoyable one," he said with a wink. Aemilia blushed.

"Back to business, if you please," I said. "I am after some *psilocybe* mushrooms. I would trust no one but you to do the correct identification."

"And which would you like? If you come to me, I assume you are not in need of the garden-variety *semblances*. I have *psilocybe semilanceata* in stock and at a good price, but if it's *cyanescens* that you want I'm afraid the price will be rather higher."

Being on an all-expenses-paid commission, I normally would have preferred the finer stuff and bluntly charged it to Valerius Flaccus, but I was conscious of Aemilia's watchful eye. "*Psilocybe semilanceata* would do just fine. Although," I paused for effect, and felt Aemilia's gaze on me. "Perhaps in this instance we should go instead with the *cyanescens*. I will need all the refinement I can get for the use I have for it. I was thinking maybe even letting the young girl try it, and her uncle surely would approve of the extra cost for the sake of his adored niece."

Akhirabus raised an eyebrow and turned to appraise Aemilia anew. She looked surprised, and her lack of understanding was plain. "Are you sure?" he asked me. "The lady seems too young, too —" he waved a hand in the air, looking for words, "— *Egretian*, to know what do with it."

"I will be there to guide her. She was adamant that she needs to report to her uncle that I am not cheating him out of his money, but with theory and no practice she can't quite follow in my footsteps. I thought this way she would gain the perspective she so strongly desires."

"Very well." Akhirabus chuckled softly at Aemilia's puzzlement and addressed her as he said, "I shall give you my best *psilocybe* practically at cost — provided you return one day soon and tell me of your experience."

***

"What was that all about?" Aemilia persisted as we made our way out of the shop and down to the Porta Fulvia.

"You wanted a taste of *magia*, right? And I need to be able to detect the traces left by the nightly hauntings. I have explained to you that I don't have the *visus verum*, so I cannot just follow the invisible marks from an animated mural to the source of its power. Even the vision of graduate *incantatores* is coloured by their specialisation, and most would find it hard to concentrate on the effect we've seen. But there are ways to enhance this. These methods, while based on folk remedies, are actually used by the Collegium. The masters and teachers use it in a controlled environment to open the students to the perception of *magia*. While the folk recipes are inexact and have dubious, sometimes even fatal, results, the Collegium has refined the practices. Instead of wild visions, the apprentices get an insight. They can then practice with it in mind. Attaining sensitivity to *magia* is akin to finding a black cat in a dark room while wearing a blindfold. This way, you at least know what a cat looks like."

"And how would that help you now? I thought you've already been through basic training at the Collegium."

"True," I said, "but it can help me in two ways. First, when used carefully, it can heighten my sensitivity to the flows of *magia*. It won't be quite like the true sight, but it will be enough for me to track the source."

"And the second way?" Aemilia asked.

"It will keep me employed by fulfilling the promise to both your mother and you. I will let you try some this afternoon. It will not be the full guided tour of an apprentice at the Collegium, but it will give you a taste of the true nature of *magia*, without the risk of exposing you to anything too dangerous. Now hush, for the place we are about to enter does not normally see women of your class."

We were standing in a narrow alley off an odd-shaped public square near the Porta Fulvia. Above the door hung a sign of an *amphora* with eels sticking out. This was the Pickled Eel tavern, the favourite haunt of my old army buddy Crassitius, and where he ran his business.

We entered and Aemilia made a strangled gurgle at the overpowering smell of rancid wine, old boiled-cabbage, and overly-garlicky sausages. "So far, all the places you stopped at were cheap but decent. What is this place? It smells horrid."

"We're not here to eat anything," I answered. "We are here to pick up some help for tonight. My friend Crassitius owns a stable of ex-gladiators."

"Why not get one of my mother's bodyguards?"

"Because I don't trust them. You've seen how your uncle's agent's enforcers reacted. I need someone I can rely on to pull me away, if things get ugly."

We shuffled our way to the back, where I found Crassitius engrossed in a game of *tali*.

"How is this game played?" Aemilia asked.

"There are four dice made of sheep knuckle-bones. Because of their uneven shapes, they can roll on one of four sides. Those are numbered from the largest to the smallest as one, three, four and six. The value of the throw depends on the combination."

Crassitius' turn came. He scooped the knuckle-bones into a wooden cup, exclaimed "Vultures circle to the left, Venus keep my hand deft!" and tossed them from the cup onto the table.

The gathered men leaned in and peered at the dice. By the loud groan that escaped Crassitius' lips and the chuckles from the rest of the group, I knew I would not be getting a discount tonight.

"Why don't you take a break, Marcus Crassitius, and earn some honest money instead?" I called to him.

"Ha! Felix! The day you make recommendations of honest work is the day the gods piss fire down on us!"

"Still closer than the day you win at *tali*," I retorted. "Calling upon Venus to guide your dice. If that goddess had any consideration for you, she wouldn't make even the ugly whores charge you double!"

"Well, she certainly has been smiling at you recently," he said as he turned his gaze to Aemilia. His eyes went up and down her youthful frame, missing nothing. His leer made her blush.

"That," I said, "would be the honest work I mentioned. I will need some muscle for tonight, but one with some brains as well. Not overly superstitious would be a preference."

"Muscles, easy; brains, a possibility; but not superstitious? Unlikely."

"What about Borax? He was quite alert and useful when I hired his services the last time," I said.

"Borax has been tentatively commissioned for tonight. I could perhaps change his booking — if the price is right." Crassitius then proceeded to name an astronomical sum.

"You always were a *mentula* of a sore loser when it came to dice. For that amount I should be able to buy a trained gladiator outright!" I said.

"Possibly, but none so accomplished and not in time for tonight," he retorted.

We argued a bit more, but Crassitius knew he had me. I needed a bodyguard I could trust and he played on it. No mention of our shared army past would sway him.

"This is ridiculous," Aemilia suddenly piped in, turning to Crassitius. "You like betting on dice, yes? We each throw the dice once. If I win, we pay you half of what you ask, which is still probably twice what the gladiator is worth for one night. If you win, we'll pay the full price, in cash, without further delay."

Crassitius eyed her for a moment. "The money I can already get," he replied. "How about you pay full price — and I get one kiss from you?"

"Done," said Aemilia before I could object. I gazed at her and then at Na'ama standing a step behind. I could only imagine what Cornelia would do if — when — the slave girl reported this.

Crassitius produced dice and a wooden throwing cup.

"Let the host go first," said Aemilia.

Crassitius gathered the knuckle-bones, shook them in the cup, exclaimed "With libations of wine and honey, Iuno Moneta protect my money!" and threw the dice. "Ha! A triple *Senio!* Three sixes! Beat that!" he exclaimed gleefully.

Without a word Aemilia gathered up the bones and placed them in the cup. "Magna Mater make this right, aid your servant in her plight!" she intoned like an expert, and cast the knuckle-bones on the table.

The dice stopped rolling and I started to laugh. "One of each number! The Venus Throw, the luckiest of them all! You were right, Crassitius, Venus must be smiling down on us."

"This is not my day for bets," Crassitius grumbled. "I'll send Borax to your place by nightfall. Now go away already and let me get pissing drunk."

Chapter IX

"Where to now?" Aemilia asked as we climbed to the crest of the Meridionali.

"I thought we'd stop by my house, so I can prepare the mushrooms for tonight. I will let you have a taste, as promised. I'm afraid you will have to make your way to your mother's *domus* by yourself, though, as I have to preserve my strength for tonight."

"Could these mushrooms let me experience the *visus verum*?"

"Under competent guidance, yes. But I think you would be the first to point out that I hardly qualify as competent," I chuckled at Aemilia. "No, tonight's experiment will let you experience some of the *magia* flows, but in the same way that riding an unbroken mare is like driving a chariot at the races. It's going to be a wild ride, so don't expect refinement or control."

She knitted her brows. "And you're sure it's safe?"

"What happened to your eagerness to try real *magia*? Don't worry, people have been using those mushrooms for visions for aeons. Of course, not everyone retains their sanity, but we will only let you try a tiny amount — hardly enough to risk damaging your mind. Entirely up to you, of course," I said, and sped up my pace a little so she wouldn't catch my smile.

We soon reached my home, where I unlatched the front door and let Aemilia, her slave girl, and the bodyguard in. "Dascha! We have guests for dinner!" I cried.

Dascha ambled into the vestibule, and croaked, "One lady for the dining couches, *domine*, and two to dine with me in the kitchen? Oh, this one looks saucy. Probably too good for you. I'll cook something nice, then. Oysters should do the trick." She leered a little.

I was amused at Aemilia's sharp intake of breath, though whether at Dascha's impertinence or her appearance, I wasn't certain. My housekeeper was in her late seventies with but a handful of yellowing teeth and a permanent squint.

"Was that your slave or some strange crone?" Aemilia asked.

"Bit of both, really. Dascha has been with my family for years, since my father was a child. Perhaps because of this, she never quite accorded me the respect a master should expect from his slaves. Right now, she is my cook and house-keeper."

"She looks like something that belongs far away in a hut in some sacred grove," said Aemilia.

"Ha! I doubt any *numina* would want her as a priestess! But it does explain why she's still with me." And to Aemilia's puzzled expression I added, "Because no one would buy her off my hands."

***

Aemilia sent her bodyguard to the kitchen, but her girl stayed with her as decorum dictated. In my study, I cleared a pile of scrolls from a chair for Aemilia and placed the packet of mushrooms on my desk, before assembling the necessary paraphernalia.

Despite summer's heat, I lit a brazier and fanned its flames, then placed a skillet on it and started to work.

"Do you need to chant anything?" Aemilia asked. "Are you channelling the *magia* into the mushrooms? Activating them in some way? The spices you're adding, are they a special mix, your own recipe? And why eggs? Don't folk incantations require blood sacrifice?"

"I don't need to chant or activate anything, the *psilocybe* will do that for us," I answered as I washed the mushrooms, selected one and sliced it finely. "Some incantations work better with blood, but this isn't an incantation. The spices are nothing more than salt and pepper, and a touch of oregano. You could probably chew on the mushroom by itself to the same effect, but they are rather vile unless cooked. The only secret here, as any campfire cook will tell you, is a splash of milk with the eggs. I am, in fact, making nothing more complicated than a mushroom *patina*."

I prepared a single portion from one mushroom and an egg. I needed to calibrate the potency of the concoction for tonight, so a single bite would give me an idea of the quantities I should use. I didn't want to take too much at the *insula* and end up a gibbering idiot while the ghosts that haunted the place ripped off my limbs and eviscerated me.

"Are you ready?" I asked Aemilia. She nodded, and I handed her a tiny bite of the mushroom and eggs on a spoon.

She took it gingerly and sniffed it. "Smells almost like a regular *patina*, though there is another faint smell that comes with it, which I can't quite place"

"The word you're looking for is farinaceous. It's a starchy smell, in addition to the normal earthly, dank smell of fungi. Now chew and swallow."

Aemilia took a breath, closed her eyes, and placed the morsel of food in her mouth. She chewed carefully before swallowing. "How long until it takes effect?" She asked.

"Not long. Describe what you see and feel."

"Well, I see you and this room. There is nothing special. Except that the light outside seems a bit brighter. Why is it so bright suddenly?" Aemilia rose and walked out of my study and into the garden. My house was modest, using a traditional floor plan. In the first section were the utility rooms and slave cubicles around the atrium, and in the other half was a cosy peristyle garden, surrounded by family rooms and the kitchen at the back. My study separated the two halves. From the garden, there was no view to speak of — just a patch of washed-out blue sky.

As Aemilia stepped out from under the colonnade, she froze and made a strange gargling sound. I followed her gaze and saw her staring at my fountain. One can only imagine what she saw in her state of mind, but the thing was horrendous even without the heightened awareness of the *psilocybe*. The brass fountain was shaped like a faun, done in exquisite detail but horrible imagery. The faun was waving a lyre in his right hand and holding his erect member whence the water came in his left. Its face, on which the nameless artist skilfully crafted each eyebrow and wrinkle, held a mad leer that would make even old goats fear for their virginity.

But Aemilia's artistic sensibilities were not the ones being offended right now. She stepped beyond the columns and started at the sky. "Why are there two suns?" she asked.

"What do you mean?"

"One is there," she pointed to the westering sun, "and there must be one just above the horizon over there," and she pointed north-east toward the bay's entrance.

"That would be the Pharos lighthouse. The sun is a natural source of *magia*. It's where Sol resides and is the manifestation of his *numen*. But the Pharos with the eternal flame fixed at its peak is a local focal point as well. It radiates *magia* so strongly that our *incantatores* have learnt not to gaze directly upon it with the true sight."

"And it colours everything. I can't see a single white cloud in the sky, but I see streaks of blue, and purple, and cyan, and pink, and lavender." She had a smile of wonder on her face, like a child discovering coloured chalks. She turned her gaze down from the sky to me, and said, "Why are you green?"

"Probably because I was handling the *psilocybe* mushrooms. Now, let's get you back inside."

I took Aemilia's elbow and gently guided her to the *triclinium*. I let her settle on a couch, pouring her water from a nearby pitcher. She kept babbling and staring at her hands as they moved and traced invisible patterns in the air. Eventually, her stream of chatter slowed. I called to Dascha, who brought us fresh bread, spicy olives, pickled cabbage, and semolina honey cakes. The trance the mushrooms induce leaves one thirsty, famished, and usually in a mood for strange combinations of food.

When Aemilia had calmed down and was feeling well enough, I walked her up to the Vicus Petrosa. There on the main road it was easy to hire a single-person litter to carry her up the mount to her mother's *domus*. The time was mid-afternoon, with plenty of light and traffic, and her girl and bodyguard would keep her safe.

Throughout this, she was uncharacteristically quiet and pensive. The effects would have worn off by then, but the impact of sensing the energies that course through and power our world would stay with her for a long while.

CHAPTER X

It was late at night, the streets on the way nearly abandoned. Human noises still drifted around the city — a drunk argument spilling from a window and the noise of wagons delivering produce to city markets. And yet, the courtyard of the *insula* I chose for tonight was dead quiet.

This was the one still sparsely populated. My choice was influenced by two factors. One, to prevent further harm to the remaining tenants; two, to face a curse not yet fully established. Though I believed Araxus' direction, I was facing a largely unknown opponent. Tackling a malignant incantation that has taken firm hold of a whole tenement building while not sure of my methods was less-than-wise, even for my reckless norm.

I imagined the tenants to be either sleeping, in the old lady's case, or absent, in Elpis' and maybe Memmia's case. Yet the house did not feel sleepy, and as I stood there I realised it wasn't as quiet as I first thought. There were noises. Different noises. Noises one would expect to hear in dark caves or under dense canopy of trees at midnight. No, that's not quite the right description. The sounds were city sounds. Just not the kind that belong in a building at a lively neighbourhood at night. These were sudden, grating noises, coming from unexpected directions.

Borax was standing beside me, looking apprehensive and trying to check all directions at once. He had his sword drawn, and the sack of supplies I brought was at his feet. His drooping red moustache was swinging, following his turning head. My instructions to him were simple. I was to concentrate on locating the source of the curse, but if anything appeared life-threatening and I wasn't in a condition to deal with it, he was to drag me outside to the street.

This *insula* was a slightly better affair than the others we had seen, with the inner courtyard dedicated as private gardens to the ground-floor apartments. This meant each apartment had to have its own cooking facilities. This kind of fire-hazard usually has landlords worried silly, so they put up their rents. A self-reinforcing cycle, ensuring only the upmarket ones have them.

I walked to one of the ground floor apartments at random, lit some kindling in a kitchen's hearth, and set up my skillet on it. I brought out the mushrooms and eggs and prepared them more carefully than I had earlier. Contrary to what I had told Aemilia, I put in some focused incantation, to build up the vision to desired effect.

When the *patina* was ready, I took a large bite.

Then another. And another.

I didn't have long to wait. What was black a moment ago, brightened. It wasn't light *per se*, but I could see objects framed by some inner glow through the different shades of darkness that permeated the spaces between them. Every time I turned my head, the swam with the motion of a sea alive with phosphorescent algae, then settled back to the normality of bricks and cement.

I needed to find the source of the paranormal occurrences, so I searched the inner courtyard until I reached the bas-relief of the house's *lar*. The *lararium* was done in the way common to household shrines — two fluted columns mounted with a triangular pediment at about a short man's height, projecting a hand's width from the wall. The alcove inside was painted dirty white as opposed to the faded ochre splattered with mud that covered the rest of the inner courtyard walls of the *insula*. The image of the *lar* was sculpted in crude but unmistakable lines, a young boy symbolising the guardian spirit of this house. The altar served as a focal point to the spirit's contractual obligation to protect the people who reside here in exchange for the appropriate sacrifices.

In the statue's right hand was a knife, and in his left he held a bowl like those used in religious ceremonies or by street beggars. He wore a tunic and a decorated conical cap, and at his feet were a dog and a snake.

Under the influence of the *psilocybe* mushrooms my mind both heightened and mixed sensory perceptions, so that as I approached I could sense the residual energy imbued in the statue from years of services and libations. I touched the plaster image and my eyes were suddenly blinded by bright colours and scenes from years of human contact with that primal energy that powers our world.

Snatches of events flashed before me in quick succession — births, childhood illnesses, marriages, work, money, and even death. Joys and sorrows. Decades and generations of people striving to gain what little control they could to steer their lives in directions slightly less miserable and dreary by appeasing the gods and begging for their favour.

As these scenes whirled before me, I could sense something else — old, unfathomable — making its curious enquiry into my mind, my life. Intermixed with the scenes from the lives of those unknown strangers, images of past events in my own life rose unbidden in my delirious mind. My father flushed with wine, proclaiming to all how I would rise far beyond the reach of anyone else in my family; my mother, sitting on the last of our good couches in a room bare of any artwork, eyes red from tears, refusing to go on with life, even though it had been a year since my father took his own life to spare us from debt collectors and exile; the day I met Helena, her golden hair shimmering in the sunlight and her smile eclipsing the sun in brilliance; and the day I found her mutilated body, floating bloated down a well.

I jerked my hand away as though the plaster snake at the *lar*'s feet had lashed out and bit me. But now, even without the touch I had a connection to that representation of the household's god. My mind flooded with images from its alien presence. It was seeking paths through the walls, seeking entry into our world. It skittered, fretted, and tried to communicate with those it encountered. These were the noises and screeches that the tenants heard.

I scrutinised the *lararium* and noticed gossamer threads of *magia* leading away from it. They wrapped all around the *insula*, shimmering like a spider's web revealed by a tilt of the head, sunlight glinting on what a moment ago appeared empty space. And like a spider, I traced the web to its centre, wary of what manner of thing I might encounter.

The shimmering silver threads led me to one of the dried vegetable patches. Dropping on my knees, I scrambled to dig in the corner with a spoon instead of a trowel until I uncovered a folded sheet of lead. I lifted it with tongs, careful not to touch the folded metal with my fingers. I could sense the dark energy throbbing from it, like the red entrails of a gutted animal convulsing in the throes of death. In my feverish state, I could smell the tablet radiating its malevolent acrid energy, the tendrils of which were by now firmly rooted in the grounds and walls of the *insula*. Though the tablet was folded, the etched writing squirmed like salted slugs, first crawling out and on top of the lead sheet, then skirting back under the folds.

A sudden crash made me jump.

Borax fell to the ground next to me, grappling with the animated statue of the *lar*. As a gladiator trained to fight for his life on the arena sands, Borax knew every trick to fighting, but the childlike sculpture was animated by forces far greater than mere mortal strength. What was made of moulded plaster and should have crumbled, was suddenly as hard as granite. Borax managed to throw the statue off him and roll to the other side. Both rose to their feet. Borax's sword lay a few paces away, bent to uselessness from hitting his stone opponent.

"Use the skillet!" I yelled, as I ran to the sack of supplies lying next to the fire-pit. From the corner of my eye, I saw Borax grab the heavy skillet from the grill. Behind me came loud clanging as heavy iron met granite-hard limbs, the strikes interspersed with Borax's grunts and muttered curses. While Borax sounded his frustration, the statue moved quietly, uttering not a single word. I busied myself with the necessities of what I had to perform, trusting Borax to keep the unnatural menace away from me. I had never advanced in my studies to the level of mastery required to bend the energies of *magia* purely by willing it, but I have studied enough theory and learnt much of the folk-ways so I could distil the semi-superstitious rituals to their essential elements. That way, with just a few crutches, I could achieve modest effects as I desired.

I dumped the contents of the sack before me and by urgent necessity thought up the quickest way to dampen the energies animating the statue of the *lar*. Its muteness gave me the idea that its tongue was bound. I took a lump of tar and placed it next to the fire pit to soften and melt. Of the three sacrificial offerings I had brought — a bloody chop of lamb, a whole fish, and a dead pigeon — I selected the fish and gutted it. I mixed the guts with wine in a wooden bowl carved from the core of a dead willow tree, then cut off the fish's head, stuffed the guts into its mouth, sewed it shut, singed it in the fire, and smeared the head with tar.

I began my incantation, calling upon Dea Tacita, the mute goddess of the dead. Her silent and chthonic nature, as well as her association with curses, made her a natural focal point. I poured the blood and guts on the ground as a libation, gathering the forces to me and opening the channel to the underworld. The appropriate gestures and the right words of power transformed the fish's head to a charged symbol of the silent goddess.

The statue, meanwhile, was steadily pushing Borax into the corner. The gladiator was getting tired, using the pan now more as a shield against the *lar*'s fists than a weapon. I yelled and threw the empty wooden bowl at the statue. When it turned to me, I cried, "Catch this," and threw the fish head. The *lar* caught the missile by reflex, and the black tar stuck to its white plaster fingers, sending dark tendrils snaking up its arms and over its shoulders, torso, and head.

Borax didn't hesitate. He brought the heavy iron skillet down on the head of the *lar* with all his might. The statue exploded in a cloud of choking white dust, as though it had dropped from the top of a tall building.

***

Borax laid me gently next to the garden fountain at my house. I was weak, dizzy as a drunken lamb, and I vomited twice that I could remember on the way home. The daze induced by the *psilocybe* lasts far longer than their effects — one reason I hate using them.

When a master in the Collegium guides a cadet with hallucinogenic mushrooms, they use them to give the aspirant a boost to their senses. They gently manipulate the energies of *magia*, so the cadet is not overwhelmed. The young men experiencing this are mere observers.

Naturally, some students will try the mushrooms for themselves. Most who do find the results too intense and learn their lessons. Some react so badly they burn their minds, which acts as a lesson to others.

Of the common folk who try *psilocybe* mushrooms without guidance, most will just experience vivid, colourful hallucinations and grow out of it. A few lose their sanity, while others claim to be oracles receiving visions from the gods. These groups are not mutually exclusive. Very, very few manage to walk the fine line that allows them to manipulate their perceptions according to their desires, directing delirious dreams to answer specific questions in a meaningful way.

Naturally, as a youngster I experimented with the mushrooms, especially after being ejected from the Collegium for my inability to pay the fees. Perhaps because I had already developed some sensitivity under the guidance of a master, or perhaps because I was just as lucky as my *cognomen* implied, I managed to learn how to use them effectively. I had watched both Collegium masters and folk practitioners, experimented with preparation techniques, and found a recipe that worked for me.

The amount I gave Aemilia was minuscule — just enough to make her hallucinate a bit. I could not guide her experience and I certainly did not want to risk her life or sanity. I imagine she saw nothing more than pink skies with purple clouds. The amount I took myself was far larger, plus I performed ceremonies and incantations, effectively forcing *magia* through my already sensitive skin.

There was a price to pay for that.

I was in no condition to do much the next day and sent a message saying as much to Aemilia at dawn. I expected a reply by mid-morning, but instead Aemilia herself came to my house. I must have looked worse than I felt, for what was undoubtedly a snarky remark died on her lips as she walked in. She spent the rest of the morning by my side, administering cold compresses to my forehead. I let her continue well after my dizziness passed.

I gathered she did not suffer many after-effects beyond vivid dreams. In turn, I told her about the events of the previous night and explained about the lead tablet. I could not risk taking the *tabula defixionis* with me for fear it would bring the curse down on my own home. I left it at the tenement building inside a special pouch, the insides of which were coated with tar and the ashes from a funeral pyre where a dog had burned with its master. My plan was to find the locations of such tablets in all the other *insulae* first, contain them, then gather and dispose of them all during daylight, safely outside the city walls.

I got her to agree it was far too dangerous for her to accompany me, and that I would tell her of my progress each day. I sent a message to Valerius Flaccus with her, indicating that security around his other *insulae* should be tightened. Now that we were certain it was a curse initiated by humans, no unknown guest should be allowed to wander into his other properties, lest they plant a curse tablet there.

CHAPTER XI

Women should never be trusted.

I chose to tackle the *insula* at the Vicus Fabricii next. It didn't matter which one I chose, but this one was a shorter walk from my house. I accompanied Aemilia a short distance and saw her depart, then Borax and I turned in the opposite direction

We began like we had the night before. The building's rectangular courtyard had a classic layout. There was a fountain in the centre with a cheap statue of a dolphin spraying waters that collected in a shallow pool. Around the pool were beds of earth for tenants to grow plants, which were now dried and dead. A shrine to the house's guardian spirit stood behind the fountain and across from public fire-pits where tenants could cook their meals. These were built of brick and placed well away from the walls to reduce the chance of fire — a hazard in any city.

With Borax keeping watch, I set up my pan and other necessities in one of these fire-pits, prepared the *psilocybe* in eggs and intoned the right words. I took one bite, then a second. It didn't take long for their effects to take hold.

A silvery, slimy trail like that of a slug led me to the apartment where the painting's snakes had eaten a baby alive in his crib. The place was abandoned, everything gone except for the crib and the picture still hanging on the wall above it. I have only a vague recollection of my baby sister. When she died of the ague during her second month of life, my mother had completely removed every trace of her from our home. Standing in that room, I was overwhelmed by the indescribable loss, a feeling I hope never to feel first hand.

The walls shimmered, acquiring a liquid, multi-coloured quality, like the faint rainbow of oils floating on a river downstream from where the washerwomen do their chores. The painting attained a depth, grew larger, took on a life beyond what could have been accommodated by a recess in the wall. I looked at the forest glade where the baby Hercules had been painted, and now showed only a grassy patch fringed with ominously dark trees. One could almost hear the rustling of leaves against an absence of bird noises that was somehow alarming. It stood as a window unto another world, yet I was not in the slightest tempted to reach into it, expecting the snakes would come biting me soon enough.

After a while of moving between the crib, the mural, and other apartments where atrocities happened, I located the silvery spiderweb of power that led me back towards its centre.

I explored the hall, stumbling occasionally but carrying on. . I ventured down the steps, carefully balancing myself with a hand on the wooden bannister which felt rough, scaly. Down and down, the tread of my feet on the stone steps echoed in the dark hallway, the stone walls closing in on me as I descended.

Stepping through one of the ground floor apartments, my eyes darted from side to side to catch the apparitions hovering at the edge of my vision. The snaking silver webs of power were multiplying, coming from all directions, passing through family shrines to the *lares* and *di penates*, and climbing the walls like suffocating vines, to converge on a potted tree in the corner.

Borax was standing at the ready, his pose the relaxed posture of a fighter about to pounce, but his fingers drummed lightly around on the iron cooking pan in his hands. He looked askance at any statue or bas-relief that might suddenly come alive. It says something about my life when the gladiator I employ to guard it prefers a heavy iron skillet as his weapon of choice.

The tree that sprouted from the clay pot was a leafy bay, its roots packed tightly in the knee-high container. I searched the base of the tree, thinking to unearth something from the dirt, but I should have looked at the tree. As my fingers dug into the earth, a branch snapped down with the head of a snake, biting my arm. I jumped back, staring at a tree that was now a coiling mass of snakes, snapping at me, like the head of Medusa the Gorgon.

Without thinking, I grabbed a discarded folding chair and threw it at the branches-snakes, then jumped into the opening and hacked at the snakes with my dagger. Borax joined me with a yell, stabbing at the tree trunk with his sword and swatting the snake-heads away with his pan. The heads made satisfying crunching sounds when he managed to smash them.

After a particularly big swipe with the pan cleared an opening, Borax aimed a mighty kick at the terracotta pot. He managed to tip it over and it cracked on impact, spilling the earth from inside it. Something metallic shone in the dirt and I kicked the object, moving it away from the snakes.

While Borax kicked and stomped with his heavy boots, the snakes appeared less fearsome as their tails remained connected to the fallen tree trunk. I took out another specially prepared leather purse from the sack of supplies and dropped the *tabula defixionis* into it. This device wasn't enough to completely block the strong *magia* of the curse but dampened the enchantment sufficiently to turn the snakes' scales back to bark. As they slowed, Borax took pleasure smashing them to bits. I tied the cords of the purse in a ritualistic knot, mumbling a few words of power and a supplication to the gods.

***

So, there I was, standing in the courtyard of the *insula*, as dizzy from the *psilocybe* as a legionary drunk on a brothel's cheap wine, and possibly poisoned from a snake bite. My breath heaved from the exertion of the fight and from performing all kinds of incantations that were guaranteed to play havoc with my system the next day, and who should I see standing in a doorway?

Aemilia.

She was dressed in a heavy cloak on a hot summer's night that didn't hide the hem of her fine tunic or her expensive sandals, looking every bit as the upper-class-lady-trying-to-masquerade-as-an-anonymous-traveller that she was. Considering she was unescorted by any bodyguard, I was surprised she had managed to make it there without getting mugged, killed, raped, or worse, in any particular order.

"That was quite a show!" she said, her eyes alight with excitement. "I watched you battle those snake-branches and yet I was perfectly safe. You needn't have worried."

She smiled, took a step towards me and fell flat on the floor.

With a startled cry, she turned to look behind her, and my gaze followed hers. Around her feet was entwined the biggest snake I had ever seen. It had come from the stairwell, and by the faint light that penetrated there I could see from whence it came — the wooden railing for the stairs was missing. Well, not missing, exactly, just transformed. When I leaned on it coming down it had felt scaly — now it was fully alive.

And angry.

It wrapped its body twice around Aemilia's legs, with plenty of scaly thorax left to rear up and hiss at us.

We rushed it. Borax swiped at the triangular head with his pan. The snake was too quick — it tilted back, and Borax missed. In one sinuous motion, it brought its tail around and swept Borax's feet from under him. The big gladiator crashed head first on the pavement, and lay still, sprawled on the floor.

I took the opportunity to circle the snake and jump on its upright back, Aemilia still entangled in its coils. It was thick as a tree trunk, smooth, and rippling like one giant muscle. I hugged it with my left arm and tried to stab it in the belly. My arm was weakened by the tree-snake bite and the giant scales proved too hard. My dagger bounced off. The snake convulsed, and I heard a sickening sound as its body tightened around Aemilia's legs, crushing them. She was screaming in pain and terror.

I stabbed again, aiming upward to get under the scales

but my dagger slipped, and I almost cut my own left arm. The snake crashed its body to the floor, trying to scrape me off. His midsection was still twisted around Aemilia, dragging her with us, and I was wary of his whipping tail.

We thrashed on the ground, and I had to roll off to the side to avoid being crushed. The snake did not hesitate, and as soon as I was off its back it raised its head high then darted towards me, his giant mouth wide, ready to swallow me whole. I stabbed straight at his mouth, in the classic movement that had been drilled into me by my centurion in the legions. Never waste time swinging a sword, just stab, stab, stab in straight lines. My arm met the snake's head half-way. As I plunged my dagger into its throat slicing its maw, the force of its charge carried it through almost to my shoulder.

It convulsed.

Aemilia screamed.

The snake closed its wide mouth on my upper arm, but there was no power to the bite as its life had ebbed away.

I yanked my arm, covered in the creature's blood and saliva, out of its gullet, clutching my dagger and ripping what was left of its jaws. I kicked its head away from me in a mix of horror and disgust.

My right arm was numb, yet I worked to free Aemilia. She was whimpering as I fumbled with my left hand to untangle the monster's massive, muscular body from around her legs. When I put my arms around her waist to pull her away from the creature, she just clutched me and sobbed. We sat there almost on top of the dead snake hugging each other, while Borax's unconscious body lay a few paces from us. With my heightened senses, I could feel the *magia* ebb and dissipate around us, but as much as I wanted to relax into Aemilia's embrace, I feared yet another monster would sneak up on us.

***

Eventually, she released me, so I could check her legs for damage. Her shins were lacerated by the rough scales, her blood an angry crimson against the milky skin. No bones appeared to have been broken, although both her ankles were twisted. There would be bad bruises on her legs, and I doubted she would forget this experience soon. But, with a bit of luck and some expensive unguents, she might escape without a scar.

I managed to revive Borax enough to stagger upright, while Aemilia groaned and leaned on me for more than just stability. I was so dizzy that I felt drunker than the night I was discharged from the legions.

Somehow, we made it to my house.

Limping along and bumping into each other like inebriated comrades, we'd arrived without further misadventures.

I treated Aemilia's legs with unguents.

I concocted an antidote for my snakebite.

I put a cream on the nasty gash Borax had on his forehead and bandaged it as best I could.

Dascha served us all soup, a portion of which I poured on the ground in the garden, in silent offering to the *di penates* of my house.

By midday on the following day a double litter and a veritable phalanx of bodyguards were sent by Cornelia to take us to her *domus*.

At their doorstep, Cornelia and Aemilia collapsed in each other's arms.

I just collapsed.

Chapter XII

They told me I slept for a day, a night, and a day. In fact, Aemilia and her mother thought I had died, for my breathing was so shallow and pulse so faint, they were hardly detectable. Sparing no expense, they called a physician — a real *magister carneum* — to check on me.

Apparently, in return for Aemilia's brief and highly censored account of events, the physician concocted a potion to help my body combat the snake venom. Regardless, they could not manage to force it down my throat, for which I was thankful. No telling what the mix of *psilocybe*, animated-tree-snake venom, my own antidote, and his medicine would have done to me.

So instead, I simply woke ravenous. I joked that nothing would make me miss another dinner prepared by Cornelia's master cook and we spent the evening talking lightly, avoiding the horrors that had been visited upon us and commenting instead on the snail-stuffed quail.

The lack of vocal arguments told me Cornelia and Aemilia must have decided to spare me so soon on my recovery. I imagined the past day had involved many emphatic assertions by Cornelia that she was right all along, with Aemilia being too afraid and overwrought to argue.

Despite my best efforts at jollity and light-hearted conversation, the atmosphere was strained. Aemilia was limping slightly, and the skin of her legs was raw, with red blood seeping through the bandages. Her slave girl, Na'ama, had a subdued demeanour and remained not more than a step away at all times.

I imagine Cornelia lashed out at her for letting her mistress slip away at night.

Dinner was over quickly. As soon as the plates of honeyed egg custard were cleared, Aemilia was escorted to her quarters by Na'ama with a bodyguard trailing them even inside the house. I stood and aimed to follow suit, when Cornelia's voice, low and seething, echoed in the room. "How could you?"

She was standing, fists clenched, shaking with anger.

"*How could you?*" she said again with more vehemence.

"She was not meant to come. I didn't think —"

"Of course you didn't! Not for one moment! You were too concerned with trying to impress her. Did you really think I wouldn't find out about the *psilocybe?*"

"That was a tiny amount, a taste to scare her away from real involvement."

"Well, it didn't work! I thought you knew her better. Her curiosity was only piqued, and then she followed you the next night. Followed you almost to her death! You men are all the same. A pretty young face and you can no longer think straight! Or did you tell her your plans in the hope of impressing her into your bed? You *mentula!* You *verpa!*"

"Really, there's no need for —"

She slapped me.

"I'll let that go," I said coldly, "but —"

She tried to slap me again, but I caught her hand. Although she growled in frustration, I just drew her close to me, gathering her in my arms.

According to romantic literature, she was supposed to collapse sobbing on my shoulder.

Instead, Cornelia tried to knee me in the groin, saying much about the literature she was reading.

I ignored the attack and held her closer still, in a bear hug tight enough to immobilise her.

She turned to bite me, but that became a harsh kiss, one that drew blood from my lip.

We made love, if one can call it that. It was wild, and

heavy, and rough, almost violent. She scratched my chest with her nails and I twisted her arms away. We fought for who would be on top.

We broke one of the dining couches.

Eventually we collapsed next to each other, lying on pillows amidst the broken couch — panting, spent.

When her breathing calmed, she began sobbing. I gathered her to me, hugged her, stroked her hair. Her salty tears stung where they dropped on the scratches she left on my chest.

She pushed herself up to look at me. "I nearly lost her," she said between sobs. "I found she was not in her bed and all the memories of last time just flooded back."

My own demons roared to life, the image of the love I lost to atrocious crimes. To her, I said, "No harm was done. Not really. I was there, and now she will have a memento to stick in her memory, to keep her away from such business."

"You're an ass, Felix."

I was about to object, but she kissed me, this time tenderly. We kissed, caressed, and made gentle love for what felt like hours.

When we finished, we tumbled into deep sleep and my last thought was that perhaps she was more fond of me than she was letting on, that my status was no longer that of just a toy — though the cynical voice in my head whispered that I was merely the tool for her relief, nothing more.

***

The third and last *insula* was almost anticlimactic. Almost.

I had Borax accompany me, for despite his head wound, I trusted him above all. On Cornelia's insistence, I took one of her private guards as well. She also left bodyguards standing outside Aemilia's door, giving me some peace of mind I would not be interrupted.

The night was warm even for Sextilis, the streets filled with people too hot to sleep. Yet when we stepped inside the *insula*'s courtyard, there was a chill in the air. It was as quiet as the dead family of squatters whose remains still occupied the ground floor apartment.

We spent more time in preparations that night. I placed all the requisite paraphernalia within easy reach and set up defences. Borax and Cornelia's bodyguard stood well-armed and positioned, although the bodyguard scoffed at Borax's iron skillet, choosing to carry a traditional oval shield.

I was tempted to just dig around, to skip the *psilocybe* and save myself the nausea and other side effects. But, not using the substance would make us more vulnerable to the curse and keep me from knowing where to dig. Under the influence of the hated mushrooms, I at least had the benefit of heightened awareness to the flow of *magia* and could sense where the next attack might come from.

So off I went, chanting and cooking my charmed *patina* and getting myself into a state even the most experienced of *incantatores* try to avoid. At least I remembered to bring fish sauce to improve the taste.

My senses heightened and mingled, touch coloured by hearing and scent flavoured with sight. Finally, a brownish smell of chimes washed over me and when my skin tingled with a breeze that wasn't in the air I knew to follow it to the ground floor apartment the family of squatters inhabited briefly. Walls shimmered and rippled like light on the surface of a pool after a stone has been dropped in.

The tramps were the last humans to inhabit the apartment. Since they were persons of no consequence, no one cared to retrieve their bodies — even when the smell became too putrid for the neighbours to bear. The mangled, desiccated remains were exactly as Aemilia and I witnessed, spilt innards plastered on the walls and undisturbed even by rats or crows. But now I could sense another layer to them, one too faint to have seen in the light of day. Four argentine figures huddled in a corner, staring mutely as I approached their translucent shapes, through which glimmered their bloody, very human, corpses.

"Who did this to you?" I asked. Although their blank

faces did not change expressions, their eyes stared with flickering emotions that were both human and unfathomable.

"I am here to find out who — or what — has done this and deal with them. Can you tell me anything?"

A pause, then without moving her eyes from mine, one of the figures lifted a translucent arm, unfolded it and extended an index finger, pointing in the direction of a bas-relief image of the *insula*'s guardian deity. The *lar* was depicted in the traditional way, as a young child dancing, holding a knife and a libation bowl in his hands. The shimmering lights that infused my vision gave his face a constantly shifting expression. Like the stories we heard from gossiping neighbours and my experiences at the other buildings, the dead seemed to corroborate the accounts of statues and murals wreaking havoc upon the living, somehow related to the ancestral and household gods that were supposed to be their protectors.

The statue was just plaster and did not threaten movement. I touched it gingerly and felt the atrocities the *lar* had committed, but with them came an understanding that it was not the *numen* who wished them or performed them, merely the animated bits of stone and plaster that constituted his image. It was a strange thought, and it appeared in my mind like a wood-louse popping from an unseen hole in a familiar cabinet. It wasn't mine, yet in some odd way it belonged there.

Before searching for the curse's source, I did what I could for those poor souls, still huddling in death as they did when life was torn from them, with no one left to care for their shades in the afterlife. Ignoring Borax, who could not divine my reasons nor understand my actions, I set to work. The skillet went upside down on the floor and I popped five dried black beans into my mouth. I spat them at the iron skillet one by one, making five loud clangs of noise, to scare away evil spirits. Some red wine from a wineskin became a libation to Dis Pater when I poured it the ground where the shades lay and mumbled a prayer for purification. I gathered dry leaves that the winds had swept into the corners, heaped them, lighted them, and let the smoke rise as an offering to Iovis Pater. Finally, I handed copper coins to the shades, which one by one they took, placed in their mouths as payment for Charun, and faded into whatever lies beyond the veil of life.

The shades freed from their earthly prison, I stepped back to the courtyard. The night air had taken on the familiar silvery luminescence, the walls glinted in flashes reminiscent of the tails of foxes disappearing in the forest, while colours acquired the vibrancy of leaves in fall. I found the spiderweb of power vibrating all around and traced it to a far corner — to the spider that sat at its centre.

It stared at us with the inscrutable blank expression of insects, the light from our torches reflected in its eight eyes, its mouth opening and closing, sharp mandibles vibrating.

The bodyguard made a choking noise and froze, but Borax and I picked up ready spears and went at the giant arachnid with well-practised stabs. We confused it by attacking from different directions with wild yells. I've seen small spiders jump to a man's height and didn't care to find if this monstrosity could do so as well. The bodyguard was not much use, terrified as he was and barely managing to hold his spear levelled. He stabbed hesitantly at the spider, but the monster reared on its four hind legs, mouth open and hissing, then pounced forward. Borax and I took the opening and stabbed up while bracing the spear butts on the ground. As the spider came down it impaled itself on the sharp points, and, though the wood shafts broke, its momentum was halted.

The arachnid from the pits of Hades thrashed for a while on the ground, hissing and shrieking, while the three of us stood panting a safe distance away, watching green ichor ooze out together with its life.

We found the *tabulae defixiones* lying undisturbed in the ashes of the fire-pit above which the monster nested. Unsurprisingly, this one was in a common space — whoever laid them was consistent in the way they used the tablets. It was probably done by the same man, following the same set of instructions — sneak in at night, find a hidden patch in the courtyard, bury the folded lead tablet, activate it, and run away.

I dropped the tablet carefully into another leather purse lined with tar and dog's ashes and buried it in a shallow pit in the central garden.

This measure would not hold the curse for long, but it would buy me the time I needed to collect all the tablets in the morning and dispose of them all — somewhere far away from the city, preferably.

How had the *rhones* of the Collegium Incantatorum not noticed these curses? Or, if they had, why had they not done anything about it?

Our magistrates usually keep an eye on such activities and try to curtail the less savoury kind. Being public officials elected only for a single year, they would look for any opportunity to make a splash, increase their public *auctoritas* to further their careers. They are not always the most diligent in the execution of their duties — there have been many cases where elected officials preferred to fatten their own purses or spend budgets on lavish festivities to ensure future elections as they rise up the ranks in their public careers — but they will not pass an opportunity to stand on the rostra and declaim their achievements.

However, being politicians, they don't often care about the inhabitants of remote corners of our city. The Subvales are populated by nonentities — people whose economic circumstances ensure their votes will never be called upon in any election. Even I've gotten away with more than I should have by carrying out illicit activities in places the *rhones* would be hesitant to check — like the sewers. Unless the problems affected someone with money, they would have picked easier issues to contend with.

Still, this year's crop must be remarkably inept if they failed to notice the festering curses that drew enough *magia* to power animated statues and living murals — or else they had a stake in this matter.

Just one more piece in this puzzle to file for later inspection.

As always, Fortuna likes to remind me why my name is Felix. She likes to point out that I should trust in her instead of the best laid plans. Those never seem to work. In fact, it was when I shook myself from my reverie about our ruling officials and was about to congratulate myself on a well-executed plan that Lady Luck chose to demonstrate I am forever in her thrall.

The noise from above began as a faint buzz. It grew in volume till it set my teeth rattling and my ears felt as though they would explode. In the square patch of night sky between the enclosing walls of the *insula*, the stars were visible — twinkling, blinking, appearing to move in their firmament. As they descended upon us we saw them for what they really were — a swarm of angry bees, each the size of my fist, the light from our torches and fire-pit reflecting in their translucent wings.

The bodyguard lost all pretence of self-control and ran away screaming and blabbering. From the sounds that followed, he did not make it out of the building. Borax and I took up fighting stances, but quickly discovered the futility of traditional weapons against a cloud of fast-moving insects.

I waved a torch furiously, but it was Borax who had the right idea. He grabbed the empty sack of supplies from the ground and began waving it in wide arcs. It created a space around him, where the monstrous bees could not approach without being swatted. I crouched near him and on the third attempt managed to light the edges of the sack with my torch. The fire and smoke angered the beasts, but also kept them at bay.

One day I'd buy Borax from Crassitius outright. As Cornelia's bodyguard demonstrated so eloquently, good help is hard to find. Someone who could remain calm in the face of the unexpected, and not due to lack of reasoning faculties, was a lifesaver.

We sidled closer to the fire-pit. An *incantator* once told me of an enchantment that could send bees to sleep without smoke, but, alas, I never learnt it. So instead, I heaped everything I could find on the fire — leaves, bits of cloth, dead bees. Fortuna must have wished me to survive, as I found a juniper bush. The smoke of juniper leaves is known to calm bees, so I added them to the fire. While Borax waved the burning sack, I used a reversal of an incantation I knew and caused the courtyard to fill with thick smoke.

We started to cough and retreated inside, but the smoke drove the giant bees away.

I heard distant alarm bells as the smoke drifted up and out of the courtyard. Borax and I dropped to the floor, crawling under the billowing clouds out to the street. We made a hasty escape just as the *vigiles* bore down the road toward what they must have thought was a tenement building on fire.

I was sure that once the smoke cleared, the *vigiles* would have more questions than answers. They might then try to rouse a *rhone* from the Collegium Incantatorum to investigate the *insula*, or at least report this through their ranks to the *aediles* or even the *praetor urbanus*. The higher up the report went, the more pressure would be placed on the Collegium to do something.

I needed to warn Valerius Flaccus about this develop-ment and, since there was smoke but no fire, ensure it would be recorded as a mere prank.

CHAPTER XIII

We were sitting in Cornelia's *triclinium* again, the sumptuous couch we broke now replaced, with Valerius Flaccus due to arrive any moment. I had planned to make my way the previous morning to Valerius' *domus* and report to him like any other client reporting to their patron, but on the way, I stopped at Cornelia's house to apologise about the dead bodyguard. When she heard my brief report, she was adamant she would invite Valerius over. Though she didn't say it, I knew she wished to hear my report in full and voice her opinion on the questions it raised and the next steps. Being a rich widow has its advantages, but plenty of limitations, too. If she wanted to be a part of anything important, it had to be behind closed doors. Hosting Valerius was her way of catching up on all the juicy gossip and feeling involved in our city's affairs. Since Valerius could only come the following night, I got another day to tie up loose ends and prepare better.

The dinner was a formal affair, with three couches arranged in the traditional U shape, facing the door. Cornelia reclined on the left of the middle couch, the place normally reserved for a male host. To her right in the *locus consularis* was the guest of honour, Lucius Valerius Flaccus, who somehow managed to recline rigidly — a man that never relaxed. I assumed he was used to Cornelia by then, his uptight moral sensibilities suffering a woman reclining next to him.

I occupied the left-hand couch, the place of the second guest in terms of social rank — quite above my normal station.

Aemilia, looking properly chastised, sat with her back to me in a traditional women's chair. I have never seen Cornelia's dinners fall on this outdated formality. Aemilia tugged at the long tunic she wore under her *stola* despite the summer warmth, no doubt to cover her still-raw legs.

Opposite me was Flaccus' wife — a certain Claudia Pulchra, no less. A union of the Valerii and Claudi Pulchi gave that family nobility and ancestry to times before the foundation of our city.

At her side was Quintus Aquilius, a budding and promising lawyer, the son of another of Cornelia's friends. He was in that stage between army campaigns and the start of the *cursus honorum*, when so many young men take to the law courts to gain notoriety for the coming elections.

I knew Cornelia had designs of marrying Aemilia off to the young man. I imagined Cornelia hoped that when the conversation turned to the matter of Valerius Flaccus' *insulae*, Claudia would keep Aemilia and Quintus Aquilius focused on each other. That may be another reason why Aemilia was relegated to a woman's chair, rather than reclining on the couches.

As soon as the slaves cleared the plates of leafy salads, figs stuffed with cheese, and salty farina cakes, Cornelia exchanged nods with Claudia. The latter engaged Aemilia and Quintus in a discussion on his last court appearance, while Cornelia got Valerius to recline closer, and asked me in a low voice to give my report.

I gave a full account, keeping my promise to the agent Aburius and not discrediting him. Certain aspects were superfluous — lines of investigation that did not prove fruitful such as some of the still resident tenants and Aemilia's surprise appearance and her injuries due to the snake. My goal was to make sure Valerius appreciated the efforts I carried out on his behalf.

"If I might suggest, you should bribe the *vigiles* or the urban cohorts to file the fire at the *insula* as a prank. I am almost certain someone bribed the *rhones* of the Collegium to ignore the curses. I'm not sure what they would do if the *vigiles* reported the fire in your *insula*, and word of it reached their ears. They will most likely ascribe it to the curse. But there is a chance they are aware of what goes on there and might warn whomever set the curses."

"I understand completely," Valerius responded. "I will deal with this quietly tomorrow."

"You will be comforted to know that the tablets have been safely discharged. I collected the *tabulae defixiones* in their special pouches yesterday and hired a cart to take myself and an old acquaintance with experience in such matters to the hills beyond the Purgamenta. There, we carried out the necessary rituals to unbind the *magia* of the curses, channelling it safely away. Now the tablets are merely harmless sheets of folded lead." I produced the three of them from a carry bag I had stashed under my dining couch, much to the desired effect.

Throughout my conversation, I noticed Aemilia and Quintus Aquilius were far more interested in my account than in anything Claudia Pulchra had to offer. While everyone was staring at the inert lead tablets with a mixture of curiosity and fear, Aemilia piped up, "So is it really all over?"

I had to chuckle. "Oh, no! My dear, the real case has just begun."

SCROLL II - INQUISITIO

CHAPTER XIV

There were three questions left to resolve. While Valerius Flaccus paid me handsomely for removing the curses, his commission didn't end there. I now had the more mundane aspects of investigation to consider. Or, what might, on the surface at least, appear mundane.

First, I needed to find out who had crafted the *tabulae defixiones* and ensure they went out of business, quietly and permanently. My civic duty, as it were.

Second, I had to discover who commissioned them and why, providing sufficient evidence for Valerius to take the responsible party to a court of law.

Lastly, I had to find the reason the Collegium Incantatorum was surprisingly quiet on a matter that was a festering boil — one our elected *rhones* were supposed to handle.

The path of progression for the investigation was clear. Start with the how, work out the who, and end up with the why. There were no takers at dinner when I suggested a bet that the last question was connected to the first two. The answer to it was almost a given — a bribery by the culprit behind question number two. And number two would be unmasked by resolving number one.

Quintus Aquilius became animated as soon as we explained the prospects of a lawsuit to Aemilia. A very keen young man, he must have smelled the makings of a case that could boost his career for the next decade.

Valerius was supportive of a lawsuit. A public disgrace,

especially one with such lurid details of using *nefas* incantations within city bounds, would send his political enemies into exile and enhance his own *auctoritas* — his standing as an upright citizen and senator. This was as much a game of public appearances as it was about property or ghosts.

Throughout the discussions Aemilia sat there, her internal struggle plain to all. She was still smarting from the encounter with the curse, her legs bandaged over the scrapes left by the snake. But her curiosity and spirit would not lie down quietly. Her plight reminded me of my own when my apprenticeship at the Collegium was terminated. True, my circumstances were financial, while hers were due to her sex and position in society. Yet, she was a kindred spirit with an unquenchable thirst for knowledge, a wish to participate in public life on an equal footing — all while facing the blank stone wall of a closed society.

And I've met a similar spirit before — my Helena was indomitable, a trait which cost her her life. As Aemilia's mixed emotions crossed her lovely features, I wondered which path I could take that would protect her, so she did not end the same. Would distancing her from it help, or would she just stumble on, unaware? Would trying to educate her allow her to avoid trouble, or would it draw her closer?

In the end, my heart and mind settled on the same path. After clearing the *insulae* from curses, my position in Valerius' eyes was sound, enough that I no longer required a chaperone to keep me honest. I suggested I could use an assistant, someone literate, intimate with the case details, and trustworthy. Someone who could carry out both academic and social research without raising questions where my own nosing about might.

The look of sheer, incredulous hopefulness in Aemilia's eyes when I suggested it and the excited joy and gratitude when Valerius agreed, were quite enough compensation for the freezing cold shoulder I got from Cornelia for the rest of that night.

***

I paid Crassitius for the gladiator's time, plus an additional charge to keep Borax in reserve for me. To Borax, I left a purse of coins as a bonus. Finding an ex-gladiator who could keep his wits facing arcane manifestations was hard. I wanted to stay his favourite contract employer.

From there I went to collect reference material which occupied all the morning. I had some at home, got more from Sosius, and arranged for him to contact Fonteius Capito for a specific scroll to be sent after me.

I carried it all back up the hill to the house where I seemed to have been spending more time than in my own home. After settling Aemilia in the library with all the scrolls and codices, I requested a light meal and drinks to be delivered and we delved into our studies.

"Are you sure they are safe?" she asked as I took out the three *tabulae defixiones*.

"Certain. I told you, I saw to the discharge of the *magia* from them."

"How does that work?" Her eyes sparkled as she picked one up.

"It varies. Essentially, the curse tablets are made from thin lead sheets, upon which a petition to the gods, the *numina*, or even to the spirit of a deceased one, is made. The target can be named, or generic. A specific effect can be requested or just general retribution. Once inscribed, the tablets are rolled, folded, nailed, buried, or otherwise disposed. At least, this is how the common variety, done by people without knowledge of the flow of *magia*, are created. If they work, it's only because the gods take favour on the petitioner."

The role of pedagogue didn't come naturally. I kept shifting in my chair, unsure of knowledge I built from practical observations and experimentation, rather than proper philosophical education. "A skilled *incantator* can channel magical energy into the tablet and bind it in such a way that the effect is guaranteed. Well, as guaranteed as anything to do with *magia* is. It still flows from the *numina* to our world, by my reckoning."

"These must have been made by a powerful *incantator* to

achieve such nasty effects," said Aemilia.

"Well, yes and no. They certainly had raw power in them. However, these *tabulae* are not the preferred choice of our own Collegium-educated *incantatores*. While they might offer a few benefits, such as the delayed effect, the mechanics are far too crude. A knowledgeable *incantator* would have better tools at their disposal and would consider their usage demeaning."

"So, a foreigner, then?"

"Perhaps. Someone with understanding and ability, certainly, but our *collegia* are not the only path to attain such. There are plenty of curse tablets done around Egretia, on an almost daily basis. The orator seeking to hamstring his opponent, the victim seeking divine retribution for petty theft — as long as no real power is involved, no one cares. It's certainly cheaper and easier for the *rhones* to turn a blind eye than waste their time chasing charlatans, while giving the populace an illusion of control over their fates. Anyway, we'll find more about how this one was activated when we open it up."

"But you haven't answered my question!"

"Which one?" I was regretting being made the lecturer.

"How did you nullify the curse?"

"*I* didn't. I took them to someone who could."

"Araxus?"

"Araxus."

"But he's mad!"

"On a good day. I found him when he had his reason about him. He has always been a brilliant *incantator* and the curse that afflicts him has, in a way, augmented his powers. That single black eye of his has the most refined *visus verum* I have even known. Sadly, he cannot turn it off, which must weigh heavy on his fragile mind." I spoke fast, as I didn't wish to examine his state — and our past — in detail.

"He was able to leach the *magia* out of the tablets in a way that would not fry us on the spot. He released it into the ground and the air, returning it to the *numina* from whence it came. I'm afraid we left a rather charred tree stump next to a creek that is now brackish and foul. In years to come, that gully where we carried this out will acquire a reputation of evil spirits, bad omens will be attributed to some *dryad* or *lar*, and people will learn to avoid it. But that should be the extent of it. Nothing more sinister. Now, let's get on with our task."

We carefully unwound the lead sheets. To create the curses, special sigils and formulae had been inscribed upon them with a hard stylus. Someone would then have chanted, made sacrifices, invoked the *numina,* and otherwise channelled the energy into the *tabulae.* At that point they were still dormant, in a sense. To activate the curses, the sheets were either folded or rolled, hammered, and often a nail driven through them, to anchor them to a particular location. This deformation released the imbued energy into a shaped effect.

The sheets we recovered from the three *insulae* had been prepared by the same hand. All were meticulously rolled rather than simply folded and had an iron-tipped bone shard driven through them in precisely the same angle and location for the activation.

Once opened, the symbols that had been etched into the sheets bore similarities to one another. Upon closer examination, traces of dried blood in the grooves and folds of the sheet became obvious. I scraped as much of the dried flakes as I could and kept them in a closed jar. Finding the kind of animal from whence the blood and bone fragments came — if it was an animal, rather than a person — might prove useful.

The last task was to prepare copies in wax. I didn't wish to leave the originals under the roof of people I liked, inactive or not. The wax tablets could be destroyed far more easily, if the need should arise.

As we worked, I pointed out certain features for Aemilia — which intersecting lines might bear meaning and which I thought were artefacts of the folding. Why certain terms appeared in foreign languages. What letters in the handwriting looked out of place and whether the *incantator* who prepared them missed, or whether it was an intentional, meaningful deviation.

She was a fast learner and a steady hand at calligraphy. We'd made decent copies by sunset, after which I instructed Aemilia in the research I wanted her to carry out. She would spend the next few days with the wax facsimiles and the scrolls and codices I brought and learn as much as she could about how the curses were created and how the effects were called into being.

I am sure, deep down, Cornelia appreciated my assigning Aemilia a task that should keep her homebound and under supervision. I never found out, as I countered the lack of a dinner invitation with a proclamation that I must remove the tablets — inert though they were — from the *domus* to be stored safely away and would therefore sleep that night in my own home.

CHAPTER XV

Working on the basis of Araxus' hint, I made my way to the Campus Civicus and the Emporium Sempronicus. The emporium holds stores and offices for many merchants and traders dealing with imports and exports from around the Mare Sepiae. It was a bustling centre of commerce, with diverse crowds from powerful business magnates in blindingly white togas to grubby dock-hands in filthy tunics.

Some of the most crucial commodities were metals, from iron and tin ores to refined silver and gold and from base metals used in construction to precious metals to adorn the statues of the gods.

And lead.

A very curious metal, lead. As soft and malleable as gold, yet grey and lacking lustre. Hardly as precious, yet far more useful. Our engineers used it to construct the great aqueduct, the Aqua Sextiae, and the associated plumbing that brought fresh water from six sacred springs to a city of a million bodies and carried their waste away.

It was used in vats for wine making, as a wine sweetener and food preserver, as a component in women's makeup and other countless unguents, as weights for fishing nets and lines, in household pots, in cheap ornaments and toys, in inks, in the manufacture of glassware, and even in an ingenious contraption pumping fresh seawater to tanks on boats allowing the transport of live fish over great distances.

It was considered the Father of Metals and — strangely

for our patriarchal society — the basest of metals at the same time.

My interest in this all-purpose substance went beyond the purview of regular lead merchants. I was not constructing aqueducts, nor manufacturing household pottery. So, I bypassed the impressive shop-fronts of respectable wholesale brokers and wandered to dingy back-alleys and their insalubrious — and unscrupulous — purveyors. These were ones who would craft a sheet of lead to obviously nefarious specifications, without burdensome enquiries. Ones who might be confused by such literary loquacity, but not by the jingle of coins.

It was late in the morning when I stepped into the fourth lead merchant's decrepit store. The first three yielded nothing suspicious, their proprietors only dealing with mundane writing equipment not possessing the required knowledge or facilities to create exotic lead alloy sheets.

I was greeted with a gruff, "Yeah, what d'ya want?" from the proprietress, a woman in her fifties.

"Sheets for writing."

"Papyrus in the boxes on your left, wax tablets on the bottom shelf."

"Lead ones, actually."

"Top shelf on the right." The woman didn't even bother to look up from her task. She was busy weaving a leather thong through the sides of two wax tablets, to allow them to hang together and close as a diptych.

"Only... I need to write quite... specific... sheets."

The proprietor paused her work and turned to look at me for the first time since I entered her shop. She stared at me for a long moment, and I stared right back. A much-wrinkled woman, grey hair held in a tight bun, with the appearance of one used to heavy work. I wasn't sure I would win against her in an arm-wrestling match. Instead I gave her my 'experienced dealer in contraband' look — not a hard pretence, considering I had on more than one occasion dealt with items best kept away from the authorities.

"What d'ya have in mind?" She finally asked.

"A mix of nine parts lead to one part tin in exact proportions, with a bit of crushed cobalt. Stretched and folded seven times," I made the opening gambit.

It didn't faze her. Where the other lead merchants asked me if I was an idiot or thought them even bigger ones, this proprietor simply said, "Now what's an upstanding citizen like you going to write on a thing like that?"

"Oh, just a bit of this and a bit of that. I have it on good authority that you are the one to contact when assured results are desired. Word on the street is that it was your products that were used on those Subvales *insulae*. You know, the ones now standing empty."

"That *matris futuo!*" she slipped between clenched teeth, but recovered quickly. "Look, I don't know who you are or what idiotic rumblings you heard from some *mentula* on the street. For all I know, you're from the Collegium, and this isn't the first time I've been set up by Afranius. That *verpa* always envied my business."

I noticed that, between all the invective, she didn't deny it. Good sign. "I assure you I hate the Collegium just as much as you do," I said. "My name is Felix, known as Felix the Fox. Ask around. You'll find I have no love for those greedy bastards." That wasn't enough, so I added, "Here, give me a plain sheet and I'll show you."

She was hesitant, so I grabbed the nearest wax tablet and stylus, scratched a few symbols, and uttered the right words. It wasn't much. I can't summon extensive *magia* quite that fast — but I'm good with parlour tricks.

It was enough.

I handed the woman the tablet. Her eyes widened as she read the symbols, even as the wax melted and ran down her hands.

"I can see there ain't no love lost between you and the Collegium," she said, scraping the wax away from her fingers. "What's to stop me from reporting on you?"

"Well, for one, you no longer have any evidence. A bit of melted wax won't be enough to get me in trouble with anyone but my laundry lady. But more importantly, I think you won't report me because you supply people like me with what we need. You are a businesswoman, after all." I emphasised that last point with a rattling of my money pouch.

"Even if I'd agree to create such tablets for you — and I ain't saying I will — it'll take me some days. I'm all booked out, so why don'tcha come back next week?"

"I need it as soon as you can make them. Name your price."

She did. It was exorbitant.

We haggled. I knew Flaccus would pay it without a flinch, but if I didn't haggle it would have been suspicious. When I negotiated her down just enough, I said, "Look, instead of half now and half when the sheets are ready, I'll pay you three quarters now and as a bonus you'll tell me the names of anyone who bought these exact same tablets in recent weeks. If he's the real man behind the *insulae* jobs, I might employ him too."

"You pay me four-fifths now, and the other three-fifths when the sheets are done. And you don't ever mention me if anyone asks how you found him."

Her maths skills may not have been an accountant's dream, but I left with a name.

Gaius Hirtuleius Ambustus.

***

Finding a man in a city of a million people takes some skill. Luckily, according to the description I got from the merchant, he was true to his cognomen *ambustus*. The man had red burn-scars on the left side of his face, neck, shoulder.

Armed with this knowledge, I set out to do the task we detectives do only slightly less than legionaries — wear out our sandals by traipsing all over the place.

At the end of the second day I found myself sitting in a public tavern nestled between the *fora* Bovarium and Piscium, gazing at The Siren's Song — one of our city's most notorious brothels. The Siren was the kind of place where, even from across the street, one could smell the old sweat and semen that permeated the walls.

Though I had never seen him before in my life, when Ambustus arrived I was sure I had the right man. The burn scars on his face held the colour of hot coals, even though he had sustained them years ago. His left eye was set above melted cheekbones and rimmed by angry red folds of skin, giving him the appearance of some cursed chthonic deity, still on fire.

I finished my drink and went in after him. After fending off attempts by the nearest attendant to foist an obviously syphilitic girl on me, I paid him to send an *amphora* of his best wine after Ambustus and tell him it was on the house.

I washed my hands in a public fountain outside the brothel and went back to my table. I hoped the whore Ambustus was with got some of the wine too, for surely she needed it more than he.

It took a while, but Ambustus stumbled out adjusting his tunic and humming a merry tune. I walked after him and called his name, and he turned and peered at me blearily.

"Gaius Ambustus!" I repeated with a smile, "I finally have the honour of meeting you!"

"Do I know you?" he asked.

"I doubt it. I'm hardly as renowned as Ambustus Magnus. Allow me to introduce myself. My name is Felix, sometimes known as Felix the Fox. It's a pleasure to finally meet you. Will you do me the honour of allowing me to buy you dinner?"

I herded Ambustus towards a nearby tavern and ordered the best wine and a lavish meal before he could mount a serious objection or question my motives.

As the taverner brought us bread and dishes of stewed squid in herbs and garlic, I toasted Ambustus with cup after cup of wine.

"You keep calling me 'the great,' but I am not sure what I've done to deserve this epithet," he said.

"Why, it's your work on the *insulae* in the Subvales, of course!" I feigned surprise at his question. "It's the talk of everyone in the know. Those curses were the best executed of their kind for a generation. I am sure they will be talked about for decades to come."

In his wine-befuddled state he didn't think to deny this; his first reaction was to nod his agreement. When I saw his brow furrow and questions start to rise, I simply poured him more wine and talked faster.

"Anyone who knows anything worth knowing in this city, tells about your great skill and audacity. Your name will go down in the annals of Egretia as one of the greatest *veneficitores* of our time. I dabble a little in the *magia* business myself, but my skill would hardly compare. I would love to know how you managed to be so precise in scope and effect, though you will probably think me a rank amateur who couldn't possibly understand your work. Still, to be able to learn from a genius such as yourself is an incomparable opportunity."

And so, compliment after compliment, one cup of wine after another, I stoked his pride and vanity and broke through his reluctance and suspicion. I learnt his method of getting the curse tablets into the *insulae* without being observed with his distinctive visage. His plan was simplicity itself — he'd disguise himself as a travelling merchant, wait around till he saw a young child going in and out, and entice him with a charm for growing bounty fruit or perhaps playing a trick on a mean neighbour. The child would then take a tablet and bury it in the garden for him. He hinted at having invented new mechanisms for activating the curse tablets.

Now came the trickier part — finding out who commissioned him. "Your employer must have pleased Fortuna greatly, to hire a virtuoso like yourself and get all those curses done so masterfully! I imagine him rich, too, to shower you with gold for such services."

"Ha! Rich he may be, but a greater skinflint has never graced our shores." His speech was heavily slurred by now. With each wheezy 's' his rancid breath sprayed me with wine and spittle.

"But surely he recognises your service?" I feigned my best incredulity. "Or, he might be afraid that you would turn your terrifying powers on him."

"Now that is a thought... perhaps I just might. He paid adequately for my services, you see, but not when I requested money for more experiments. There was this thing I wanted to try, you know. My powers have grown enough to turn a person's own *lares* against him."

"He would be a fool to cross you. A high-ranking senator like him, such a scandal could destroy him."

I got a hiccough of assent in reply.

"I wonder how he keeps his clients. A patron must give lavish rewards if he is to maintain loyalty."

"Oh, he spends enough on them. He practically owns the college up the street from here at the Vicus Greges. He rents it cheaply to the dock-hands, provides free drinks, and those *verpae* are ready to do any violence for him for the sheer delight of it."

That was something I could work with, but I decided to push my luck. "I know," I slapped my hand on the table. "I have a brilliant idea. Why don't I register as his client and then whisper in his ear about how all your great deeds are appreciated by anyone in the right circles, and how you are courted by powerful men with offers of money who'd like to have you as their client. I'll let him understand that you are steadfast in his service, appreciating him as a good patron."

"You would do that for me? You are a good friend, Felix." He put his arm around my shoulder and nearly knocked me unconscious with the admixture of sweet wine and tangy fish sauce on his breath.

I toasted our little plot with another cup of wine, then furrowed my brows. "What's his full name again? I want to make sure I get his right address in the morning."

"Gaius — *hic* — Gaius Nu — *hic* — Gaius Numicius," Ambustus managed to say before the third-loudest belch I have ever witnessed escape a man's lips overtook him.

"That's right. Of course. Pretty soon you should be expecting a whole bag of golden *aurei*," I smirked. "Now where was that barkeep? Disappeared right when we ran out of wine. Let me go get us another *amphora*."

I went to the rear, yelled for the proprietor loudly to get us another *amphora* of his best, then went to pee in the gutter outside the door. With my back to the world, no one saw me get my pouch of supplies from my inner tunic pocket and select those herbs I needed along with a few strands of hair from a shaggy dog. Attempting to poison a *veneficitor* is not a wise course of action, but I was willing to bet he was too drunk to notice. All I needed was a little something to push him over.

I went back inside the tavern, demanding clean cups. I carried them myself to the table where we toasted each other again and drank deeply.

"I'm afraid I'll have to return home to my nagging wife now," I said. I took a pinch of my herbs, mashed them with my right thumb into my left palm, blew a slow breath into my fist, and sprinkled the contents into my wine. I drank deeply and made a face.

He peered at me curiously. "What was that?"

"Ah, just a hangover cure I picked up from a beer-guzzling Capilani. The stuff they drink is horrible, but this ensures that there will be no headache tomorrow. I couldn't possibly stand having a hangover with my wife's shrill voice screaming at me to get the slaves to clean the latrines. I never go drinking without it. But what am I thinking? How unkind of me not to offer you some. Here, please allow me to return your kindness tonight. This will leave you fresh and sprightly tomorrow."

I picked up another pinch of the herbs, mashed them with my left thumb into my right palm, inhaled a breath, and sprinkled the mix into his wine. "Tastes dreadful, I'm afraid, but it's worth it."

We toasted, drank the spiced wine and then a clean drink to wash the taste. I bid him farewell and left, whistling as I made my way up the Via Petrosa to the crest of the Meridionali towards my home. I was safe in the knowledge that my little charm would leave me fresh in the morning, while tonight's debauchery would be amplified for Ambustus by my reversed process — to the point his hangover would leave him with no memories past the previous day's breakfast.

Chapter XVI

I spent the next morning revisiting Valerius' three *insulae*. I found those I spoke with before and in some cases new neighbours with curious noses. I enquired whether they had seen a man matching Ambustus' unforgettable visage. A few remembered, which confirmed he was sniffing around the *insulae*, in case I needed more evidence than his drunken confession.

It was time to report the new name to Valerius Flaccus and check up on Aemilia's progress. I was already halfway to Cornelia's house, so made the hike up Vergu and showed up just after midday, unannounced, at her *domus*.

The mistress of the mansion was in, but she avoided me. I was allowed to meet with Aemilia, though. I innocently asked whether I could use one of their house slaves to send a missive to Valerius Flaccus, whose mansion was not far away. I requested to see him for a private meeting at his house outside normal hours, and perhaps arrange for Quintus Aquilius to be present if that promising young lawyer could be found.

I expected nothing would happen in Cornelia's house without her knowledge, and that her curiosity would get the better of her current disdain of me. Nor was I disappointed. By early afternoon, the slave returned to inform us that, indeed, Valerius Flaccus and Quintus Aquilius would be happy to join us all for dinner at Cornelia's.

In the intervening time, Aemilia and I pored over the scrolls and her notes. She had been diligent in deconstructing

the complex etching on the lead sheets, copying the sigils indi-
vidually on wax tablets, and keeping associated notes with them.
The work to decipher and analyse Ambustus' curses was significantly more difficult than one would expect. Curses are almost
always written as a petition to the gods. "*Titus has lost two gloves
and beseeches Venus that the thief responsible should lose their mind
and eyes.*" Or "*Marcus begs Iovis' favour, and promises him a rich
sacrifice of lamb, if he should strike Gaius dumb during his trial.*"

Ambustus' tablets, however, were drawing the *magia* to
them rather than attempting to influence its source. That necessitated the use of far more complex formulae. They involved
symbols not found in the *Quirite* alphabet, and, as is often the
case, words and phrases which had been appropriated for different, symbolic meanings and allude to things outside the normal
sphere of human experience.

Deciphering these required significant cross-referenc-
ing of treatises on the subject, which were also written in the
same oblique language. Though Aemilia lacked my education on
the subject, her memory and skill at reading was far superior to
mine. We worked together, me providing her with direction and
instruction, and her noting down options and quickly retrieving
and recalling the reference material.

With all this concentrated work, a pattern was beginning
to emerge. "See here?" I grabbed a couple of wax tablets. "These
symbols appear in tandem on the other *tabulae defixiones*. He
uses a few recurring themes. Does anything strike you as odd
about these supplications?"

"You mean the references to the *lares*? I thought appeal-
ing to the major deities was the usual practice."

"It is. But by invoking the household gods, any of the *dii
familiares*, he is focusing the curse. This is his method of limiting
the curse and concentrating it on the premises of the particular
insula. You'll note also that he specifically mentions the *lares loci*,
not the *lares familiares* — the place, not the people."

"Wouldn't the household gods be less grand, and therefore less effective, than the major *numina*?" she asked.

"I think we've all seen the efficacy of Ambustus' curses," I said drily, glancing at her legs. She shifted in painful memory. I wanted to impress on her never to underestimate practitioners of forbidden arts and the havoc they might wreak.

"These are his anchoring points," I continued. "He channelled powerful *magia* into the curses. You can see it in the incantations here and here," I pointed out the relevant sections. "I believe this is how he was able to get a powerful, yet localised, effect."

Aemilia was as excited as a puppy exploring its first meadow. She asked me about the meanings of various symbols, how one executed an incantation both in chanting and with inscribing symbols, what feelings the various branches of *magia* evoked in the practitioner, and so on.

It was the opposite of how I wished her to feel about it — but it was contagious. I couldn't quite keep up with all her questions, my education being incomplete. We both rummaged through the scrolls and codices I brought, flicking between them, theorising about meanings and explanations, talking fast, and letting our intellects run wild.

Things other than my intellect stirred. I could not but be enchanted by her smile and by her large, grey eyes with the circles of dark blue around the irises. The faint smell of roses that came from her marble-white skin reminded me too much of the lost Helena, but this time I felt no pain in the memory. Aemilia was making my insides flutter in ways I never thought I'd feel again.

I kept on talking about the curses then, to drive away those distracting emotions. Better to concentrate on the disasters brought upon the unfortunate denizens of the cursed *insulae* by rampant household gods than dwell on more earthly things that could not be.

***

In what was becoming a standard for the case, we gathered for another dinner party hosted by Cornelia. The important figures reclined on couches, Valerius (sans his wife) next to Cornelia, and Aemilia was allowed to recline on the couch with Quintus Aquilius. Thankfully, Cornelia did not invite her vacuous friend Icilia, which made conversation about the matter at hand easier.

The food, even on such short notice, was superb. I can only imagine that Cornelia's cook was used to impromptu feasts and knew who to contact for fresh supplies. The spicy snails were particularly exceptional, while the squid in nettle sauce was an eye- and mouth-pleasing classic.

We didn't waste much time with pleasantries. In between courses, I gave a detailed report to Valerius Flaccus about how I tracked Ambustus and confirmed the tablets were his doing. When I got to naming Ambustus' employer, Flaccus drawled "Numicius!" like someone who has just discovered a half-eaten cockroach in his food.

"I gather you know the man?"

"I do indeed. Cursed be the day I first laid eyes on his miserable, bloated carcass! We have been on opposing factions in the senate a few times. He doesn't even pretend to uphold the business restrictions of senators and actively participates in enterprises all around Egretia."

"Do you think this move against you was political or business-related?" asked Cornelia.

"Who could say what goes on in that snake's mind? Probably a bit of both," answered Valerius. "Come to think of it, earlier this year he was suing to get the Via Arborea extended past Arbarica. Entirely not his place to do so. The public works contracts are the purview of the censors and should not be forced through legislation. His impassioned speeches about 'spreading our noble culture deeper into barbarian lands' fooled no one — he was after some personal gain. As for the *insulae*, he's probably trying to prepare cheap housing for clients he acquired during his praetorship in Arbarica. I'm guessing he's interested in buying my properties, but without paying their true worth."

"Has he approached you?" I asked. "I imagine that despite

Ambustus' complaints, he paid handsomely for those curses. Both to be cast, and to be ignored by the authorities. He might have tried his luck with you first."

"Oh, he should know what my reaction would have been. He knows better than to try and buy anything from me."

"Hmm," I pondered this for a moment, "I wonder if you are the first one he tried this tactic on. I have not come across any other such rumours."

"Well, you haven't heard of the curses afflicting cousin Lucius' *insulae* either, till he hired you," said Cornelia with what I thought was unnecessary smugness.

"No, but neither had anyone else." I tried to avoid getting dragged into argument and to stay on point. "This would strengthen my assumption that Valerius is the first such victim, which speaks to motive and opportunity."

"Numicius' usual tactics are straightforward," Valerius said before we could continue the banter. "He takes aim at the owner or leverages the tenants — a few broken bones usually get him the results he wants. If he has tried curses in the past, it must never have progressed so far. I wonder what might have pushed him to resort to *nefas magia*."

"I'll add it to my list of open questions," I said.

"Good. I'll have another chat with Aburius about doubling guards on my other properties."

"And now?" asked Aemilia. "What's next?"

"Now we need to collect evidence against Numicius," Quintus Aquilius spoke up. "If we are to have a hope of convicting him in court, we would benefit by having more than just Felix's testimony based on hearsay from Ambustus."

"What kind of evidence?"

"A confession in front of witnesses would do," said Aquilius.

"I think you'll find people willing to testify against Numicius are few and far between," said Valerius. "In the past, those who dared rarely made it alive to the trial. People learn from others' mistakes, surprisingly."

"Why not do what you suggested to Ambustus?" asked Aemilia. "Register as his client and get him to talk to you about it."

Valerius retorted even before I could. "I would never ask that of Felix!"

I saw the confusion rise on Aemilia's face and softened my tone before replying. "In our system of patron and clients, there is no shame in accepting bribes. But once a man is bought, he stays bought. To do otherwise would be to close all doors. If I were to do as you suggest and officially register myself as Numicius' client whilst working for Lucius Valerius, I would never be able to find employment in Egretia again. No one would ever trust me."

"So, what then?" from Cornelia.

"The usual. Start with his cronies and work my way closer. Gain his confidence. Attempt to get a confession or at least witnesses willing to testify. And all without becoming his client."

"And how would you do that?" asked Aemilia.

"I will think of something," I replied. "If he's employing *incantatores* with a loose understanding of the law that could be one angle. Or perhaps something more directly related to the *insulae*."

"There is one matter we should probably address first," said Aquilius. "We should file the case with the Urban Praetor sooner rather than later to avoid delays."

"Isn't it premature?" Cornelia interjected.

"By the time we deal with the preliminaries, the praetor will not be able to set a date for the trial sooner than a month hence."

"And I trust that would be sufficient time for you?" Valerius addressed me.

I nodded confidently.

"Are you filing a charge of sacrilege?" Aemilia wondered. "For using *nefas magia* within city limits?"

"It will be harder to prove, unless we know for a fact he was involved in the creation of the tablets," answered Aquilius.

"Besides, there haven't been many successful sacrilege cases. It's too easy to weasel out of them."

"Why not *maiestas*, then?" asked Cornelia. "Surely this is a kind of treason, even if he merely ordered the curses."

"That won't do. While perhaps easier to prove, if we succeed the state gets the lion's share of the spoils. We would only be eligible for a tiny fraction of Numicius' estate. We'd better make it a *nummaria poena*, a fiscal matter resulting in a hefty fine."

"So, you file a property case, *in rem?*"

"*In personam*," answered the lawyer. "It's not a thing that is being contested, but rather his personal actions against Valerius to which we can attach a bill of damages."

"Do you need me to be registered as a *quadruplator?*" I asked. Being listed as a formal informer in the case had its benefits — such as a quarter of the spoils.

"An *index* would be better," said Aquilius. "If you plan to get close to Numicius, it's best to keep your name in reserve until we are ready for the trial."

Same task, less profit. Par for the course for me. Still, Valerius was paying me handsomely for my testimony. Greed is not a pretty trait.

CHAPTER XVII

For connoisseurs, the preliminary motions of a court case are almost as much fun as the eventual trial. None of the *comitia* were due to meet that day and a regular senate meeting was convened in the curia. This made it easy for Aquilius.

As soon as the morning session was over, senators drifted out of the building, chatting animatedly in small groups. Aquilius must have arranged things with the Urban Praetor, as the latter hastened to set up his stool and desk in the closest shady colonnade to the Senate's doors. When Numicius made his way out, Aquilius stood on the curia's steps and declared in a loud voice, "Gaius Numicius, I hereby summon you to trial!"

The gathered senators, as well as any passers-by in the Forum within hearing distance, stopped to gaze and then settled back to watch the show.

"Let us step before the *praetor urbanus*, so that your vile deeds against Lucius Valerius Flaccus — nay, against the whole of the good people of Egretia — may be made known to all, your shame exposed, and restitution of the good name of an upright citizen made."

"He's suicidal," said one greybeard behind me. "To oppose Numicius like that in public — he'll never live to the trial."

"Nah," responded another, tapping his nose. "He's smart. He's doing it in full public, see. Right in front of the *praetor urbanus* too. Too many witnesses — too many curious minds who'll remember."

"He might survive today but getting any witnesses to trial will be like getting live octopi to walk across a snowy mountain pass," countered the first.

The second greybeard spat on the ground. "I wouldn't bet a dried fig on any witnesses living through it. But the young 'un will live. Numicius will clear his name in court. *Then* he will deal with him."

I tuned out the gossips and returned my attention to the legal tableaux. Having done the verbal summons *in ius vocatio* as needed and according to custom, Numicius was bound to appear with Aquilius in front of the Urban Praetor or be declared *indefensus* and forfeit the claim.

So far, so good.

The main part of filing a lawsuit came with both of them standing before the magistrate. Aquilius had to define his claims according to the prescribed formulae. First the *demonstratio* — "*Quod Valerio Flacco...* Whereas Valerius Flaccus owns three *insulae* represented here by these three stones taken from their courtyards, and Gaius Numicius has impinged on Valerius' ownership by committing delictual acts of vile character, against the laws of gods and men..." After this came the actual claim, the *intentio* — "*Quidquid Numicio...* If it appears that Numicius by his actions has violated Valerius' rights under Quiritary law, then he is to pay the sum of..." Aquilius added an *adnotatio*, to indict Ambustus in the proceedings as well, making the connection as being Numicius' client and henchman, his hand acting on Numicius' direction.

And so on, and so forth.

The two greybeards next to me — whose names I gathered were Statilius and Valdrius — were rather impressed with young Aquilius, from the authority he projected in speech to his choices in legal forms. He used all the right words (and trials were lost for misuse of the ancient formulae), he presented his grievances clearly, and he chose the right form for the trial, given the complexities of the apparent case.

When his turn came, Numicius responded by first trying

to dismiss the suit as a false claim, to which the praetor replied that *prima facie* there was nothing wrong with the application and final decisions would be by the judge. Numicius then tried to object to having been ambushed to appear before the praetor immediately after the summons. The Praetor responded that he would be agreeable to allowing more time until the trial. Aquilius then requested a larger sum to be put in bond, as delays meant financial harm to his patron.

This went on for a while, all according to custom and formula. They haggled over the dates and the urban praetor set it to ten days to the Kalends of October. The praetor then consulted a list and picked a judge — some hapless senator who would probably be cursing his luck with this trial. Jury lists were exchanged — a roll of one hundred names handed by Aquilius to be approved by the praetor, of which Numicius chose fifty-one.

Observing these proceedings from my vantage point in the crowd and listening to the chatter around me, it became obvious that Aquilius was correct in the choice of trial subject. The case was already drawing attention and there was no benefit in filing for sacrilege or treason. The two greybeards providing a running commentary throughout were giving me wonderful insights, especially concerning who might be siding later with Numicius. A complex game lay ahead of me.

***

And so, I began sniffing around to get the measure of Numicius, find his weak spots, and devise a way to entrap him. I spent the rest of that day in the Forum, listening to gossip about the public spectacle at the urban praetor as well as the debates in the Senate. When evening descended I went to the docks, bought wine for longshoremen, and learnt about their colleges and landlords. I visited myriad places around our city, picking up conversations, buying honest meals for dishonest people, and pouring liberating wine by the jugsful. I found a whorehouse belonging to one of his clients that was frequented by several of his cronies in which I spent some of Valerius' money on bribes and prostitutes.

I worked my way up the ranks. From old chinwaggers in the Forum to clerks and scribes, from longshoremen at the docks to the leaders of their respective colleges. I made the acquaintance of people closer and closer to Numicius himself, without association to Valerius Flaccus or a mention of the Subvales *insulae*. Just seemingly idle chatter about politics and business opportunities.

It was a tedious, time-consuming business involving walking from one end of town to the next and back again in the sweltering Sextilis heat, made only slightly less laborious by the wine, food, and prostitutes.

What I found out about Numicius after three such days was that he was your regular land-owning senator. That is to say, he had as many businesses on the grey side of the restrictions as he could safely get away with. Superficially, those esteemed members of our society who dedicate their lives to public service by becoming senators are too noble be dragged to earthly affairs, and earn money solely through the acquisition and rent of land and properties. Realistically, they engage in the grey area of silent partnerships in businesses, providing investment funds and back-room advice, but not public involvement. Cynically, they do everything shy of hawking wares loudly on the streets, using their power and influence to pass favourable laws and garner more money and power.

Very few and far between are the exceptions, those truly upright citizens — like my current employer — who adhere to the traditions of the *mos maiorum* without deviation. Their low numbers are lucky for the rest of the senate, as they are invariably insufferable uptight prigs who use moral superiority to annoy everyone to tears.

As for Numicius, he was perhaps on the darker end of the grey spectrum, but nothing outright illegal that I could find. Well, nothing besides using curses within the sacred city limits against fellow citizens.

Still, I gathered enough information to get the measure

of Numicius, and to plot how to gain access to the man himself.

***

It was the first time I had to wear a toga to a brothel. Most such establishments are quick in-and-out affairs — no affront meant for my male readers — where a tunic is preferred for ease of access.

Venus' Swan, however, was a different thing. A sprawling mansion behind high walls not far from the Forum, its doors were located in a secluded alley and entry was by invitation only. I had to cash a favour long owed me by a former client and see Flaccus' banker about an advance to get access. I also had Borax with me, for appearances as well as security.

Mentioning a certain name I was given to the guard at the gate got me shown in. I waved my hand dismissively at the sycophantic attendant before he even opened his mouth and strolled leisurely past him. From behind me came the jingle of coins as Borax dumped a pouch of silver *denarii* in the attendant's hand then walked briskly after me.

The atrium was exquisite. A pool of clear blue water with mosaics of frolicking nymphs; green marble columns, with potted vines climbing up them; and frescoes of meadows and natural life in the making. Gilded decorations were everywhere. As I circled the shallow pool, a bare-breasted slave walked in and deferentially handed me a cup of wine. It was an amazing vintage the likes of which I have rarely tasted — so flavourful that it hadn't needed aromatic herbs or sugar-of-lead.

As I glanced after the retreating slave, I noticed cleverly hidden openings that allowed the staff to move behind the walls. As I walked toward a wide archway at the other side of the pool, a man stepped in front of me. He smiled openly, showing brilliant teeth. He was polite and warm — yet blocked the way nonetheless, and his posture made it clear he would not be waved aside easily.

"*Ave*, Spurious Vulpius. I'm Titus Pompilius, the manager here. How may we please you tonight?" The gate attendant must have relayed my name via the invisible network of slaves behind the walls.

"Just the man I want to see. I'm planning a private party and I would like to hire a few of your girls and boys."

"Certainly, my good man. Let's go to my office, where we can organise everything for you." He led me past the archway and to the left, down a colonnade. From the gardens and rooms beyond I could hear music, laughter, and the occasional squeal or a moan. We stepped into a side room set as a *tablinum*, with a desk, chairs, and many scrolls in pigeonholes.

"Tell me your needs and I shall arrange all," he said as he poured wine and water into silver cups.

"It will be a private affair, a *convivium* for a few select guests. I will need a handful of skilled girls and perhaps a couple of boys to cover everything."

"Will you be hosting this party with us? I'm afraid that we never let our girls leave the premises with first-time customers."

"That will be fine. We could have it here, so long as you can guarantee me a private suite."

"We certainly can." There was a sparkle of gold in his eyes. "We can also cater food and wine. Just leave me your wishes and I shall see them fulfilled."

"That will be much appreciated." We discussed the specifics, haggled over the price a bit, and I left him with an advance in coin. For the price of a house or the freedom of few slaves — a mere pittance for Valerius Flaccus' bank account — I arranged an evening of exquisite pleasure.

"Lastly, I shall need to speak with your girls before the event. Just to, *uh*, prepare them with specific instructions pertaining to some of the guests."

"Certainly. Is there anything else I can do for you tonight?" Pompilius raised a brow.

Well, what was the harm? I was already there, and Flaccus was paying.

That was when Fortuna smiled upon me.

Livia, one of the girls I sampled at the Venus' Swan, struck me as brighter than the average breasts-and-giggles type one expects to find at such establishments. I was lying sweaty and satisfied on her bed, and after I got my breath back, I asked whether she'd be interested in earning a bit of money towards her freedom fund by assisting me in my planned activities.

"Is there someone to whom you'd like Venus to grant a special blessing?" she asked in perfectly correct Quirite.

"A prospective employer. I will need him fulfilled and in a good mood, and there is nothing better than Venus' blessing for that."

"Any idea what he likes?"

"No. Experiment."

"I hope you will be generous with your donation to Venus, then." She stroked my chest with her fingers. "The goddess prefers gold, given directly to her humble priestess."

I laughed, she laughed, and it was some time again before I could explain to her what I needed. The twinkle in Livia's eyes at the thought of mischief convinced me she was the right girl for this.

***

The orgy was planned for two nights hence. Now for the second part of my plan, getting Numicius there. I knew his routine sufficiently well from the past few days and I learnt enough to take an educated guess at what would catch his ear.

The Senate met an hour after dawn. The great wooden doors with the bronze nails stood open and a crowd of some three hundred men were standing on the steps in front of the Curia, resplendent in their brilliant white togas with purple hems and buckled crimson shoes. Being the month of Sextilis, the junior consul had the *fasces*, and was therefore responsible for the Senate's sessions. The consul, a man by the name of Aulus Gabinius, approached the marble altar at the top of the steps and to the right of the door, pulled the fold of his toga over his head, and chanted the traditional prayer to Iovis Pater.

Two young boys marched from the side of the building towards him, one leading a dazed goat and the other carrying the instruments of sacrifice. In the appropriate time, and without breaking his prayer, the junior consul reached out, took an obsidian knife handed to him by the boy and with a deft motion slit the goat's neck. The beast shuddered, its knees buckled, and it fell on its side, dead.

The consul used a different knife to cut open the goat's belly, poked about for a bit in the spilt innards, and declared the liver auspicious and showing the gods' favour for the day's meeting.

The gathered men ascended the steps and entered the Senate hall while the junior consul washed his hands in a bowl of water and made his way last to the big auditorium. The Senate's doors are normally kept open during meetings, and from my vantage point amidst the columns on the Basilica Antonia's portico, I could see the gloomy interior. The men were finding their places on the three marble tiers: current office holders in the first row, minor notables in the middle row, and senators who never rose on the *cursus honorum* past *quaestor* as backbenchers on the top row. Servants, slaves, scribes, and clerks were hurrying around, setting folding chairs, delivering scrolls, and whispering updates and gossip.

One such man, paid handsomely, delivered a folded papyrus to the hands of a clerk. The clerk carried it to his master, who glanced at it abstractedly, then paused to examine it more closely.

He lifted his eyes, spoke briefly with his clerk, and they both looked around. They couldn't locate the man who had delivered the papyrus — the messenger having long disappeared in the throng of people getting ready for the Senate's session.

The senator broke the seal, unfolded the paper, and read the message. A slow smile arose on his face. He carefully folded the missive back and put it in the sinus of his toga.

Having little interest in the proceedings of the Senate that day, I calmly strolled out of the shadows of the colonnade and walked away from the Forum. Getting Numicius to the party turned out to be far easier than I first thought it would be. A quick forgery, a message drafted as though from one of his senatorial opponents to another, a quick exchange of coins, and the appearance of a confused scribe delivering the message into the wrong hands. The contents of the fake message referred to a certain exclusive party where back-room deals would be struck and properties would change hands.

My leads and estimates led me to believe the temptation to crash the party would be too much for Numicius to resist. I fervently hoped I was right, or I would have a very large and unnecessary expenditure to explain to Valerius. I stopped in front of the Collegium Mercatorum, at the fountain of Juno Moneta. This being a fiscal matter, she was the appropriate deity to beseech. I prayed briefly and tossed a silver *denarius* into the waters for her assistance.

CHAPTER XVIII

The eve of the orgy was quite busy for me. High-society parties were never my thing — or, to be more precise, I was never invited — so I had left most of arrangements to Pompilius. My task was to gather a few respectable collaborators — or at least able to appear so — who wouldn't mind providing a background cast to the orgy. Considering the people with whom I usually associated, that wasn't as easy as it might sound. High on interest, low on respectability. I needed a crowd who would fit in well with the Venus' Swan decor, not the kind that would land me a bill for damages. But I bartered a few favours — managing to give out more than I had to cash in — from some of my more respectable acquaintances and got the right mix of people to be present and advance my master plan.

I arrived early, made sure Pompilius had everything arranged, and briefed the girls about what favours should be paid to whom and what to pay attention to. Livia would see to the guest of honour, and the others knew to follow her lead if needed.

Nothing left to do but wait.

It was well after sunset and the sky was a dark, rich purple. The musicians were going at full blast, plates of delicacies were scattered around the rooms half-eaten, and enough wine had gone down thirsty throats and started to stain togas and tunics. My own guests were already on the tipsy side and I heard the unmistakable sounds of enjoyment from side rooms. If Numicius didn't show up soon, I'd have a hard time explaining this expense to Flaccus.

I was starting to get worried about my scheme when Numicius finally made his appearance. He must have timed his arrival to that stage of the party, since he was not formally invited. Numicius was a short, rotund man, with a vast waist and thick jowls. His short, curly, black hair framed a face with sharp teeth and dark, beady little eyes. He was almost a caricature of the quintessential unlikable person. Yet, he exuded undeniable energy and he knew it — smiling warmly around the room as he walked in, as if in benign ownership.

I gave Livia a discreet nudge and assumed my best bored and disappointed expression. I watched as she greeted Numicius, her scantily-clad curves swaying like a kitten riding a pendulum behind a silken curtain. She guided him to one of the couches near me, caressed his legs as she removed his sandals, then clambered into his lap and fed him peeled grapes.

"Fetch me some of those nuts instead, *meum mel*," he told her. Livia obediently stood up, stepped to a nearby low table, bent down from the waist in way that must have afforded Numicius unparalleled views of her exquisite behind, and scooped up a handful of glazed nuts. She curled back in his lap and hand-fed him the delicacies. In between servings, she nibbled on his earlobes.

I turned a wearied look in his direction, and on the second attempt caught his eye. I gave him a jaded half-smile and turned away.

"Quite the girls they have here," Numicius said. "Or are you waiting for the boys?"

"They better be pretty," I answered, "for what I'm paying. Though it seems all for naught."

Livia pretended to accidentally drop a candied almond down Numicius' toga and started to search for it. With her lips.

"Oh, they are, they are. I've been here before and I can assure you, your party will be a success."

"It won't be a success unless the guest of honour arrives," I retorted.

"Guest of honour? I cannot imagine anyone of worth would miss an orgy at the Venus' Swan."

His eyes glazed briefly, as a muffled 'found it!' came from deep in the folds of his toga.

"Who, *ah*, who… is this guest of yours?" He feigned ignorance, though I knew better.

"Valerius Flaccus. I meant to impress him with the party and to discuss some property deals in the Subvales."

"Flaccus? That dried twig will never appreciate the delicacies offered here," he fondled Livia's buttocks in emphasis. "I'll tell you what. I have a few property interests in the Subvales myself. Why don't I see to this, *ah*… enthusiastic young lady here and if Valerius doesn't come by the time I'm done, we could discuss it between ourselves."

I turned to face him fully for the first time and put on what I hoped was an expression of only mild interest. "How kind of you, though I fear I really will need Valerius Flaccus for this. But do enjoy the girls. Someone should. Shall I send any more girls for you…," I waved my hand in the air as if hoping to grasp his name from it, "Uh, I'm not sure we've been introduced."

"Gaius Numicius," he said as he stood and hoisted the giggling Livia on his shoulder. "And don't worry, I think this one will be enough," he said, giving her buttocks a gentle smack.

***

I waited patiently while Livia entertained Numicius. The various moans and cries from the other guests provided a backdrop while I plotted the rest of the night. I hoped to speak with Numicius while Livia was busy distracting him, so I just had to adjust my tack slightly to account for him already being satisfied.

He took his sweet time about it. Livia was instructed to ply him with wine and delicacies as well as any other pleasure he might crave to ensure a good mood and dimmed sensibilities. I gave the signal and the supporting cast cleared the central room. The stage was set for private discussions.

Two hours later, he returned. His toga was draped impeccably around him, and, but for a slight rosiness of cheeks, he appeared as though he had just spent the time in philosophical discourse about the origins of the *Lupercalia*.

He seated himself next to me with a satisfied sigh. Livia joined us and curled in his lap, but not before pushing a cup of wine into his waiting hand. She winked at me as she bent forward to choose some grapes for Numicius.

"I see that Valerius has not come," he commented nonchalantly.

"Sadly," I lamented. "All this expense for naught. I will need another way to lure him."

"What's that deal you mentioned?" He put on a nonchalant face as Livia fed him peeled grapes.

"Oh, I had a property transaction to propose to him, something that will at once reduce his headaches and improve his cash flow. It's a good deal, completely legit on his side, if only I could get him to listen."

Numicius hummed while I munched on some nuts. Then, "I could certainly use a property trade with improved cash flow and reduced headaches. I happen to own a few properties around town, so I could well appreciate such a transaction. Tell me more, and perhaps you could interest me instead."

"I know of certain… difficulties Valerius has been experiencing, with finding tenants for his Subvales *insulae*," I opened. "I was hoping to broker a deal with him. Clear out his troubles just long enough that he could either find new tenants or sell the properties, should he wish to get rid of them altogether. I'm willing to work on commission — reduce his risk and increase my gains."

"Are you a real estate specialist?" Numicius asked me, with the most genuine look of disinterested ignorance I have ever seen on the face of someone who was sure to have made enquiries about me and my trade.

"Uh… not exactly, Gaius Numicius. My name is Spurius Vulpius Felix, commonly known as Felix the Fox. I specialise in solving uncommon problems for common people. Or, at least, common people with enough money to afford my services. A while ago I noticed certain *insulae* standing abandoned in the Subvales, not far from where I live. Only rarely will our landlords stop leasing a property and our *aediles* are unlikely to declare a building unfit for living even as it collapses. While the situation was unusual by itself, I then discovered those apartment buildings were completely abandoned — even squatters or neighbours would not go close to them. Word on the street is that they are haunted by *lemures* of the dead. It sounded just like the kind of unusual problem I could solve for Valerius."

"Mmm. Well, his loss, no doubt." Numicius was scanning the murals on the ceiling.

We were playing a game of cat and mouse, or rather fox and cat, each trying to bait the other. I used a tactic that worked well for me in the past — I sighed deeply, swirled the wine in my cup, sipped listlessly, and said nothing.

"Those deals…" Numicius began again after a while, and I had to suppress my grin. "Those deals can be rather expensive. Are you sure you could solve Valerius' 'unusual problems' as you call them?"

"Quite certain, my dear Gaius, quite certain. I have seen similar infestations in the past. A bit of purification, a sacrifice to the gods, some smoke and mirrors for the neighbours, and Valerius would be able to get tenants and sell the *insulae* before anyone was wiser. They'll fetch a better price than he could get now, and I'd enjoy a better commission. I just need to get his attention. If an orgy is not his inclination, I have other ways to gain his confidence."

"Persistent, aren't you?"

"That is how I get results for my customers," I replied.

"What if you just brokered a real estate deal? For the *insulae* as they stand now, empty?"

"Not only would I have to find a buyer with more money than savvy, but my commission would be smaller. No, I can't see how that would work," I shook my head.

"I might be tempted to buy. You see, I wish to build a

shrine to Bona Dea in memory of my mother. I plan to spare no expense in the building, but I am still a businessman. Getting a good-sized plot of land on the Vicus Bellonae for a reasonable price would allow me to spend more later on the temple. I'm sure any problems will be over once we consecrate the land to the Good Goddess. I'd even be willing to fund your commission as if I paid full price."

"A sound plan, one I will be happy to assist you with!" I put in as much eagerness as I could muster into my voice.

"I'm sure we could come to a mutually agreeable arrangement. Why don't you visit me an hour after dawn tomorrow and we shall discuss the details?"

So Numicius planned to draft me as a client, a minor inconvenience I was sure I could get out of. A more interesting revelation was the confirmation from his own lips that he knew of the curses — he mentioned the address of one affected *insulae*, even though I never named them.

When I queried Livia after everyone left about what happened while they were secluded, whether Numicius had blabbed anything pertinent, all I got out from her was that he was "a surprisingly gentle and considerate lover," and an enigmatic smile.

Chapter XIX

I presented myself at Numicius' *domus* at the appointed time. This was the hour rich patrons dedicated to the clients — dispensing favours, assigning tasks, keeping and building their public image. While I had no plan to register myself as his client and didn't wish to be seen like one, I had to balance that with maintaining an air of eagerness for the deal.

Mercifully, there weren't many others to observe me or take up Numicius' time. I gave my name at the gates, the door-slave checked me against his list and ushered me in. A secretary asked for my name again, made a note of it on a wax tablet, and waved vaguely at a few folding chairs as he turned and went inside.

Several minutes passed, during which I got to examine Numicius' atrium decorations — all in good taste, opulence without decadence. Three *imagines* were mounted in alcoves, a shrine under each one. I couldn't remember whether they were consuls or achieved other public distinction. There were marks of old fires on the marble for the *lararium*. The Numicii might not have had as many consuls as the Valerii, but it was obvious that Gaius Numicius was a man of taste and piety, worshipping his ancestors and family deities. Admittedly, not what I expected when I first met the man. He kept surprising me, in ways which made me uncomfortable.

While I was admiring a particularly exquisite white marble statuette of Diana the huntress, Ambustus walked in from the street. He glanced at me, but kept on walking inside, without a pause or any sign of recognition.

A moment later the secretary called me in. Numicius' *tablinum* was large but crammed with so many pigeon-hole shelves and tables holding scrolls, that space to move was limited. Some of the tables held astronomical and other devices I didn't quite recognise with a quick glance. Though it was hectic and jumbled, I got a feeling there was a method to the madness. Numicius had his hand in many things and stayed on top of them all. I needed some quiet alone-time in his office — I was sure I would be able to dig up incriminating evidence for various acts amongst all his scrolls.

"Ah, my good Felix — come in, come in! Please have a seat," Numicius waved at the client chairs in front of his desk. "Archaeon! Wine!" he yelled.

Numicius was sitting behind his massive desk, his wide buttocks resting on a chryselephantine chair worth more than my house and all its contents. If I found him energetic the previous night, that morning he was positively brimming with enthusiasm. Ambustus, on the other hand, had a more typical attitude towards mornings. He was leaning casually on a wall to the side, sipping his watered wine slowly, his face blank of expression. He was at an angle that allowed him to observe me clearly whilst remaining at the edge of my vision. It was all I could do to refrain from glancing openly at him, attempting to guess whether he recognised me.

Once I was seated with a cup of watered wine in my hand, Numicius continued. "I am intrigued by that deal you alluded to last night. I am, as I have mentioned, in the market for a decently sized plot of land in the Subvales. My late mother was a devotee of the Bona Dea. She saw the rise of Magna Mater amongst the noble women and traced it to the slaves and handmaidens these women employed; slaves who often grew up in the Subvales or associated with others there. On her deathbed," — and he actually had a catch in his voice when his said this — "she made me promise to do my best to promote our own Egretian gods to those who live within the city limit. A shrine to her patron goddess, dedicated in her name and giving free solace to women of lower status, will achieve just that." He leaned forward and placed his elbows on the table, looking at me intently. "And so, to execute my grand design, I require a good-sized property in a central location of the Subvales. I will convert it to the grandest temple in our city dedicated to the kindest amongst the *numina*, spread the word I have been charged with, and my mother's shade will rest with her beloved Good Goddess."

An amazing performance. As someone who outfoxes people for a living, I consider myself a connoisseur of the perfectly spun lie. I admired his tale — both in content and in delivery — for professional reasons. I just didn't buy a word that came from that money-hungry thug, who cursed whole buildings and brought death to babies.

Still, I had a job to do. "I recall you explained how a lower land price will allow you to build a grander temple," I said. "Without affecting the intermediary's commission, of course."

"Precisely," confirmed Numicius. Throughout this, Ambustus leaned quietly against the wall, sipping his wine and staring at me impassively as a snake watches a mouse.

"I would very much like to be that agent, then. I have ways — several of them, in fact, already in motion — to gain Valerius Flaccus' attention and get you his *insulae* on the cheap. However..." I let it hang for a moment.

"Yes? However?" said Numicius.

"However, my plan was always to help him rid his properties of whatever afflicts them, or at least temporarily suspend the effects while the sale is in progress. Now, I am certain I could spin this into a simpler real estate brokerage and still gain Flaccus' trust. But, as my benefactor in the matter, surely you are aware that this might leave you with buildings afflicted with supernatural phenomena? Even demolishing them could bring the curses down upon you and your engineers. I do not want you to come after me claiming I deceived you later."

"I won't," Numicius waved his hands animatedly. "I know full well what I am buying. What I need from you is to broker the deal without letting Flaccid Flaccus learn I am the final buyer. Do not worry about the state of the buildings. You will be well recompensed for your part."

"Oh?" I raised my brows, and added slowly, to press on Numicius' impatience, "Political rivalries, is that it? Opposing sides on some matters of foreign policy and suddenly he's refusing to do business with you?"

"Quite, quite. As you say. So, the key will be to get him not only to sell, but to do so to a straw man. I would enjoy the look on his face when he finds out I got them from under him."

"And would you require just one of his *insulae*, or all three? I know of three that are afflicted. Surely you need but one to build a shrine, but the buyer I had in mind before would want all of them."

"I will buy all three," Numicius waved his hand expansively. "Might as well realise some profit at the same time."

"But have you looked at these properties? Do you understand what you are getting into, what with all the gruesome deaths that happened there?" I sucked air through my teeth.

Numicius drew a deep breath and spoke slowly. "I know, I know. That will just be a wonderful leverage on Flaccus. I am sure this is nothing but mere superstition that I could deal with in time."

"But, they say the *lares* of the buildings have woken up!" I pressed. "That the *numina* run out of control and hurt the very people they're supposed to protect."

"Your concern is touching," he said with forced calm, "but I assure you I know what I'm buying. I have men who could purify it."

His eyes made the tiniest flicker towards Ambustus, who, in turn, contributed his first comment that day. "Whatever the problem is, it will go away when we consecrate the properties as temples to the Bona Dea. The goddess' power will override any mere local *lar* or any other nonsense. Hortensia — Gaius Numicius' late mother — will be guaranteed a temple that will make its name as the quencher of curses."

"Very well then," I said as brightly as I could. "You get everything in readiness and I shall proceed to procure you the deal as quickly as possible. We just need to set up finances through the straw companies and men of your choice, and your construction will commence well before the rains comes."

"Excellent, excellent!" Numicius gave me a wide and toothy grin. "I just need you to register as my client so that we can set your extended commission from this deal into formal agreement." He pushed a leaf of paper towards me, on which I could make out a patron-client contract.

"I think it might be better if I don't sign that just now," I said. "If I were to make this transaction with Flaccus, I need the appearance of a completely impartial, or at least unaffiliated —"

"Don't worry!" Numicius interrupted me. "The details will never come out. They will simply be filed in my office."

I gave a sceptical wave at the mess of scrolls strewn about the room and said, "The contacts I have to pave my path to Valerius Flaccus will make far-reaching enquiries. I have built my reputation on being impartial, independent. Since you made the imperative condition that you must not be identified as the buyer, I must raise absolutely no suspicion of being connected to you." I saw him open his mouth to cut me off again, so I pressed on. "A client agreement would be for my benefit as well, but I will put my trust in your late mother. You wish to build a shrine in her name. I will trust that Hortensia and the Bona Dea will keep us both honest for its sake."

He paused, blinked, then slowly withdrew the paper. "Very well. We will make this arrangement on word of honour for now. But be warned — dishonour the deal and you dishonour my mother. You will be begging for a death a long time before it will come to you." The cold steel of his voice ensured I did not doubt his words.

***

By the time I left Numicius' *domus*, the sun was striving to reach its zenith. It was only when I stopped to wash my face at a public fountain that I realised how tense my shoulders were. Throughout our discussions, I was in constant fear of Ambustus shouting a sudden '*aha!*' and bringing up our night of drinking. While I had my cover story ready, Ambustus' serpentine demeanour unnerved me.

After Numicius and I shook hands and toasted that deal of 'honour' with wine, he regained his exuberant energy and we flew into a flurry of activity. We discussed the requirements of setting up the straw companies, brainstormed who could be listed as the final buyer that would be unconnected to Numicius, and drafted letters and charters and bank notes and every other type of miscellanea that is required in the set-up of complex and opaque business structures.

Brokering real estate wasn't my area of expertise. My experience at my father's knees as he taught me about his international network of bankers and agents were of marginal relevance. My own banking experience, as Barbatus my banker would gladly attest, was more creative than legal. Numicius was a real shark, quoting legal loopholes from memory and pulling names from a vast network of connections amongst the financiers that control Egretian economy.

I was amazed at the speed he could set something like this up. I must have appeared out of my depth to him, not to say a simpleton. The benefit to me was twofold; I have received that day a condensed education in fiscal and legal matters, which might be useful later. And lowering his opinion of me served to lower his guard as well. I was not there for the real estate, after all, but to catch him slip.

And in this I was disappointed. While I had no doubt Numicius had indeed employed Ambustus to curse the *insulae*, and thereby cause the death of innocents, I was not able to get him to admit that openly. My feelings on the matter were not enough to give my testimony weight in a court of law, which is what Valerius Flaccus required of me. I would have to keep pressing him for that admission and I only had a few days left till the trial.

ASSAPH MEHR

CHAPTER XX

It had been a few days since I'd last reported to my
employer. I had been so busy night and day worming
myself close to Numicius and organising to meet him, that I
simply did not have the time. Now, however, I had to be dou-
bly careful. I couldn't be seen chumming it with someone with
whom I was supposedly finding it difficult to arrange a meeting.
Neither could I present myself as his client, for the same range
of reasons I gave both Aemilia and Numicius. My independent
good name was paramount.

And, thinking of that lovely young lady, I also hadn't
had the chance to check on her progress over those few days. I
was sure she was not in trouble — more because I would have
heard from Cornelia if that was the case rather than because I
trusted Aemilia to have learnt her lesson from the snake — but
her research into the mechanics of the curses Ambustus crafted
might provide me another piece to my eventual testimony on
behalf of Valerius.

And so, I sent a note to Cornelia's domicile requesting an
interview with Aemilia on the morrow, the Nones of September. It was the first quiet evening I had for myself in some time,
and I celebrated by dragging a couch out to the peristyle garden
and taking down the canopy sail. I gazed at the starry sky and
breathed deeply of the night air.

On a tripod table, I set jugs of wine and water — not ice
cold as Valerius was enjoying this summer, but regretfully warm
— and a scroll of Catullus' latest bawdy poetry. The quiet bur-

bling of the water arching from the faun's erect member to the shallow pool at the base of the fountain soothed me, as did the scent of the brain and pine-nuts sausages Dascha was cooking for dinner. With a contented sigh, I sunk into the old, comfortable pillows supporting my back.

The scroll of poetry was open across my knees and I was just reaching for my wine cup when there was a loud knocking on my front door. I put everything down and muttered profanities on my way to answer the call. The same messenger I had sent to Cornelia was waiting for me outside with a tied wax tablet in reply.

To Spurius Vulpius Felix, from Cornelia Rufina maior, Greetings.

I regret to inform you that tomorrow on the Nones we will be unavailable, as we are attending a meeting of society women to plan the winter celebration of the Magna Mater. With the kindest regards et cetera.

So, the high-born patrician woman has decided to put the upstart Subvales pleb in his place. An inconvenience for me, as her house afforded me a discreet location to meet with Valerius Flaccus unobserved.

Knowing Cornelia, I had a few options. I could reply tersely that her involvement is not required and that I just needed to collect Aemilia's notes before I continued discussions with Flaccus privately. Even considering her eagerness to be involved, I was not sure if that would get her to change her tack — but I was certain it would make her even more furious with me. The other option was to appeal to her self-importance. As my dear, departed *pater* used to say, 'Never leave a pretty woman spitting at your back' — advice that served me well over the years.

I smoothed the wax with the edge of my palm and wrote.

To Cornelia Rufina maior, from Spurius Vulpius Felix,

Felicitations.

I am overjoyed to hear that Aemilia is attending the planning of the Magna Mater winter celebration. Surely those are the right and proper activities for a young woman of her class and will prepare her for the life you plan for her.

I have uncovered some interesting developments in the matter at hand, and was, in fact, hoping to consult with you prior to meeting with your esteemed cousin and my employer. I feel your input on this new development would prove invaluable.

I would also like to collect Aemilia's research notes so she can move off this case and concentrate on your council's celebration planning.

I reread it and ran my finger over the last line to erase the writing in the wax. No point in promising something I couldn't keep, nor in getting out of hot water with Cornelia at the price of Aemilia's displeasure.

I signed the letter, tied the leather thongs to close the tablet, and muttered a brief prayer to Fortuna to protect me from the fickleness of women.

Two hours later, when my spirit had been refreshed by the scathing wit of Catullus and my belly revived with Dascha's brain-and-pine-nuts sausage with fish sauce, there was another knock by the same messenger, quite haggard by now.

My father's words stood me in good stead. I was invited to Cornelia's house for dinner the next day.

***

Dinner was a simple affair, the three of us and Cornelia's friend Icilia. Aemilia and I were each reclining lengthwise on our separate couches, while Cornelia and Icilia shared the centre couch. I would be flattering myself if I said she needed moral support against my charms; a likelier scenario was that Cornelia wanted an audience for her rebuking of me. I took this to mean that I was still on uneasy footing with Cornelia.

Cornelia and Aemilia were dressed modestly in tunics and shawls which did nothing to mask their natural beauty. Cornelia had no need to impress Icilia and no doubt instructed her cook not to waste anything expensive on me, but he was still a master of his craft. The delicious and slightly sweet quail and asparagus *patina* was well-complemented by the garden salad with anchovies and eggs and its tart dressing.

"The reason I asked to see you first," I opened once we were all settled with watered wine, "is that I would appreciate your insight and craftiness on what is becoming a delicate matter."

"Flattery will get you nowhere," retorted Cornelia, though my experience with women suggested otherwise.

"I have managed to get close to Numicius with the pretext of brokering a deal with Lucius Valerius for the afflicted *insulae*. That, in itself, is not a problem, though I will have to be careful not to appear in public to be acquainted with Valerius. My goal is to get Numicius to confirm he is behind Ambustus' curse tablets, preferably with more witnesses that just I. That will be the linchpin of a court case against him. I know you keep tabs on the Senate and are intimately familiar not only with their official discourse, but also with their public and private personalities. Surely you have some insight on how to approach the man — what I can use to gain his trust and push him to confess."

Cornelia pulled a quail apart and sucked on its bones in thought. "Numicius is not a great public figure, as you must know. He was a plebeian *aedile* a while back and ran a couple of times for the *praetorship* before finally getting elected. That's enough to sit in the middle tier of the Senate, and I suspect he'll be aiming even higher, though I wouldn't give a dried fig for his chances at becoming *consul*."

"His chances aren't that low," said Icilia. "His father was a *praetor* and his grandfather one of the minor *flamines*. The priest for Pomona, if I recall. I think they also had a *consul* once, but that would have been a long time ago."

"Yes, yes, I think so," agreed Cornelia. "You always had a great memory for genealogy." She paused again, helping herself to some of the eggy *patina*. "His wife is a Faucia, a woman of no consequence. Her family comes from Ausculum, where their fortunes grew on pig farming." She snorted. "Well, her manners are not much better than the pigs'. She has been trying to worm her way with gifts and gossip into every little clique of high-society women."

"Oh, rather!" Icilia interjected. "She has been hounding me and some close friends, seeking admittance to our circles. Very regrettably she has managed to gain influence on certain ladies whose families are down on luck and low on fortunes."

"She is insufferable!" continued Cornelia. "We were recently discussing the winter celebration to the Magna Mater at some unrelated party. I don't know who invited her, but she wandered over and prattled on and on about the Bona Dea, and how the Great Mother was not a native to Egretia. I gave her a quick history lesson — how it was written in the sacred Sibylline scrolls that the Magna Mater would save our city in the time of war, and how the chaste Claudia Quinta, that great patrician woman, saved her statue from falling to the river and thus saved our city from calamity. We sent her home with her skirts aflutter! I can assure you she will not make it into any circle of women who matter in this city."

"What could you tell me of her relationship with Numicius?" I asked in a vague attempt to get back on topic.

"Oh, no scandals. Neither of them strays, at least not enough to make the gossip. He needed money and her family needed an entry into Egretia."

"Both got less than what they bargained for, if you ask me," Icilia snorted.

Slaves took away the *patina* dish and brought in a tray of fresh and dried fruits. Before Cornelia and Icilia could dive back into the intricacies of female politics, I said, "I doubt Faucia would provide me an angle to get Numicius. Even if he confided in her, and she then confided in either of you —" both Cornelia and Icilia shuddered at the thought — "the courts will not accept the testimony of a woman. I'm afraid I will need something more direct."

"Perhaps the nature of the curses…" Aemilia began, her first comment since greeting me that evening.

"Don't bring that up at dinner, dear," Cornelia cut her off. She tightened her shawl around her shoulders. "It's bad enough you spend your daylight hours with those awful things."

I could see Aemilia had recovered from her ordeal with the snake. She was positively bouncing at the prospect of discussing the curses. Only the dark looks from her mother kept her from continuing that discussion.

"I would leave you to mull it over," I addressed Cornelia. "What motivation might a man such as Numicius have to use curses, and how we might tempt him to admit to being behind them."

"But I thought last time you explained that everyone uses *tabulae defixiones*. You said some lawyers would not appear in court before first cursing their opposing counsel," quipped Aemilia.

"There is a difference between selling ineffectual lucky charms to the gullible and using *nefastum scientiam* to wreak deadly havoc within city walls. I am hoping your mother — and Icilia — will be able to shed some light on his motivation behind this. Understanding the man's motives will help us bring suit against him."

"So, what do you plan now?" from Cornelia.

"Three things. First, I need a discreet way to meet with Valerius outside of some public performances for Numicius' sake. What before was merely your graciousness, has now become critical to this case. There is no way we can meet in his home or any of his offices around the Forum without his clients noticing and tongues wagging. I hope we may still rely on your hospitality and discretion, both for meeting and for passing messages."

Cornelia nodded, her mouth twisting into a tight smile.

"Second," I continued, "I will keep searching for evidence

Valerius can take to court. A confession would be ideal, but we must not neglect other avenues." My gaze flickered towards Aemilia, who clearly understood. I waved my hand gently at her and turned back to Cornelia, who was pulling her shawl tight again.

"Lastly, while Faucia might be a country bumpkin and not in your circles, I'm certain that through the women's gossip network we can learn more about Numicius and his plans. He made quite a point of mentioning the shrine to his late mother. I would love to know anything you could find out about the woman, and any advice you could come up with on how we could press him with it, unbalance him. When a man is provoked, he acts in fear and anger — reactions which will cause him to make mistakes that might cost him the trial. You could be the one providing us the key to his eventual defeat."

**

Soon after, it was time to disperse the dinner party. I had written a message for Valerius which Cornelia sent with a courier, and still had the curse tablets to discuss with Aemilia. I managed to get Cornelia to thaw her attitudes towards me with the flattery and scheming over dinner and didn't want to ruin that by being too open on a subject she considered taboo. After Aemilia kissed her mother goodnight, I got up and proclaimed I needed to continue with my work.

Cornelia did not invite me to remain behind, but neither did she have me ejected from her house, for she surely knew where I was heading and what subject Aemilia and I were about to discuss. I took it to mean that, while I was perhaps not back in her good graces just yet, she was willing to overlook things for now. A safer bet, based on my knowledge of women in general, was that between the sulking treatment of the past few days and any resumption of cordial relations, would be a scathing discussion of my faults and failings in this — and, potentially, many other — matters. I never could understand why men married.

I didn't need to call after Aemilia. She was waiting for

me a few paces from the *triclinium*. "My mother doesn't like to even mention the workings of *magia*. I really wasn't expecting her to be so old-fashioned about this."

"I believe she just doesn't want to dwell on your involvement with it. She isn't happy that you are exposed to such shady dealings."

"But why is it wrong of me to want to know more? And it's not like I'm exposed to anything besides the occasional woodlouse, being cooped up with the scrolls!"

"You've met Araxus and seen what careless run-in with *magia* can bring. I've witnessed worse — much worse. I won't see you come to a horrible end. The only reason I'm involving you in this at all, is that I know you wouldn't listen otherwise. You should learn the risks and dangers for yourself if you are to avoid trouble in the future."

My outburst made her take a step back. It's a lesson she needed to learn — I wasn't ready to have her on my conscience. Like Helena.

Having just barely pacified Cornelia, though, I didn't wish to antagonise Aemilia. I continued, "Anyway, it's a good compromise between you and your mother, as both of you seem equally unhappy with it." Aemilia only harrumphed in return. "Let's talk about your research, then. Come and tell me what you found."

Aemilia led me to the library — her girl and guard never more than two steps away — where we lit an oil lamp and settled at her desk. I didn't need to prod her. As soon as she started talking about the research, her eyes lit up and the pace of her speech quickened. She was covering all I had asked of her — the language used, the particular words of supplications, the gods both mentioned and alluded to, promises, vows, contracts between humans and *numina*. She referenced material beyond that which I gave her and brought out academic treatises and obscure poems. She talked animatedly, gesturing, shuffling the scrolls for the latest quote, jumping up to pace about, then sitting back down abruptly to open another wax tablet with scratched notes.

It wasn't, strictly speaking, necessary for the case. We knew the how and the who. But her references could still prove useful when I delivered my testimony. Courtroom oratory is an art unto itself and her research would aid me in delivering the necessary flowery allusions to carry more weight. Linking my observances to the curses, to the gods, to history, and to literature creates a powerful speech — one more likely to sway the listeners with my authority on the matter.

I was, I'll admit, in awe. Without any formal education, at least in the arts of incantation, she had a breadth of knowledge in a variety of fields of philosophy. From theological to medical and oratorical to metaphysical, she seemed to have read — and remembered — more than some of my old tutors. But even beyond that, I was in awe of her ability to make connections. She cross-referenced a turn of phrase in a curse tablet with a similar phrase in a two-century old translation of an Hellenic play, and linked it to the god discussed in the play. From there she jumped to an aspect of that deity in Ovidius' Metamorphoses, then back to the curse tablet to show how that aspect might be enticed by a promise of a specific sacrifice mentioned. Her research into the science of effective cursing stretched from the advance preparation of the tablets to the phenomena we observed.

The real *tabulae defixiones* are half-way between folk magic and proper incantation. They rely on a supplication to the gods done to specific measures for real effects. They still depend upon precise words and formulae — an essential requirement to any working of *magia* — but are more forgiving than, say, an *elementor's* specialised incantation to freeze water into ice. This technique of supplication — and it does not matter whether you believe the *numina* to be conscious gods or merely forces of nature — allows the magia to slowly accumulate in the tablets, to be shaped by the particular words and symbols, and cause their intended effect without burning through the *veneficitor* using them.

Aemilia was brilliant in picking up on that science. Some

of the connections she made I knew to be wrong; others I was unsure of. But many I knew or suspected to be correct. And she had managed to do this based solely on classical tutoring and a short instruction by me — a man who never finished his own education. It made me wonder how our society would turn out if women were allowed to study at the *collegia*. Only the gods know for sure, though I suspected the result would be a more orderly world.

As her lecture was drawing to an end, I felt desperate to keep her going. Her slave girl had curled up in a corner and fallen asleep, while the bodyguard was leaning against the wall outside the library. We sat, heads together and open wax tablets all about, as we worked on deconstructing incantation terms from flowery embellishments.

Every *incantator* leaves his mark in incantations, like a signet seal in wax. Some might take pride in it while others might try to hide it, but just like a woman wearing makeup, the reality is always the same underneath. One can discern this personal signature by how an *incantator* builds up his charms.

And, more importantly, once extracted by a discerning individual, this signature could be used to incriminate Ambustus in a court of law.

I would like to blame the wine for what happened next, though that would be disingenuous. As we were poring over the tablets, leaning close, talking animatedly, Aemilia absorbing my clumsy teachings and building upon them, both of us excited at the intellectual exercise, some part at the back of my mind kept its attention on other things — the dark blue circles around Aemilia's gold-flecked, grey irises; the way her cheeks dimpled and blushed when I paid her a compliment; the jangle from her ankle bracelet as she shifted her legs under the table; the caress of her tunic against my shins. Even the dark subject matter could barely dissuade my mind from noticing everything about her.

But the most piquant — and cruelest — of all was the scent of her hair. Attar of roses, a touch of cinnamon, and something else I could not identify. The Fates had her wear the same oils as Helena, the only woman to have stolen my heart. I thought Helena kept my heart with her when she passed from our world to that of the dead, yet now, for the second time in my life and over a decade later, Aemilia evoked in my chest the same fluttery feeling.

And so, with the wine, the excitement, the proximity of her eyes, and the overpowering scent of the familiar perfume, I kissed her.

In the middle of her sentence, engulfed by the heady aroma of her hair, I put my lips to hers, felt her stiffen in surprise, then her lips' soft, inviting warmth melted into mine. We were both lost in that kiss. Nothing else existed — no light, nor sound, nor any sensation, bar that overwhelming explosion from the gentlest caress where our lips touched.

I found enough of my senses and leaned back, staring, my mind numb and my heart racing. She had her eyes closed and an ethereal smile dimpled her ruddy cheeks. I pushed myself backwards, the chair dragging on the floor, making an ugly sound. She opened her eyes as I stood.

"I'm sorry," I mumbled as I scrambled out of that room, out of that house.

CHAPTER XXI

Trusting my message from the previous night had reached Valerius, I went to the Forum the following morning. The day after the Nones of September that year was marked as *endotercissus* and the Forum was taken over by priests and acolytes of various colleges preparing sacrifices for that night. While business was permitted in the middle of the day, no Senate meeting was called. This curtailed the public speakers and spectacles, but hawkers and vendors compensated to keep the noise level constant.

I put the time to good use — talking to everyone who would listen, pretending to have great interest in understanding when the next Senate meeting would take place, and 'accidentally' letting it slip that I was looking for Valerius Flaccus for a property deal. I worked from one end of the Forum to the other and trusted the gossips to spread the word for me. I was vindicated when news of my quest reached the other end of the Forum before I did.

That done, I walked up the Clivus Incudis to the Clivi Ulterior and Valerius' *domus*. In a quiet moment, I knocked on the gate and verified the door-slave had his instructions. Then I waited across the road in the shade of a fig tree till a passing senator and his retinue rounded the corner. I swarmed into action, knocking and attempting to berate and bribe the door-slave to grant me admission and enduring his rebuff. I repeated this exercise twice more, for the benefit of other important-looking passers-by.

At the ninth hour, the door-slave opened the gate, jerked his head in my direction, then shut the gate quickly. I got up from the shade and made my way unobserved to the slaves' entrance.

My second interview with Valerius at his mansion was conducted in his study. Like the rest of his house, it was neat and orderly, with understated decorations that demonstrated his family's security in its generations of good fortunes and tastes.

Once pleasantries were exchanged and I had given him an account of my talks with Numicius, we discussed strategy.

"I'm still not sure where you are heading with this. This deal could never actually go through, as we both — and probably Numicius too — know well."

"I plan to draw out Numicius, giving him false hope then frustrating him repeatedly," I explained. "We will put on a bit of a show for him in public and then I will go back to him with some new complication. He is an impatient man — that's his flaw. Forget the curses and what we deem lack of moral fibre. It's his temper that will make him burst out and that's how we'll get a confession out of him."

"Temper or not, he is not stupid. We are suing him for taking illegal actions in those *insuale*. How can he possibly buy them, without giving the public the clear impression that this was his plan all along?"

"He is intent on you not finding out that he's the buyer till much later," I replied. "He was quick to set up straw companies and proxies, so his name won't come up till it's too late and he can gloat publicly. I believe this was his plan all along — to make it known he gets what he wants, and to show what happens to those who resist him."

"I have my misgivings about this. I have seen him in the Senate. He can play a long game when he has his mind set on something. I fear either your strategy will fail to get us something in time — and it's now impossible to delay the lawsuit against him — or that he'll grow tired of this game, dismiss you, and move on to nastier actions."

"Oh, I am confident I can string him along. Playing into

his plan will make him feel more secure, and therefore more careless. It won't take long to get an outburst out of him. It might not be in public, but I would have enough information to testify convincingly about him. The whole play is geared towards getting as many incriminating details as possible. I just need you to gather your clients tomorrow."

"I hope you know what you are doing," Valerius replied. "Make it happen properly, though. I do not want this matter dragging — I want my good name cleared!"

***

The day after was a well-orchestrated public performance. I had, since the crack of dawn, been walking nervously about the Forum Egretum, casting glances in all directions. When Valerius and his retinue of clients arrived and crossed the Forum towards the Senate — nobody wondered why they would arrive from the opposite direction of his house — I waded into the crowd of people surrounding him. I waved a sealed scroll above my head and cried loudly, "Let me through, by Iovis! Your master will reward you when he hears my message! I have the solution to the problem *insulae* that have been plaguing him for months!"

None of his clients, sycophants, and guards knew anything, of course, so acted with their usual zeal towards their patron by enforcing layers of controlled access. Some were a tad too enthusiastic in stopping the clamouring madman talking loudly about their esteemed benefactor's real-estate problems, and I did sustain a few unnecessary slaps and light bruises. But, I got through.

By the time I forced myself close enough to Valerius' inner circle, business around the Forum had all but stopped. Say what you will about the chariot races in the circus or the gladiatorial games at funerals, when it comes to public performances we Egretians value an emotional debate above anything else. All around the large open space of the Forum, people were gawking at the commotion we were staging for their benefit.

Valerius, born a nobleman and educated in the art of oration, raised one hand dramatically and, in a voice that would put stage actors to shame, spoke, "Let that man through!"

The throng of clients around him separated, and I walked down a clear corridor towards him. Doing my best to project my voice without yelling, I declared, "Senator, I know all about the properties that have been haunting your dreams of late!" I bowed slightly as I handed him the scroll.

Valerius broke the seal with a flourish, scanned the text quickly, and rolled the scroll back before anyone near him could glimpse its contents. "Intriguing." This single word reverberated around the Forum. "Walk with me, and I will grant you a private audience."

Safely behind closed doors in a nearby office, we toasted each other with cups of watered spiced wine.

"I doubt anyone missed that performance," I said. "Numicius will have heard all about it by now. I daresay your voice would have carried through all the way to his house."

"Let us hope his hunger for money drives him to carelessness. I have to say, I am impressed with your ability to get through my men. I do hope they didn't cause you much grief. They are rather dedicated."

"Think nothing of it. Their dedication is a testament to you as a patron. My bruises are merely a part of the job and will be gone in a few days."

"I will see you well recompensed for them. I'm not sure if I should reward my men or not."

"Reward them." I was generous with his money. "They played their unwitting part beautifully. Your clients would not have seriously harmed me and no normal messenger would have been this persistent. Were I wishing you harm, I have no doubt they would have been effective."

"Very well, then. I will set their minds and wallets at ease, as I am sure this will also add to the gossip flying around. Here's to our success!" He toasted again.

***

The next morning, I set out to meet Numicius. I had to build his hopes up and then crush them. Perhaps repeatedly. I wanted him frustrated enough for a public outburst, an admission of guilt or any slip-up that would reveal incriminating details.

I lurked about his home but did not join the queue of clients inside. When he came out later I followed him, then skirted through side streets so I could bump into him as he reached the Forum.

"Gaius Numicius! Gaius Numicius!" I cried enthusiastically as I made my way towards him and his retinue. "Excellent news, Gaius Numicius!"

He beckoned me closer and I fell in step beside him. I could not see Ambustus amongst his retinue. "I have managed to get through to Lucius Valerius Flaccus," I said loudly enough so no one could miss who I was talking about, "and got his attention at last."

"Yes, I've heard," Numicius said dryly. "You mentioned you had contacts to introduce you, not that you had to fight your way through his guards."

"I had the letter of introduction, but I got tired of waiting for an appointment. I had to be rather abrupt about it, but when I got through and gave him the letter, the introduction worked! He has granted me an audience and I was able to hook him on the deal for the *insulae*."

We reached the steps leading up to the Collegium Mercatorum, and Numicius slowed and stopped. "That is good news indeed," he said, his sharp teeth punctuating his smile. "So, are we ready to proceed?"

"We certainly are! You will soon be the proud owner of three perfectly empty *insulae* in the Subvales," I beamed at him.

"Excellent, excellent. Now you must excuse me, as I have business with our *rhones* about a shipment of grain."

I let him get half way up the wide steps before I added, "There was only a small matter of Valerius Flaccus' insistence on some due diligence with the bankers, but I am sure our arrangements will withstand any scrutiny." I smiled at Numicius, waved goodbye, and disappeared into the crowd before he could respond.

Rather predictably, I received a message to meet Numicius that same day at dusk. I was not keen on so late and private a meeting, as my designs preferred a public outburst. Still, the more emotional highs and lows I could put him through in a short span of time, the grander this eventual drama would play out.

I spent the afternoon visiting Crassitius and arranging for Borax's services that night — for both appearances and security — after which I stopped at the baths for a good shave and massage.

CHAPTER XXII

The meeting that night took place at Numicius' *domus*. The door slave had me on his list, and we were shown into the atrium immediately. The front of the house was empty, which was not surprising. Visitors had long gone, and deep in its interior the household was concentrating on evening activities.

Numicius' clerk came to escort us. I nodded at Borax to follow, an unusual act for a guest. The clerk said nothing, though, and Borax padded after us — his huge bulk, drooping red moustache, and blue tattoos incongruous with the highly refined Egretian decor.

We were led to Numicius' *tablinum*, where the clerk bowed me in. "Please go in," he said, putting up a hand to stop Borax, "and I'll send some water for your bodyguard."

Borax raised a brow, but I walked on without him.

"Ah, Felix! Have a seat. Wine?" Numicius gestured at the side table and the clerk poured me a cup. Numicius already had a fine blue glass goblet in front of him. Ambustus, leaning against the wall as before, was slowly sipping his.

"Now, tell me about this good news you have," Numicius said when I was seated with my spiced wine. The dim lights from the lamps on the table lent his face an eerie appearance, his sharp little teeth gleaming and the fire's reflection dancing in his eyes.

I faked my best enthusiasm and delivered a fictitious account of my handling of Valerius. I described the letters of introductions, my frustration at Valerius' schedule, my resolution to break through his encircling layers of clients, the encounter in the Forum, and the meeting afterwards. I gave a flowery account of his facial expressions, of his moods changing from disbelief and distrust into guarded optimism at my cajoling. In short, I spun a tale like no other, leading Numicius through an emotional wringer to highlight my negotiation skills and dedication on his behalf. At several points, Numicius tried to interrupt and get to the conclusion, and at each point I assured him I was about to, yet continued with my tale. It was, despite my own words being as the butcher vouchsafing the contents of his sausages, a tale worthy of the theatre. I walked the fine line of building Numicius' investment without getting him overly annoyed at the meandering story. He became visibly restless, yet engrossed, as my story unfolded.

Once I described Valerius' grudging assent to the deal, we toasted each other on a plan well executed. Numicius was flush with wine and excitement.

"But wasn't there a mention of some complications with the bankers?" Ambustus made his first contribution, a perfect segue for me.

I let my face darken momentarily, then forced a smile. "I'm sure it is nothing we can't get past. He was merely being cautious, a standard procedure of financial due diligence, no doubt."

"And what did that *cunnus* want?" Numicius asked.

"Just to ensure the deal is legal and to avoid problems later. Under the *Lex Claudia*, as surely you know, Valerius Flaccus cannot profiteer from large sales to foreign entities. He requested to trace the origins of the money, so as not to end up being ejected from the Senate under the *Lex Cassia*." I went on to reassure Numicius that Valerius was highly unlikely to uncover our scheme, and in the process highlighted the weak links in Numicius' setup, to increase his consternation. "I am sure Valerius would never be able to trace the straw companies to the banker we used," I reassured Numicius, "and even if he did, so what? It's only the banker. He has no power over him."

"You promised me you could deliver these *insulae* to me,"

Numicius said with an amicable tone but narrow eyes. "I have set up the necessary business arrangements, locking up money that I could have put to good use elsewhere. If this deal does not go through, it will be a pain — a pain I will be sharing all around!"

***

I left Numicius satisfied with my work. I could think and plan my next move as we walked back to my house, Borax watching the streets and scaring shifty characters away by growling menacingly.

Numicius' threats were a signal my scheme was working. I was not concerned by them, as I had offered him a quicker resolution to his land-grabbing attempts and he was invested in my plan.

Cornelia was passing messages between Valerius and me, but I heard nothing from either her or Aemilia. I knew that at some point soon I would have to deal with what happened between us. Not a task I relished and one I preferred not to dwell upon.

And so, two days later, I presented myself before dawn to wait for Valerius with his clients. I was pacing around, chatting to others, making my presence known, and only vaguely hinting — to anyone who wouldn't move away fast enough — about the important property deal I was brokering for him. His clerk was under instruction to keep me in the atrium until all his other clients had finished and left, for maximum exposure. We wanted the word to leak and circulate.

Once we were ensconced privately in his library, I gave him an update on my last meeting with Numicius. And, to counterbalance how I was trying to build Numicius' emotions, I had the task of assuaging Valerius' impatience about the deal. Both were men of power, both concerned with their own public standing and position, their *dignitas* and *auctoritas*, and both with egos that needed massaging. Not too different, in many respects. Employers like Valerius pay well, but I was starting to miss the simple cases, which could be resolved with a bit of chanting and the sacrifice of a chicken.

In the end, I set him on the right course and ensured he would put forward the deeds to the *insulae* — under escrow — so that Numicius' bankers could vouch for them. I wanted Numicius to smell those millions of *denarii* worth of properties he'd be getting for a ludicrously low price before we withdrew them. I deemed that would be his breaking point, the act which would push him to expose himself.

I spent the rest of that day and the following one dealing with various bankers around the Forum. The days were right before the Ides of September, the city was full of people coming for the *Ludi Egretani*, and half the time those I was after were at the games or just plain too drunk to care. I waded my way through the throngs, walked countless miles back and forth on sun-baked streets, dealt with people that smelled so offensively even the dead would turn in disgust, and — worst of all — missed the opening chariot races.

But by the end of that second day, I had the paperwork I needed. Talents of silver were recorded and assigned, the certificates notarised, conditions of sale stipulated, reviewed, approved, signed and countersigned. I had a letter from Numicius' banker, guaranteeing the money was ready to be picked up in exchange for the deeds. All I had to do was take the letter to Numicius, let him read it and get his hopes up, and then crush it with some ridiculous last-minute demand.

And do it in public, preferably.

CHAPTER XXIII

As befit my schemes, I set out to meet Numicius that same day. I planned to run into him as though by accident on the way back from the *Ludi Egretani*, draw him to the public baths, and have our private chat turn into a public spectacle.

Considering the hustle and bustle of the city — with all the country folk flocking for the games, and the pickpockets, thieves, cut-purses, cutthroats, brigands, boisterous drunks, filthy beggars, maimed veterans — both from the legions and the circuses — and other charming and picturesque characters whom the poets love that were out to greet the visiting simpletons — I arranged with Crassitius to hire Borax to accompany me.

I spotted Numicius on his front-row seat for the final chariot race, but he was in a different section of the Circus Magnus than my clay token allowed me to access. Instead, I exited the stadium to wait, keeping an eye on the throngs milling about outside and an ear on the roar of the crowds inside. From what I could make out, the Red faction won the day, with their newest *quadriga* driver finally beating the veteran driver of the Blue team after five bitter years of losses. An historic and momentous victory for fans of the Reds, such as myself. I worked hard on my employers' behalf, so I could afford the (admittedly subsidised) tickets for the races — work that seemed at cross-purposes to actually attending said races.

Borax and I discussed the games while we waited. As an ex-gladiator, he was keenly interested and followed all manner of

sports. He was, it turned out, a fan of the Green faction of char-
ioteers. He countered my jibes about them being ousted on the
first day of the games by pointing out the Reds' illustrious five-
year losing streak. Though the talk was mere banter, it cheered
me a little from the gloom of having to miss the games.

Eventually the racket inside calmed and people spewed
forth through the *vomitoria*. When Borax spotted Numicius, we
trailed him at a distance. His path home would normally take
him on the Via Lutia to the city gates, but I had a plan to draw
him to the Baths of Mauritius to stage our little drama.

All for naught. Before I could reach him, another
acquaintance hailed him, and they headed towards the wharves,
no doubt for a ride in one of the many private yachts moored
there.

I rushed after them, Borax pushing people out of my
way. I tried calling out to Numicius, but it was of no use, as the
crowds were cheerful and boisterous after the races.

Despite ruining my plans, Fortuna must not have been
too angry with me. When Numicius and his acquaintance
reached the gangplank of the waiting *bireme*, they let their reti-
nues board first while they continued their animated discussion.
I got there almost out of breath but put on an enthusiastic smile
for Numicius.

I only got out the first 'Gaius Numicius!' before he began
talking excitedly.

"Felix, what a day! Were you in the Circus? A great day
for the Reds! We won! After five years of the most embarrassing
losses, we won!" His face was flushed with wine and excitement,
his speech an unstoppable torrent of words. His natural energy and exuberance were amplified tenfold. "I was the one who
brought Appuleius Diocles, you know." He tapped his finger on
his nose. "I donated a sum of money to the Reds in the beginning of this year and arranged for him to come from the Steppes
of Massau. It was a risk! He won local races but was virtually
unknown outside the Shangarii. And you can never tell how
these provincials will do once in a big city. I didn't want to make

a big fuss about it in case he flopped, but now that he has carried the day so beautifully, Marcus Tometius here will make a public announcement shortly."

I glanced at the man next to him and all thought of my business for the day flew out of my head. Marcus Tometius was the captain of the Red faction, a legend amongst fans. Egretian-born, he was one of the best drivers ever to race in the Circus Magnus and the bright beacon of hope for fans of the Reds. When he was critically injured a couple of years back, we had thought all hope for future resumption of glory had gone. But the *magistri carneum* managed to save his life, if not his legs. He came back, took the reins of the club from the previous disappointment of a captain, and brought us to the present historical win.

Numicius kept talking as these thoughts raced through my mind. He was bragging about the sums he had to pay for the physicians that cured Tometius, how he orchestrated his return as captain, and about the acquisition of Diocles. Tometius was just as animated, each reminiscing and regaling the other with shared memories.

This man, whose downfall I was about to bring, was apparently the greatest benefactor to the sports faction I have cheered for since I was a child on my father's knees. All of Egretia would be talking of the Reds' win that day and Numicius' name would be associated with it. The jury in his trial might find it hard to vote against his popular status and the crowd might react poorly to those who bear witness against him. But even if I assumed the jury would be composed of fans of the Blue faction and that people's memories are short, even then — I felt a twinge of uncharacteristic guilt in taking down the man who elevated my sports faction to glorious heights.

Eventually I regained both my wits and the control of my mouth. I professed my abject adoration to Tometius — which did not require any acting. When he grasped my forearm like a friend, I held on perhaps a tad too long.

Later, I turned to Numicius and said, "More good news:

I finally have the bankers' letters for the purchase of the *insulae*. This deal is all but done and sealed! Truly a blessed day."

"Oh, excellent news! I had my doubts about you, Felix, but I'm glad you managed this transaction. You worked well to a swift conclusion. Now, come! Sail with us on my ship. I'm throwing a party to celebrate the Reds win today, and you deserve to join us for a treat — for arranging the deal and for being a fellow fan."

***

Sea traffic was busy, with the many private yachts getting in between the regular merchant and supply ships. Sounds of celebrations drifted on the water from the Campus Civicus and around the bay. We boarded Numicius' *bireme*, which cast off and sailed leisurely to the middle of the harbour. The deck was laid about with tables holding platters of rare delicacies and fine wines. The outriggers where the galley-slaves were seated with their oars were tastefully hidden behind curtains. Numicius directed his captain towards the entry to the bay, where we cast anchor and milled about on the deck, toasting each other and the games.

Amongst the people were a few faces I've seen with Numicius before, but none I recognised by name except Ambustus. His complexion was ruddier than usual, the flush of wine and excitement setting the burn scars on the left side of his face aglow with inner fire.

Amidst talks about the spectacular chariot win for the Red faction and their future rise to the glory they deserved, I recounted the details of the banking arrangements to Numicius. Ambustus was never far away, listening with an insectile expression.

It was hard to catch Numicius alone. His guests kept coming to congratulate and toast him in the jovial atmosphere. If my mind wasn't on my task, I would have enjoyed being surrounded by fellow Red fans, drinking wins and observing our great city from a pretty vantage point. Sailing on the bay offers one unparalleled views of the great temples, *basilicae*, porticos, and other important buildings as they rise up the side of the mountain. The Pharos with its eternal light is, for our people, a most comforting sight, signifying homecoming. The solid marble spire with its bas-relief images of our ancient history always takes my breath away.

But my mind was on the case, not the view. It was the perfect opportunity to bring up the 'little hitch' I concocted, to push Numicius into rage and get him to utter something damning in front of all the guests. The trick was to hit the right level of inebriation, and to push him hard enough. Numicius kept drinking, displaying the capacity of commercial *amphorae*.

The sun sunk behind the tip of Vergu and the bay was cast into twilight shadows. The various lights around our city turned it into its own version of a starry night. As Numicius directed the ship towards the shore of the inner bay, I decided the time was right.

"Why all the *insulae*?" I asked Numicius. "You mentioned a shrine to your mother. The three are not next to each other, and surely one would have provided ample grounds for it."

"Told you, I'm a businessman. Valerius had three to sell, and I have money to buy them all. And you came to me with them, I'll remind you. I just took the opportunity to make some profit," he said, following it with a massive hiccough.

"Well, you would have your choice for the shrine then." I smiled my best. "One is quite close to the Via Alta, so would be a perfect location for a temple. Oh! That reminds me. At the last-minute, Valerius' brought up the *Lex Papiria de dedicationibus*. Because there have been recent deaths on the premises, he wanted the buyer — *id est* your esteemed self — to know that the properties could not be legally consecrated as altars or temples for a few years."

"*What?*" Numicius exclaimed loudly, and I knew I had him.

"Oh, I'm sure it will be nothing," I said. "All you need is for one of the *consuls* or *praetors* to pass an exemption through the popular assembly and you should be able to circumvent it."

"Must we listen to this drivel?" Ambustus said behind me, nearly making me jump out of my skin.

"No… no, we don't," said Numicius, his smile never wavering but eyes suddenly hard and cold like steel. He gazed at me in a calculating way that sent shivers down my spine. "You're right. This has gone far enough. Restrain him, and we'll deal with him after the party."

I opened my mouth to respond, but Ambustus lifted his hand and blew some powder from his palm onto my face with a muttered incantation and the world went black.

CHAPTER XXIV

I woke up in the hold of the galley to someone nudging my leg. I opened my eyes to the gloom and Borax muttering *"Domine! Domine!"* while kicking me awake. Wood creaked, and in the dim light I saw we were in the ship's cargo hold. My hands were tied behind my back and when I tugged I could feel the ropes anchored to a ring in the wall. Borax was trussed next to me. From above came the sounds of people alighting from the ship, still merry and congratulating each other on the day's win.

Numicius boomed out, "Go on! More wine and refreshments at my *domus!* We shall celebrate this night like it deserves. I shall join you all momentarily."

Heavy steps crossed the deck, and then a narrow hatch opened and Numicius clambered down into the hold, followed by Ambustus and an extremely large gladiator.

"Ah, you're awake," he said when he saw me. "I was hoping to have this little chat more leisurely — actually, I had hoped you would see sense and we wouldn't need to have it at all."

"I don't know what you're talking abou —" I started to say.

"Please, don't insult me," Numicius cut me off. "I know who you are and what you do. Did you think we wouldn't find out when you tampered with our little... *set-up?"*

In between frantic thoughts of how to save my skin, it crossed my mind that this was as close as I had ever gotten to hear Numicius admit his involvement in the curses. Pity there were no witnesses.

"The companies? Bankers? I was just ensuring the money was in the right hands, I never gave any instructions to change or divert anything —"

"You're an arrogant fool, Felix," Ambustus spoke. "We know who you work for and what you aim to do. We knew since the moment you approached Gaius Numicius. Did you think your little powder and charm would affect me? You really thought you could catch me with mere wine and garden-variety incantations? Never try to poison a *veneficitor*, Felix. Your mind cannot conceive of the venoms and toxins to which I have built immunity while you were wasting your time getting drunk in whorehouses! My constitution rivals that of Vulcanus."

Numicius raised his hand to calm Ambustus and squatted down so his eyes were level with mine. "Still, I hoped we might salvage the situation and use you. My interest in buying those *insulae* is genuine. I was willing to play your game if it led to acquiring the properties. Still am, in fact. I will give you one last chance to complete the deal as we discussed. You will not be cheating Valerius — he will receive his money. Your conscience and *dignitas* will remain clean."

It was hard not to jump on the opportunity and promise him anything that would keep me alive. But I suspected he would have ways to enforce it, to bind me in some unbreakable, unspeakable way. "Just broker the deal?" I asked. "Just let it go through and you will let me walk free?"

"In essence. My good man Ambustus has ways of ensuring your cooperation and compliance. He can be somewhat creative and overzealous, but as long as you stick to our agreement, no harm shall come your way."

"But why?" I blurted out, my last-ditch effort to get an admission from Numicius. "Surely you had a plan to get the buildings without my involvement? And why curse three *insulae*?"

"Three *insulae* with three variations," said Ambustus. "I like to experiment, you see. There were more I wanted to try, but Gaius Numicius said it was enough to put the pressure on Valerius to sell."

Numicius caught Ambustus' eye, who then resumed his passive expression. He fixed his gaze back at me. "Overly creative, as I said. Regardless, you were just a bonus. Didn't you wonder how we set up those straw companies so quickly and had sizable sums of money at the ready? I was going to buy that property anyway. When you first came to me, I suspected you might be trying to play us, but I was willing to go along for the sake of the deal. So far, I have been honest with you while you came to me under false pretences. So, make your choice now — will you still broker this to completion and walk away, or will you persist in interfering with the affairs of your betters?"

My mind was racing. Not to accept his offer surely meant death. Yet I did not like his inference about Ambustus ensuring my compliance. I did not want to end in his thrall under some incantation.

I didn't have time to vacillate, so I went with my gut feeling. "I will carry your message to Valerius, but I will not consent to any enchantment — either on myself or on Valerius. I will not be your agent in illegal incantation."

"You are not in a position to negotiate, Felix. I could just proceed in a month or two. I could keep any other buyers at bay until Valerius will be glad to sell to me. Or, I could have you killed now and let Ambustus do that final experiment he wanted, directly on Valerius. Dealing with heirs is often easier. I always get my way, in the end."

In hindsight, my gut feelings and cocksure attitude had led me to this mess.

Numicius raised his hand to silence me. "Twice I have offered you to come to my side. Once, when you became my agent I offered you to become my client, and again just now. And twice you have refused my genuine offers. I am disappointed, but that is your choice in the matter. Life, as the philosophers say, is a series of choices and their echoing ramifications. So now for the consequences." He stood up from his crouch next to me and stepped back. "Milo, break his legs, please."

The silent brute Numicius brought with him made a pass at grabbing my right ankle. I tried to kick him, but he simply caught it in his ham-like hands and hoisted me upside-down till all but my shoulders were off the ground. In the swift and practised motion of a wrestler, he stepped over me so my right leg was between his two and sat down with all his weight, holding my ankle and twisting my leg on the way.

My scream was not enough to drown the squelching sound my ankle made as bones and ligaments tore out of their natural set. Milo stood up, still holding my ankle, then let it drop to the floor. I screamed again when it hit, as waves of pain and nausea travelled from my mangled foot through my body.

"I'm afraid I'll have to take my leave now," Numicius continued in pleasant tones. "My guests are no doubt getting anxious to continue our victory celebrations, and there is only so much time a gracious host can steal away to deal with business during his own party. Gaius Hirtuleius," he addressed Ambustus, "would you kindly stay here and finish the job? I know you'll prefer your little 'experiments' to social hobnobbing, and for once I have no reservations. I'll make sure the cook won't serve the sea-urchin before you come back."

Ambustus grunted and turned his beady eyes and evil smile on me. "I'll just get Milo here to help me set up before he accompanies you. What I'm about to do will probably make even gladiators squeamish."

While Numicius was making his way up the ladder to the fresh air, Ambustus and Milo approached Borax and hoisted him by his elbows. With his hands tied behind his back, Borax tried to resist by shaking free and slamming his shoulder into Ambustus. He knocked him back, but Milo elbowed Borax in the jaw before he could turn against him and I heard teeth crack. Milo shoved Borax against the wall, then grasped his shoulders and sent a knee into Borax's groin. The force of the blow made the ship rock. Borax doubled up and Milo grabbed him by the hair, dragging him forward. I could do naught but wriggle gently to sit upright as each movement of my leg sent fresh waves of burning pain through my body.

"Truss him," Ambustus said. Iron rings were set in the walls of the under-deck hold to secure cargo. Borax was still winded, but Ambustus and Milo were taking no chances. They slapped him around as they unfastened his ropes, splayed him against the wall, and fastened each of his hands and feet to a ring. They further secured his waist, elbows, and knees, to fully immobilise him. Borax's head was lolling and bobbing. He was dazed from the beating, and I could see a trickle of blood from his mouth where Milo had elbowed him.

"Right," said Ambustus, "I think we're set here. You better go and catch up with Gaius Numicius. Even today, he can never have enough guards about him. We," he turned to me, "can now proceed to further advance the scientific research into the lore of *veneficium*. Two live subjects will make a great contribution."

***

Above us, the gangplank scraped against the wooden deck and the noises changed tone. A rhythmic drumming began, and we could feel the reverberations as the galley slaves pulled on their oars and the ship lurched and launched back into the bay.

Ambustus busied himself in the corner of the hold, fussing with jars, pouches, and metal implements, and muttering under his breath. The burning in my ankle was replaced by a throb. Each movement of my leg, whether voluntary or not, was like coals coursing through my bones. Fastened to the wall, Borax was coming out of his daze. He caught my eyes, then silently strained against his bonds. His huge muscles bulged, but the ropes held.

"Right," Ambustus said as he turned towards us. "We will shortly be making our way out of the Bay of Egretia, where you will be assisting me in the advancement of the frontiers of learning and knowledge. You were right to call me the greatest *veneficitor* of our time, even though you were merely pandering. Working with me on this little project is an honour which you should be proud of, even though — for practical reasons — you will never be credited," he said without a hint of sarcasm. He was like a metaphysics lecturer, excited to conduct some new experiment with his students. The garish red scars on the left side of his melted face marred this image, a constant reminder that his interest was not purely a mental exercise.

"I thought you cared not for the restrictions on the practice of *magia* within the city limits," I said. "You seem to have gotten away with the *tabulae defixiones* and the hauntings of the *insulae.*"

"Ha! Though I guess you're right. This is the second time you've seen me advance past the frontiers of knowledge. What I did at the *insulae* demonstrated a delayed application of focusing *magia*, of controlling when the *numina* will respond, as well as how. I have actually advanced in my research. I prepared another *tabula*, but had not the opportunity to try it... A pity. You would have appreciated my new developments." He strode back and forth before me, his hands clenching and unclenching with unbridled energy.

"Back to the business at hand. We're lucky — we have all my ingredients on board. I was going to sail away to experiment tomorrow. What we are about to do here goes well beyond even Numicius' ability to bribe the *rhones* and thus will be carried out on the open waters. And since we're already underway and you're so keen to find out, why don't we start? It will give you a sample of what to expect. It's a little thing I've been working on that will come across as *magia vita* to any stray eyes that might be attuned in our direction. Pay attention, I will be curious to hear your thoughts when you have the chance to experience it for yourself. For now, just watch. You'll enjoy it."

He ambled to the table at the back and began mixing ingredients in a mortar, gently mashing and chanting over them. There were jars, pouches, *pyxis* boxes of unguents, strange tools of metal and wood, and a lit brazier on the table. My dagger was lying on a table-corner too far to reach with my broken ankle, even if I could free myself from my bonds. As he worked,

I could feel the drafts of *magia* on my skin and smell the crushed ingredients at a higher register as they were used to channel and shape the forces of nature. With each ingredient added, the scents alternated between spring flowers and honey to a rotting, swampy smell. Back and forth, back and forth, life and death.

"Now observe," Ambustus said as he turned to me. "Form your thoughts so that you could describe them later to me when it will be your turn. I so rarely get to work with someone familiar and attuned to the *magia*, so your contributions will no doubt help me reach a breakthrough in our understanding of science."

He strode to Borax and with a stone spoon started to dollop and spread the mixture from the mortar on Borax's right hand. Borax flexed his fingers and tried to avoid it, without success. His thrashing managed to flick a little of the sticky cream at Ambustus. He got a resounding slap for that, and Ambustus carefully cleaned himself before continuing.

"Watch this," said Ambustus, and began to chant. Borax hissed, strangled a scream, and then roared in pain as his hand aged to that of a man twice his age. The hairs became white, the skin wrinkled further, and muscles atrophied, till his became the hand of a corpse, shrivelled and desiccated, without a speck of life left.

My stomach heaved, and my hands twitched in sympathy. I broke out in clammy sweat at the thought of whether Ambustus might be tempted to try this on my broken ankle, and to what level would it elevate the pain.

"It's a similar process to what the Mitzrani use to mummify their dead." Ambustus turned to me, ignoring Borax's whimpers. "Same components and analogous principles but refined and controlled beyond their ken. Yet my powers do not stop there — I have brought the forces of *magia* to my will and can manipulate them to exact results. In contrast, the Mitzrani mummification is no better than a tanner attempting taxidermy. Let me now show you an even greater achievement — one of my own innovations!" he smiled broadly.

He stepped back to the table and busied himself with

ASSAPH MEHR

the ingredients, mixing and chanting as he went. The tip of the Pharos was visible through the hatch at the ceiling of the hold and I knew we were exiting the Bay of Egretia.

Ambustus began treating Borax's left hand with the contents of his mortar. Borax strained and wriggled, and I suddenly understood why they bound him at the elbows, waist, and knees as well. Try he might, Borax could not avoid Ambustus applying the cream to his hand

"Don't fret," Ambustus cooed, as if talking to a frightened animal. "This will all be over soon. Your contribution to the science of the *magia vita* will save many lives, and what slave can dream of a better fate?"

Ambustus stretched and carefully wiped his hands. "Now for our demonstration. I have never quite managed to practice this on a human before, even a slave, so you are witnessing a breakthrough! Our idiot *rhones* with their taboos on the practice of *magia* around death — as though life and death are separate things. It's a shame you won't live long enough to see it, but I do hope to one day change these rules."

He chanted as before and at first the results appeared similar. Borax's left hand began to wrinkle, acquire the brown spots of age, shrivel. "Now watch!" Ambustus said and changed the tone and tempo of his incantation. Borax's skin began to stretch, fill up, the muscles crawling back, his complexion becoming pink and vital again. Even the hairs on the back of Borax's hand went back from white to brown. Borax stared incredulously, the tendons in his arms twitching as his fingers regained their movement.

Ambustus concentrated steadily on his chant. Sweat beaded on his brow and his half-closed eyes never wavered from his target. I took this time for a quick chant of my own, even though it was nothing remotely in the same league. A mere cantrip, in comparison, one that I learnt during my brief stint with the legions. One of the *incantatores* attached to the engineering corps of the legion had developed it and taught it to some of us grunts. Egretians should fight honourably, he held, yet there is

175

no honour in remaining a captive. But I digress.

I used this charm while Ambustus was distracted, to loosen the bonds and free my wrists. I kept my hands behind my back, holding the piece of rope that had bound me. A moral victory rather than a practical one, in light of my broken ankle and lack of weapons, while facing an opponent who could wither limbs at will.

CHAPTER XXV

"Look at this!" Ambustus marvelled at his own work.

He glanced at me, the incongruence of his smile and facial scars chilling. "Flex your hand," he barked. Borax was staring incredulously at his left hand, moving his fingers. I could see his right forearm twitch too, as tendons pulled on decayed digits, but those remained as devoid of life as Orpheus' wife.

"See, I can feel the pulse, strong and steady," Ambustus placed his fingers next to Borax's bound wrists. "I could continue to make it even younger, get rid of old scars and wrinkles," Ambustus traced his index finger along the lines of Borax's palm. "It's an interesting question what would happen if I continued past that point."

Borax surely knew that there was no way this day would end well for him. In a final act of defiance, he grabbed Ambustus' finger and twisted hard. The finger made a sickening, cracking sound and Ambustus screamed. Borax held on, twisting the broken digit and screaming back at Ambustus as if they were gladiators in the arena.

Ambustus flailed wildly, first at Borax's hand and then at his face, but it is a lot harder to pull one's finger away from a trained fighter than one would imagine. Our minds recoil at the pain of each movement and prevent us from what feels like tearing the finger off.

I didn't wait for Ambustus to wise up. I stumbled to my feet, pulling on the rings in the walls with my hands, then launched myself at Ambustus' back with my one good leg. My lunge was enough to cover the short distance of the hold. I looped the rope from my bonds over his neck, then crossed my arms and pulled hard.

Ambustus freed his finger and staggered backward. He knocked into me, forcing me to step back. My broken ankle crumpled, shooting waves of pain up my body and we crashed to the floor. I held on to the rope as we thrashed together, Ambustus flailing his arms trying to dislodge me. I was screaming in pain and frustration, but still I gripped the rope, pulling it tighter, tighter.

In our scramble, we knocked into the table. The jars and boxes on top came crashing down and the brazier toppled, sending burning embers scattering on the wood floors of the hold. A pile of hessian sacks in the corner began to smoulder.

Within a minute it was over. Ambustus' limbs became heavy and his movements slowed, his face acquiring a deep shade of purple as his tongue hung bloated outside his mouth.

I stretched the rope past the point when he stopped moving and went limp. When I finally let go, his head lolled, and his bulk lay limply on top of me. I rolled him over and stood, leaning on the wall for support. I would have kicked his lifeless body, if my ankle wasn't broken.

***

Orange flames sprouted from the sacks in the corner, and black smoke billowed up. I grabbed my knife from where it fell, and, holding on to the wall, limped towards Borax to cut his bonds. Even in full health this would have been faster than an incantation, and I wasn't in a state to perform unnecessary feats of *magia* now. As I came to free Borax's right hand, the desiccated fingers crumbled to dust as I worked on the ropes. What remained was a charred stump ending at the wrist, like a thick branch that has burned to its middled. At least he wasn't bleeding.

From the deck came alarmed yells at the smoke rising through the hatch. We grabbed some of the sacks by their corners and flung them out to increase the panic. Fire onboard a ship is deadly. We hadn't moved far outside the bay, so were still close to the shores of the Septentrionali. We heard people abandoning the ship, jumping overboard to swim to shore rather than fight the fire.

"I think we should run now," I said to Borax. "Just rush out, cross the deck, and jump into the water. The island of the Pharos is close enough."

"I can't swim, *domine*," said Borax, "but I can carry you to the water."

"Neptunus' wet willy, that's not good. Could you float? If you held on to an oar or something, could you keep your head above water? I'll get us to land."

"I guess," came the tentative reply.

"It's either that or burn and then drown." I knew how to swim, of course, but with a broken ankle I wouldn't go far. Certainly not if I had to drag Borax, who only had one good hand to hold on.

We exited the cargo hold under cover of the smoke. Staying any longer would have meant suffocation. We emerged to a scene of panic and chaos. What was left of the crew were swimming ashore. The galley slaves in the outrigger seats were rioting, pulling on their chains and kicking the seats to break them. Each wore a neck manacle connected with a length of thick chain and secured to rings at the end of their rows. There were two rows of twenty men on each side, eighty slaves in all to power Numicius' private pleasure ship. Their oars were the best thing we could hold to float ashore.

Two hundred paces. That's all that separated life and death for us. Two hundred paces of choppy waters to the waves hitting the rocks at the base of the Pharos Island. To make it to land, we must find something to float upon, manage not to get dragged out to sea, make it to the rocks, avoid being smashed on them by the waves, and climb the slippery things with three legs and three hands between two beat-up men.

I got the message, Fortuna — I got it.

I needed help and the slaves were my only option. I didn't know how many of the eighty chained men knew how to swim. I didn't know how many of those who could wouldn't just swim away at the first opportunity. I didn't have a choice except to find out.

I knew any number of incantations to open locks, as well as traditional lock-picking techniques. I even had lockpicks with me, but not enough time to open eighty locks.

We were right across from the Pharos, the mystical lighthouse of Egretia. It was erected five hundred years ago by the *incantator* Iunius Brutus. Standing on the top of its island, its high spire was mounted by a marble statue of an egret holding the eternal flame in its beak. The bound forces of *magia*, burning in the same spot for centuries, formed a focal point, an entry gate into our world from that of the *numina*. Its light was blinding to the eye, and to the sensitive ones the energies buffeting from it were just as blinding. I've seen before a man who channelled that *magia* to give his incantations powerful energies. He died in agony in the process — practising incantations is not just about power, but about control.

Options were in short supply, though. At the stern, all four chains holding the slaves came together, two from each side of the galley. I limped between them, stretched my arms out, and laid my hands on the ring to which they were attached. Letting the invisible winds of *magia* wash over me, I basked in the power of the Pharos, drawing it in, concentrating it and storing it before speaking my incantation. It wasn't long or complex, just a nuanced variation of the charm I used to break my bonds in the hold. It's lot harder to concentrate standing with a broken ankle on a rolling, burning ship, but I was proficient with the charm, having performed it many times in my line of business.

I shaped the *magia* borrowed from the Pharos to the best of my abilities and released it into the chains. Like a crack of thunder, every lock across every neck of the eighty slaves burst open. At the other end, the chains snapped the ring out of the ship, splitting the wood asunder. Even the thongs of my sandals became undone.

The whiplash from the chains and the *magia* hurled me back against the wooden stern. My breath was knocked out and I slid down to the deck. Luckily, the crack of the exploding metal locks stunned the slaves. I recovered first, and yelled, "If you want to live, listen to me!"

Some didn't wait, jumping into the water and swimming away as soon as they could. Enough stayed. I had them bundle the oars — those they hadn't broken — and tie the bundles together with lengths of rigging rope to make thick logs. These would float better than single oars and could be powered by several men holding on and kicking to propel themselves, giving us better odds to reach the shore.

I put Borax with one group of slaves and myself with another. The fire was roaring furiously by then, heavy smoke billowing from below deck. Other ships were mostly steering clear, not keen to chance a burning wreck at dusk, but a few edged close.

Nothing was left but to hold on to the oars and jump overboard. When my ankle hit the water, the shock nearly made me let go. I cried out in pain. Only luck kept me from swallowing seawater till I drowned.

My group kicked and paddled with our hands, aiming towards the *Insula Laridae*. I caught occasional glimpses of Borax hugging his oar-bundle tightly among other groups making their way to the island. We found a spot where fallen rocks created protruding shelves at water level. The rocks were slippery and the waves vicious, but we managed to claw our way atop. I yelled and waved to those in the water, and men angled towards us.

"You can run the length of the Vicus Caprificus and try to exit the city at the Porta Rupis," I said to the slaves as they clambered up, "but the gates are closed by now. You can try to disperse and hide in Egretia, but you'll get picked up as runaway slaves. Or, help me get back to the city centre, and I'll handle any questions till we reach the temple of Asylaeus. I'll vouch your master left you to die, chained on board a burning ship. An asylum may not be freedom, but at least you won't be declared *fugitivo* and hunted down."

Some slaves ignored me, scrambling up the island as soon as they caught their breath. Whether they tried to exit the city that night or hide and escape later didn't matter. A few stayed behind to help others on the rocks.

By the time all had made it to the shore, about fifteen of the original eighty were with me. I would have liked to set my bones but getting away was a higher priority. I led the slaves across the viaduct bridge from the Pharos island back to the city. Taking turns, they supported me in hobbling. Borax tried to claim that position, but I insisted he let the others help. I wasn't sure of his condition and how the loss of his hand would affect him. Stalwart as ever, he walked next to me, growling when anyone jostled me or one of the slaves on whom I leaned tripped.

The commotion in the harbour was evident. Ships were circling closer to the burning wreck. I could hear the *vigiles* on the shores. Their firefighting skills were mainly geared towards clearing buildings, but this wasn't the first fire on the bay. They had rowboats and instructions to protect the wharves while assisting survivors.

Their organisation was nominally paid for by the city, but more often was supported by the public officials of the year, usually the *aediles*. Those running for public office invariably run expensive election campaigns. Those are financed in exchange for favours — such as secondary tasks for the *vigiles*, like hunting runaway slaves. I could see a *decury* of them roughing up some of the wet galley slaves that ran away ahead of us, nabbing them and tying them with ropes.

I didn't feel like arguing with them. The way I looked and felt, I doubted they would stop to listen to my claims of citizenship. As soon as we crossed, I directed my group northward, towards the open sea. The promenade next to the shore doesn't go far, as it meets the cliffs which rise out of the sea. But where the road turns to snake up the steep hill, one can take a disused path to the egress of the *Cloaca Maxima*. The sewers spill their contents, which are then carried away by sea currents.

We waded in, holding to the walls to avoid slipping. Not a pleasant walk at any time, the stream of foetid, cold waters made the pain in my ankle excruciating.

Borax and the slaves supported me as I led the way through the tunnels. The lines were fairly straight, but it helps if one knows which turns to take. I seem to have had far too many cases which took me down there. I imagined some god found it hilarious, landing me in foul-smelling, sticky sewage. I'm certain he was taking enjoyment at the offences against my nose and the shudders induced by slimy things brushing against my legs in the dark.

And in the dark we trudged. We had no torches, and nothing to burn for illumination. Only the occasional overhead grill suffused with moonlight and the feel of stones marked with symbols at intersections gave me hints to navigate by.

I was aiming for the Forum. What was normally an hour's walk overland took three times as long. My fervent muttered prayers to Fortuna, Cloacina, and — considering what we were stepping in — Sterculius, must have been answered because I found an exit behind the Porticus Aemilia. From there it was a short hike up the hill for the temple of Asylaeus.

At the temple, the slaves huddled close to the altar. Holding on to it would give them asylum, the protection of the god. The priests were not surprised by our wet and bedraggled appearance. I gave the chief priest my account of what happened, or at least the pertinent details, without revealing my hand in causing the fire. For a master to abuse slaves to the point they seek asylum was considered shameful. If found true, and the testimony of a free citizen would weigh the balance in their favour, their owner would be forced to sell the slaves. Not freedom, but at least a legal way for them to escape the galleys.

One last task remained that night.

CHAPTER XXVI

The wooden door was adorned with a glazed clay tile bearing the image of Aesculapius, holding out his staff with the snake coiled around it. I knocked loudly. Yelled his name. Neighbours were surely used to it, given his profession. He had been a *medicus* with the legions, where we met when he was working on a comprehensive treatise of first-aid and tried to give lessons to the legionaries. Predictably, our centurions viewed this as a waste of time. A soldier's role was to fight until dead. If merely wounded, they maintained, his comrades should kick him back into action, not mollycoddle him with bandages. I guess the centurions were afraid close association with the medical staff would give the grunts ways to feign illnesses better — a not-unfounded suspicion, considering how I extricated myself from the army. But we did strike a guarded friendship back then, with me being the one bright soldier who took an interest in his teachings.

A slit in the gate opened, then his wife unlocked the door. Although approaching middle age, she was still slim and fetching, with long blond curls and horrendous *Quirite*. Originally from a local tribe out on the border, I knew her as his housekeeper, though Petreius eventually married her despite her dubious origins and atrocious cooking. Her restorative stews, which she offered occasionally to her favourites amongst her husband's patients, were an affront to both culinary and medical arts.

"Is Gaius Petreius at home, Tilla?" I asked.

"You are in need of patching up again, Fox?" She replied. "Indeed. I've also got an interesting case for him." I pointed at Borax.

Tilla appraised him, then spoke rapidly in her own language. Borax answered in the same. She said something to him that made him blush.

While we waited in the atrium, I asked Borax what she told him. He blushed an even deeper shade of red and shook his head, refusing to answer.

"*Salve*, Felix. Still up to no good?" Petreius, a classically handsome man despite approaching sixty, had mellowed with age — I was expecting sterner words.

"All in the service of our city, Gaius Petreius. I hope your new private practice for the rich and their digestion has not dimmed your field-medic skills. Got a couple of patch-up-and-get-back-in-there jobs for you."

Petreius led us to a large room off the atrium. In the middle was an examination table, and the walls were lined with cabinets holding the various instruments of medics everywhere — from bandages and salves, to scalpels and bone-saws. In the corner was his desk and favourite folding chair.

"Let's start with the easy case," I said as I hobbled to the examination table and lifted myself to sit on it.

Petreius walked over to peer and my leg, and quickly took a step back. "Where have you been, man? You smell like you just cleaned the Augean stables."

"Close enough. We had to take a detour through the sewers."

"Don't tell me — I don't want to know." He called for slaves to bring him a basin and warm water, and to help wash my feet.

Once cleaned, he peered closer, *hmm'ed* and *tsk'ed*, said, "I thought I taught you first aid," and went about setting my ankle. "Bite on this," he handed me a piece of wood. I obediently placed it in my mouth and closed my eyes. Petreius removed my sandal and prodded the swollen ankle, bringing tears to my eyes. "You're soaking wet. Did you go swimming? Got drunk at the races and fell in the sewers, did you now?"

"I missed the races, as a matter of fact," I mumbled around the wood in my mouth.

"Ah, double shame then. I heard the Reds' victory was legendary. Or at least, that was the drunken singing outside my window recently. Can you imagine the *quadriga* in full gallop?"

My answer was a scream, which didn't quite mask the squelching, grating noises as he used the distraction to pull my bones into place. While I regained my breath, he proceeded to bandage the ankle with strips of linen soaked in plaster. Despite my pain, or perhaps because of it and the heightened sensations it brought, I felt a slight tingling on my skin. The mixture of plaster contained other elements, with traces of *magia* that would speed my healing.

"You'll have to wait until this dries before you can go anywhere. Now, you mentioned two cases?"

I motioned Borax to the table. "Show him your hand."

Borax cautiously extended his right arm. Flakes of ash wafted from the charred stump of his wrist. Petreius sucked in his breath, then leaned closer, peering. He took Borax's arm gently in his, carefully turning it around as he examined it and scraped it delicately with a thin, metal instrument. "This was not done by any ordinary fire," he stated. "There are no red burn scars around it. Just living flesh one point, charcoal the next. Does it hurt?"

"Not now," Borax shook his head. "Only when he'd done it."

"It was a new kind of incantation. An unguent of some sort and a rather tricky chant to activate it," I told Petreius. "I saw a variation of it used — and then reversed — on his other hand."

He perked up, moving to examine Borax's left hand. He compared the dead wrist to the pink hand. "I don't suppose you've kept any samples of any of it…?"

"Unfortunately, no," I answered. I knew Petreius well enough to know that his interest was in the healing aspect, and that I could trust him with any samples. He was certainly good enough to attempt to deconstruct what Ambustus had performed. "Whatever there was went up in flames, before sinking down into the depths of the bay — together with the man who made them."

"Right. Never a simple case with you. I'll no doubt hear all about it tomorrow, when my patients gossip. Do me a favour and don't tell anyone you stopped here," said Petreius, while scraping charcoal skin samples from Borax's wrist into round dishes, no doubt for future research.

In the end there was nothing much he could do. He cleaned the stump, working gently as if it were a scab or a real burn wound. Since it was effectively cauterised and did not show any signs of bleeding or oozing pus, he simply applied some general healing salves and bandaged it with clean linen.

We waited for my cast to dry so I could walk, as it was far too late to find a litter to carry us. We continued chatting, reminiscing about army life and gossiping about past acquaintances. Petreius was sitting behind his desk, rocking the front two legs of his chair off the floor.

I could see him torn between professional curiosity and the desire not to get involved in dark dealings, but he didn't broach the subject. He had the samples from Borax's skin, and would no doubt investigate them for himself, safely and discreetly.

The wait also meant a dinner invitation. I am sure Petreius could afford a cook, but apparently Tilla had insisted on cooking something herself. No doubt for the benefit of Borax, her erstwhile countryman. She instructed a maid to set the dishes for all of us at the examination table, serving Borax — a slave — together with the free men. I've heard her speak her mind before and knew better than to point this out.

"This gives men strength," she said. It was a thick, roundish, greyish, sausage-y kind of blob, filled with what smelled like minced offal. Then boiled. Possibly fried again. Tilla herself cut thick slices and served them on plates, together with vegetables that had been needlessly sacrificed by being boiled to death till they turned to mush. Petreius' face became completely impassive when he saw the dish, and he averted his gaze. He was extremely cautious not to indicate even the slightest opinion about it.

Borax's face lit up at the sight and smells of the dish. He attempted to eat it by breaking it with a fork. Using just his left hand was awkward, though, as the sausage casing was a tad rubbery. Tilla clucked, took his fork and knife, and started to cut pieces and feed him. He made feeble attempts to complain, but was silenced by a short staccato of foreign language.

"Men of my tribe walk many miles driving cattle, eating just this for days," Tilla told us. I don't know if this dish was the origin of the legendary strength and stamina of the Arbari men, but I certainly could see them walking for days eating just that. After a single bite, I was willing to walk any distance needed to get away from it. There was not enough fish sauce in the world to make it palatable.

SCROLL III - JUDICIUM

CHAPTER XXVII

There was nothing left for me to do. The curses had been removed from the *insulae* and I had extracted as much evidence as I could out of Numicius, though it still didn't amount to much beyond my word. Valerius would call me as a witness at the trial, but until that time my involvement with this case was done.

I attended to neglected facets of my life. I sacrificed to Fortuna, donated current profits and pledged future profits to her temple. I returned Borax to Crassitius, weathered his abuse at damaged goods, and forfeited my deposit. Borax, never talkative, was practically taciturn. His future was in doubt, as the only thing he was trained to do was taken from him. I knew Crassitius would not throw him out on the street, but there was nothing more I could do for him.

I hadn't been to Cornelia's house nor exchanged any notes since I kissed Aemilia. All I had to do was stay home and nurse my broken ankle back to health.

Or so I thought.

Valerius was not satisfied with the written report I sent him. He wanted to meet in person, together with Quintus Aquilius, to discuss details and plan the speeches for the trial. All items of evidence must be reviewed, their strengths and weaknesses debated. Arguments need to be presented in the best sequence during the speech and oratory tricks must be assigned to distract the jury and crowd from weak points and enhance the strong ones. I have worked with lawyers before, and knew of their obsession with drafting, redrafting, and practising their delivery in terms of pitch of voice and gestures of hand for hours at a time. The final performance in court would be like a well-rehearsed play, adhering to the strict rules of rhetoric and aimed at achieving maximum effect.

My objection on the grounds of my leg was summarily dismissed. Valerius would send a litter to carry me. I just needed to make myself available the next day. Since he was still paying — very handsomely — for my time, I had no choice but to agree.

**

I made myself comfortable in Valerius' *tablinum*. A couch was brought into his study for my benefit, so I could put my leg up. Valerius was seated at his desk, on which piles of scrolls and wax tablets lay open. Quintus Aquilius had a backless seat next to the desk, but kept jumping out of it to deliver impromptu snippets of oratory. He was practising his delivery, discarding phrases that didn't work and jotting down the sparkling ones lest he forget.

They were working on the opening segment when I arrived, so I waited patiently for their questions. "We must pre-empt any attempt by Numicius to bribe the jury," said Valerius, drawling his nemesis' name in disgust. "It's almost a given he would buy votes."

"How about this, then." Aquilius strode to the middle of the room, closed his eyes for a moment. He then raised his hand dramatically, gestured towards me as though I was a senator sitting with the jury, and spoke in the clear, slightly high-pitched, orator's voice.

"That which was above all things to be desired, O noble conscript fathers, and which above all things was calculated to have the greatest influence towards putting an end to the discredit into which your judicial decisions have fallen, appears to have been thrown in your way, and given to you not by any human contrivance, but almost

191

by the interposition of the gods. For an opinion has now become established, pernicious to us, and pernicious to the republic, which has been the common talk of everyone, not only at Egretia, but among foreign nations also, that in the courts of law as they exist at present, no wealthy man, however guilty he may be, can possibly be convicted.

"Now, at this time when men are ready to attempt by harangues to increase the existing unpopularity of the senate, Gaius Numicius is brought to trial as a criminal, a man condemned in the opinion of everyone by his life and actions, but acquitted by the enormousness of his wealth according to his own hope and boast. I, O judges, have undertaken this cause as prosecutor with the greatest good wishes and expectation on the part of the Egretian people, not in order to increase the unpopularity of the senate, but to relieve it from the discredit lest I one day share with it. For I have brought before you a man, by acting justly in whose case you have an opportunity of retrieving the lost credit of your judicial proceedings, of regaining your credit with the Egretian people, and of giving satisfaction to the gods. This man is the betrayer of public trust, the petty tyrant of the docks and people of our city, the violator of ancient laws, the disgrace and ruin of all that we hold sacred.

"And, if you come to a decision about this man with severity and a due regard to your oaths, that authority which ought to remain in you will cling to you still; but if that man's vast riches shall break down the sanctity and honesty of the courts of justice, at least I shall achieve this -- that it shall be plain that it was rather honest judgement that was wanting to the republic, than a criminal to the judges, or an accuser to the criminal."

"Oh, I like that!" Valerius exclaimed and scribbled furiously, capturing Aquilius' words. "You have just equated a verdict of innocence with tacit admission of bribery." When he was done, he handed the wax tablet to Aquilius, who in turn scanned the written lines and made some adjustments. He then placed the tablet on a side table, presumably with others he wanted to keep.

"Let us put this aside for now and concentrate on Felix's testimony," instructed Valerius. "I want to be sure the meat and bones of the evidence are as solid as they can be. The jury and crowd must have no doubt left in their minds both of the atrocities done in Numicius' name, but also of his ultimate involvement. It's such a pity we could not string his toady Ambustus together with him at the same trial."

I personally thought Ambustus got off easy and was not sorry to see him gone. Trials are unpredictable at best, but I thought better than to voice that opinion.

"You are an experienced witness as I understand it," said Aquilius. "Why don't you act as though you're giving testimony at the trial? We'll build up from there."

"Very well," I replied. I took a moment to place myself in the right frame of mind and began. "I was hired by the noble Lucius Valerius Flaccus, whose illustrious family's patronage any citizen would be consider an honour. Not finding tenants to fill up his excellently maintained *insulae —*"

"Maybe we can just skip to the facts, for now," interjected Valerius. "We'll worry about the flourishes later."

"As you wish," I said. "I started with canvassing the three properties, the neighbours, and the remaining residents in one of them. I wanted to hear for myself what transpired there to scare off tenants. I wanted to form a hypothesis regarding whether this was the work of hooligans and gangs scaring your tenants, or whether there was indeed more to it. While some of the stories, such as random voices and screams in the night, could be explained by work of human agents, others could not. A skilled burglar might be able to sneak a snake into a toddler's crib, but when I examined the blood-stained walls at one *insula* and the claw marks at another — it was plain no mortal hand could have traced those. I could feel the traces of *magia* left behind by unholy incantations."

"Could you expand on this?" asked Aquilius.

"Explain the tracing of *magia*?"

"No, elaborate on the atrocities you found there."

I did. He paled at my description of blood-spattered walls and unnatural hoof-prints in the blood. He turned green at my description of rotting human remains, lying broken and mangled in dark corners. It was Valerius who asked me to stop, when I reached the baby being eaten alive by animated snakes.

"I think we heard enough," Valerius said. "Felix can spin a yarn well enough. I am sure the jury will be just as horrified by his testimony as we are. Let's move on, and tie this to Numicius."

I moved on to describe how I uncovered to cause of the unnatural events. I never once mentioned Aemilia in my account. "The trick I used with the *psilocybe* will be understood by any who have attended the Collegium Incantatorum and by dabblers in the mystical arts. It will be looked down upon, though. It is not nearly as precise as the *visus verum*. Yet without it, and having never graduated from the Collegium, I could not explain how I located the *tabulae defixiones*. What would you have me say?"

"Your credentials will come under scrutiny no matter what. You might as well mention it and give the weight of known techniques to your testimony," replied Aquilius. "Make it 'at great personal risk', to show your dedication to the cause. Here, when you introduce the subject of the mushrooms and where they led you, do it like this." He strode to the middle again, placed his left hand on his heart as though holding the toga, and gestured with his right.

"I seem to myself to have done an action acceptable to Valerius Flaccus and his tenants in seeking to avenge their injuries with my own labour, at my own peril, and at the risk of incurring enmity in some quarters; and I am sure that this which I am doing is not less acceptable to all Egretian citizens, who think that the safety of their rights, of their liberty, of their properties and fortunes, consists in the condemnation of that man."

"Oh, jolly good!" exclaimed Valerius. "Elevating this to a

case of public safety and justice, not merely property squabbles."

"And not far from the truth, either," I added. "Shall I brandish the lead tablets? I can pull them out at the right moment as the cause of the bloody events. Once that stirs a commotion, I shall, of course, assuage any doubts that they have been properly neutralised, again at great personal risk. When everyone has their attention on the tablet in my hands, I could gesture with them at Numicius to help strengthen the connection."

"You should have been a lawyer, Felix," Aquilius commented after a short silence.

"Moving on then," Valerius continued. "After removing the tablets and rendering them inert, you had the task of finding who placed the curses — and, in turn, who ultimately commissioned him."

"Before that, there is a matter I think was neglected. It could affect the case. It is rather delicate, so I am not sure if you would wish to bring it up."

"Well, what is it?" asked Valerius.

"In the last *insula* I treated, I had to start a fire to combat some manifestation of the *nefas magia* of the curses. While the fire was fuelled mainly with leaves, so would not have damaged the property —"

"Think nothing of it," Valerius gestured grandly, which I took to mean he already knew that no serious damage was done.

"— but mixed in the fuel were some incantations to increase the smoke. Now, it's quite possible that the *vigiles* never entered the *insula*, for fear of the curses or of collapse. Or, that their report got filed under pranks. Or, that no one with sensitivity was around to sense the fire and smoke had more to them than belongs in our world. It's possible, for that matter, that no one of sensibilities and rank had been near the *insulae* in the weeks they stood empty under the influences of the curses. Even, perhaps, that this year the *rhones* of the Collegium Incantatorum are even more inept than usual. But my guts scream there are too many implausibilities in this chain of events to explain without resorting to the simpler explanation — namely that Numicius owns one or several of this year's *rhones*."

"You mentioned that before," said Valerius, "and I made sure the matter will be buried with the *vigiles*. Do you think the *rhones* could make matters complicated for us?"

Aquilius cleared his throat and said, "I doubt this would matter much. As a former praetor with his eyes on the consulship, Numicius would no doubt have some *rhones* as clients. We do not have the time to start investigating them, even if that were advisable. In the unlikely event we were to find conclusive proof of bribery, there is no gain in taking the *rhones* to court. And anyway, a bribery trial would have to be next year, after they step down from office. They cannot overtly influence the outcome of this trial, no more than Numicius would do himself in any case. What I can do is raise some general questions about the authorities' lack of response without naming names, thus avoiding making us vulnerable to a calumny suit. Just enough to cast doubts, but without lingering on it."

"I concur," from Valerius. "If this becomes an issue, we could prosecute next year. But for now, we need to concentrate on Numicius. Tell us how you traced the curse tablets to him."

I gave a short summary of how I tracked Ambustus. "He did boast of the *tabulae defixiones* to me, an admission of guilt. However, should you think the word of a dead man is not enough, if perhaps it could be dismissed as empty bragging, we can use some of the material Aemilia had uncovered in her research here. The signature of each *incantator*, as they create the enchantment."

"Do you have sufficient evidence to tie him to the curse tablets?" asked Aquilius.

"I didn't get written samples of his other works on the boat, but no one needs to know that. Alternatively, I could... *acquire*... some examples from his estate. His death is recent — I am sure I would be able to bluff my way in," I said. Then added, "It is a risk, though. Numicius' men will no doubt be there. In my less ambulatory state, I would have to hire competent assistance."

Valerius, apparently reading my mind, said, "There will

be a bonus for you, if you could find conclusive proof amongst his artefacts. Anything that would positively indicate Numicius had ordered the curses."

"With all due respect," Aquilius interjected, "I do not believe that would be a wise course of action. The risk to Felix is great and we cannot afford to lose our star witness. You just narrowly escaped their clutches — we shouldn't send you back there, in your condition. Conversely, we would have trouble explaining how he came across such evidence. We would be exposing ourselves to ridicule as employing thieves and thugs."

Valerius agreed. "Perhaps you are right. Though it might make the testimony shakier, it is, as you say, too risky."

I didn't mind being called a thief and a thug as much as I minded my evaporated bonus.

"The next step, that of trying to entrap Numicius with the proposed real estate deal, was a failure," I admitted. "I never once heard him utter anything explicit. He was forewarned by Ambustus and was too careful around me."

"I think it's safe to omit this from your testimony," said Valerius.

"It would be brought up by the opposing counsel," retorted Aquilius. "I really wish you had consulted with me prior to approving this scheme. We would, again, be portrayed as dishonest citizens. Our best bet now is to spin this as if it was a genuine attempt. Felix trying to settle the dispute between the two of you."

"Understood," I said. "I can testify — without bending the truth much — that after I disarmed the curses and figured out Numicius was the one ultimately responsible, I got the idea of scratching out a tad more commission out of this case. Guessing that Numicius was interested in buying and that you would be keen to recover losses, I attempted to broker a deal. I can then use Numicius' attack on me on the ship to portray him an unbalanced and dangerous man, a murderous villain who would turn on free citizens providing him an honest service."

"Perfect!" Aquilius exclaimed. "That would leave a confused jury facing two distinct versions. Numicius' own tale, portraying him as an innocent victim of prosecution, and ours, depicting him as a greedy brute. Reminding the jury of the murder of children with illegal *magia* should then nudge them to our side and make any who took bribes second-guess whether supporting a man who turns on his associates is a good move."

And, with that, my testimony was covered.

We chatted a while longer, discussing fine points of law and rhetoric. I was to be the star witness, though a few others were mentioned as potential support. Valerius' role as the wronged party was mainly to sit stoically and look respectable. Aquilius would be the one delivering the main speeches for the prosecution, in opening and in closing. A couple of other orators were suggested as well, to provide support. A decision about it has not been reached while I was there.

In the afternoon, Valerius' litter carried me comfortably back to my own *domus*. I made myself comfortable in my garden, reading poetry, sipping watered wine, and drawing physical and emotional nourishment from Dascha's simple cooking. I set to enjoy the lull before the storm.

Chapter XXVIII

Two days later I was disabused of this notion, my idyll disrupted.

In the mid-morning came an insistent knock on my front door. Dascha was out at the markets, so I had to shuffle to the vestibule, supporting myself with a walking stick. Through the viewing slit in the door, I saw a messenger holding a large crate and flanked by bodyguards. No doubt a mistaken address.

I opened the door and froze. Hiding on the side where I could not have seen her was Aemilia.

"Uncle Lucius said you are now preparing your testimony on his behalf. I thought I would bring you all the research notes we worked on. He mentioned you had a broken leg — he said it would raise sympathy during the trial, so you have to keep your cast on — but he was rather scant on details about how it happened. I was curious as to what kept you away."

She brushed past me into the atrium. Her entourage filed in behind her through my narrow vestibule — her maid-servant, an older chaperone, the slave carrying the box, and two bodyguards. I closed my own front door, and shuffled after them. Aemilia was undoing the straps of her wide-brimmed hat as she sauntered into my peristyle garden, the *domus'* inner sanctum.

At the sight of my faun fountain, almost a *sopio* with his enlarged manhood, her girl blushed and giggled, while the chaperone clucked, pulled out a fan, and started flapping it furiously. Aemilia stood in the shade of the colonnade, her servants arraying themselves behind her — the picture of a young lady on a socially-acceptable visit — except I could scarcely pass as another young lady of her class on whom she might make a call.

I still had not uttered a word. My mind was occupied with trivialities, such as arranging refreshments without a servant in the house, how to carry a tray while balancing on my broken leg — anything rather than face the inevitable consequences of our last meeting. What was it about the women of that family, both mother and daughter, that left me speechless?

"Come," she invited me to my own couch, "it must be hard getting around with a broken leg."

"My ankle, not my leg. Does your mother know you're here?"

"Don't be daft," she replied, without answering my question. "Shall we begin? I've brought with me all the research material," she indicated the crate. "We should start with my most recent discoveries."

I lowered myself onto the couch, hauled my leg up, and let her carry the conversation. As she talked about the *tabulae*, what she found and gleaned from them, her cross-references and sparks of inspiration, I let my mind wander. Her research was not really essential to my testimony. I had already defused the curses with Araxus' aid, and the courts would care little about the technical details. The task I set for her was merely to distract her from interfering and safe in her mother's house — not an unwise choice, considering what happened on Numicius' ship. I did not have the heart to tell her that, so I feigned interest.

The rest of my mental faculties were occupied with the memory of our last meeting. She hadn't brought up the kiss. She also hadn't answered my question about Cornelia, so I had no idea in how much trouble I was with that lady. Was her presence here against Cornelia's wishes? Did her mother know I kissed her daughter? Why was she here at all?

***

An hour later we heard Dascha return from the markets. Soft murmurs from the atrium were soon followed by her uneven footsteps as she came into the garden.

"Will you stay for dinner?" I asked Aemilia. "It won't be as refined as you are used to, but Dascha is a decent cook."

"As long as it is not another *patina*, I look forward to it," she smiled.

"Dascha, would you please cook something nice for our guests?" I said.

For once my elderly housekeeper refrained for making any lewd comments, and replied simply, "I'll have to go out for some more supplies, *domine*."

"Thera," Aemilia addressed her chaperone, "why don't you go with Dascha and help? Take the two bodyguards with you, to help carry baskets. And Na'ama," she said to her girl, "why don't you bring a glass of water to Titus? You must be bored by now, and I know Titus would love to chat with you. Felix and I still have a lot of dull issues to discuss."

And thus, neatly and efficiently, we were alone. I moved to pick up the next wax tablet from the crate, and Aemilia leaned in. She placed her hand on mine and gazed into my eyes, her face a foot away.

I spent an eternity drowning in her storm-grey eyes that must have taken no more than a heartbeat. If ever the gods offer me the gift of knowing what thoughts run through women's minds, I shall decline. Perplexing, infuriating, unfathomable, unpredictable — yet magical creatures in their own way. I suspect life would be terribly boring without moments such as that.

Aemilia shattered my reverie by speaking in a business-like tone, "Now, then. We have better things to speak about than my research. You left rather suddenly last time we met and have been avoiding me since."

"I've been busy on behalf of your uncle," I replied weakly.

"So busy you couldn't even send a note?"

I indicated my broken and plastered leg.

"That happened only four days ago," she replied with infallible feminine logic. "You kissed me almost two *nundinae* ago."

"Kissing you was a mistake," I said. "My business with your uncle is almost done. Best forget about it and move on."

"Mother said you were harsh. Then again, she likes that. But kiss me you did and ignore it you can't."

"You might not. I can."

There was a sharp intake of breath as she stared, searching, into my eyes. I had to disabuse her of any notion, any imagined possibility of a future. Egretian society allows for mobility, but even if the gods delivered me a sudden fortune, a Subvales boy could never marry a daughter of the Cornelii and Aemilii.

I expected tears. I expected a slap. I did not expect another kiss.

Leaving me gasping for air, she leaned back. "Deny this!" she exclaimed.

"This is a mistake —" was all I managed before she lunged and kissed me again — her mother's daughter.

I put my hands on her shoulders and pushed her away, feeling her tremble. She reminded me so much of my lost Helena. I wanted nothing more than to draw her in and kiss her gently, properly. Instead, I said, "Everything in life, my dear, has consequences. If we continue, your infatuation with me will pass — and an infatuation is all this is — then you will be faced with a tarnished name. You are in a better position than most young women of your class. You are not bound to a father who will marry you off to some ageing political ally. Didn't your mother say you were to marry Quintus Aquilius? A fine young man..."

"Phaw! Quintus will marry whomever his mother tells him. A lion at court, a kitten at home. My mother has very old-fashioned ideas when it comes to *my* life."

"Your mother," I said, "would have me castrated and feed me my own testicles if she thought I touched you in any way."

"I can handle my mother," Aemilia replied. I shuddered at the memory of their last argument.

I tried the Socratic method. "What future do you see for this? For us?"

"What do you mean?" She seemed suspicious of this

change in tone.

"You kiss me. I kiss you back. Then what?"

"We don't need anyone's approval. We could have a life together. You could teach me the workings of *magia* and incantation. I could assist you in your investigations."

"And how do you see your mother taking me jumping straight from her bed into yours?"

"Told you, I can handle my mother."

"What about the *rhones* of the Collegium Incantatorum? Teaching women incantation is expressly forbidden by the *mos maiorum*."

"There are plenty of wise-women, fortune-tellers, healers, witches, and other women who practice *magia* all around Egretia. Besides, it's not like what you are doing is in strict adherence to the *mos maiorum* or to the expressed rules of the Collegium. If you can get by now under the noses of the *rhones*, this will hardly be any extra burden."

"Look around you. You have led a sheltered life filled with learnt idealism but removed from street reality. Would you give up your comforts so easily? Your slaves, your girl, those who handle your every bidding?"

"I am not so pampered that —"

"Would you trade your life amongst the *nobilitas*, the people who matter in our society, for a life when even your next meal is uncertain, let alone anything further in your future?"

"If we were together, that is all that would matter. Like Baucis and Philemon, Daphnis and Chloë."

The trouble with Hellican philosophy and logic is that it is completely lost on infatuated nineteen-year-old girls. And on women in general. Fortuna, my name-sake goddess of fickle luck, is commonly depicted as a woman. Explains a lot, I thought to myself, and took a mental note to sacrifice to her more often.

Time to play my harshest move. "When you talked about a future with me, you had me as a teacher — someone to teach you incantations, to excite you with mysteries. You have the chance to marry for love, have a happy life. Happiness, in my experience, is far rarer and more delicate than mere worldly knowledge. Life with me will only lead you to misery and ruin. I don't need such a responsibility in my life."

She stared at me for a long moment. Tears welled up in her eyes; one rolled down her perfect cheek. I thought it best to shut my mouth. Let her face the futility of her plans, hate me if she needed to, but grow up and get on with her life. She was a strong woman, an indomitable spirit like her mother. She would survive this, just as most adolescents do.

"I thought you had a heart, Felix," she said, her voice catching. The tears came faster, and she collapsed sobbing on my chest. I hugged her gently.

She looked up at me, the kohl running from her eyes, her hair in disarray. When Helena cried, I let the tears persuade me, and the vile circumstance that followed were her undoing.

As if reading my mind, Aemilia said, "What happened to make your heart as hard as stone? What did that girl Araxus mentioned — that Helena — what did she do to you?"

She didn't leave me time to answer about my guilt, about the goodbye I never bade Helena. Aemilia ever-so-gently put her tear-stained lips to mine.

And just like that, the last vestiges of my resolve evaporated.

CHAPTER XXIX

Not long after, we were interrupted by a commotion from the atrium. Dascha and Aemilia's chaperone had returned from their shopping, and the latter was busy loudly chastising Aemilia's slave girl. Apparently, we were not the only ones occupying time with an illicit tryst. While the chaperone was lecturing the girl about the appropriate behaviour for a young woman and what her mistress would think, we quickly recomposed ourselves. Lacking anything better, Aemilia washed the ruined makeup from her face in the fountain and dried it on a cushion cover I handed her. Stifling a giggle, she dabbed my face with the wet fabric to remove the traces of her makeup clinging to me.

By the time the chaperone was satisfied Aemilia's slaves were properly remorseful and made her way to the garden, we were back in our seats — Aemilia with reading aloud from a wax tablet and myself reclining on my couch and nodding vigorously.

Our hearts weren't in discussions about inscribed curses and comparative metaphysical reviews of ancient sources. Thankfully, we didn't have to pretend long. Dascha had bought some ready-made dishes from nearby shops. My neighbourhood being what it is, those consisted of fresh bread, cured cheese, and fried dormice. A bodyguard set up a tripod table in the garden on which Dascha placed the dishes together with bowls of honey and poppy-seeds to drizzle on the meat. I noticed she used my best remaining bowls and plates — the ones not chipped — and she brought us wine and water in silver jugs and cups. I had no doubt that if she could, she would have organised a lyre player to regale us with romantic tunes and recitals of raunchy poems.

Despite Dascha's best efforts, we were constrained into discussing weather, food, and other trivialities. Aemilia's slaves lingered at her back and I had no illusions Cornelia had sent the chaperone for more than just social protocol.

The slow conversation gave me a chance to reflect on our situation. I could pretend this was the work of Cupid, but I suspected Priapus was a likelier culprit. Unprofessional was the least of the epithets for my actions. Moronic would be more appropriate. By continuing along this line of action, I would be making my life complicated, on both professional and personal planes. Worse, I would be ruining Aemilia's life.

And yet...

She was different from my Helena and yet so similar. Dark auburn hair rather than blond. Grey eyes to green. Similar age, but ten years had passed for me. Aemilia, the product of two old and noble Egretian families. Helena, a recent immigrant — a foreigner. One with prospects of a constrained life amongst the elite, the other with control of her own life, but few prospects. Yet both full of enthusiasm, indomitable spirits. The same dancing smile, the same mischief in their eyes.

Aemilia was smiling at me, blushing lightly, and not even the painful memory of Helena's dead and mutilated body could stop my heart from melting.

***

All things come to an end, whether enjoyable or deplorable. At the eighth hour of the day, Aemilia's chaperone started to fuss, reminding her mistress that Cornelia was expecting them for dinner well before dark.

I escorted Aemilia to my front door, limping along with my crutch. When the guards stepped outside to the alley first and were followed by Aemilia's girl and chaperone, the latter eager to get going, I took the opportunity to steal one last kiss. She froze, her eyes widening in surprise before fluttering shut.

She melted into my lips, my arms.

It was a gut-wrenching thing to tear her away and push her gently to the street before anyone was the wiser.

I leaned against the wall, deflated, confused. Well, perhaps not confused. Many conflicting emotions ran through me, to the point I was shaking as I stood, but I knew well enough what I was doing, why, and what was wrong with it. Aemilia was both an inescapable lodestone and a living, breathing reminder of my loss. I was furious with myself for letting this happen, for making it happen — yet at the same time unable to stop myself.

And, if I did not want her to end up like Helena, I had better back away. My life, with its danger and subterfuge, was not fit for young girls, a lesson painfully learnt.

I straightened up, forcefully exhaled a deep breath, and made my way inside, relishing in the pain of stepping on my ankle while resolving to find myself something to occupy my time away from women.

***

As if to reinforce my resolve to protect Aemilia, in a grim reminder of my past, the next morning I found Araxus knocking on my door. He was bedraggled, stooped, unwashed, unshaven, but his green right eye was looking at me openly and the mad black one seemingly under his control.

"Do you have a pig?" he asked before I could say anything.

"Ah..."

"Never mind, you will. It's about the *tabulae defixiones* that we disposed of the other day. Do you still have them?"

"Yes," I replied. "Why?"

"I wanted to check something."

My hackles rose. "Do you think they are not inert? I thought we disposed of their *magia* safely."

"We did, we did. They are nothing but plumber's supplies now. Could I see them, please?"

"Did you think of some new aspect?" I asked, motioning for him to follow me to my study. I dug out the curse tablets and handed them over.

He unfolded one carefully and examined the engraved signs. As he read, his green right eye clouded, darkened, became as black as his mad left eye. Clouds drifted past my window and the room acquired a chill.

"Well?" I asked. "What is it?"

He turned both black eyes on me, his gaze boring into my soul. Shivers ran up my spine and my broken ankle began to ache and throb.

"It's as I feared," he said, voice rasping. "There is more baaa to this than a baaa curse. It's not a mere supplication to the major baaa gods, it's almost a love sonnet baaa to invite them to procreate. Do you realise what this baaa means?"

"It means you are insane."

"No! It means that the black sheep has three bags of wool! Baaa!" And with this he broke into a mad little jig, reciting a silly children's ditty about lambs. After a while I gave up trying to restore his reason, and — somewhat fearful that in his mad state he might reactivate the curse tablets — escorted him out of my house.

After Araxus left, I needed some time away from everyone and decided I would not be getting it at home.

Given my impaired mobility, I could not take on another case. I was in no condition to walk far, but I limped down to the docks between the grain and fish markets, found a good corner, and left a honey-cake in the shrine of the nearest crossroad *lar*. I chalked 'FORTUNES TOLD, CURSES IDENTIFIED' on the wall, sat down on a folding stool under it, put on airs, and busied myself with a scroll by Thrasyllus on star-gazing which looked impressive with all its strange and foreign symbols.

People being what they are, especially sailors and dock-workers, I scraped enough *quadrans* and *semis* that day to cover a night of drinking. Calculating people's horoscopes is tedious, but at least cleaner than haruspicy. One sailor wanted me to write a curse against his fellow, whom he swore stole his lucky *fascinum* when they were asleep. I scribbled a supplication to Hygieia — about as magical as a bucket of piss — to withdraw her protection from the thief's health. I also sold him a mild laxative in the guise of 'special medicine' and told him to slip it in the evening meal whilst at sea to reveal the guilty party to all. On the off-chance he was wrong about the culprit, the laxative was to go into the main pot and the supplication into the fire. I taught him meaningless doggerel to repeat, so I could claim it was his fault for botching it. Thoughts of future winds generated below decks by an overly flatulent crew cheered me up.

It also kept my mind away from Aemilia and what I needed to do with her.

On the way home, I could feel my ankle getting stronger. Whatever charms Petreius had weaved into the cast were working their magic. Still, limping on a plastered leg, a crutch in one hand and my folding stool and scrolls in the other, was hard enough without impairing my balance further. So despite a strong desire to forget Aemilia, my better judgement prevailed and I only had one drink on the way home. I sat in a tavern, ordered some fried and stuffed bread, and sipped a half-decent vintage that required just a pinch of cloves and sugar of lead to make it palatable.

I was about to leave for home when Araxus walked in and, with a heavy sigh, sat at my table. Without looking at me or any acknowledgement, he took my cup and poured the dregs of wine from the jug into it. There was barely a quarter-cup left. He dipped his finger in the little saucer of sugar, then swirled the wine with it. As he did, the wine rose, filling the cup. I was still in shocked silence when he lifted it up to his lips and drank deeply. While that spoke volumes about his table manners, it gave me little clue about his mental state.

"And hello to you, too," I finally said. "What brings you into the town?"

"I need to find my friend Felix," he said. "He needs my help."

"Oh? Do tell. What trouble has 'Felix' gotten himself into this time?"

"He needs a priest."

"You are no priest," I said.

"And neither is he. You see," he leaned close to me, his reek overwhelming, "we could never worship the *Magna Mater* — we love our testicles too much!" At this he erupted into inane giggles which turned into hiccoughs.

Still, he could be prophetic at times. Not for nothing is the power of prophecy linked to curses and madness. "Why does he need a priest?"

"How should I know?" he said.

"So how do you know he needs one?" I asked through gritted teeth.

"Who?"

"Felix! You said he needs a priest!"

"Felix, what are you talking about? Who needs a priest?"

I took a deep breath. "You just walked in here, said you were looking for me because I need a priest."

"Did I? No one in your family left to die, so perhaps you're getting married soon?"

I had enough of him, and stood up to leave, dropping a few coins on the table. Araxus' hand shot out and grabbed my wrist. His green eye was still looking at the wine cup, but his black one looked straight at me, through me.

"I will be there when you need me," he said in a hoarse whisper. "I still have much of my debt to repay you."

CHAPTER XXX

The alley leading to my front door was packed. A closed litter was resting on wooden blocks, its eight burly, dark-skinned slaves standing idly next to the poles, staring into space. More worrying was the detachment of armed guards giving pointed looks to passers-by.

I might have kept going, pretending I was someone else, but the hour was late and there was no other way to get to my house. So, I made my way to my front door — or tried to. A short man wearing a well-tailored tunic stepped in front of me. "Spurius Vulpius Felix, I presume?"

"Who wants to know?" I asked.

"Marcus Romilius, sent by Lucius Valerius Flaccus. I have a letter for you." He handed me a wax tablet, Valerius' signet of the aurochs imprinted in the wax seal that matched a circular emblem on his tunic.

I broke the seal.

To Spurius Vulpius Felix, from Lucius Valerius Flaccus, greetings.

My sincere hopes that this letter finds you in good health. I would not disrupt your recuperation so close to the trial, but new evidence has come to light — evidence on which I would greatly appreciate your opinion. Please make yourself available immediately. I have sent a litter to provide you with all the comfort of travel, so you should not need to exert yourself overly much.

I was glad I sacrificed yesterday to Fortuna Redux, her aspect that promises a safe return to home. I had a feeling I would need it.

I climbed into the litter with some assistance, made myself comfortable on the cushions, and closed the curtains. This was a different litter than Valerius had sent for me before and, judging by the number of pillows, presumably this one was used by his wife. There was a bit of a rocking motion as the slaves bent down and hoisted the litter up and soon we settled into a rhythmic jostling as the little convoy made its way up the sides of Vergu. Valerius' *domus* was on the highest reaches of the Clivi Ulterior, so I prepared myself for a long hour of leisurely travel. From the selection of scrolls I had with me, and in consideration of the upcoming trial, I picked *De Legibus Magiarum*, that classical treatise about the laws of incantations and man.

With the curtains closed and with my concentration devoted to reading in the rapidly fading light, I missed how the litter took the wrong turn once we were halfway up the mountain. When the slaves stopped and lowered it gently to the blocks of wood and I opened the curtains, I was facing Cornelia's front door. Valerius had neglected to mention the location of this urgent meeting.

I was completely unprepared. For a moment, I wished I sacrificed yesterday to Fortuna Atrox as well as Fortuna Redux. The savage goddess of blind fate surely had a say in what was about to happen.

There was nothing for me to do, except let the valet assist me in climbing down and make my way inside the lion's den.

***

I was escorted by Cornelia's majordomo to the *triclinium* for what I hoped was nothing more than a session of panicky gossip. I could not imagine what might come up so close to the trial. Valerius' sounded concerned, but our presence at Cornelia's indicated some juicy gossip in preparations for court.

True to my assessment, I found Cornelia reclining with Valerius and his wife Claudia at the central couch; Aemilia and Quintus Aquilius at the right-hand couch; and the left-hand couch occupied by Icilia, meaning the last spot for me to recline was next to her. Cornelia fussed as soon as I hobbled into the room. As I allowed myself to be seated and pampered with soft cushions, Icilia joined the clucking and fussing, hindering more than helping me settle my broken leg. Aemilia and I exchanged a surreptitious glance, but I forced myself to look away. I didn't want to encourage a bout of inappropriate blushing from Aemilia. Nor encourage her in general.

"It's quite alright, I assure you. I am very comfortable."

"It's a shame it's too late to list you as an additional *accusator*," said Aquilius, "or you would have been entitled to compensation from his estate."

"It must have been so harrowing! I am sure Cousin Lucius will look after you," Cornelia shot a quick glance at Valerius. "When he told us what happened on that ship, we were all quite distraught! You could have lost your life."

"True," I said, thinking more of my bonus than her peace of mind. "Ambustus turned out to be completely deranged. Though trained as a *veneficitor*, his skill of combining *veneficium* with the *magia vita* was phenomenal — even if borderline *nefas*, forbidden."

Said Cornelia, "Well, I'm glad he's dead. Which brings me to the reason I invited you all here. Quite by chance, we have come across the most shocking news. We spotted Faucia — Numicius' wife — in the Forum yesterday. On the off chance Numicius had ordered her to avoid me, I sent Icilia after her. Why don't you tell us what she told you, my dear?"

Icilia preened at being the centre of attention. "I made it seem as though I had run into her by accident. She was quite flustered and in a hurry, but I knew the way to her heart. A strange woman, overly keen, and definitely doesn't have the breeding to join the right circles. I enticed her with talks about social events, even hinted at possible inclusions in the Magna

Mater planning committee. The poor woman lapped it up and we ended up having a drink of mint tea and sharing a cake in the nearest shop."

Cornelia coughed lightly. Icilia hurried to the point, lest she lose the focus of the group. "It turned out she was on her way out of the city to visit her family in Ausculum. Apparently, upon hearing of Ambustus' death and the loss of his ship, Numicius flew into a rage like she had never seen before."

"Oh, good," said Aquilius, "that will no doubt impair his judgement at the trial."

Icilia shot him a dark look for interrupting her and continued. "She said that although she is used to his flamboyant and overly dramatic moods, she had never seen such anger in him. She said he was throwing things around in his study, overturning his table, wrecking furniture and shelves. But that was not what made her decide to run away. It was when he stopped his invective and swearing of revenge. He suddenly got quiet, his face contorted into an ugly smile and his eyes took on a mad focus. According to her, he muttered he knows just the thing to avenge Ambustus and ensure no one will ever dare oppose him like that, ever again. He said the wrath of the gods will be as child's play compared to what will happen to you." With that, Icilia looked at Valerius, but I caught Cornelia glancing sidelong at me. Icilia resumed, "She said he sacrificed a grown bull to Mars Ultor, the avenger."

"He already tried his best to kill me," I said, indicating my cast, "but that didn't turn out well for him or his men. The trial is three days from now. I've dealt with his 'enforcer.' Anything he could throw at us now could be avoided by staying at home and increasing one's bodyguards."

"You nearly got killed!" Aemilia said a little too loudly, then blushed.

"Your concern is touching," I responded gently, "but, really, this is what I am paid to do."

"Even more concerning," Icilia wouldn't let the focus shift away from her, "is that Numicius has managed to hire for his defence none other than Marcus Tullius Cicero!"

That got sharp breaths and hisses from everyone but Aemilia.

"Wasn't he a consul?" asked Aemilia.

"And even before that he was the best authority on Quirite law," said Aquilius.

"I was just reading his *De Legibus* on the way here," I added. "Between his knowledge of history, philosophical proclivities, and courtroom experience, if anyone can find a loophole or otherwise sway the judge and jury, he is it. He is our generation's — or any generation's — finest orator."

"Rather than sink into doom and gloom," said Valerius, "I am looking for ways to counteract this news."

That was met with a gloomy silence.

I cleared my throat. "Would you consider bribing the jury?"

"What, and have our own opening statement turned against us?" said Aquilius. "We built the theme of acquittal meaning bribery into all our speeches. It is too late to change strategy and redo them all."

"Then I am not sure what you can do, Lucius Valerius," I said. "Quintus Aquilius will have to write and orate the best damn speech of his career. If he wins, his future is assured. If he loses, there is no shame — and probably will still be quite a step up in his reputation. You have my testimony, with the additional charge of kidnapping and detaining an Egretian citizen. We have all the speeches and everything ready and just enough time to put a final polish on them. Beyond that, it is in the hands of Fortuna."

And that was that. Or it should have been. I was expecting some vigorous discussion to follow but, barring any further revelations, my assessment stood correct. What I was not expecting was Cornelia's following suggestion.

"Even with Ambustus gone and Cicero in his employ, Numicius might still strive to sabotage the case. He's got gangs of ruffians at his disposal. Since much of the outcome relies on

Felix's testimony — he's our star witness after all — it would be best if he stayed here with us till the trial. The best way to protect him is if he were ensconced here; the bodyguards will have just one house to watch."

"Surely that won't be necessary —" I started to protest, but was overridden by Valerius.

"What a great idea! We must guard you, after all. Not only am I protecting my investment, I also have an obligation to you as your employer."

"But —"

"And don't worry, I'll station a few guards around your house to prevent mayhem and damage, just in case."

"Really —"

"Valerius is right," added Aquilius. "Numicius is notorious for getting out of trials when witnesses suddenly choose to leave town. Or worse, are never seen again."

"I assure you —"

"And we could nurse you to health," said Aemilia, smiling sweetly at me.

"That's not —"

"Don't nurse him too well, *deliciae meae*," said Aquilius. "Appearing haggard and with the cast on his leg will make his testimony all the better."

"I'm quite —"

"It's settled, then," from a smiling Cornelia. "You will stay here with us. We shall take care of you until the trial. Cousin Lucius will provide extra guards, both here and for your own *domus*." Valerius nodded at that. "Though, really, I don't think you should venture out. We have all you need right here, and we'll help you practice your testimony."

And thus, I was stuck in a situation promising to rival the best comedies of Plautus. My mind was reeling with all the possible scenarios of night-time romps and mistaken bed-partners. Although my objections failed, I swore to myself to at least lock my door. That, and a big sacrifice to Fortuna, Venus, Juno and any other female goddess.

If I survived that long.

***

After that, the conversation meandered, with people talking in twos and threes about Cicero's glorious and inglorious past, the sorry state of law and order in our times, the decline of public mores, *et cetera*. Wine was flowing freely, and together with the sweet deserts it helped restore and fortify our spirits.

It was then that Icilia jumped to fill a momentary silence.

"Let us not forget Felix," giggled Icilia. "Just imagine the looks on the faces of both Numicius and Cicero, when we spring you on them. They think you're dead! That's what Faucia told me. Your testimony will be spectacular, I just know it." This garnered a murmur of assent. I drank deeply from my wine, not happy at being the centre of attention.

"True," said Cornelia. "And now —"

"This trial has people excited," Icilia, all flushed, continued oblivious to Cornelia's glare. "Everybody knows it's coming! Legal connoisseurs are expecting a grand show. The audacity of working *nefas magia* within city limits! Everyone is observing carefully to know what the new life will be, what they can get away with. I think there will be a lot more of that in the coming days. I predict the *rhones* of the Collegium Incantatorum would make a big show of arrests but will net none but the sellers of trinkets who've sprung up all over town."

"What trinkets?" I asked.

"Haven't you seen? They are everywhere. With the notoriety of the case, some quick-witted individuals have decided to capitalise on the public attention. Word leaked out about the details and they are now selling mock curse tablets out in the open, to amuse the rich and idle. Some admit they are replicas, though they swear they are just like ones used on the *insulae*; some pretend they have managed to procure the original ones — now inert — from the case; some even pretend to sell the real thing! Nonsense, of course, but amusing."

"This is a disgrace," said Valerius. "Our *rhones* have been becoming more concerned with personal glory over the recent years than the good of the city they are elected to administer. We really must pass a law in the assemblies to correct this."

"Good luck with that!" retorted Aquilius. "Between the plebeian tribunes keen to veto anything that simple people might take offence with and the *rhones* and *aediles* currying public favour with lavish feasts, you would be hard-pressed to pass any restrictions on them."

Icilia, sensing the conversation was slipping away from her again, interrupted rather loudly. "I almost forgot! Speaking about all those trinkets reminded me. In her rush to flee her murderous husband, Faucia stole something from him. While Ambustus may be dead, Numicius had in his possession the last curse tablet he prepared, the one he boasted was the most powerful of them all. She overheard him planning to activate it somehow and then use it against Valerius. She gladly gave it to me so that we could dispose of it."

She withdrew a folded sheet of lead and I recoiled in horror. Even in my wine-addled state I could sense the *magia* imbued in that thing. Icilia held it out for all to see, and waves of nauseating malevolence emanated from it, washing over the room like the poet's wine-dark sea.

CHAPTER XXXI

"Put… put that thing down," I said, my voice shaking.

"Oh, don't worry, Felix," Icilia was still smiling, "She said it's completely inert. She stole it before he could activate it and curse us. It will just be something to remember your famous case by. Here, take it," she extended her arm towards me.

"It's real, you stupid woman!" I yelled even as I cringed away. "It's Numicius' revenge! It was all just a ruse to get you to bring it here!"

Her extended hand, still holding the tablet, started to shake. "But… but… how can it be? His man is dead."

The room was spinning, the lamp-cast shadows on the murals dancing like satyrs around bonfires. I knew it was not the wine. I said, "I don't know, Ambustus must have left some instructions behind and Numicius found someone to activate it. Now please, put it down."

But she didn't.

She dropped it.

As the soft metal hit the tiled floor, it bent. Though it's usually done by driving a nail through the sheet, Ambustus had embedded some device in the *tabula* so that the dent was enough to fully release the pent-up curse. A ripple spread from where it lay, sending waves and creases through the floor, walls, furniture. When it hit me, the sensation was like being immersed naked in a barrel of wet slugs; I could feel it crawling over me, leaving slimy trails on my skin as it sought its way into my spirit through every bodily orifice.

I retched, rolled to the floor on my knees, and vomited. The others, less sensitive to *magia*, were becoming ill as well. Worst was Icilia. Her skin erupted in boils and bleeding pustules, oozing out and soaking her clothing. She tried to stand up but collapsed on the floor, convulsing like a fish out of water.

On the walls, the murals became alive. The ripple that went through the room — through us — left them as windows to the scenes they were depicting. And just as perversely, those worlds were corrupted. What was an idyll a moment ago, turned garish — nightmarish. Wolves tore into the lambs, birds fell dead from the ceiling unto us, the ocean water became red when sharks ripped the mermaids apart. I tried to rise and take a step but slipped back down. The floor mosaic of wholesome foods had turned into plates of putrefied, rotten, oozing messes.

Reactions varied from shock to screams. "Out!" I cried. "Everybody out!"

That got them going. I managed to stand with the aid of my crutch and follow suit. I had to limp around the rapidly decomposing, still whimpering mass that once was Icilia.

In the hallways pandemonium reigned. Slaves were running everywhere, terrified and screeching, trying to get away from horrors that had awakened all over the house. A maid wrapped in bed sheets tumbled out of a sleeping cubicle, the sheets slithering about her like snakes. They constricted her chest, muffling her screams, as they tightened until we could hear her ribs crack, forcing her last ragged breath out.

Crossing the garden was sheer lunacy. The bronze statue of the boxer awakened and was beating everyone who came near it to a bloody pulp. We had no choice but to risk it and run under the colonnade on the other side while it was busy with one of Cornelia's bodyguards. It had caught the man, an ex-gladiator, in a wrestler's hold, then managed to slip under him and catch his legs. The statue lifted him by his ankles and swung, crushing his head against a column. Bone shards and brain matter spattered everywhere. The bronze statue made a grab at Valerius' wife, but Valerius picked up a potted plant and smashed it into the statue's face. The pot shattered, covering the boxer's face with dirt and giving Valerius and Claudia the chance to escape.

We made it to the atrium, where a water spirit playing in the *impluvium* was laughing joyously while the door-slave thrashed at her feet in the shallow pool. The silver-bell tinkling of her laughter was a stark, incongruent contrast to the desperate gurgling of the drowning man.

Aemilia supported me as we skirted the pool. She stepped into the vestibule ahead of me, and something flew at her head. She clawed at her face, staggering and falling to her knees, nearly dragging me with her. I stared in horror as the animated wax-mask of one ancestor wrapped itself around her face, choking her. I drew my knife to scrape it off — a feat easier said than done. Cornelia rushed to help me restrain her daughter, lest I scar Aemilia. I slid my knife along her jaw, working the tip toward the mouth rather than her eyes. The *imago* hissed at me in voice as dead as the ancestor it represented. It slithered onto my knife hand, and while Aemilia gasped for air I stared numbly the face of a nameless dead senator wrapped around my fist, looking back at me with hatred in its painted eyes.

I stuck my fist close to the nearest torch, heard and felt the shade scream as the wax of its face melted. I kept my hand in there as long as I could, singeing the hairs on the back of my hand.

In the vestibule, the other masks were fluttering about like a flock of disembodied harpies. Aquilius had the right idea — he covered his head by pulling up his tunic and ran straight through to the main gate, which he managed to unlatch and force open. The rest of us followed him out into the moonlit street.

***

We stood on the other side of the road, opposite Cornelia's *domus*. I could see the building shaking and heaving. Ambustus' previous curses had taken a while to build up their effects and dissipated when the tenants left. This one was different. I witnessed it reach full power almost immediately and I was certain it would remain around for a long time. There was a disparate quality to it, one I just couldn't place.

Some of the slaves remained faithfully by their mistress' side while others ran, never to be seen again. Valerius and Aquilius tried to organise the survivors.

"Are you sure it's safe here?" Aemilia asked me, again. "I have half a mind to keep running, like the slaves."

"It seems to be limited to the building it's affecting," I replied. "Ambustus managed to localise the effect, which doesn't appear to leak beyond the boundary of the estate. I can sense it, but it's as if it's walled in."

"Gods above and below, mother will be devastated," Aemilia said.

I looked at her young face. Her pale skin was marred with a thin red trail where I pried the living wax mask off her. "You should go to her," I said. "She needs you. Just send Valerius and Aquilius over. I need to have a word with them."

She went, and I limped on my crutch back across the street to stand next to the *domus*. My broken ankle was throbbing. While we were making our escape, I had no option but to lean on it heavily, and now I was paying the price.

I put my hand on the outside wall of the house and immediately recoiled, as though I touched hot iron. I could feel the power thrumming, potent, evil. But like hot smoke roiling inside a glass jar, it did not seep outside. Some view the *magia* as a manifestation of divine will, others claim it is mindless forces of nature. Whatever the source, the power held inside Cornelia's house felt angry.

And yet, it felt different from the residues I have witnessed in the other *insulae*. Distinct in a way I could not quite define. Same origin, same pattern — but deeper.

Aquilius and Valerius came to stand with me. "This cannot be ignored," I said. "Your *insulae* suffered far less powerful curses and are situated in a lowdown area where there aren't any voters the *aediles* and *rhones* need concern themselves about. But here, we are right next door to the rich and influential. There will be talk."

"Good!" exclaimed Aquilius. "We can bring it against Numicius in the trial. We'll place it right at the doorstep of the jury, too close for them to overlook."

"Except that you will need to explain how Numicius had done it without Ambustus. Our prosecution is based on proving the link between them."

"But we know it came from him," said Aquilius. "Icilia —"

"Is a woman," I interrupted. "And a dead one at that. Cicero will tear us to pieces with her demise, claiming Valerius is dragging the wrath of the furies about him, causing the deaths of innocents."

"Then, what would you suggest?" asked Valerius.

"Give me a day to see whether I can contain this. For Cornelia's sake, if nothing else. If there's a chance to clear her name in public and restore her *domus* to liveable conditions, it's worth the delay. Take them all with you — Cornelia, Aemilia, and their household. Let me have a litter or a sedan chair and some guards so I can get around to collect what I need. Tomorrow night, I'll have a better story for you to tell."

Valerius stood a moment in thought. The susurration and murmurs emanating from the house were interrupted by a loud crash.

"Agreed," he said. "You have one day. Make it good."

***

This was over my head. I never completed my training in the Collegium Incantatorum. I hadn't built up the skills to deal with such phenomena — though I doubted many living *incantatores* did, either. The years after I left the Collegium I spent learning other trades, performing many tasks. Whenever I had the chance, I practised and furthered my understanding of *magia*. But that was in snatches from various sources, mostly folklore, which I worked to distil to its true essence. Hardly what one might call comprehensive philosophical learning and wisdom.

So why did I beg Valerius for this assignment? Partly due to some sense of duty to my hostess and to my employer. Partly due to some inner indignity, at the callous disregard to our traditions, our gods, our people.

And rage. Seething rage. As my breathing calmed after the rush of events, reflection caused my anger to rise like bile. Aemilia's face would heal with nary a scar, but the memory of her choking gasps as the mask of her own ancestor tried to kill her would remain with me for the rest of my days. The spirits of ancestors are there to protect a family, not turn against them. Had Aemilia succumbed to the mask, it would have been a horrible end, one that would carry its implications into the next world. It also echoed too much of the death of Helena. That old crime might be beyond redemption, but I wanted to make sure whoever tried to cause this one would not only pay, but never produce anything like it again.

There was only one man I could call for help. It was the middle of the night, the streets deserted of honest people. I had no time to waste. As the slaves carried me in a sedan chair from the heights of Vergu to the docks next to the commercial *fora*, I prayed to all the gods I would find him in time.

And find him sane.

CHAPTER XXXII

It was pitch black when I found Araxus, some hours past the middle of the night when the moon had already sunk behind the mountain. Travelling by sedan chair was easier than limping on a broken ankle, but not much faster. I had the slaves carry me around to all sorts of unsavoury places, the bodyguards helping avoid unnecessary trouble. I poked far too many sleeping beggars awake trying to locate the rubbish heap on which Araxus slept.

But find him I did. It wasn't too far from the tavern where I encountered him only this afternoon. I could smell the cheap wine as the guards turned him over and shook him. He grunted, burped, coughed, rolled back over. They shook him again, and he flailed his arms in the air.

"Lea'me alone," he mumbled.

"Stand him up," I said, and two of my bodyguards picked him by his arms and held him upright. His shoulders slumped, his feet dragged on the ground. They gave him a gentle shake and he rewarded them by vomiting at their feet.

I wished I had some water to throw at his face. Instead, I slapped him lightly. "You said you wanted to repay your debt, that you would help me when I was in need. Now is your chance."

His black left eye focused on me and gave me a keen look, but the rest of him still appeared drunk. "Jusht lemme gather my wits, will ya?" he mumbled. "Lead on, brave legate, lead on."

"Carry him," I said to the bodyguards. Though tall, his frame was slender. Years of living on the streets left him thin,

225

almost emaciated. I doubted the beefy guards would have trouble dragging him with us. A third guard carried Araxus' meagre possessions — his walking stick and a bundle of rags. I climbed into my sedan chair, and we started the way back up the mountain to Cornelia's *domus*.

We stopped at several public fountains on the way where I had the slaves splash water at Araxus. Little by little, he came to his senses.

The sky was beginning to pink when we reached Cornelia's. The street outside the house was deserted, bar the few guards Valerius had left behind. They were huddled under a tree on the opposite side of the road, not keen to be any closer to the cursed house. By this time, Araxus was walking under his own power, leaning on his staff. I hoped his mind came back to him, as a deranged *incantator* was the last thing I needed to add to the scene.

"This is the latest of the curses," I said. "Do you remember the ones you helped me dispose of about a month ago?"

He nodded.

"This one is different. The same *verpa* of a *veneficitor* crafted them, but he did something strange. The power burst out of it all at once, instead of gradually." I gave him as accurate an account as I could about events over dinner and what sense I could make of them.

Araxus stood in quiet contemplation for a moment, letting his black eye roam over the cursed building. Susurration and murmurs could still be heard from inside, as well as scratches, screeches, and heavy huffing. It was as though the building had become the holding cell for some exotic menagerie.

"Only one way to find out," he said at last and shuffled towards the gates. I limped behind him.

***

As soon as we crossed the threshold, the sensation of *magia* was palpable, visceral. The force of it hit us full in our faces like a thousand screaming barbarians. The most immediate sensation was the stench. Smells of death and decay assaulted our noses, making me retch. Torches were torn from their sockets and braziers overturned, giving the place a dim fiery glow, as though we entered the domains of the underworld. Strange noises emanated from random directions, making my heart jump. But the worst thing was the feeling on my skin. I cannot put into words the feeling of invisible insects that ran all over me, tingling and itching and almost driving my reason away. I could not imagine — nor did I wish to — what Araxus was seeing with his *visus verum*.

The fluttering flock of Cornelia's ancestors' wax masks dove straight at us from the dark heights. I covered my head with my arms, afraid one would latch on and choke me to death. I drew my dagger and waved it over my head to keep them at bay. Araxus kept his calm and bent down to pick up a dying torch. He whispered to it, and its flame sprang to roaring life. It gave off far more light and searing heat than a torch's natural wont. He waved it around and the wax masks withdrew, fearing the magnified fire.

"That's better," said Araxus. "Let's go."

As he led us deeper into the house, I walked close behind, afraid to find myself cut off from him. My legs were shaking, and not solely due to my throbbing ankle. We skirted the *impluvium* in the atrium. The water spirit had caught three more slaves, drowned them, and arranged their bodies in grotesques postures on the edges. It sat in the middle, humming to itself, its translucent, girlish body reflecting the torch light. Occasionally, it sent tendrils of water to rearrange this corpse or that, like a child playing with clay models. It didn't seem interested in us, and Araxus didn't stop to examine it. I made sure to not step in any wet patch on the floor as I passed by.

The atrium opened to the first of the gardens, ringed by a colonnade. The *triclinium* where we dined was on the other side and I knew beyond it lay the inner parts of the mansion, the family's private quarters. The statue of the boxer was seated on the stone ledge around a fountain. It had removed the bloody bandages from its hands and was washing them in the basin at the base. In the firelight, the waters acquired a deep and menacing red.

Blood spatters covered everything. A few battered corpses were scattered around the garden, only recognisable as once-human by their general shape.

When the statue spied us, it smiled without a trace of guile and began to wrap the bandages around its hands again in the classic boxer's wrap. I remembered Borax dispatching the last animated statue with his iron skillet, but then that one had been made of cheap plaster. This one was bronze, and even with a proper hammer I doubted Borax would have dented it.

Araxus stood quietly, facing the boxer. What he saw I could not fathom. It was then that the similarities between the boxer and the water spirit struck me. Though their actions were horrifying, there was a quality of childlike wonder to them. A child without reason to be sure, playing with some poor insects without understanding the torment it was causing them. It didn't do much to my mood knowing I was one of those insects.

Bandaging completed, the statue stepped towards us. On its third step, the flagstones under its feet shifted and it found itself facing to the side. It stopped, turned back to us, and tried to take another step. The flagstones shifted, and again it was facing away. It cried in frustration, a grating noise that no human throat could make, and tried to charge us. The stones under its feet slid rapidly, rearranging themselves in a tight geometric pattern, causing the statue to run in a little circle. With each step, it sunk lower until it was up to its knees in the ground beneath the floor. It flailed its arms and bellowed in rage and frustration.

Araxus winked his green right eye at me, his left eye never wavering from the animated figure. As we walked away, the statue sat down heavily in place, its legs immersed in the solid floor as though sitting on the side of a pool. As we left it behind, it's fading bellows became lost, forlorn.

We made our way past the peristyle garden to the *triclinium* where the curse tablet exploded. Icilia's body lay where it had fallen, her skin cracked and blackened. Occasionally, a new pustule would pop and burst, oozing pus and blood. She looked deflated, as though her bones had melted inside her body, like a wax model of a woman left in the sun. When Araxus' staff clicked on the tiled floor, a whimper escaped her lips and she shuddered in ragged breaths. She wasn't dead, but trapped inside a decaying body.

Araxus navigated the mess on the floor and extended his staff towards the *tabula defixionis* to draw it to him. Crouching next to Icilia, he considered the tablet. I found it hard to concentrate on anything with the sensations of wild *magia* buffeting my skin. Instead, my mind was filled with thoughts about poor, dim-witted Icilia still alive in her own rotting body.

Araxus' black eye scanned the tablet, reading the inscription through the folded lead. "Do me a favour, will you?" he said. "Go back to the family's *lararium* at the entry and see if there are any ashes and crumbs left from the offerings to the *lares*. Bring whatever you can find there."

To say I did not wish to leave his side and wander alone in the cursed *domus* would be an understatement. I drew a deep breath, picked up a discarded napkin, and made my way back. The boxer was sitting where Araxus has trapped him, picking up pebbles and throwing them listlessly at the columns. Not taking any chances, I hobbled as close to the walls and as far from it as possible. In the atrium, the nymph was still absorbed with the cadavers, like a girl enacting a dinner party with dolls. I skirted her, too, as widely as I could.

The *lararium* was tucked in a corner. It was done in the traditional way of such shrines. An indentation into the wall at waist height, about three feet tall and one foot deep, with an arched top. On the flat stone at the bottom were remnants of candles, ashes from burnt offerings, stains of wine libations, crumbs of broken salt cakes — all the things a family offers its ancestors daily as provisions in their afterlife, and as gifts when beseeching their protection. I gathered all I could into the napkin, folded it carefully, and made my way back.

Araxus was still crouching next to the curse tablet, oblivious to the whimpering Icilia and the rotting mess around him. He handed me the torch and took the folded napkin.

He gently unfolded it, pinched up some of the contents and sprinkled them on the tablet. They sizzled and popped like water sprayed on hot iron. Araxus hummed a happy tune.

"I was right," he said, "you need a priest."

"What are you talking about?"

"Earlier tonight. I came to you and told you you'll need a priest. I was right."

"Yes, I understood that," I said, though our meeting at the tavern seemed days ago. "But can you please explain *why* I need a priest?"

"The way he crafted the *tabulae defixiones* was quite ingenious. Both for effect and his innovative triggering, but mostly for the way he concentrated them inside a single house. Most curse tablets petition the gods above and below, to strike someone wherever they may be. Instead, he petitioned the gods of the household, the *di penates* and the *lares*."

"We knew that from the other tablets," I said. "Why would the household gods and the ancestral spirits turn on the ones they are revered to protect? And how come this curse exploded in full force, while the previous ones built up slowly?"

"That is the second part of his genius. He didn't just petition the household gods but gave them extra vim and vigour by channelling *magia* through spirits which are not used to it. He borrowed the drifts from the major *numina*, gave them to a sleepy little spirit, then poked it with a sharp stick, as it were, to enrage it. Here, he managed to codify in the tablet a quantum of *magia* heretofore unheard of. I dare say, we have barely begun to see the full extent of the curse's effects."

It took me a moment to digest all that. I wanted to query him further, but Araxus cut me off. "Shall we perhaps defer the philosophical discussion about celestial matters to another day? We have some more pressing things to attend to." As if in emphasis, a loud crash came from deeper in the house.

"So how do we deal with it?" I asked. "And what does any of it have to do with priests?"

"Because this time he gave the household spirits too much power. Rather than merely making the extant spirits annoyed, he — intentionally or not — created something bigger. We are witnessing, my dear Felix, something few mortals have ever seen. The birth of a god."

***

I admit I gaped at him with slack jaws, like a country bumpkin. When I found my wits I said, "I doubt our *Collegium Sacrorum* would have much knowledge of this either. First, they'll argue, then they'll confiscate everything, and finally a temple will be erected here. We'll see the start of a new cult. None of which particularly helps anyone. Well, except the neighbours, but you know who I mean."

"All we need," Araxus said, "is to appease the god. Right now, he's like a babe — an angry babe, stronger than Hercules, but still just a newborn. Give him the right offerings and keep him sleeping."

"We'd need a priest to do that."

"Which is what I came to tell you about," he beamed up at me.

"And we're back to dealing with the priests of the *Collegium Sacrorum*."

"You could do it," Araxus said.

"I'm no priest," I replied.

"Isn't every man the master of his own household?"

It took me a moment to understand what he was talking about. When realisation dawned on me, Araxus added, "Think like the big spectacles, but choose something appropriate for a newborn. I'll hold things at bay here, while you gather the necessities."

With that, he sat cross-legged and leaned his shoulder on his walking stick. He closed his eyes, though I knew it would not stop his black eye from seeing. With a smile, he started to hum a childhood ditty softly. And, like a strange puzzle with moving pieces, floor tiles, wall dados, and discarded miscellanea, moved and slid and rearranged themselves continually. It was like being inside a paper as it is folded; inside a kaleidoscope.

I rushed off to collect what I needed.

Chapter XXXIII

My first stop was Valerius' *domus*. It was not far away from Cornelia's and I got there at the beginning of the second hour of the day. The house was in uproarious commotion. Valerius had taken Cornelia, Aemilia and their entire household into his home. The more hysterical of Cornelia's slaves had run off, but even those who stayed behind were finding it hard to function. Valerius' own staff were trying to find places for everybody, people were running around, and gossip was rampant.

I found Cornelia ensconced with Valerius, Aemilia, Aquilius, and Valerius' wife in the master's study, hiding from the ruckus.

"Felix!" Cornelia exclaimed. "Have you been able to remove the curse from my home?"

"Not yet, but I know what needs to be done. I'll need to officially rent your house. I'm afraid I can't pay its worth, but this is only for a night or two."

"What are you talking about?" Aemilia asked.

I took a deep breath. "This curse is not like the others. Ambustus managed far greater damage. It's not just about removing the tablet and rendering it inert. I'm afraid I will need to consecrate your house."

"Why not get a priest to do it?" Asked Aquilius.

"Because then there will be too many questions," I replied, "and Cornelia might be forced to donate her house to become a temple. If, on the other hand, I am the man of the house, it is within my right to sacrifice to the gods inside it. I've spent the night there before, but only as a guest. This time, I should do so as a *paterfamilias*."

"Have you thought of the other half of your promise?" Valerius asked. "Did you find a good story for us to spread about those events?"

"I'm still working on it," was all I could respond.

"What do you need, then?"

I addressed Valerius, "Ask one of your scribes to draft a simple rent agreement. Let's say two nights, just to be on the safe side. I'll pay Cornelia a single gold *aureus*," I smiled meekly, "which, symbolically, should be a high enough price. Then we sign it here in front of you all as witnesses. That will give me the moral right under human and divine law to carry out the necessary duties."

"And what are those?" Asked Aemilia.

"That's the other thing I need to ask of you, Lucius Valerius. Please dispatch a slave to the market, and buy me a piglet, a lamb, and a calf. They should be as perfect, as unblemished, as possible. The younger the animals your slaves can find, the better. Alive, of course — not a carcass from a butcher. I need young, flawless, male lamb, piglet, and calf."

There was a moment of quiet as the implications of my request sunk in.

Aemilia broke the silence. "I thought this was done with adult ram, pig, and bull, and for the lustration of the temple of Iovis Pater."

"It's actually performed quite often. Farm owners do it routinely to consecrate their farms and beseech Mars for protection."

Aquilius cleared his throat. "I may not be an expert on these matters, but might I suggest something? Cornelia, if you trust this man, then best make the contract not for rent but for the sale of your *domus*. It'll give Felix more rights and powers within it, which surely will give his actions more legitimacy over the property — in this world and otherwise. For your protection, we would also draw a counter-sale contract, to be fulfilled in a day or two, when Felix will sell you back the house."

"And probably a will too, leaving the house to Cornelia," added Valerius. "Just in case."

***

And so, I found myself the owner of a lucrative city mansion worth a million times more than what I paid for it. I liked to think Valerius was merely being methodical when we drafted my new will as I certainly had no plans to test it by refusing to sell the house back. Assuming my survival, of course.

I stopped at my house briefly to pick up some personal belongings, enough to symbolise my residency and ownership. I got my toga, that most conspicuous symbol of Egretian citizenship. I didn't have any wax masks — none of my ancestors achieved noble status to earn the rights of *ius imagines* — but I picked up a plate painted with a dancing child and a dog that belonged to my grandfather's grandfather; my family's *lares*.

Valerius had lent me some bodyguards, some of whom I left in the care of Dascha, to ensure Numicius wouldn't lay a curse — or plain old violence — on my home.

I led the slaves in a procession back to Cornelia's house: a couple of guards at the front; myself, riding as master and leader in a sedan chair carried by four hefty men; two more guards; a slave holding a squealing piglet; one carrying a lamb, frantically trying to jump off so it could prance around; a third, leading a calf with a rope — the calf was quite interested in the wares of every flower merchant we passed, and the slave had to tug the rope to keep it from munching their produce and my money; a last slave carrying some wrapped packages of what might have appeared as kitchen utensils; and a final pair of guards brought up the rear.

Processions are an important part of our life. Every event worth mentioning begins with a procession, from a bride travelling to her husband's house to priests making a show of their offerings as they make their way to a temple. I tried instead to appear as merely a man of eccentric tastes in pets or cuisine.

What we were about to do was borderline between religion and magic, and neither side of that equation liked the other much.

When we reached the *domus*, things in the street had calmed down. I didn't glean any gossip — travelling by chair or litter removes one from the street — but I got the impression none of the neighbours had yet picked up on anything beyond some wild party. Araxus had been keeping everything under wraps. Regrettably, those errant runaway slaves would spread unsavoury rumours. Perhaps there was still a chance to claim it was just the wrong kind of mushrooms in the soup.

The time was past midday and we still had a lot to perform before nightfall. I left my entourage on the street. I didn't want to bring the animals in until it was their time and there was no point in the slaves and guards coming in at all. The constant shifting of tiles and walls was still going on inside, but at a more languid pace. A picture of a young couple left the wall on which it was hanging and slid in front of me as I crossed the atrium. It moved from the wall to the ceiling, then down a fluted column, and even its wooden frame acquired the contours of whatever surface it was sliding along. Yet, it moved in an almost listless manner, as though unsure of its destination. It finally came to rest half-skewed at the bottom of another wall, one of its corners folded unto the floor. Whatever Araxus was doing to direct and redirect the flow of *magia* around the house was slowing down.

I found Araxus exactly where I had left him. His countenance, never healthy since the curse, had taken on a grey pallor, worse than I'd ever seen. Keeping the forces of *magia* at bay in the house was taking a heavy toll on him. Since the curse had begun at night, the coming darkness would cause a resurgence of its power. I needed to complete the ceremony before sundown, lest Araxus would be overwhelmed and the wild *magia* consume us.

I reached out to touch his shoulder, but he opened his eyes before I did. The pupil of the right green eye, the sane one, was dilated so only a thin ring of green was visible. The black curse inside him was taking over his mind, his spirit.

"I have what we need," I said. "It will take me some time to set up and perform the *suovetaurilia* properly."

He stared at me for a long moment, his face slack, before nodding.

I hurried back out, limping as fast as my broken ankle would allow.

CHAPTER XXXIV

Suovetaurilia. A pig — *sus*, a sheep — *ovis*, and a bull — *taurus*, are sacrificed together in an act of purification, a *lustratio*. The public in Egretia is aware of the big spectacles, of the sacrifices to one of the main deities carried each five-year *lustrum* period, or when consecrating a new temple. But out in the country it is a common practice to purify a piece of land for good harvest, beseeching Mars — the protector of fields, not the warrior — for his favour.

I had to adapt this to fit a personal scope in a city-scape and for the purposes we had in mind. But first things first. I needed someone to handle the beasts, as even baby animals are too much for a man with a broken ankle.

I stepped outside and offered a large purse of coin for any slave or guard willing to assist me. Valerius, I was sure, would not mind the extra expense. They all looked away. I doubled the sum. The four who accepted first got in, the remainder I instructed to stay outside — not that they would have come in of their own will, but rather that they wouldn't use the opportunity to make a hasty retreat back to Valerius.

None of the ones who came with me knew how to drape a toga properly. They were kitchen slaves and guards, so, really, I shouldn't have expected them to know. But with enough instruction, one of them managed to drape me in it till I was dressed as a free Egretian citizen. I pulled a fold of my toga over my head like the priests do. That was not a requirement to work the *magia*, but symbolism helps in concentration, I found.

I placed the image of the dancing boy and his dog in the *lararium*, broke a bread bun, poured a drop of wine, and prayed briefly. I thus installed my own family *lares* into the house, further affirming my ownership and rights.

Next, the actual purification ceremony, the *suovetaurilia*.

And immediately I hit a snag. According to the manual of *De Agricultura* and the custom I had observed, the sacrificial animals should be led in a procession around the perimeter of the site — be it a farm or a temple. This was not possible in a house inside the town where inner walls touched the outer ones and gardens were on the inside, leaving no space to walk around the circumference. Instead, I led the slaves throughout the building, visiting all the rooms and ensuring we passed next to the outer walls as often as possible. We visited all parts of the *domus* — public, private, slave quarters, kitchens, storage. Everywhere were the signs of the bloody mayhem the *lar* wrought when it first awakened. Worst were the latrines, though. My stomach still revolts at the memory of what happened to the young scullery maid caught there.

It took us a long while to complete the circuit. The house was large, its rooms many. I had to stop often for rest, as my ankle was wearing me down after the tiring day and night without sleep. The animals, at least, became subdued inside. As if sensing the ambient danger, all playfulness left them. They huddled close to the slaves who held their ropes tightly, themselves unsure and disturbed.

As we walked, I kept repeating the charm

Cum divis volentibus quodque bene eveniat, mando tibi, Mani, uti illace suovitaurilia fundum domum terramque meam quota ex parte sive circumagi sive circumferenda censeas, uti cures lustrare.

That with the good help of the gods success may crown our work, I bid thee, Manius, to take care to purify my house, my land, my ground with this *suovetaurilia*, in whatever part thou thinkest best for them to be driven or carried around.

Manius, for those unfamiliar with our rural colloquialisms, is a generic name for the *Di Manes*, the chthonic spirits of dead ancestors who could intercede with the gods on our behalf.

Once the circuit was complete, we led the animals back through the central courtyard to the *triclinium*. The sun cast long shadows, Sol guiding his fiery chariot to its nightly hiding place behind Vergu.

First came the offering to Ianus and Iovis Pater. Ianus, the god of beginnings and endings, of the old and the new, of transitions. Iovis Pater, best and greatest of the gods, the patron of our city, our people. Nothing could change without the blessings of these two. I offered them hard salt cakes and libations of wine.

This was followed by the traditional prayer to Mars the Protector.

> *Mars pater, te precor quaesoque uti sies volens propitius mihi domo familiaeque nostrae...*

Father Mars, I pray and beseech thee that thou be gracious and merciful to me, my house, and my household; to which intent I have bidden this *suovetaurilia* to be led around my land, my ground, my house; that thou keep away, ward off, and remove sickness, seen and unseen, barrenness and destruction, ruin and unseasonable influence; and that thou permit my business, my livelihood, my family, my standing to flourish and to come to good issue, preserve in health my progeny and my clients, and give good health and strength to me, my house, and my household. To this intent, to the intent of purifying my house, my land, my ground, and of making an expiation, as I have said, deign to accept the offering of these suckling victims.

The original prayer is about harvests and plantations,

but I fitted it to more mundane city business. Normally, when adapting such common practices into practical incantations I would strip them to their bare bones — often literally — and imbue them with proper *magia*. I would gather the forces around me and use the quintessential elements of the folk practices to give intent to my desired effect. Not this time. These forces were beyond my ability to control. I acted merely in priestly duties and left the incantations and manipulation of energy to Araxus and his superior knowledge.

I could feel his work around me, manipulating the flows of *magia*. He did so with but a few muttered incantations, hardly audible. My skin tingled as though I was standing in a draughty room with light breezes buffeting me, constantly changing direction, temperature, scents. It made it hard to concentrate, but I did my best to let it flow through me and guide my actions.

Then came the meat of the matter, so to speak. The sacrifice of the pig, the ram, and the bull. Or piglet, lamb, and calf, on this occasion. When Araxus nodded at me, I held my knife in one hand and took hold of the piglet. I had to almost lie on top of it as I could not hold the squirming animal and balance on a broken and weary leg. I held it down, said, "Father Mars, to this intent deign to accept the offering of this suckling victim," and slit its throat.

The blood spattered warm over my fingers, gushing out in spasms as the animal gave up its life. I felt, more than heard, Araxus enchant an incantation in tandem with my actions. The pig's blood ran over the floor mosaics, draining from the little stones into the grooves between them. It ran in channels, spreading like tendrils out and away from us, up the walls, the columns, and onto the ceiling. When it reached the *tabula defixionis*, still lying where Icilia had dropped it, it hissed and bubbled and steamed. The mosaics around it blackened like a piece of paper marred by a fiery brand that failed to light it. I sensed the sacrifice take a tentative hold on the room and a certain calmness enclosed us inside that cocoon of fine spiderweb made of blood.

The custom dictates that after each sacrifice we must look

for signs of the gods' approval. Normally, an augury of watching the skies for the flights of birds. We would step outside, mark an area in the sky, and observe which birds the gods sent, how they flew, in which direction, and a plethora of other signs. Such signs take their time to appear, and we just didn't have the time this close to sundown. So, when the piglet ceased its spasms, I slit its belly and separated its liver from the rest of the organs.

It's ironic, given my chosen profession, that augury was my weakest subject at the Collegium. Many times since I began working as an investigator, I wished I had paid more attention to my tutors. While I was still trying to make sense of the bulges and splotches of colour on the bleeding liver, Araxus proclaimed in a deep and raspy voice, "The omens are good. Proceed."

The thought struck me that, as I had been cocky and rash throughout this case, I was here once more. If the sacrifice was not accepted, if the omens were bad, the instructions were to repeat it again, using a slightly different formula of prayer, or — in our case — of incantation. I could only hope Fortuna had had enough of toying with me.

The lamb was bleating piteously when I took hold of it. It must have been a month old, still suckling, no doubt wishing to spend its life prancing in a sunny meadow rather than receiving the honour of showing human reverence to the gods. But just like we are in the thrall of the celestials, farm animals are here to serve us.

I held the lamb tightly, repeated the incantation of "Father Mars, to this intent deign to accept the offering of this suckling victim," and cut the animal's throat in one swift motion. Yet again I could feel my skin buffeted by unseen flows of *magia* as Araxus was shaping them around the sacrifice and sending them into the house.

The forces felt different now, though I could not say how or why. On the physical plane, the blood tendrils rushed out again. This time they elongated in thin rivulets. Two went to encircle the curse tablet, flowing in the spaces between the mosaics in tightening concentric circles. They managed to envelope the tablet, though the blood dried, cracked, and blackened almost immediately. The rest of the blood, rather than climb up the walls and ceiling as before, rushed out the door to spread into all corners of the house.

When the time came and life left the lamb, I slit its belly open and laid its innards for Araxus to inspect.

He was silent for long moments. He spoke, again his voice rasping, "The signs are ambiguous. Repeat with the second formula."

"I didn't bring another lamb…"

His green eye looked up at me and rolled in its socket in exasperation. He did not speak though, his voice and body taken over by his black aspect. I stared mutely at him. I was about to ask if I should go and procure another lamb, when he spoke again in that chthonic voice, "Sacrifice the calf, but beseech the wife, too, and your patroness."

An unorthodox sacrifice, to be sure, but none of what we were doing here appeared in the orthodoxy of the collective *mos maiorum* or the accumulated knowledge of the *incantatores*. I took the calf by the rope and led it closer. I prayed.

> Father Mars, if aught hath not pleased thee in the offering of those sucklings, I make atonement with this last victim; Lady Venus, I pray and beseech thee that thou intercede on our behalf with your husband, make my land, my ground, my house a place of hearth; Fortuna, she by whose will all endeavours rise or fail, I implore thee as thy faithful servant, to grant us success and clemency in this lustration.

I cut the animal's throat, letting the blood gush over my hand and out onto the floor. As Araxus pushed his incantation hard through the flow of blood, the poor calf nearly exploded, its body drained in a single heartbeat. The blood rushed out, not trickling into rivulets but spreading aggressively into the house. Where it met the curse tablet, it rose up like a wave in a storm and crashed over it, as if hitting a breakwater. It drained over and through it, filling the etchings in the soft lead. Then another such wave of blood crashed over the tablet, and a third. Where the blood ran through the symbols, it blurred and effaced them rather than pooling in the grooves.

With the destruction of the *tabella*, it was as though someone closed a shuttered window to a busy street. A hum that had been present since last night suddenly dimmed. It was not extinguished, but muted, sleeping. I could feel the rest of the *domus* settling as well, like a ship moored at night in a calm berth.

The calf's carcass lay on its side. I gripped my knife, lest my anxiety make me botch the cut, then I sliced it open from groin to sternum. Its viscera flopped out, drained of blood. I let Araxus examine the liver in silence, holding my breath.

At long last he proclaimed, "The omens are good. The sacrifice has been accepted. Now seal it by burning the offerings, partaking in the meat, and allowing the smoke to permeate the house."

And with that, Araxus keeled over and lay unmoving.

***

His skin was a blueish-grey. I could not feel a pulse. Only when I put my ear to his face could I detect a faint, wheezing breath. The effort of sedating a newborn god had almost cost him his life. I snatched the flask of wine brought for libations and forced a bit into his mouth. I could feel his pulse then. Weak, erratic, but beating. His chest moved in slow, shallow breaths. I placed a discarded cushion from one of the dining couches under his head, tucked a cover over him, and made him comfortable. Even if he survived till morning, there was no telling what effect it would have on his mind, his curse.

I couldn't let Araxus' sacrifice be in vain. The ceremony had some final tasks to be completed before sunset. I cut up a piece of meat from each of the sacrificial victims and gathered the offal as well, keeping it separate. Leading the slaves in yet another procession, we headed to the mansion's kitchens. There we built up a fire, burned the offal completely and roasted the pieces of meat. I cut a bite of each meat, prayed, chewed, and swallowed. The slaves who accompanied me took a bite of each as well, as a representative feast by me and mine.

The burned offal went with some live coals into metal bowls and I instructed the slaves to walk around the house and waft the smoke into every room before I made my way back to the *triclinium* to check on Araxus.

His body was not there.

I searched to no avail. He was no longer in the *domus*. Eventually I gave up, dismissed the slaves, and sent them back to Valerius with a hastily scrawled missive. My night would be spent sleeping in the house to further cement the ritual, to ensure that human ownership was restored. If things went amiss with the ceremony, if the gods did not accept my supplication, if Araxus failed in shaping the *magia* of the rampant *lar* — the slaves would not help me. There was no point in endangering them.

It had been a day, a night, and a day without sleep, traipsing on a broken ankle and exerting myself, and still sleep did not come easy. I lay on the bed in the master's cubicle, the bed on which Cornelia and I had spent pleasurable nights, and looked around in the dim light cast by my single candle. Though the house was nominally mine, her stamp was on everything from wall decorations to the boxes of unguents on a side table. Would the ceremony work? With all the adaptations and shortcuts Araxus and I took, would the gods be offended? This was no hedge wizardry, a modification of folk ritual with some minor incantation principles. No — this was the fabric of our religion, of our mutual relationship with our gods.

And if it did work, come morning I would have to find an explanation for Cornelia and Valerius, something to put gossiping tongues to rest and assuage nosey neighbours calling on the *rhones* for protection.

CHAPTER XXXV

I don't know at what hour I fell asleep, but when I woke up the sun was high in the sky. A lark was chirping happily. I clambered out of bed, my leg almost as sore as on the day Numicius broke it. I found my crutch and limped outside. Dappled shadows danced around the inner courtyard, cast from trees sighing in the gentle breeze. The sun-warmed flagstones were invitingly pleasant under my feet. A bird was splashing happily in a bubbling fountain. And yet, deeper in the shadows of the colonnades, I could still see broken furniture and bodies of dead men and women, reminders of the *lar's* violent awakening.

All around the house, an incongruent sense of peace lay over the wreckage. The ritual had worked, but earthly matters still needed attending to. I lit a taper from the embers in the hearth and limped to the atrium. At the *lararium* I lit incense, broke a salt-bread cake, and prayed to my ancestors and to every spirit that would listen.

Valerius' slaves with the sedan chair were waiting patiently for me outside on the street. I climbed in and they carried me the short distance to his house.

Seated in the loggia and enjoying the view and the fine watered wine, I recounted the previous night's events for Valerius, Cornelia, and Aemilia. Their relief at the restoration of their *domus* was obvious. I cautioned about work that still needed to be done, such as clearing the home of all signs and remnants of the violence.

Aquilius arrived just before midday and I had to retell

the story. He quizzed me at length with his lawyer's eye for detail. Snacks and wine were brought in, consumed, and cleared, before he satisfied himself that he knew everything pertinent to the trial.

"What shall we tell inquisitive minds?" Valerius asked.

"On the assumption that, as previously discussed, we will not be referring to this last curse in the case," Aquilius nodded assent at my words, "we still cannot hide events — gossip will be rampant by now — and so, without sullying the good name of Cornelia, I would suggest we take the offence, and neatly lay the blame at the feet of this year's *rhones*."

My suggestion was met by open stares.

"Icilia was, like you, a devotee of the Magna Mater, am I correct?" I continued, and Cornelia hmm'ed an acknowledgement. "The very same goddess Numicius claims his mother was discomfited by and the reason he wants to erect a temple to the Bona Dea. Yet aren't they both maternal goddesses? Caring and terrible at once, but, in essence, similar? We shall say that this occurrence is merely a failure of our priests, our *rhones*, our *incantatores*, and, indeed, of the senate itself. They failed to honour this new aspect of an old goddess. The Great Mother's statue was imported to our city when our ancient enemy was at the gates, when the gods were sending stones from the skies as signs. Our women were the ones to pull her into the city, and still organise a yearly feast for her. Yet, clearly, she has not been fully accepted. I think it's time for Valerius to stand up in the senate and deliver an impassioned speech about this. Whether we win or lose at the trial, he could allude to Numicius' usage of illegal curses within city limits and the events which transpired at Cornelia's house, and beseech the Senate and the *collegia* to lay their differences aside and take divine matters in a firmer state hand. We should accept all the gods who helped us, rather than let dissent about worship bring the wrath of the goddess down on us. After what we'll expose at the trial, whatever the result, they'll love taking a poke at Numicius."

It didn't take much more convincing to sell them on

the idea. Valerius and Aquilius were accomplished orators and grasped the value in this approach. Cornelia and Aemilia, lacking a formal voice, understood there were slim chances to escape official enquiry, but at least this way offered a diversion away from them, and potentially — with some luck — they might even turn it to social capital amongst their peers.

"So, what now?" Aemilia asked. "Can we move back into our house?"

"I'm not sure I'm ready to," Cornelia shuddered.

"The contract to sell it back to you can be executed whenever you wish," I said. "The house has been purified and is fit — at least in that respect — for habitation; but it still lies in chaos. I would like to perform certain ceremonies, both before and after you buy it back. Then there is also the mundane aspect of cleaning up the mess left behind. I can take some of the slaves with me — as many as you can spare — and have them remove the dead bodies and scrub the place down. Although…"

"What is it?" Cornelia asked, with a tremor of anxiety.

"Icilia was a citizen and, I believe, a widow. Are you certain she has no male relatives left? Her remains are in no condition to be viewed publicly. And what about the other dead? Do you know who were freed and who were slaves? I'd like to give them all a proper cremation and last rites, as due."

In the end both Cornelia and Aemilia elected to come back with me for the gruesome task of identifying the dead of their household.

* * *

It was a harrowing experience, but one we managed to deal with swiftly. By late afternoon, the contingent of slaves we brought collected their dead comrades under the colonnades of the peristyle garden and covered them with sheets. Slaves to one side, freed men and women to the other.

That just left the body of Icilia. The poor woman finally passed away overnight. I wished to protect Cornelia from the gruesome sight, but she made her way through the house and to the dining room before I could stop her. She screamed and collapsed to her knees, vomiting. Aemilia started to her mother's side, but I grabbed her by the hand, staying her. I gently helped Cornelia up, and brought her to Aemilia, who embraced her and lead her away.

With the women gone, I flagged a passing slave to assist me with Icilia. I did my best to cover her body myself. Her skin was raw, eaten away by oozing boils and open lacerations. And, though her cheekbones were poking out, her face was recognisable. The look of abject misery in her dead eyes would stay with me till the day I die.

I laid the sheet on top of her body, but when I tucked it under her the skin broke, rancid bloody goo soaking through the linen. Her insides flopped and wobbled, turned into a wine-coloured gelatinous mess. I called for slaves to bring more sheets and a stretcher. We managed with some effort to roll her — scoop her, more like it — onto the stretcher and cover her with fabric. It was hard to recognise that a human body lay there. She, unfortunately, had to receive a quick and hasty cremation, without the usual observances that befitted her social status.

I offered Cornelia to send the slaves with Icilia's body to the funeral plateau on the path up Vergu that night, but she insisted on being present for her friend's final rites.

"We'll do it first thing tomorrow then," I said. "Valerius' men will take the slaves and freedmen to the temple of Libitina for cremation and we shall arrange a private ceremony for Icilia. You should go now to Valerius."

"Are you not coming with us?" Cornelia asked.

"I should stay. There is work here yet to be done and every night I spend sleeping under this roof and sacrificing for the new *lar* which now inhabits the *domus* will further strengthen the incantation Araxus put in place."

"I am not leaving without you," she refused flatly. "It was my home and will be again."

"Mother, you should listen to Felix," Aemilia implored her. "There is nothing but death and decay here. Let him finish his work."

"I don't care." Cornelia was adamant. "I would feel safer with him here, than without him anywhere else."

"You would have to sleep in a guest room," I tried a different tack. "The house is formally mine and I must sleep in the master's bedroom. Take Aemilia and let Valerius and Claudia's girls pamper you this night so you get some rest."

But she wouldn't hear of it. And, of course, Aemilia would not leave her mother behind. And so, the three of us ended jammed together on the master's bed. I slept between the two women, engulfed by the warmth of each.

Or attempted sleep. I lay in bed for long hours, awake and listening to the women' soft breaths, thinking circles about my situation. There were only two days to the trial, and with the mess at the house we had no time to prepare further. The addition of Marcus Cicero was bad news for Valerius and Aquilius. Although past experience taught me happy customers tend to be generous with bonuses, my fees were not contingent on the trial's outcome. Likewise, Numicius' avowed revenge did not worry me. One does not survive in my business without making the occasional enemy, and he played his strongest moves already.

What did worry me were the two lovely ladies sleeping next to me. Cornelia had, in the past, regarded me as entertainment, though her concern tonight seemed genuine. Could she have developed deeper feelings towards me? Even so, if she found out I kissed her daughter, then Numicius would not be the only one trying to kill me before the trial. Add this to the fact that I still had to deal with Aemilia, resist her charms — and the pull of my heart — and direct her towards Aquilius. That was an unbearable thought as she nestled against me, the perfume in her hair tantalisingly warm and close.

I am no Cupid, nor do I wish my life to resemble a tawdry comedy. I might one day fathom the mysteries of the *numina*, but I doubt I will ever understand women. Best to just sacrifice to every female goddess out there and pray for protection for the women and me, then leave them both to their own lives.

CHAPTER XXXVI

After breakfast — consisting of whatever the slaves managed to buy from nearby vendors — I went to the family's *lararium* with a chunk of bread, some salt, and a cup of wine to perform the rites as befitting the *paterfamilias*, the master of the house, praying to the *lares* for appeasement.

For those less familiar with our home culture, our attitudes towards gods and *magia* can appear confusing. On the one hand, our *collegia* are all about teaching and disseminating knowledge in a practical manner. From military engineering to medicine, from mathematics to rhetoric, we put abstract ideas to worldly use. Both philosophy and folklore present enchantments that are woven throughout our life, but while Collegium graduates perform precise and scientific incantations, the common people attempt to influence the world via the ubiquitous gods.

Every street has temples and shrines to deities large and small. We claim our providence and the worldly success of our great city to be the *de facto* blessing of Iovis Pater, especially in his Optimus Maximus guise, the protector and patron of Egretia. We hold annual events and sacrifices. We consult the gods about everything, see them at every corner. We bring out their statues to the games, even as the *incantatores* use enchantments to create fantastical shows in the arena.

Inside the home, daily life is governed by an equal number of deities. Outsiders know that the great god Ianus is the god of beginnings and endings, and by extension the god of doorways. Yet to an Egretian householder, the doorway is under the rule of Forculus, but Limentinus is in charge of the threshold while Cardea is the goddess of the hinges. Ianus also has a role in the beginning of life — but so do thirty-odd others. From Dea Mena who ensures the menstrual cycle to Prema the goddess of the sex act — though Innus is the god of sexual impulse, lead-ing Mutunus Tutunus the phallic god (not to be confused with the over-sized one, Priapus) to enter the female by the grace of Pertunda. Ianus allows the seed of man to go in and for the baby to go out, but the seed — provided by Saturn — is ejaculated on the command of Liber Pater. And that's even before conception, and pregnancy, and birth, and infancy.

Yet are these gods separated from the *numina*, their divine spirits? Are the gods real, human-like in their attributes as the Hellicans depict them, or is that merely a human failing of reason, a misunderstanding of the powers and energies which swirl about our world? To whom are we sacrificing — spirits that care for us and grant us favours, or forces of existence, which, like eddies and currents in the ocean, are no more conscious than a sea storm?

A question for philosophers.

I concentrated on my observations and applied knowl-edge. That the *magia* emanating from the *numina* could be felt and used to manipulate our world was obvious. That the gods could be bartered with, pleaded to, and entered into contract with, was also evident. Whether they were one and the same, two roads up the same mountain, or even something else entire-ly, concerned me not. I used each when it presented the best opportunity.

And right then, the opportunity I had was to safeguard the women whose house I was purifying, to preserve them from harm. To achieve this security, I supplicated the ancestral house-hold gods to accept the new one as a *genius loci*, a spirit of the place. Araxus started the binding process, but it was up to me to complete it for posterity.

That my feelings for both women were mixed and that their — and my — well-being required each remaining unaware of the other's affection towards me was a mere detail.

So, in breaking the bread, sprinkling the salt, and pouring a libation of wine, I added just a little extra intention, a gathering and shaping of *magia* to power the protection beyond a mere uninformed prayer.

Whether my focusing of *magia* for the *lar* helped or not, my requests were answered. While both Cornelia and Aemilia spent time with me that day — attending to the funerals and the tasks of cleaning the house, assuring my comfort with my broken leg, helping prepare for the trial, and anything else they could think of — there were no embarrassing incidents. Both were affectionate, but not overly so while in the presence of the other. I wondered how long it would last until someone slipped.

***

Icilia's funeral was carried out without a hitch. Only our close circle attended to save her the embarrassment of being cremated in shrouds. I myself placed the coin between her teeth, though I blocked the view with my back when I reached inside the linen bands. No priest was present, so it fell to me to say the appropriate prayers. Stupid and naive as the woman was, and despite the misfortune she brought down on Cornelia and Aemilia, I still performed her last rites to the best of my abilities. No one deserved her fate; she paid dearly enough already, and her shade should rest in the underworld.

On the way back, we stopped at Valerius' house to execute the counter-sale contract — signed, witnessed, sealed, and paid for with the same gold coin I gave her — restoring Cornelia as the owner of her family's ancestral *domus*. Later, at her home, we checked that all bodies had been carted away to the necropolis, the bloody stains scrubbed from the walls, and wreckage cleaned from all rooms. It's amazing what slaves can achieve when promised freedom.

"One more thing I would do," I said. "Though the house had been purified and the new *lar* bound to protect it, I wish to carry out a last ceremony to help turn this house into a home."

"Should I send slaves for more sacrificial offerings?" Cornelia asked.

"No need. This is for the *dii penates* and the hearth, so we'll use whatever can be found in your pantry." I hobbled in the direction of the kitchen.

"Last time you were there, you bent my cook's favourite pan," she answered, "and with no results."

"I am not trying to do anything as complex as last time. That was an incantation which ran afoul of more powerful forces. No, this time it's merely to propitiate the gods, bring a blessing on the home, and help ensure our success in the trial." I refrained from adding 'and my own safety once you discover I kissed your daughter.'

"Isn't the time better spent honing your testimony to face Cicero?"

"I have gone over it backwards and forwards several times and I know it by heart. I'll remind you Valerius hired me, indeed on your recommendation, since this case has elements of the metaphysics. Let me do what I do best and attend to everyone's interests."

We reached the kitchens and cleared them of confused slaves. The cooks were busy in preparations for dinner and I hoped my actions would not spoil the pre-trial meal.

I gathered what I needed — flowers, figs, grapes; the carcass of a young lamb the cook had skinned but hadn't yet roasted; wine, salt, bread; knives. I already wore a toga from this morning's funeral.

"So, what exactly are you doing?" asked Aemilia.

"An incantation to appease the gods. Or goddess, in this case. It's dedicated to Maia, the most ancient of female divinities."

"Why her?"

Because sleeping next to both you and your mother raised impure thoughts in all concerned and I'd like her protection, I did not say out loud. Instead, "She is the protector of life and home for our people. This case started with tenants being haunted in their own homes. Their *lares familiares* failed them, the *lares loci* turned on them. I shall ask for her assistance in avenging the crimes against her children."

"But aren't such rites best performed by women? She is a goddess, after all."

"In some cases, yes. Vesta's priestesses are her Vestal Virgins, yet they are under the official jurisdiction of the *pontifex maximus*, a man. Your mother is a follower of the cult of Magna Mater, the Great Mother, who is served by both women and eunuchs."

"You are certainly neither," said Cornelia.

I ignored the comment. "Though your mother might disagree — as the mysteries of the Magna Mater are strictly closed to men — in certain ways the Mater is similar to Maia. I would hazard she is a different interpretation of the same manifestation of *numina*. No matter what name you give to the goddess, the divine female spirit behind it is the same."

Cornelia harrumphed, but left it at that.

Said Aemilia, "So is this like the *patina* you cooked, to enable us to see the flow of *magia*?"

"Not quite. More like a religious ceremony, but with added focus of proper incantation."

"But combining them has been disallowed since the days of Numa Pompilius! The *mos maiorum* expressly forbids priests and *incantatores* to mix."

"Luckily, I am neither," I smiled, in what I hoped was a reassuring manner. Aemilia's eyes glittered, and Cornelia, despite attempting a disapproving look, was clearly intrigued as well.

"So, you will attempt a sacrificial offering to Maia, but pour the *magia* into it, to make it work?"

"The principle is simple. With prayers and sacrifices, priests rely on consecrated altars and prescribed formulae to carry their intentions to the realm of the *numina*, for the gods to reflect it back on earth. With incantations, the *incantator* has to focus the ambient *magia*, the power. Prayers are neither precise nor assured of result, while incantations are localised and less encompassing. That's why the priests can serve the gods who assure the safety and prosperity of the city, while *incantatores* do flashy, yet ultimately short-lived, effects."

"And mixing the *magia* in a prayer?"

"This gives the intent behind the prayer more power. Maybe it is a way to shout louder and draw the gods' attention to one's prayers. Though our ancestors forbade the two from mixing, perhaps religion is just another form of incantation, not much different at all. Imagine climbing up Vergu, versus being carried up in a litter — you'll end up at the top, but someone else does the work."

"And the reliance on symbols and sacrifices, on rituals and supplications? Is it like using a staff, a crutch to aid you in climbing?"

"In a way. Priests rely on the trappings of ceremony, in contacting and contracting the gods. In a similar way, the *veneficitores* concoct exceedingly potent poultices and potions, but it takes them significantly longer than for a pharmacist to blend your medicine. Within the realm of incantations, you can go about it quickly or carefully. If you do it all at once you will achieve great things on the spot, but it will drain you, might even burn you. If you do it slowly, your exertion is small, so you are not exhausted, but it takes weeks of preparations. To continue the analogy, it's the difference between climbing the path up Vergu at a leisurely pace and taking stops to refresh yourself,s versus taking it at a dead run. On that extreme are the *elementori*. Everyone appreciates their flashy magics and incantations, bringing about fire from the sky or water to fill the circus. What folk don't realise is the price those who use it pay, the early death they come to."

"Mayhap this is why our ancestors forbade it," Aemilia extrapolated, "if religion is the magnified effect of a small manipulation, imagine the divine cataclysm that would follow an *elementor* calling forth fire."

"Quite. Now, let's begin. If your mother will allow, I will extend the ceremony to Vesta as well. As the protector of the hearth, her interest and aid in the matter would help. And you, dear Aemilia, are the only one present qualified to serve her."

That last comment made them both blush, though I imagine for different reasons. I hurried with the ceremony, before my mouth got away from me.

I pulled a fold of my toga over my head as the priests do, and began my supplication to Maia, chanting traditional hymns yet interweaving them with words of power and making both sacred and purposeful passes with my hands. Squeezing blood from the lamb chops, I mixed it with wine and poured it as a libation on the edge of the fire, to sizzle on the hot stones. The morsel of lamb went into the fire, and I imbued the smoke it gave off with *magia* as it dissipated and was absorbed into the house. As household spirits are symbolised carrying cornucopias, I took a fig from a platter, broke it open, offering the halves to both women. I instructed them to bite the fruit, but flick a few of the seeds onto the fire. Finally, I passed the petals of the flowers through the smoke, heating them lightly so their colours brightened but their edges did not singe. Those I would tuck into nooks and crannies around the *domus*.

One can never be sure of these things, but it felt to me as though the house was filled with warmth and scents of cooking and a strong, motherly love permeated the spaces.

"Would you do the honours?" I indicated the salt and bread still on the table. Aemilia took a linen towel and rolled it into a cylinder, wrapped it around her forehead, and tucked the rest at the nape of her neck. The Vestal Virgins wear seven such tiers in their headdress, but it was enough to get Aemilia in the right mood. She broke off a piece of the bread, sprinkled it with salt, and chanted traditional prayers to the *lares* of the ancestors and place, to the gods of the pantry, and to Vesta. She placed the bread on the stones of the fireplace, pushing it close to the fire to let it singe and smoke. She couldn't work the *magia* by herself, and I was certainly not good enough to pass my intent and concentration and imbue her actions with it. But she was a woman of the house, carrying out an age-old rite of home and hearth and using a fire which I had just used for power. Again, no signs were visible, but I imagined the light was brighter, yellower, warmer, the dance of dust motes in filtered beams more joyous.

"And that should be that," I told the women. "From now on, the trial is in the hands of Aquilius and the gods."

CHAPTER XXXVII

O n the day of the trial, we arrived bright and early at the Forum. Because the event promised to be a worthy spectacle, a special wooden dais had been erected. Seats were provided on opposite sides for the prosecution and defence, and tiered benches built at the back for the jury. The judge would bring his own folding chair, according to his station. Rows of wooden seats surrounded the stage for the watching crowds. Interested affluent people sent their clients or other household members to reserve front row places for them. The Forum's usual gossips were fluffing their cushions, and industrious traders were already hawking pastries and watered wine. Second only to chariot races, a trial of notorious personalities is our city's favourite spectator sport.

I sat behind the dais, on the side of the prosecution. On corner seats near me I heard, even before I saw, Valdrius and Statilius — the two greybeards from the Forum. I hoped the running commentary and occasional outburst from them would not distract me from the proceedings.

I had the chance to observe the processions of the parties as they wended their ways to centre stage. The prosecution was led by Quintus Aquilius, his bright white toga draped immaculately. Next walked Valerius Flaccus, head held high, back straight. He wore an older toga, the purple at its hem fading. His senatorial crimson leather shoes were scuffed, and the crescent brass buckle tarnished. A picture of the suffering respectable citizen, holding to his *dignitas* despite the emotional and financial hardships inflicted upon him by the defendant. His wife and daughters walked deferentially one step behind, dressed similarly in older-style *stolas* that covered them modestly. They took their place at the spectator benches, the daughters supporting the mother, accompanied by Cornelia and Aemilia. Aquilius and Flaccus climbed the three steps to the dais and sat at the prosecution bench. Busy scribes, like a cloud of gnats, buzzed around them.

From the other side of the Forum came the defence. Marcus Tullius Cicero strode at the head. He was a man past his physical prime, but with unmatched personal *dignitas* and public *auctoritas*. A former consul — though his year had its share of scandals — and the city's foremost legal authority. His pate was completely bald, and he had gotten heavy in his later years, but I doubted that would diminish his courtroom oratory and theatrics.

Next, ambled Numicius, wearing a moth-eaten toga to cover his girth, his hair in disarray, and sending bewildered looks all around. His wife Faucia walked demurely behind him — so much for fleeing town to escape his wrath. Her hair was covered in ash and she wailed and stumbled dramatically, only to be caught by her companions. The picture of a family distraught by the unfair and untrue allegations brought against them.

They, too, arranged themselves with the women close behind the dais — still wailing — and Cicero, Numicius, and their scribes on the bench opposite Aquilius and Valerius. Numicius gave a casual glance at the prosecution. When he noticed me behind the dais his eyes widened, then narrowed, and his face hardened. I got the impression he was not expecting to see me alive after the fire. I also got the impression his mind was racing with options to rectify that.

The jury were dressed each according to their station. All fifty-one were either senators, wearing togas with wide purple borders and buckled crimson shoes; or equestrians, dressed in white togas of the finest quality, tunics with a narrow purple stripe showing over the right shoulder, and bedecked with rings and jewellery to show their affluence. They wended over in small groups and sat on the benches assigned to them.

Last came the presiding judge. The Urban Praetor had nominated an ex-praetor, one Titus Ampius, who I knew had designs to run for the consulship. I wondered whether assigning Ampius to the trial was an act of political kindness by the Urban Praetor — Numicius would approach this case, the judge, and the jury with an open purse. The right result could net Ampius a hefty sum towards his election fund.

Since he wasn't in office that year he was not entitled to *lictors* or a curule chair, but he brought enough of his retinue of scribes and aids to compensate. His slave placed a folding seat in the appropriate place on the dais — an ornate, backless affair that was a hairbreadth short of being an official *imperium*-holding magistrate's chair. Ampius sat in it confidently. He kept his back straight, his left arm clasping the folds of his toga, his left leg tucked under the chair and his right leg out, in the classic pose of the upright Egretian citizen-of-rank.

And thus, when everyone took their appropriate places with the right level of theatrics, the show began.

***

Ampius raised his right hand to hush the crowd. When things settled, he initiated the trial. At his signal, court slaves carried a flat stone in front of the dais. A lamb, bought and paid for by Aquilius, was brought at the end of a rope to the makeshift altar. Two special attendants from the *Collegium Sacrorum*, the *popa* and *cultarius*, proceeded with the sacrifice. The *popa* stunned the lamb with a hammer. He held its head up while the *cultarius* cut the beast's throat with a brass knife and caught the blood in a *skyphos*. The *cultarius* raised the vessel, murmured a prayer to Iustitia and Prudentia, and spilled a libation on the ground. He cut open the belly of the lamb, poked in its entrails, and then declared that the ladies Justice and Prudence had given their blessings to the trial. Those of us with sensitivity could also feel the subtle shift in the flow of *magia* around the makeshift court. This ancient rite performed by priests, while perhaps not powerful enough to prevent a determined witness from lying or juror from accepting a bribe, still gave the proceedings a nudge in the right direction.

"I'll go now, but I'll be back," said a voice in my left ear and made me start. I turned around to see Araxus' grinning face. "The priests will soon burn the lamb, and it gives the *magia* a funny taste. I'll swing by for your testimony later." He got up and shuffled in the direction of the latrines. He always had the worst ways of unnerving me, but right then I had to focus my attention back on the proceedings.

Ampius cleared his throat. "This trial will be carried out according to the prescribed formula for *in personam* matters. We shall hear the opening speeches, both limited to one hour as measured by a water clock. Witnesses shall be presented by the prosecution, examined and cross-examined. Witnesses for the defence shall follow in a similar manner. Lastly, both parties shall deliver their closing speeches. Two hours for the prosecution and three hours for the defence, measured by a water clock as prescribed by law and custom." He waved his hand expansively at Aquilius. "The brief given to me by the *praetor urbanus* indicated two defendants. I see Gaius Numicius present here, but where is Gaius Hirtuleius Ambustus?"

Aquilius stood up, fussed with his immaculately draped toga, and strode to the centre of the stage. "It will please the judge and jury to know that the gods have already avenged the deplorable, delictual deeds committed by Ambustus against that virtuous fellow, Valerius Flaccus. Giving the man the fate his name prescribed, Vulcanus and Neptunus both acted in tandem, and that despicable degenerate burned down on the ship in the bay not a *nundinum* ago, an incident fresh in the minds of all citizens. And, although we are spared the presence of that corrupt creature, that reptilian reprobate, just like the gods chose a light-filled spectacle to bring about his death in public, so shall we bring to light the abominable atrocities perpetrated by that parasite —"

"In short," interrupted the judge, "he died before the

trial began. Clerk, please make a note of this. You," he addressed Aquilius, "may now begin your opening speech."

"I like his style," said Statilius from his nearby seat.

"His oration is definitely off to a strong start," replied Valdrius. "He might even make Cicero sweat a little."

Back on stage, at a nod from the court clerk in charge of the water clock, Aquilius raised his right arm and began the formal oration.

I will not bore my readers with the verbatim transcript of the trial. I have already described the major gist of the prosecution's opening, and full transcripts are available at some libraries. I understand this case became somewhat of a standard *quaestio*, which aspiring law students must study.

I will say Aquilius delivered his speech flawlessly. His pointed comments equating acquittal with bribery went down well with the crowd. My two favourite commentators were not shy in pointing out which of the jury shifted in their chairs uncomfortably — useful information to note and remember.

He expounded on the crimes of using *nefas magia* within the city limits. He made his claims that Ambustus was acting at Numicius' behest when he put those curses in the *insulae*, to drive tenants away and hurt Valerius' finances. Here are his words on the crux of the matter.

"While, I admit, a patron is not immediately guilty of the acts committed by his clients, in this case we shall show, by calling upon witnesses to testify on the ultimate culpability, and by demonstrating the obvious gain for Numicius rather than his miserable minion, that the case here is one of conspiracy.

"When a patron sends out his client to commit crimes, is he any better than a conspirator, an accomplice? By condemning the man who acts but ignoring the one who sent him, you are summoning to destruction and devastation the temples of the immortal gods, the houses of the city, the lives of all the citizens. For if we order only the one man to be put to death, the rest of the conspirators will still re-

main in the republic; if, as I have long been exhorting you,
you order him to depart, his companions, those worthless
dregs of the republic, will be remain in the city to continue wreaking havoc with their foul deeds."

Aquilius made the best use of his hour. By the time he
was done, the gathered spectators were salivating at the prospect of heinous deeds exposed, of juicy, embarrassing tales of the
depravity of men and affronts to the gods being brought up for
their amusement.

Then came Cicero's turn. He strode to the centre stage,
wearing his toga, that large and unwieldy garment, with the
ease of a man born into politics. His every movement, from
the waving of arms to the twitch of his brows, was practised for
maximum effect in accordance with the rules of rhetoric. The
crowd needed no command to hush, waiting with bated breath
for what promised to be another of his famous performances.

"Formerly, O judges, I had determined to conduct this
cause in a different manner, thinking that our adversaries
would simply seek to implicate Numicius in such violent
and atrocious acts of *nefas magia*. Accordingly, I came with
a mind free from care and anxiety, because I was aware
that I could easily disprove that by witnesses. Yet the accuser's shameless impudence, which has much less power
in the Forum and in the courts of law than audacity has in
the country and in desolate places, seeks now, in this trial,
to implicate all patrons in the actions of their clients.

"I have observed, O judges, that the whole speech of
the accuser is divided into two parts. One of which appeared to me to rely upon, and to put its main trust in, the
inveterate unpopularity of practising vile and forbidden
magia within the city, touching very lightly and diffidently
on the method pursued in cases of accusations of poison-
ing. The other, just for the sake of usage, concerning which
matter this form of trial is appointed by law, yet attacking
the very *mos maiorum* which dictates both legal proce-

dure and the relationship of citizens and benefactors. And, therefore, I have determined to preserve the same division of the subject in my defence, speaking separately to the question of unpopularity and to that of the accusation, in order that everyone may understand that I neither wish to evade any point by being silent with respect to it, nor to make anything obscure by speaking of it."

He went on in such manner, promising witnesses to clear Numicius of any links to forbidden curses and use of magia, painting him like a pious boy wearing a pristine toga, devoid of mischief or malice. But far worse was his treatment of the second aspect, the conspiracy between patron and client. He defused this by calling on our collective ancestors, equating Aquilius' charge to an attack on the *mos maiorum*, the revered ancestral way of things. Neatly and effectively, he reminded both jury and spectators our social order relies on a system of benefaction, without which our political and social structures would be thrown into chaos. Worse, he implied that a conviction would potentially hurt them all where it pained the most — in their money pouches.

CHAPTER XXXVIII

The first witness for the prosecution was Aburius. The only remarkable thing about him was that he managed to be even more smarmy than usual. He described the tenants leaving, his difficulties in getting new ones, and the fate of the guards he positioned within the *insulae*.

"Ooh, nicely done," said Valdrius. "I could believe his hand wringing was about the poor occupants, not just about lost rents."

"I don't know," said Statilius. "If you tighten that toga of his, I bet you could squeeze out an amphora of oil."

"Granted, but did you see the tears he shed when describing his deceased gladiators?"

"Crocodile tears."

"Still," insisted Valdrius. "I maintain that for a man used to extracting the last *sestertius* out of starving families, his performance in a civilised court was quite adequate."

"You're fooling yourself if you think he hasn't done this before," retorted Statilius. "It's part of the job of the agent, to give good performances to match the crowd."

They hushed when Cicero took the stage.

He strode to the front and centre of the dais, faced Aburius, and took a deep breath. He held it for a long moment as if collecting his thoughts, his arm raised only slightly as if about to commence his oration with a grand movement. The watching crowd held its breath in sympathy.

He then exhaled, said simply, "No questions for this witness," and turned away.

"Wha...? Are you sure?" asked Ampius, over the loud murmuring of jury and spectators.

"Quite. We do not deny a grave wrong had been done, that possibly even *nefas magia* had been practised within city limits. We only maintain the wronged party here is Numicius, a man of such rank, and authority, and virtue, and wisdom, innocent of any misdeed, carried to court merely by a vindictive political opponent. We shall show Numicius was uninvolved in the matter. It is no matter for us, or for any Egretian court, why Valerius had incurred the wrath of the gods and the ways in which they chose to show their displeasure with him."

He sat down amongst gaping jaws and unbelieving stares. Statilius was the first to recover, with a piercing wolf-whistle. The crowd clapped and talked excitedly, so that Ampius had one of his slaves bang a staff on the dais for silence.

***

Ampius adjourned the proceedings, declaring a break until the sixth hour. Hawkers immediately moved to ply the hungry crowd with snacks, while the queues to the public latrines stretched lazily on the stone paving of the Forum and through the shaded colonnades.

My two commentators, Valdrius and Statilius, were quick to grab lamb-stuffed *lagana* flat-bread from a passing vendor. Stuffing their faces with it did not slow down their commentary, only added the extra dimension of flying spittle as punctuation.

"And here I thought young Aquilius stood a chance," said Statilius.

"If I didn't know better," replied Valdrius, "I'd say it sounded like Cicero had advance copies of Aquilius' speeches."

"He's a political weasel. I wouldn't put it past him."

"Political weasel, but genius jurist. He doesn't need to stoop to that."

"Might I remind you..."

Aemilia drifted into my view, and I lost interest in their

bickering. "Are you ready for your testimony this afternoon?" she asked as she sat down next to me.

"Ready and eager."

"Should I get you something?" She caressed the cast on my leg lightly. "Let me get you a pastry and watered wine. Can't have you collapsing from hunger or thirst. You need to be at your best for us to win this case!"

She jumped up and stalked off after a vendor. I watched her shapely behind as she walked away. When I returned my gaze to the dais, Cornelia was exchanging words with Valerius. She saw me alone and approached. Maia was cutting it thin with her divine protection.

"Are you prepared for your testimony?" She asked. "Do you need to review your notes?"

"There is nothing in them I don't already know by heart," I smiled at her. "According to the gossips here, Aquilius is doing a remarkable job. With anyone but Cicero for the defence, our victory would have been assured. We must trust in our preparation and in the gods."

"Humph."

The way she looked at me, though, gave me the distinct impression she was asking something else, something I didn't quite answer. By her body language, she was keen to sit down next to me, but was wary of how that might be seen by the crowds observing the trial.

"Well, just make sure you groan and limp on that leg of yours when you go up. I want Numicius to pay for what he did to you. And to Lucius Valerius, of course."

She was gone before I could respond, which was just as Aemilia came back with the snacks and wine.

CHAPTER XXXIX

The next testimony was mine.

I climbed the few steps to the dais with visible difficulty, leaning on a walking stick and stumbling. Aquilius was swift to come to my aid. I sat down on the witness bench with a groan and adjusted my casted leg with both hands into position. Only after straightening my toga did I turn to the judge with an expectant look.

At a wave of his hand, I began. Readers of my memoirs up to this point are already familiar with the facts of the case — I filled the previous two scrolls with them. I had, as per the discussions with Aquilius and Valerius, focused my testimony on two aspects: the vileness of the deeds, and the links to Numicius.

"I shall tell you, dear jury, that Aburius before me has done a disservice to his employer, the virtuous Valerius. Out of respect to your august selves, out of respect to the positions of leadership you hold for our city, he perhaps thought to spare you from the vivid descriptions of the consequences of Numicius' nauseating enterprise. With his grubby, grabbing greed, the accused had brought death and destruction to many Egretian citizens. I shall describe to you the atrocious, heinous horrors this man has committed inside the sacred city limits, so you can appreciate the gravity of his crimes."

I proceeded to do just that. I recounted all my encounters with the various neighbours and denizens, described in gory details the stories of the survivors and the remains of those left dead behind. Riling the jury up with horrid tales of atrocities would motivate them to condemn any man before them to appease the public, rather than sink into fiscally-motivated doubts. When I reached the part about the babe's half-eaten corpse, Cornelia swooned loudly and theatrically, with Aemilia fussing and wailing, all catching the jury's attention. Whether real or acted, it provided an emotional underscore to my testimony.

The next part of my speech was about the curse tablets. "It may seem, at this point, as the counsel for the defence has alluded, that the gods have shown their displeasure of Valerius. And yet I maintain the esteemed Cicero has done a disservice to the man in whose defence he speaks, and to his profession, by omitting to question the previous witness. For someone whose very name is synonymous with courtroom oratory, and, indeed, from his consular days, with defence of our republic, I can only assume that he is aware of Numicius' guilt, and, being true to himself, cannot stomach his acquittal." I caught Aquilius' eye at that point and saw him exhale and smile as he realised where my improvisation was going.

"What I am about to show you, O brave Egretian citizens, will shock and dismay you! Cicero, a pious man, cannot imagine such vileness would come from anywhere but divine retribution. But that is not the case before you today. Today we are dealing with the atrocities of depraved men. For who but the most depraved, the most perverted, the most deviant of degenerates, would use potent *magia* to power such corrupt *tabulae defixiones* as these!" With this I withdrew one of curse tablets from the sinus of my toga and waved it emphatically.

It had the desired effect.

There were gasps from the crowds and uncomfortable shifting from judge and jury who did not appreciate being in proximity to such an item of evil purpose. I went on to expound on the power of real curse tablets, as opposed to the garden-variety ones. I built up the case of how all the effects and horrors previously described appeared in the symbols etched and scratched into the lead. I made it clear this was all the work of one man, aimed at mimicking godly displeasure, and committing sacrilege. Aemilia's research notes had helped me here, her literary allusions aiding me in building up the case in a way even laymen could understand. As I talked, I waved the tablet around, hypnotising the watchers who could not stop staring at it, however much they wanted to avert their gaze.

Finally, I settled back into my chair and put the *tabula* away. I let the crowds murmur, and release their pent-up emotions before continuing. The sight of Araxus sitting next to Valdrius and Statilius — looking like another greybeard — gave me pause. I could not hear what they were saying, but all were nodding heads in agreement with each other, which I took as a good sign. Any good feelings I might have had were mitigated by Numicius, who, from his bench at the other side of the dais, stared at me with unadulterated hatred.

Time for the last part of my testimony — implicating Ambustus and Numicius. "Tracking the one who crafted the curses was no mean feat. These people, and those who support them, know full well what they are doing does not belong within the sacred perimeter of the city, or in civilised society. They cling to the shadows, make their deals in dank alleys and windowless rooms. They walk amongst the underbelly of our noble society, with the criminal element, hidden from upright and innocent citizens, hidden even from the *aediles* and *rhones* administering our city." I stuck to Aquilius script with those words, trusting to his better judgement about influencing juries.

"And yet, like all animals, they leave tracks for those who know where and how to look. At great personal risk — and at great personal cost, as my broken leg here testifies — I braved these pests of the state, these vermin that skitter underfoot, to find the most corrupt and evil of men, who would carry out such heinous crimes. Like a fox that hunts the weasel, I found all those who, unwittingly or not, have aided in the creation of the curse tablets. And all pointed at one man — one man so vile, that the gods had already punished him once with a monstrous visage. The man with half his face burned in divine retribution for his impious acts, his affronts to our sacred *mos maiorum*, the man named Gaius Hirtuleius Ambustus."

With the preliminary character assassination out of the way, I could then move on to show how I linked the man to the curse tablets. I listed all those who have identified him to me, from the lead merchant to the guards and neighbours at the *insulae*. "One would assume, but would be wrong, that this skulduggery is carried out at the dark of night, hidden from sight. No! The man, the loathsome toad, confessed it all to me in glee. Over a cup of wine, as though in civilised discussions, the man intimated the most horrific of crimes. He would bribe a mere babe with sweets, get them to bury the *tabulae* for him at the central courtyard of the *insulae*, and thus seal their own fates, and the fate of their beloved families. He kept visiting the buildings, observing the effects of his deplorable curses, claiming himself a philosopher advancing the study of *magia*, but, in reality, deriving sickening pleasure in the misfortune of his victims. All this he was proud to admit."

Now Aemilia's research helped me again. Not only in the references she found, but also, in forcing me to explain it to her, I found the words to use in my testimony. "And, if some of you be naive and consider his boasting the act of a charlatan, taking credit for skills and acts far beyond his ken, know you this. Studying the art of incantation is no different to learning the arts of the muses. As one studies, grows in understanding, perfects his techniques, one acquires a signature, just like on a signet ring. Each incantation has the mark of the *incantator* who effected it, just as surely as each picture has the brush stroke of the painter, each sculpture the chisel marks of the sculptor.

"I analysed the curse tablets for such marks. Later, in circumstances I shall relate shortly, in which I, a free Egretian citizen, was unlawfully imprisoned by the defendant and an attempt made on my life, I had the displeasure to examine Ambustus in action. I witnessed him perform his craft — his art — I heard him speak again of himself as a philosopher advancing our understanding of the *numina* and their *magia*, while performing horrendous, proscribed incantations. There is a good reason why our revered ancestors declared it *nefastum scientiam*, forbidden knowledge. Ambustus used the powers of the gods that permeate our world to meddle with the very boundary between this world and the next. He was using his incantations to decay living tissue unto death, and then infuse that dead matter back with life. Sacrilege of the highest order, an execrable deed by a deranged man. And yet, in his actions he sealed his own fate. Not only did it confirm the *incantator's* signature embedded in the *tabulae defixiones* was his own, the gods had also chosen me at that moment to deliver their divine retribution."

Giving testimony was parching work. Normally, when I did that much talking, wine was involved in sufficient quantities to lubricate throats. While I was recomposing myself and preparing to launch into the conclusion of my testimony, I glimpsed the watching crowd. Both Cornelia and Aemilia looked at me with mixed emotions. Fleeting glimpses of distress at hearing again about the crimes, concerns for each other's safety — my safety too, I presumed — and approval of my delivery of the testimony — all these I recognised, as well as other, unfathomable, female emotions.

Valdrius and Statilius were more straightforward in their commentary on my testimony. Their gasps, groans, and exclamations at the right points of my speech were sure indicators that I was delivering an emotional and effective oration. Araxus was with them, and though I have not been able to read him for many years since he brought on himself the curse that afflicted his mind and changed him physically, I felt he was goading them on my behalf. A public outcry is known to affect the jury's disposition.

"All this is well and good," I continued, "and even the esteemed Cicero, counsel for the defence, dares not deny the horrid nature of the crimes. So, allow me now to get to the crux of the matter, of why Numicius is sitting here before you, wearing a moth-eaten toga, as though this prosecution is a great wrong, when all know of his fabulous riches acquired through unscrupulous acts. And this, this atrocity, this abominable act, this transgression against the laws of both men and gods, are just the peak of his depravity, his sacrilege in the name of greed."

I went on to describe Ambustus' confirmation to me that he was acting on commission by Numicius his patron, that all his acts were done with full knowledge and upon instruction from him. I went on to describe how I approached Numicius, and while I glossed over the finer details of attempted entrapment — those did not concern the jury — I was explicit in repeatedly stressing the close relationship of the two men.

For the finale, I told of my imprisonment of Numicius' ship and the attempt on my life. In our society, the punishment for severe crimes was execution or exile. The *carcer Tullianum*, the one public prison, barely had doors or guards and was used for detention of debtors sold into bondage or wayward politicians during trying times. To deprive a citizen of his freedom to move about was anathema to our republican society — a thing for kings, not for a republic of free men. To kidnap and assault a man was a crime, albeit hardly as serious as using forbidden magics to cause deaths and mayhem within city limits. It gave me the opportunity to vilify Numicius even more, complain and moan about my broken leg at his hands, and the damage to my property — namely Borax.

I was careful with this, though. I had to be. I was testifying under formal auspices at a trial and would be swearing upon my deposition at its conclusion. These things have a meaning, both in earthly and divine records. Stretching the truth was expected, and, outside of consecrated proceedings, truth had an even more fluid nature, but doing so under oath was borderline blasphemy. My existing record with Minos, Rhadamanthus, and Aeacus was already dubious and I didn't want to give the judges of the dead another excuse to send me to Tartarus.

"Ambustus had intimated to me that he was acting on behalf of Numicius when he crafted those curse tablets and activated them with puissant *magia* to doom the inhabitants of the *insulae*. Yet, I wanted to get the measure of the man himself. By all accounts, Numicius was ruthless in business, relentless in the Senate, remorseless in all his dealings with fellow men. When he had his slave break my leg, he all but admitted aloud his involvement in the nefarious plan to rob Valerius of his rightful property. He may present a persona of piety, wishing a public perception of a devoted son honouring the memory of his mother, but it is my sworn testimony here that in all my observations of the man and his actions, he is the mastermind behind all of Ambustus' misdeeds. He is naught but a common lawless landlord, a greedy ghoul who would sentence innocents to death even while praying to the Bona Dea to preserve his mother, who surely never wanted such a son!"

This was met with a grating, scraping noise, as Numicius jumped to his feet so forcefully his stool scratched the wooden dais. His face was red, and he was sputtering incoherently. Cicero was quick to rise and restrain Numicius, aided by some of their scribes. I finally managed to get a public outburst out of Numicius, but the shaking heads of Valdrius, Statilius, and Araxus seemed to say I had gone too far.

CHAPTER XL

When the judge managed to restore order, it was Cicero's turn to cross-examine me. I knew what was about to happen, so I composed myself and put on a calm smile.

"We have just heard, O noble jury, the sworn testimony of the defence's star witness. A man, by his own admission, who digs amongst the dregs of society. Calls himself a fox, but I ask you would not ferret -- weasel -- be a better term? What need has Aquilius of his assistance? Why, I hear you ask, has Valerius not resisted his enemies with his own resources? Why call upon that ferret, Felix?

"Could it be because he was in so wholly desperate a condition as to consider himself not only safer if he had that man for a protector, and more ready for the struggle if he had him for an advocate? Why is he anxious to lean on the counsel or protection of that piece of comatose cattle, of that bit of foetid flesh? Why does he seek for any support or ornament for himself from that contemptible carcass?"

So far, so good. I held my smile.
Cicero continued.

"This is a case not about personal damages, or property damages, or of anything but mere political vindictiveness. Valerius, upon being defeated in fair and open proceed-

276

ings of the Senate, sought to blame the divine retribution he had brought upon himself on this, his honourable senatorial opponent. For that he dredged this witness before us, as if an expert. But I ask you, from whence did Aquilius bring him here? He dragged him out of some dark and dirty cook-shop, this *saltatrix tonsa* of his, to testify against a righteous senator of the Egretian people."

I gritted my teeth and clenched my hand around my walking staff. I've been called worse things, but not often. To call a man a shaved dancing girl, to impeach his masculinity like that in open speech, is not a light offence against one's *dignitas*.

In the perfect timing he was renowned for, Cicero both avoided the judge's impatience and capitalised on my upset. "So, let me ask you now, Fox, as you claim expertise in matters of foul curses, where did you gain such knowledge? Are you, perhaps, a qualified *incantator*, a graduate of our noble Collegium Incantatorum?"

He sure knew how to press where it hurt. "My expertise was learnt and gained twofold," I answered. "First, in matters of investigations, I had apprenticed under the famous *Gordius et Falconius*, those two famed detectives whom you yourself have used on many occasions to bring successful suit in our courts. Were they here, they would vouch for my training, my skills, my integrity." Stretching the truth, as I mentioned, was perfectly acceptable. "As for my education in the arts of the *magia* and incantation, I was indeed a student at our Collegium. I know, I know — you are about to say I never completed my studies. True, I did not. My family fell on hard times, and I could no longer pay for the tuition. But the knowledge I acquired in my years there served me well and I can tell the theory and practice of curses."

"And so, we have here," Cicero turned to the jury, "a man with dubious understanding of the *magia*, running errands for two of our esteemed investigators yet claiming to be their equal. A man who, by his own admission, was down on his luck and on his funds, spending his days dealing with foul knowledge amongst the dregs of society, pursuing *nefastum scientiam*. A fine witness indeed."

He turned back to me. "Let us move on then, to the details of your testimony. You professed before us that, following clues given to you by nameless, dubious, odious dealers in occult supplies, you have, in your mind, identified Ambustus as the originator of the *tabulae defixiones*, the *incantator* responsible for this deleterious delinquency. Even should our fine jury choose to accept such flimsy logic and accusations, you claimed Ambustus confessed to you both his crime and his commission by Numicius. Tell us, please, how you came to extract such a confession by a man who, in your later testimony, you also claimed was so devout to his patron he would take no action without his sanction. How did you trick him to confess and confide in you?"

The bastard. My options: one, emphasise I got Ambustus drunk, thus diminishing the credibility of any confession. Two, hint at his dissatisfaction with Numicius, thus diminishing the bond between them, which was crucial for Aquilius' condemnation of the patron.

The rule of thumb for a professional witness is: When in doubt stick to the facts and keep things simple. The more you talk, the more material the opposing counsel has to confuse the testimony and lessen the judge and jury's trust in you. "I tracked Ambustus down, as you noted, by the methods taught to me by those investigators you esteem. One need not be concerned about the dirt on the hand that points the way, when the milestone clearly announces it as the right road. Over a simple glass of wine, the man admitted, nay, took pride, in the way he crafted those tablets to achieve his patron's bidding."

"Just like that?"

"Indeed so."

"Without any provocation? A loyal client betraying his patron to a complete stranger without a second thought? And yet you would have us believe that it is ultimately his patron's fault for the vile deeds? Was he a monster or a loyal client?"

"I do not know what happened between them, only what

I saw and heard."

"Ah! So, there are limits to your testimony and your so-called expertise. Let us move on. Tell us, then, about the circumstances that brought you on that fateful night to be on Numicius' ship."

"I was invited by the man himself."

"Oh? And why would he invite a complete stranger onto his private yacht?"

"It was the day the Reds won in the circus," I answered. "It seems we are both great fans of the Red faction."

"But, still — a complete stranger?" Cicero pressed.

"I have mentioned that I set out to gain the man's measure, to determine his complicity and ultimate responsibility. We had met before."

"You make it sound all so innocent. And yet, as we shall soon hear, your motives and methods were more sinister than you would like the jury to believe. Is it true," he raised his voice, "you approached that blameless citizen now sitting here wrongly accused, in an underhanded plot, concocted by the foul *accusator*, to deceive and entrap the defendant? That your entire testimony is made up of lies, half-truths, and untruths?"

"As I have mentioned," I tried to keep my voice even, "I needed to get close to Numicius. I wanted to hear a confession from his own lips before testifying to his guilt. I wished to discuss the properties —"

"But wait!" Cicero interrupted me. "You needed to hear from his own lips, you say? And did you?"

Bugger. I fell for it. "In all meaningful ways. On his boat, tied and trussed, illegally detained, just before he ordered his slaves to break my leg!" I gave an emphatic knock on the cast and winced in real pain. "When I confronted him with the atrocities committed by his man, he treated it just like another business deal! Neither of them even bothered to deny it, nor feign surprise or outrage."

"But never, in point of fact, openly admitting to complicity in the matter? I present you, O conscript fathers, how this affair appeared to Numicius, one of your own. A pious son, wishing to acquire property to honour the gods and his dead mother, is approached by a man of dubious background and unsavoury connections. That man," and he gestured at me, "worms himself close to our brother, making propositions about properties and yet in the same breath accusing one of his clients of crimes most heinous. Only naturally, he sought to deal with the obvious menace first, and with his client later, in private, as fitting. These are the acts of a righteous man, doing right by gods and ancestors, doing right by his own clients. Did he know Ambustus betrayed him, acting beyond the proper bounds? No! Would any man here turn upon his own clients immediately, upon baseless accusations from some degenerate, some borderline criminal confederate? No! You listen to those loyal to you, you give them the benefit of the doubt before denouncing them on the groundless allegation of some street trash. There was nothing we have heard this afternoon, nothing in any testimony brought forward by the craven political rival, to incriminate the blameless Numicius, whose actions were just and proper by all laws of gods and men."

He skipped saying 'your own clients will be noting at how you vote,' but it was unnecessary at that point. He had sown the seeds of fear and doubt in their minds and gave those vacillating a way out of condemning the ruthless Numicius.

***

Ampius declared the proceedings concluded for the day. We gathered in gloomy silence before making our way home. Araxus ambled over, somehow getting Statilius and Valdrius to trail behind him. He merely stood and looked into my eyes, inscrutable as a cat.

"Jolly good show," said Statilius as he clapped me on the shoulder. "I've seen Cicero reduce experienced witnesses to tears before."

"A most convincing testimony," Valdrius agreed with him. "We must congratulate the young attorney, too. Rousing rhetoric!"

"Rousing enough to raise the hackles on Cicero," grinned Statilius. "Which may or may not have been the right course of action."

They moved off to speak with Aquilius and Valerius, and left Araxus still staring into my eyes. To have both his black and green eyes focused together was more unnerving than having them wander in different directions.

"What was shall come again," he said. "The gladiator... No, that is yet to come. Today. You did well, today. The sacrificial smoke makes everything hazy... but you did well today. You kept to the truth. It is an act of piety. Like the one you performed tomorrow. Is it tomorrow? Time is funny, but the gods are immortal, so it doesn't matter. I shall help you yesterday, though I am neither priest nor sculptor."

"Uh... thanks," I replied. Despite his fragmented mind, within his broken speech I got a glimpse of the friend I once had. He meant me well, though he terrified me.

While Valerius and Aquilius were talking quietly, their scribes hovering around to help them with references, while Cornelia and Aemilia were trying to get our company moving, a break in the milling crowds gave me an unexpected view of Numicius.

As though on cue, he raised his gaze and our eyes locked. He smiled an evil smirk, his eyes radiating intense hatred. I had crossed some line with him, the mention of his mother pushing him too far. If Cicero would let him testify, Aquilius might be able to press this into an advantage. I had a feeling, though, I was yet to pay an even greater price for it.

All of that escaped my mind when the crowds closed and hid him from my view, and Aemilia came to guide me to the litter. The spectators were making their way home and Araxus had disappeared amongst them when my gaze was turned. Cornelia had chosen to walk beside Valerius and Aquilius and participate in their discussions, contributing her gossip gathered amongst the women as to whom of the jury was likely to vote which way, and how to conduct the next day's affairs.

Whilst Aemilia could not ride with me alone in the litter for propriety's sake, she fussed around me to make me comfortable before standing respectfully behind her mother. The litter gave a lurch as the slaves hoisted it up, and our party took the meandering path from the Forum to Cornelia's *domus*.

Chapter XLI

The next day the parties gathered at the court's stage in the Forum as before. Aquilius had some more witnesses testifying to Numicius ruthlessness. Cicero called them 'sore losers, who, upon experiencing buyers' remorse, sought merely to besmirch the name of a business rival.'

Aquilius then brought forth witnesses for the bond between Ambustus and Numicius, trying to claim overheard snatches of conversation about hidden plots. Cicero breezed through them, discrediting their relevance to the case with alarming ease. When he made the spectators tear up in laughter at his treatment of a banking associate claiming secret payments, Aquilius decided to cut this short. Rather than give Cicero further chances to reduce our credibility, he would have to stand on my testimony and his closing speech.

It was then the turn of the defence to present witnesses. Cicero brought forth a 'family friend' of Numicius, describing his deep sorrow at his mother's passing, and testifying of Numicius' great desire to immortalise her for her charity amongst the poor of the city.

Aquilius proved he was a quick learner. He strode to the middle of the floor, faced the man, inhaled as if about to launch into his cross examination. Then exhaled and said, "We are not here to discuss his mother, only her stunted offspring. Witness dismissed." He turned away and sat down to cheers from the crowd.

Cicero then brought forth a series of witnesses to the

effect that Numicius was a fine businessman, that he had many deals — all honest and above board — that Ambustus was merely one of many clients acting on his behalf, that he couldn't have known about every little detail, and that he was, in fact, out of town when anything untoward happened.

Harassing the witnesses, Aquilius managed to break their testimonies with the insistent question of "Are you, then, claiming to be aware, unlike all his other clients, of every one of Numicius' deals? Are you professing to know more about the details of his all-encompassing ventures and machinations, than the man himself?" When each man faltered, Aquilius was quick to dismiss his testimony as irrelevant to the case.

I saw Cicero pass a wax tablet to the fourth witness before he came on stage. I remembered the man's face and passed my own note to Aquilius. The man, Juventius, testified he was indeed the closest of confidants to Numicius, and that in all his dealings Numicius was observant of law and custom. Aquilius saw this and changed tactics. He drew the witness into a discussion about Numicius paying for Appuleius Diocles, the new driver for the Reds. The crowd became animated, the excitement of the Reds' recent wins still sending many hearts aflutter. They were wholly focused on the proceeding on the stage now.

Juventius, flushed, practically took the credit for brokering the whole deal.

"Even though I'm a follower of the Blue faction myself, still I should congratulate you," Aquilius said. "I can only imagine the pride you felt. You must have been absolutely exhilarated. Did Numicius commend you for this?"

"Why, yes, yes he did. He was mighty pleased."

"Having done this great service to him — to all of the Red faction fans — he must have rewarded you lavishly. And the celebrations! Surely you were the star of the post-victory festivities?"

The man puffed up. "I was indeed! Even before the main party, Numicius, that great man, raised a toast to me on his ship, to congratulate me."

"Ah, so you, his closest confidant, his second in command, who knew about Numicius' deals as much as he did, was on his yacht that fateful night? Judge!" Aquilius turned sharply. "I would add this witness to the list of defendants! By his own admission, he's involved in all Numicius' affairs. Confirming his presence on the ship, he is clearly guilty of complicity in the crime of wrongful imprisonment and of grievous bodily harm against an Egretian citizen!"

Juventius paled to white, started to stammer. Aquilius turned upon him, viciously attacking him, but his words were lost in the noise. The crowd was cheering wildly for this turn, laughing and booing the witness off the stage.

After that, Cicero did not bring forth any more witnesses.

Even though it was only the eighth hour of the day, Ampius declared the proceedings concluded. Both the summation speeches and jury voting would be delivered the next day. The spirits of our party were not as gloomy as previously, but tension was high. Cicero kept Numicius from testifying, not wishing to expose him to Aquilius and risk Numicius losing temper publicly. He was more than capable of delivering an exonerating oration and carrying the jury without his testimony.

It was a close race, with predictions risky and bets and stakes running high amongst the spectators. We headed home for a quiet evening, and doubtlessly a sleepless night. I imagined Aquilius spent most of it rehearsing his closing words.

***

The morning of the third and last day of the trial saw our corner of the Forum packed with spectators. Extra benches were added, and hawkers were doing a brisk business. Some enterprising ones even sold wax tablets with the previous days' highlights, for those who missed them. A few shifty characters were selling mock *tabulae defixiones*, and the memory of Icilia's slow and horrendous death brought the bile up in my mouth.

Valdrius and Statilius were the centre of a loud group, commentating and debating with anyone who would listen. This turned out to be quite the show, something that would be talked about in years to come.

The proceedings began as on the previous days, with a quick sacrifice that served to assure us the gods favoured the activities and, coincidentally, to weave the *magia* in a manner which drew the attentions of Iustitia and Prudentia, to enhance the chances of justice and prudence taking place.

Ampius invited Aquilius to deliver the summation of his accusations and the clerks started the two-hour water-clock to measure his allotted time. I shall not reproduce his words in full — that would take a whole scroll in and of itself — but I shall add my notes as someone who had a unique view of the proceedings that day.

Aquilius opened with the expected affirmation of Numicius' vile character. He recapped in sufficient details the horrors that occurred in his name within the sacred city limits to remind the good citizens of what was really at stake here. His clever allusion to acquittal meaning bribery made the jury squirm, as did his reminders about Numicius' ruthlessness in business and the senate. Longest of all, Aquilius spent recounting how I had clearly identified him as the one who commissioned the curses by Ambustus' open admission and by his own obvious complicity via his actions against me.

Aquilius' masterstroke came at the end. A few years prior — a couple of decades really, by that point — Cicero had been consul. During his consulship he eradicated an underhanded plot by a frustrated political opponent to overthrow the senate. After exposing a ring of subversive revolutionists and facing them in the senate and in armed conflicts, Cicero executed several without trial and hounded the ringleader to the final battlefield miles away from the city.

Some say this plot was of his own manufacture, that he pushed those who opposed him with merciless litigation till they faced no other option than violent resistance to ensure their own rights. Be that as it may — and I was only a child then, unaware of the finer points of politics — his speeches in the

senate denouncing the would-be reformist ringleader were some
of the finest ever delivered. One phrase in particular remained
stuck in the public's mind, and echoed down the ages — *Quo
usque tandem abutere, Catilina, patientia nostra?*

"Until when, O Numicius, will you abuse our patience?
How long is that madness of yours still to mock us? When
is there to be an end of that unbridled audacity of yours,
swaggering about as it does now? Do not the traditions
of our ancestors, do not the laws of the gods, does not the
alarm of the people, and the union of all good men, does
not the precaution taken of assembling the court in this
most vital place, do not the looks and countenances of this
venerable body here present, have any effect upon you?
What depravity of intellect possessed you, what excessive
frenzy seized on you, and made you, when you had begun your unheard-of and impious sacrifices, accustomed
as you are to seek to evoke the spirits of the shades below,
and to appease the Di Manes with the entrails of murdered boys, and despise the auspices under which this city
was founded.

"*O tempora, O mores!* Oh, the times, Oh, the customs!
For what is there, O Numicius, that you can still expect, if
night is not able to veil your nefarious meetings in darkness, and if private houses cannot conceal the voice of
your conspiracy within their walls?

"O ye immortal gods, where on earth are we? In what
city are we living? What constitution is ours? There are
here, here in our body, O conscript fathers, in this the most
holy and dignified assembly of the whole world, men who
meditate practising the foulest of *magia*, casting the most
forbidden of curses, bringing about the death of citizens,
and the death of all of us, and the destruction of this city,
and of the whole world!"

When Cicero delivered his original speech, those senators sitting next to the ringleader shied away from him, leaving
him alone. He was reduced to incoherence, forced to run from

the Senate hurling curses over his back. We paid spectators to sit in the front row behind the defence and to move away when Aquilius delivered this closing. Though the defence was not left isolated, of course, together with Aquilius' immaculate oratory mimicking Cicero in every way, the effect was grand. The crowds loved it and cheered wildly. A scathing summation, delivered brilliantly — the epitome of rhetoric. A few days later, Cicero might have appreciated turning his own speeches against him so resourcefully. Right then, he did not look amused.

***

After a short break we reconvened for the three hours of the defence summation. Cicero, it seemed to me, had not quite regained his composure from having his own words — taken from an episode in his career still considered highly controversial — brought to bear against him. When he took the stage, there was a certain set to his jaw, a certain clipping of his gestures and movement, as to imply that he was seething at the upstart Aquilius.

Was he really livid, or was that just theatrics for the spectators, to give another undertone to his oratory? He was certainly not above using every trick possible to build up his speeches and sway the public opinion.

He delivered his opening comments in the expected vein. He opened with claiming Numicius' innocence, painting Valerius as the aggressor.

"What have you given me to defend my client against, my good accuser? And what ground have you given these judges for any suspicion? My client was wishing land upon which to honour the gods and his dead mother and acted viciously in its acquisition. I hear you. But no one says what ground he had for viciousness. His aides and clients had it in contemplation. Prove it. There is no proof — there is no mention of anyone with whom he deliberated about it, whom he told of it. There is no circumstance from which it could occur to your minds to suspect. When you bring accusations in this manner, O Valerius, do you not plainly say this? 'I have had regard to that alone which Ambustus said, that there was no one who would dare at this time to say a word about the purchase of the property, and about that conspiracy.' This false opinion prompted you to this dishonesty. You would not, in truth, have said a word if you had thought that anyone would answer you."

He went on to besmirch the reputation, rectitude, and temperament of all the prosecution witnesses in the nastiest and foulest of words — words which can be found in libraries but omitted here, as they will no doubt merely offend my readers. He moved on to laud and praise all the defence witnesses, each of whose blameless character meant their word — so he proclaimed — was sufficient to acquit Numicius as a model of the upright citizen.

It took him some time to get to the main point of his argument. He had to convince the jury that — despite testimony to the contrary — Numicius was unaware and uninvolved in Ambustus' curses and then draw the link that a conviction meant a conviction of our patron-client system, and a collapse of the established social order.

"You are not now about to decide on the complicity of an innocent man, but on your own republic, on the constitution of your own state, on the common safety, on the hope of all good men. I will not say our piety, for that is lost, but it is our traditions, our social fabric, the very *mos maiorum* which hangs on a slender hope.

"From its very inception, the founders of our *res publica* cherished the greatest respect for the institutions of hierarchical and ecclesiastical ordinances. Our ancestors also enacted that the nobles should act as patrons and protectors to the inferior citizens, their natural clients and dependants, in their respective districts. And, though the patron-client relations in Egretian society are based on *fides,* on informal trust, rather than legal obligation, they are binding nonetheless.

"Our laws, the very ancient and sacred Twelve Tablets that form the basis of our laws, provide for the protection of the client from the misdeeds of a patron. It is clearly stated, *patronus si clienti fraudem fecerit, sacer esto* - 'If a patron shall have wronged a client, he is to be accursed'. But what of the reverse? What protection is there for the just patron, doing right by his clients, when they -- in their zealotry -- harm their very protector, the man they swore to serve? Where lies the boundary of guilt, for the actions of one man taken in the name of, yet unbeknownst to, another?"

The jury was composed, of course, entirely of the patron class in our society. Formally, it was a relationship of dependency and mutual obligation between richer and poorer citizens. The basic principle was that the client depended on his patron for protection and assistance, financial and otherwise, in return for a variety of services rendered, including votes in elections. Over the years, many words of fanciful rhetoric came from the patron class on the virtues of the relationship, while the miserable complaints from the side of the clients about the humiliations they have to go through, all for a second-rate meal, were largely ignored.

While I felt Cicero's speech did not directly refute any of the evidence and testimony presented, by making his closing about the relationship between patrons and clients he twisted the issue so a vote of innocence was directly in the jury's own interests. Numicius didn't even have to bribe them — it was their own money he was using as incentive.

CHAPTER XLII

We gathered on our side of the dais, nerves stretched thin. Ampius declared a recess for refreshments and restoration of spirits, following which the jury would cast votes. The jury dispersed to seek snacks and relief, talking among themselves about the merits of the case. Meanwhile, court slaves dragged a large wicker basket and set it on a low table in the centre of the stage. They had a pile of square wooden tokens, one side covered with wax for the jury's ballots. Each juror would mark either an A for *absolvo* or C for *condemno* and cast his token into the basket. The votes would then be tallied by a citizen and the results announced that very day.

Aquilius, Valerius, and Cornelia were talking in hushed voices, counting and recounting again who amongst the jury they could predict to vote one way or another. Which of the men present had a grudge against Numicius? Whose wife had been seen sporting a new black-pearl necklace, the astronomical cost of which could only be accounted for by bribery? Which senators had more clients and which needed funds the most? Which were concerned with their *dignitas* and public *auctoritas* beyond needing favours in coming elections? It was an endless discussion running in loops, keeping them busy in futile effort to predict the outcome. The defence, on its side of the stage, was similarly engaged.

Aemilia was nowhere to be seen, presumably having rushed to the nearest latrines open to women at this time after Cicero's long-winded three-hour speech. Araxus was sitting amongst the greybeards, staring vacuously at a flock of sparrows. The gossips themselves were engaged in much the same conversation as our party, analysing the speeches for rhetoric correctness, debating the weight of witnesses versus the effectiveness of their dismissal, and running a high-stake betting pool upon the outcome. They liked Aquilius' speech — odds were even.

The time came and Ampius had his slave bang a staff on the dais and announce loudly the resumption of proceedings. The prosecution and defence took their seats on opposite sides, and the jury shuffled to their benches. The spectators were riveted to the stage while last-minute bets were placed in hushed voices.

"I now call upon you, conscript fathers, to cast your vote on the guilt or innocence of Gaius Numicius in the matter of interfering with another man's rights to his property by commissioning forbidden curses within the sacred city limits and supporting illegal *magia*. On the matter of imprisoning a fellow citizen and causing him bodily harm, I will remind you that no formal allegations were made according to due form, and therefore they are not for your consideration. The formula chosen for this trial dictates a closed ballot. You will now be handed a wax token, upon which you shall carve your vote and cast it into the basket."

"Ahem!" He was interrupted by a juror.

"What is it now, Sulpicius? You know the drill," Ampius addressed the one who spoke.

Sulpicius stood up. He was seated at the front row of the jury benches and by his hair he appeared to be the oldest of them. In a calm and clear voice, he said, "Surely, O Ampius, you meant to declare the voting on the guilt or innocence of Gaius Numicius *and* Gaius Hirtuleius Ambustus."

"What? Where did that come from?"

"When we were chosen for this duty all those weeks ago, both were named as defendants."

"But he's dead!"

"Nevertheless," Sulpicius insisted, "the jury would like to vote on both."

From then on, it was a foregone conclusion. Over the loud murmuring of the gathered spectators, Ampius ordered his court slaves find another wicker basket. It was put on the table next to original one. Each was marked clearly in white chalk upon black plaques hanging on it — G. *Numicio* for Numicius, and G. *Hirt Ambusto* for Ambustus.

The jury were issued two wooden tablets each and given time to mark an A or a C on the side with wax. All spectators with monetary interest in the proceedings hastily and loudly bore down on their bookkeepers, demanding a readjustment of the stakes in the voting outcome. The bookkeepers, now the results were obvious, were doing their damnedest to forestall financial ruin.

A lively debate ensued, resulting in a few split lips and bloodied noses. Ampius roared at the crowd demanding a respectable silence, then sent a few of his bodyguards to break apart the worst of the altercations. When a semblance of order returned, he ordered the jury to cast their ballots.

In a single file, they walked past the table and put a tablet in each basket. The court officials then took the baskets and counted the votes. The tally was handed to Ampius on a sealed wax tablet.

To this day I know not who came up with the idea. Was it one of the jury looking for a weasel's way out of condemning Numicius while keeping some semblance of personal *dignitas*? Was it Numicius, uncertain about the results and fearing exile, paying Sulpicius to suggest it? Was it Cicero, afraid in his old age and semi-retirement to lose a trial to a young upstart and seeking a way to protect his name? In all the quiet conversations I held later, those close to the case either professed no knowledge and no involvement in this or were too quick to take the credit for that brilliant idea. I could never find the originator of it.

When Ampius read the tablet and announced the results there was no doubt in the mind of anyone present about the outcome. Ampius cleared his throat. "Fifty-one votes condemning Ambustus. I hereby pronounce an *aquae et ignis* interdiction against him. All citizens are to deny him — should he be found still alive — or his shade, since this is just about as silly as it gets — food and fire within eight hundred miles of Egretia. I doubt his *lemur* needs the time to put his earthly affairs in order before departing our city, so I waive the traditional *triginta dies*. ~~The prosecution may seize his estate immediately without the~~ need to wait thirty days. If his heirs object," he added in a mutter, "it is not going to be in my court. Now for Gaius Numicius." He made a theatrical flourish of consulting the tally again. "The votes sworn by the jury are fifteen *condemno* and thirty-six *absolvo*. I therefore hereby pronounce him absolved of all guilt and free to resume his life. Clerks, please record the verdicts and file them in the temple of Saturnus. This concludes the trial."

***

The crowds dissolved into groups, talking excitedly, chasing down bets with suddenly absent bookkeepers. This turned out to be the best show in town, a trial the likes of which no courtroom pundit could remember. Exiling a dead man's shade was certainly an interesting precedent. I was willing to stake that in the days to come a lot more people would recall having been there than actually were present.

Numicius and Cicero were celebrating their victory. Technically, Numicius had sold out his client to save his own skin. I hoped his other clients would take notice and think about it when considering their own funerals. Yet, I doubted they would. Memories are short and the men who swore their allegiance to him were motivated more by money and other immediate earthly benefits. A dead man's opinion mattered little.

Our party was slowly getting over the shock of the results. Everyone was talking at once, unable to contain themselves. Aquilius was both impressed and outraged at this precedent and Valerius was working himself up to declare a moral victory. Cornelia was busy chatting to anyone who would listen, how she would chase down every woman in town till she found out whose husband came up with the scheme.

Valdrius detached himself from the other gossips and walked over. He clapped Aquilius on the shoulder. "Don't be discouraged, young man. You did brilliantly well, going up against Cicero. It's been years since anyone came close to threatening his courtroom supremacy like that. The results are obvious to all who watched."

"Quite right, quite right. I see a bright future for you," said Statilius, who followed his inseparable companion. This encouragement from the Forum gossips was enough to push both Aquilius and Valerius into the moral-victory high-ground they desired.

"At least my good name is restored," said Valerius. "Spread the word, my good men, that I am a decent landlord in need of decent tenants. I shall now take the opportunity to renovate those *insulae* and make them a dwelling fitting the best of our citizens."

I tuned him out when Araxus walked up to me. He leaned close — too close — and whispered, "The gladiatrix should not fight the dwarf. It's just not right. He only has one arm!"

"Sure, friend, whatever you say," was all I could think to respond, perplexed as much by his enigmatic left eye as by his words.

"Ah, you'll forget it by the time it matters," he shook his head sadly. His eyes flashed, changing colours, even the black one washing out into a dark green. He smiled brightly and said, "Anyway, jolly good show today. Your testimony was brilliant. Top-notch oratory. I'm glad those tutors your dear departed father paid for left their mark. It was you who forced the defence into this chicanery, this weaselling out of an honest vote."

"Thank you kindly," I replied.

"No matter. Your star will continue to rise. You'll become a much sought-after witness, I predict. Just remember your old friends when you need some help. I shan't let you down, ever again."

That memory was a bit too much for me to bear right then and I dismissed him and walked away.

As though on cue, I bumped into a smiling Aemilia. "It's a shame my uncle won't receive sufficient compensation, but he won't feel it long. He's got enough money and properties. He's already planning how to maximise usage of his now-empty *insulae*. We all know it was your work, both in investigating and in testifying, that gave him this fighting chance."

"Thank you, my dear."

"I would like to think the research you made me do helped you," she said. "That it wasn't just some task you set for me, to keep me out of your hair."

"Have you not been listening to my testimony?" I asked with a smile. "Did you not recognise that the references I used came from you? I could not give attribution to a woman uneducated in the *magia*, of course, but you should know where I got them from and how essential they were."

She blushed and smiled warmly. "We make a good team, don't we? I could keep doing such research for you, help you in your cases. No criminal — whether earthly or from the next world — could withstand us."

The afternoon sun cast golden specks in her eyes and brushed her dark auburn hair with fiery highlights. The attraction was strong — too strong — and I was about to reach out for her, kiss her sweet lips, when Cornelia broke the spell.

"Come, my dear, we should be heading home. Felix, will you be joining us?"

"I should see the *medicus* about my leg," I said, "and it's time to check on affairs at home. I doubt all the bodyguards are needed now that Numicius has got what he wanted."

"You can keep them around for a few more days — the man is vile and vindictive. Either way, we'll soon hold an intimate celebration for the conclusion of the case and some other exciting announcements. Please do come by." She took Aemilia by the arm, saying, "Come now," and guided her away.

I felt suddenly alone, the crowds and acquaintances having drifted away. I looked across the dais and again Numicius caught my eye from the other side. He gave me the most evil of grins, and I swear I could see him mouth 'this isn't over between us' before he, too, walked away.

CHAPTER XLIII

Though it was but eleven days since I — since Numicius — broke my ankle, Petreius was quite pleased with my healing. He changed the cast to tight bandages, renewed the charms he wove in them, and warned me not to get into trouble or do any strenuous activity for ten more days, after which I could take the bandages off and be fit for service.

I assured him nothing would ever make me join the service again and thanked him profusely.

I walked home in the gathering dusk, feeling alien in my own city. Shadows seemed ominous, hiding criminals. Sounds, whether sudden laughter or the scuffling of cats in rubbish heaps, caused me to turn sharply. I hastened my steps.

The alley leading to my home was dark, silent. I unlatched the door and walked in quietly. No lights were lit around the entryway, though I heard muffled voices and saw a yellow glow from the direction of the kitchen. I peeked inside and saw the bodyguards, who were supposed to be at the door, all sitting at the kitchen table and stuffing their faces. Dascha was bustling about ladling porridge and bacon, encouraging them to eat. I hoped Valerius sent them together with a food budget, or by now they would have eaten all my earnings from this case.

Dascha noticed me and said, "Ah, *domine*. Shall I serve you in the *triclinium*? I can have it ready in a moment."

I was yet to see anything that would faze that old crone. "No need," I said, and shuffled onto a bench at the table. "Just get me a plate of whatever's hot and ready."

The guards were tense, seeing the master of the house sit with them in the kitchen, but soon relaxed. I imagined after all this time in Dascha's care, they would not be in a hurry to return to their old duties and regime. Not my slaves, not my problem. I enjoyed the unsophisticated company that night, swapping tall tales about short women, laughing at flatulence, and drinking more wine than was good for anyone.

***

I don't know why I accepted Cornelia's invitation for the celebratory dinner. On her part, I was surprised to be invited at all. On my part, I had a good guess at the torture that would follow. And yet I found myself in her *triclinium* one last time. She wanted to celebrate the conclusion of the case, and like a moth to the flame, I went.

I spent the morning getting washed, massaged, shaved, and put on a freshly laundered tunic. When I arrived, I noticed no signs of the previous dinner party. The floor mosaics, the wall dadoes and paintings, the furniture, all had been replaced, repainted, and redone in a different style.

Cornelia was reclining at the *lectus medius*, the honoured middle couch. With her were Valerius Flaccus and his wife, Claudia Pulchra. On the right side were Aemilia, and a couple who were introduced as Quintus Aquilius *pater*, Aquilius' father, and his mother Caecilia Metella. I found myself on the left-hand couch reclining with Aquilius and man by the name of Publius Clodius, a rather flamboyant senator, brother to Valerius' wife. This brought up the number of guests to the traditional formal nine.

Cornelia had taken pains to ensure it would be a celebratory feast, helping everyone erase the bittersweet taste of the trial results. She was determined to present it as a victory, both legally and morally. Together with traditional dishes for the first course — lettuce and fennel salad with walnut and anchovy dressing, green and brown olives, and quail eggs poached in broth and served with bread — Cornelia had also served a rare and expensive delicacy of oysters with cinnamon. A bit too much cinnamon, if you ask me. I prefer my oysters fresh, with just a touch of *garum* to enhance the natural saltiness. The wine, though, was without fault; some of the best Verguvian wine I had ever tasted.

"I still have not discovered the rat who suggested the double voting," said Valerius. "The *mentulae* at the senate are happy to discuss the trial, but none can tell me where the idea was from."

"It doesn't matter," said Aquilius *pater*. "That yours was the stronger argument was clear. Between the histrionic claims of Cicero on the death of our *mos maiorum* and the bribes offered by Numicius, they still found it hard to give a vote of innocence to a man known for his loathsome character and deplorable business tactics."

"And it's all thanks to your son," said Cornelia. "What a great oration! It will be remembered for generations."

"Thanks should go to my parents, for giving me the best tutors," Aquilius responded modestly.

"Nonsense," was Clodius' contribution. "You've surpassed your teachers. The entire Forum is abuzz with gossip of your marvellous performance. You will have keen eyes on you, expecting great deeds from you in years to come. I certainly will remember you, should I land in legal hot water."

"That shouldn't take long then," jibed Claudia Pulchra, his sister.

The banter and self-congratulations continued till the servants cleared the first course away. I had a feeling Cornelia was trying to build up to something, getting ready to make an announcement. Instead of waiting for it to come, I excused myself to the latrines.

I knew the house well by now, what with the time I spent there as its owner trying to purify it. I did my business, washed hands, came out — and nearly ran into Aemilia, leaning on the wall just outside.

"I can still stop her, you know," Aemilia said.

"Don't do this…"

"She can't force me. If I insist, she'll let me have my way."

"And what way is that? Don't be daft, Aemilia. She has your best interests at heart."

"Best interests? Ha! My best interests would be to be happy!"

"What you think you want will not bring you happiness," I retorted. "It would be better for all concerned if you followed the prescribed path."

"You are an idiot, Felix! We could be happy! You know your feelings — how could you deny them?"

"Because I am not an overly-excited child!"

She slapped me.

Almost without thinking, I slapped her back.

We stood breathing hard for a moment. Then I turned on my heel and walked away.

I reclined back at my couch, drained the wine in my goblet, and called for more. I hated myself for doing it, but I had rather lose Aemilia like this, of my own volition, than lose her in the same way I lost Helena. I could not protect my love when I was young, and if the events of this case had shown anything, it was that nothing much had changed.

The cooks brought out dishes of peacock meat in *silphium* sauce. Immeasurably expensive, it delighted everyone, yet tasted like ashes to me. A few moments later, Aemilia came back as well. Her hair was in its place, her makeup immaculate. There were no signs of what went on between us, no sign of the past few weeks and their horrors. But I knew that no matter her arguments, no matter her makeup — she still had a thin red scar, left by my own dagger as I pried off the malevolent spirit that was choking her. With Numicius all but promising revenge, slapping her away was for her own good.

"Now we're all here and done with horrors, we should turn towards bright futures," Cornelia raised her voice and her glass. "I have some happy news. It is time to formally announce the betrothal of Quintus Aquilius *filius* and Aemilia. The wedding will take place in a few *nundinae*, once we have had the chance to find the most favourable day and to sacrifice to the gods. Let us drink to the young couple's health!"

We all raised our cups and toasted the marriage. A sour feeling that had no place to be there still lingered in my heart. I looked over my cup at Aemilia, meeting her eyes. Unfathomable as women are, I knew the feeling was mutual — an opportunity lost.

EPILOGUE

I always repay my debts.

It was some days before everything returned to normalcy. I made daily sacrifices to my patron goddess Fortuna, swearing to forever trust in her to lead me on the right path. I also sacrificed lavishly to Minerva, atoning for my impetuousness and lack for foresight and beseeching her for wisdom in the future. My family's *lares*, my home's *di penates*, the *manes* of my ancestors, and many more of their ilk got their due as well. I even participated in some of the public ceremonies and sacrifices with a religious zeal I don't ordinarily show.

But there was another, more mundane, debt I had to repay. I made my way down to The Pickled Eel, to share a drink with my buddy Crassitius. When the obligatory small talk was finished — first the insults, then the memories of army life — I enquired after Borax.

He survived.

Slaves don't get first-rate treatment, not even expensive,

well-trained slaves. But the burn damage to his hand and whatever Petreius had done were enough to prevent gangrene.

"I don't know what I'll do with him, though," Crassitius
said. "He's no good as a bodyguard anymore and since he did not
lose his arm in the arena, the ladies just view him as a freak. It's
expensive to keep feeding him when I can't hire him out."

"Heh. Pretty useless to you then?"

"Unless I come up with some use for him. Can't even free
him, he'd still be my liability as a freedman. And I do have the
good name of Crassitius to think of, so I can't just let him starve.
I'll face a mutiny from the other gladiators at my stable. All ready
to die in the ring one second, and then worried for their pensions
the next." He belched loudly.

"I know! What about selling him as a door slave? Only
need one hand to operate the latch…"

"That's an idea! You were always the smart one, Felix.
Too smart, usually. Remember that time the centurion caught
you cheating him at dice and you ended up on a month of latrine
duty?"

We both laughed, drank, belched.

"You know what," I said into the middle of a big yawn,
"perhaps I could even buy him off you myself. Can't afford a
proper door slave, but he'd be able to help Dascha with her duties
too. He could carry more groceries in his one hand than she can
in both."

We haggled.

Army buddies or not, damaged goods or not, drunk and
good humoured or not — Crassitius haggled. It was in his nature.

I ended up paying more than I planned to, but I still had
some tidy profits from Valerius. I knew they wouldn't remain for
long once I had Borax to feed, but it was a price I was willing to
pay.

Crassitius sent a boy, and a few minutes later the ex-gladiator ambled into the tavern and made his way to us. His right
arm was covered with leather straps at the stump and he was still
pale. But the biggest change was in his demeanour. For someone

that large, he seemed to occupy very little space.

"Good news, Borax! I found you a good house and a post as a door slave. Meet your new *dominus*," Crassitius nodded at me.

Borax remained silent and walked diffidently behind me as we made our way up and over the crest of the Meridionali to my home.

"Thank you, *domine*," he spoke suddenly when we crossed a moonlit square. "I shall be the best door slave you ever had. Even with one hand I can make sure no one will come in who you don't want in."

"Oh, about that. You will still be my bodyguard."

He stopped and stared at me for a moment.

"But I can't! Your life would be in danger! Without my right hand I am useless."

"Well," I drawled, "We'll have to see about that."

***

It took some time to get everything organised. I needed to research certain aspects, which in turn required calling favours to gain access to private collections.

While these arrangements were being made, I also called on an old acquaintance from the days I was accompanying my father in the arts and antiques business. Quintus Mamilius had advised him on a few deals where the authenticity of statues needed to be confirmed. At least that was what my *pater* told me — I always suspected he might have assisted in the occasional forgery as well. I guess it takes a forger to recognise another's hand.

Which brings me back to hands. We went to Mamilius' workshop out on the Campus Civicus. Between rough iron hooks and the incantations of those powerful enough to regrow limbs, lie other solutions. When I described what I wanted, he called me mad. I said I'd pay. He was sceptical but acquiesced for my father's memory — and coin.

I told Borax to put forth his hands. He looked at me in

surprise and then obeyed silently. Mamilius took Borax's hand and peered at it, turning the hand and stump gently and muttering under his breath as he examined him.

He called one of his assistants, and together they devised a quick sketch of what they needed. It didn't take them long to assemble a box cut to size and fill it with plaster which they used to take a cast of Borax's left hand. While the cast was drying, Mamilius sketched a holder of leather straps, buckles, and brass studs.

"We have to make sure the ends match, though," Mamilius said. When they came to attach the contraption holding the plaster box to Borax's stump, he flinched at its touch. He said nothing, until Mamilius asked him how it felt.

"I am grateful for my *dominus'* gift to me," was the answer.

"But…" prompted Mamilius.

"I will wear it with pride."

"Does it cause you pain?"

"Nothing I haven't felt before," Borax answered.

"Is it here?" Mamilius pressed his fingertip to the red scar around the burnt stump. Borax blanched and drew a sharp breath, but did not answer.

"We'll make adjustments once we have the final cast," Mamilius said. He turned to me and said, "Come back in a few days. I'll have it ready, and we can fit it then."

We went back to doing the research I needed to complete my scheme. Borax followed me around, not questioning my seemingly unexplainable behaviour. He tried his best to appear menacing while keeping the stump of his right wrist tucked inside his tunic. He wore a permanent scowl and managed to bluster and give the impression he was ready to draw a knife from under there. Standing next to him, though, I could feel him as tense as the ropes of a crane lifting a marble statue. This was in contrast to how I remembered him, always standing in the relaxed posture of a professional fighter.

I got him to talk, and somehow the conversation drifted to his career in the arena. For the first time in days, his eyes brightened and his spirits lifted. We talked about an impressive win he scored and how he was hoping to get into the big leagues one day.

"They said it couldn't be done, but I've gone and done it! My *lanista* almost refused to let me, but I begged him. A *cestus* versus a *retiarius!* Surely no one ever condoned such a fight. Think of it! Him with his weighted net and his trident, and I had only my spiky iron gloves. They thought I could never get close enough to him, that it'd take him a mere minute to turn me into a squid-onna-stick." He stabbed a meatball with a fork and waved it around for emphasis, sending droplets of cumin sauce flying around. "But under my *lanista* I practised with some of the best *retiarii* there ever were. Their greatest strength is their mobility and having the longest weapons of all gladiators. That's how they manage against all those heavy types — run, circle, and stab. But I was lighter, and quicker! I am large, yes, which is why my *lanista* just gave me the gloves. One punch from me, and I could split a *myrmillo's* shield. But, you don't get to win as a *cestus* without being quick. They used to call me The Cleaner, because I used to leave the sands unblooded, my defeated opponents broken on the inside but not bleeding."

He paused to take a swig of his beer before continuing. "So Casidex — that was the *retiarius* — started with the usual. He swung his net, and I ducked, and he swung again. He never could catch me, and I never was where he could poke his trident. All I did was laugh and duck!" And with these words Borax moved his bulk from one side of the table, imitating a fighter ducking a punch. He bumped into a passing barmaid, who nearly lost her balance and the tray of jugs she was carrying. The girl turned to him with a curse on her lips, appraised his bulk, smiled meekly, and moved on.

"Casidex was getting pissed, I can tell you that! He started cursing that we're not there to do some wedding dance, but I just laughed in his face." He grinned showing his teeth. I could see that long-ago fight reflected in the gleam of his eyes.

"He was getting mad and careless. And then I did what

307

I'd been practising for weeks! He tried throwing the net at me not like a *retiarius* should, but like a fisherman. Not using the weights to whip around, but two hands, to spread it. But to do this, he couldn't keep his trident pointed at me. So, I ducked again — but this time forward and under, rather than to the side. I grabbed his trident in my left hand and came up with a legendary uppercut with my right…" He mimicked the movements and his words trailed at the sight of the stump where his hand should have been. He grew quiet after that. We just drained our drinks and kept on drinking without talking for the rest of the night.

***

It was around that time I learnt Numicius had managed to buy an *insula* in a respectable location in the Subvales, demolished it, and commissioned a shrine to Bona Dea in memory of his mother. Seemed as though he hadn't lied in that respect.

This fact did not deter Valerius. It took him some time to craft the perfect speech, though he could not tarry much. He hounded the *rhones*, the *aediles*, the *praetors*, driving his fight against Numicius in the guise of piety. He caused the *galii*, the eunuch priests of the Great Mother, to be banded as a minor college under the *Collegium Sacrorum*, bringing them officially into the fold of state religion. He almost managed to forestall Numicius' temple, citing obscure religious precedents, but Numicius managed to get the *rex sacrorum*, the chief priest, to support him. The gossips took to calling them the Pious Brothers — a nickname which stung and enraged them both.

Mercifully, Cornelia's house and household were spared from further embarrassment or unnatural occurrences. Valerius managed to clear her name, make her appear as a saintly matron — more than she probably ever was — and Numicius had little to gain and much to risk by dragging her further through the mud. All this I learnt from the gossips too, as I kept my distance from both her and Aemilia.

Back to the matter at hand, if you will excuse the pun.

Once I'd read all I could find by knowledgeable sources, once I'd gathered all I needed and drafted all the ceremonies it would require, I wanted to validate my design with the only other person who I knew was mad enough to consider it seriously.

Probably because he was mad by all standards anyway.

Araxus.

I found him at one of his usual haunts. I was in luck — he was in a relatively lucid state.

I explained what I wanted to do and gave him the schematics. He took the scroll from my hand and examined it, each of his eyes reading a different part of the text, a phenomenon I found slightly nauseating.

"Did it work?" he asked me.

"I haven't tried it yet. That's what I came to ask you about."

"It wasn't a question," was Araxus' response. He stared at me. Even just reading the description of the incantation made his green eye grow darker. His brow furrowed in intense concentration and his lips moved more than was required to shape the words, "It… will… work."

"Are you sure?"

His lips moved soundlessly again, till he mumbled, "Your future affirmative."

His temporal grasp was slipping. I hated him. The memory of his failure all those years ago still enraged me. But he wasn't himself, not then and not now. And some of my hatred of him, it was uncomfortable to admit, was reflected from my own failure in the same matter, my own pain. A decade is a long time for such a burden. He was trying to atone, paying a dear price for the help he rendered me in performing the lustration of Cornelia's house. And I was there to make amends.

"Do you need a place to stay?" I asked. "Come live with me."

He stared at me for a while, but the only reply I got was a single tear that rolled down from his green right eye.

After a long silence, I turned and walked away.

He followed me home.

One last thing remained for my plan.

I had all I required. I knew all the words of the incantations. Araxus even helped, in his lucid moments when his speech was — with effort — understandable.

I took Borax with me to the stews of the Subvales, the lower parts of the Meridionali furthest from the bay. I was carrying a rather heavy box, and Borax was growling at anyone coming within three paces of me. In a street stinking with open sewage, I stepped into a shop of sundries, its shelves haphazardly populated by dented pots and stale spices. I walked past the snoozing octogenarian proprietor to a cubicle at the back. The man inside was reclining in a chair, a half-eaten apple in one hand, the fingers of the other picking at his nose.

"Felix! You droopy *mentula*! To what do I owe the pleasure?"

"You finally get your wish, Brewyn. I'm here to commission a tattoo from you."

"So, the ladies have been complaining, *eh*?" he leered at me. "Just hitch up your tunic and I'll prick you where the sun don't shine."

"It's not for me, you dirty minded *verpa*. It's for him," I jerked my thumb at Borax.

Brewyn appraised him up and down. "Why, Felix, I never knew you swung that way."

"*Fellator asini*, Brewyn, just shut up and listen." I explained to him what I wanted him to do.

He whistled softly. "You're one crazy *matris futor*. Are you sure it will work? Otherwise you'll be torturing your poor boy here."

"*Mentulam caco*, of course I'm not sure. Can you do it?"

"Yeah, I can do it. Let's start."

Brewyn had Borax sit in the chair and handed him a piece of wood. "Bite on this."

Borax puffed up his tattooed chest, almost completely covered with blue woad in intricate designs. "I've had plenty done," he said.

"Not like this. This isn't going to be your regular tattoo. This will hurt more than when a gap-toothed whore bites your balls."

Brewyn took out a special set of needles. Not the fine fish-bones he normally used, but very fine needles made of shards of glass-like obsidian held in copper. He started to mix the inks needed. Not woad, but black squid ink mixed with exotic components my research indicated would be required. It resulted in a gold-flecked, foul-smelling, glistening black emulsion.

I unwrapped the straps from Borax's right stump. "Don't be a hero, now. Bite the wood."

He was bent on impressing me but did as he was told.

"Ready?" Brewyn asked.

Borax nodded.

"Ready," I replied.

Brewyn dipped the tips of the needles into the unguent he made, took hold of Borax's arm, and with a swift motion pierced the skin of the scar. Borax turned white and grunted. By the fifth stroke, a scream escaped his lips. As Brewyn continued to tattoo his stump, putting more force into working the scar tissue, Borax screamed.

And screamed, and screamed, and screamed.

I did my part. I opened the box I brought and took out the assorted paraphernalia. Nestled in straw at the bottom was a shining metal sculpture of a hand. It was the twin of Borax's left hand, inverted so that it became a right one.

I chanted. I used some of Brewyn's ink to trace runes that Araxus helped me etch into the base of the hand. I summoned the power and focused it in there.

When Brewyn finished the tangled and twisted pattern that stretched from the now-bleeding stump to Borax's elbow, I was ready. I slid the metal sculpture onto the stump. Mamilius had matched them perfectly. I held them in place with my left hand and with my right took a stoppered jar. I flicked the seal with my thumb and poured the contents on Borax's arm where the metal met the skin. It contained blood squeezed from lizards that shed their tails and essence of starfish as the main ingredients. It sunk into the fresh tattoos and ran along them to the grooves in the metal hand, the creases and wrinkles of the mimicked skin as well as the symbols of power at the base of the wrist.

Brewyn and I stepped back. Borax was flushed, breathing hard. The sudden silence was deafening.

"Try it," I said. "Lift your hand."

For the first time since we started, Borax turned his head to see what we had done. He lifted his arm — and the metal hand came up with it, firmly attached.

"Now flex your new fingers."

Borax kept staring at his new appendage. After a long moment, one finger twitched. Then two. Then they coiled together, only making a soft clink when they closed on the palm. He kept opening and closing his metal fist, staring dumbly at it.

"You saved my life on more than one occasion. I need a bodyguard, and you are now the best one in town."

Tears welled up in his eyes. "Thank you, *domine!* Thank you!"

"Here, try to use it." I put an apple on the table. "Pick it up with your new hand and take a bite."

Borax extended his hand, wrapped his fingers around the apple, and closed them. Bits of fruit splattered all over the room, juices running down his clenched fist.

"Cack! Oh well, I'm sure Fortuna will find you some nasty people to practice squeezing on soon enough."

I spent nearly all my earnings from this case buying Borax and fixing his hand. My testimony in the very public trial of Numicius had attracted attention, both of potential employers and of those who might seek to silence me. My rising career required a bodyguard as a status symbol and for practical reasons. There was no other I trusted with my life more than Borax, whose new metal hand would defend me well against any danger — bar those dangers that come of affairs of the heart.

ASSAPH MEHR

~ Finis ~

We hope that you have enjoyed this book. If you have, please consider supporting the author by leaving a review on Amazon.com and Goodreads.
There is nothing more important to an author than reviews!

Join Felix and the others in the next instalment of his adventures, In Victrix, *and visit* **egretia.com** *for short stories and news.*

Until then, don't forget about the Bonus Material (which we couldn't possibly tell you about before you read the book) at the end!

AUTHOR'S NOTES

Following are notes about the culture of Egretia and its adaptation from the ancient Roman world, followed by some bonus material that couldn't make it into the story proper. There is also a list of little 'Easter eggs' — obscure references to real-world artefacts and people. These notes are for those who wish to learn more about what goes into the construction of an historical-fantasy world. Please just remember that this is primarily a fantasy novel and do not take it as an accurate reflection of historical reality. I have conflated many aspects from over a millennium of kings, republic and empire. The calendar and gods, for example, reflect the earliest known versions, while the legions and circus games borrow more from the imperial period.

More information about the origins of the concepts and words in this book and links to relevant articles can easily be found on my website (egretia.com) or with a web search. There is only one made-up term, the title of Rhone. I just could not find an appropriate word that sounded good in both Latin and

English and would have the appearance of high rank. When making up the word, I actually went with a more Greek-sounding word, rather than a Latin-sounding one. That is an allusion to the mix of many elements of Alexandria into Egretia, in particular the 'educational' colleges which borrow from the Museon and library.

I have not replicated the notes from Murder In Absentia regarding calendar etc., but have instead made them available on the web together with the complete glossary from both books. I'll only mention that the novel starts in early Sextilis — August, before Augusts Caesar renamed the month — and ends a few days before end of September (with the epilogue going into October). Important days in a Roman month were the Kalends (1st of the month), Nones (ninth day before the Ides, counting inclusively — that is, either the 5th or 7th of the month) and the Ides (middle of the month — either 13th or 15th). Romans counted forward, e.g. three days to the Kalends.

While Romans counted days starting at midnight, they counted hours starting from dusk or dawn. There were always 12 hours in a night and 12 in a day. This necessitated changing the length of hours to match the seasons. When Felix is complaining about walking for "a long summer hour" he is not just being poetic.

Meaning of In Numina

The title of this novel is a play on words. Numina are the divine spirits of the gods (a distinction I chose to sharpen for Egretia probably more than it was in ancient Rome). In Latin, the phrase could therefore mean 'by the gods'.

In court speeches, defence speeches are *pro* someone (as in, Pro Flacco — in defence of Flaccus); however, the prosecution speeches are given *in* action against someone, e.g. In Catilinam. That could make the title mean 'against the gods'.

And then again, the title might remind readers of the opening words of the Catholic blessing *In nomine Patris et Filii et Spiritus Sancti* — "in the name of the father, the son, and the holy ghost" — with spirits (unholy ones, at least) being another part of this haunted-houses mystery.

Marcus Tullius Cicero

No introduction is needed for history's finest orator. Many tomes have been written about his life, his prolific writing, and his influence on law and politics that is still relevant to this day. I shall concentrate here on those aspects relevant to the novel.

Real-world's Cicero was an important part of the turbulent last century of the Roman Republic. Egretia isn't quite ready for those upheavals and is set at a time that corresponds to over a hundred years earlier, closer to the Punic wars. Therefore, while I alluded to some of Cicero's political highlights (such as the Catiline plot), I have made them less dramatic and more isolated. Correspondingly, the Egretian Cicero is an older man, who lived long enough to reach semi-retirement. Things didn't get quite as dramatic and he hadn't made enough enemies to cause his execution. Instead, his life is taken over more by philosophical writing than political or judicial activity.

For example, Felix reads a scroll named *De Legibus Magiorum* — *On the Laws of Magic*. This is a conflation of Cicero's *De Legibus* — *On Laws* — with his philosophical treatises *On the Nature of Gods* — *De Natura Deorum* — and *On Divination* — *De Divinatione*.

Most of the courtroom oratory in the novel is taken from Cicero's surviving speeches. I have chosen essential quotes to capture the flowery language, while still keeping the message clear and concise. Those I mashed up together, and wrote in the specific details of the case.

For the curious, the prosecution relies on *In Verrem* (against Gaius Verres) for the opening bribery remarks, and on *In Catilinam* (against Catiline) for the closing. That last is probably his finest oration, fragments of which survive in use to this day ("Oh, the times! Oh, the morals!"). I only mixed in a fragment from *In Vatinium* — the bit about the entrails of murdered boys

— which fitted this case better, and was too delicious too pass.

For the defence, I have stolen fragments of Cicero's own words from many speeches. Notably, *Pro Caecina* and *Pro Tullio* (opening speech, and first part of closing), and bits of *Pro Roscio*, *Pro Flacco*, and *De Re Publica*.

In particular, Cicero's insults directed at Felix are taken from *In Pisonem*. This speech survives only in fragments, which is a shame — it is one of the most wonderful examples of invective to survive the ages, and a classic study in how to thoroughly insult a man for two hours straight. I have tweaked it lightly for added alliteration ('comatose cattle, foetid flesh,' rather than the original translation of 'senseless cattle, rotten flesh'), because I think this captures better the essence of the creative insults Cicero came up with. He also uses the term *saltatrix tonsa* which finally breaks through to Felix. Literally, this means "shaved dancing girl" and a more modern translation might be "drag queen".

I used the names of other real-world ancient personas — Catullus, Appuleius Diocles, Iamblichus, Cato the Elder, et al. More on those in the notes below. Cato the Younger, a contemporary of Cicero who held uptight, moralistic, hard-nosed attitudes, served as inspiration for Valerius' character.

Law and Order

One cannot mention Cicero without touching on the subject of law. While the *Vigiles*, that rudimentary public fire-fighting and policing service, come from later periods in Roman history, most of the laws and legal procedures I mentioned are correct for the Republican era.

The *Vigiles* were not a police service in the modern sense. While they were given a secondary task of keeping the peace (their first duty was firefighting), that task was usually limited to breaking up rowdy drunken brawls. Catching runaway slaves was another secondary task, that they performed with ambivalent attitudes, considering that some *vigiles* were slaves themselves (promised freedom at the completion of six years of service).

Rome (and Egretia) did not have a prison. The *carcer* was a badly maintained lock-up, intended to temporarily detain people. When someone was thus detained, guards were assigned from the college of lictors to prevent them from walking out. Romans preferred either creative executions or exile as punishment. Magistrates (as in, state officials, not in the modern sense) were accompanied by lictors not just as a status symbol but also to have them dispense justice on the spot.

Prosecution was not run by the state, but rather by concerned individuals. That is true for all crimes — both personal and 'national' offences such as treason. An interested individual would raise a complaint in either the courts or the assemblies (depending on the nature of the offence and the era), and on the appointed days speeches would be given and witnesses presented. Rhetoric, the ability to sway the crowds and voters with a convincing speech, played a far larger role in the outcome than legal precedence and procedure. This is what I tried to capture in the legal battle between Valerius and Numicius.

The control of the courts in Rome kept switching between the Senate and the equestrian order. Their structure also fluctuated along the years, with many reforms. It is a subject of many tomes (the Roman legal system forming the base of most modern Western traditions), and is far beyond the scope of this work of fiction. I have simply chosen a form that was appropriate for the time. For the interested, look for the system of *actiones* (singular *actio*) of legal procedure. There were defined procedures and types of complaints that could be filed with the courts. For example, there is the distinction between *in rem* — matters of physical possessions — and *in personam* — actions resulting in damages to a person and his rights. All the other terms used by Aquilius when discussing and filing the case are original terms, though I have used them to allude to the complexity of the legal system rather than specific accuracy.

Another example is the role of Felix in the trial. He is an *index*, an informer (from which we get the modern 'index finger' — pointing at someone in accusation). There were other roles he could have filled, from a fellow *accusator* to a supporting *quadru-plator*. The latter would have meant that he was registered with the prosecution and therefore liable to a share of the estate of the defendant should he be convicted. Hence, his silent chagrin at losing this theoretical bonus.

The *Lex Papiria de dedicationibus* mentioned by Felix to finally push Numicius over the edge was a real law. It was used in the squabbles between Cicero and Clodius, where the latter declared Cicero's house a sacred place to prevent him from rebuilding it following some riots. Similarly, the *Lex Claudia* excluding senators specifically from large maritime commerce and later from general commerce were real restrictions. The *Lex Cassia* to eject offending senators from the Senate was original-ly for those who disgraced themselves and had their *imperium* stripped by a popular vote. Using such laws for machinations and political gain was fairly standard practice, so more than the content of the laws I was trying to capture the spirit of legal manipulations.

Nominally, a trial was supposed to start at sunrise and end by sunset. Often the parties would agree on some of the facts beforehand and only bring the crux of the matter to trial. Adjournments were not uncommon, though, and — in the inter-est of the story — I have set the trial at almost three full days to allow for all the witnesses and speeches. It was not uncommon for speeches to last several hours, hence the need for some limits.

Lastly, I used the modern term 'lawyer' in a few places. It is important to note that it was not a formal profession in Rome and Egretia. Officially, those delivering the prosecution and defence were concerned citizens who rose to the occasion for the common good, without expectation of compensation. In practice, naturally, this played into the system of patron-client, and those involved received indirect 'gifts' for their role in the trial. More importantly, since trials were very public affairs, they did provide the platform for aspiring young men to build a name for themselves ahead of elections to the Senate.

Rights and Women

There is one right explicitly mentioned and one implied in the novel. The *ius imagines*, the right to have ancestral wax death-masks, was granted to those who have reached high public status. There is some debate whether this included consuls only or praetors as well. This is compounded by the fact that in the very early republic, the chief position was actually called praetor, not consul.

The right not explicitly mentioned is *in sui iuris*, 'in its own right'. In the context of Roman society at the time, that right was given to women outside the control of a *paterfamilias*. Nominally, women were always under the control of a man. This was usually their father until marriage, then their husband. In cases where the husband died or the father of an unmarried woman died, this could be an uncle or another senior male relative. In some cases, women were granted *sui iuris*, the formal right to own and manage their own property.

This leads to a greater discussion of feminism and the role of women in society. A far larger subject than can be covered here, but I would draw your attention to a couple of aspects. First, Rome did not have law and order in the modern sense. Though they had a legal system, its use was limited to the rich and politically influential, and enforcement was in private hands of the suitors. Women were excluded from public life in that respect and could not openly participate or vote in senate and assemblies. Naturally, that did not stop some of the more politically-minded women in Roman history from influencing events from behind the scenes. Though we know of them indirectly and incompletely, women such as Clodia, Fulvia, Cornelia the mother of the Gracchi, Servilia, Livia, *et alia* certainly influenced Rome's politics. Our own Cornelia is modelled after them, though of a slightly less flagrant nature, at least than the first two mentioned.

That, of course, pertains to the high-born women that participated in the public life. The situation of the common folk would have been less restrictive. While nominally the concept of *paterfamilias* was prevalent at all levels of society without anyone raising objections (see the note about legal prosecution above), many women would have held jobs and managed their own business — washerwomen, seamstresses, cook-shop owners, etc. And, in the imperial-era case of Lucusta, as a poisoner to the rich.

The traditional language and descriptions of women refer to them in their place (at home) doing their noble tasks (weaving wool). However, women were responsible for the family unit in all things — home, hearth, health. They performed many tasks in and out of the home. The complex issues of gender roles — and how we interpret the surviving evidence, bearing in mind that most writers were rich males — is a fascinating subject outside the scope of these notes. I've tried to capture the essence of both their function in society as well as society's attitude toward them, without letting modern biases affect this overly much.

A last note in relation to women is the ages of the characters. Felix is 34 years old, a man in his prime. Aemilia is 19, an age a patrician woman would have been married already. It was very common for women of the higher socio-economic classes to marry men much older. Aquilius, at 27, would be considered a reasonably young husband — a choice Aemilia can get away with, as her father passed away and there was no need to marry her to one of his peers for political alliances. Cornelia would have married at a younger age as well and had her children soon after. That places her in her early-to-mid forties (Aemilia was not her first child, but the only one to survive to adulthood). Given Cornelia's family background and the death of her husband, she managed to acquire a formal status of *sui iuris*. She is rather happy to take lovers but in no rush to marry again and come under the rule of another man.

Lead and Curse Tablets

When Felix describes the uses of lead around Egretia, he is referring to our historical usage of the metal. Beyond the more mundane uses such as in ink and cosmetics, or in the ingenious contraption for transporting live fish (a real archaeological find — link on my website), I think the most surprising use for modern readers is the use in food production.

With honey being the only natural sweetener available, grape juice or other fruit juice was boiled down in pots and kettles to what was referred to as *defrutum* or *sapa*, depending on the level of concentration. The result was used mainly as a sweetener and wine preservative, as Romans liked their wines sweet and spicy. It was also added as a general sweetener in other dishes. The kettles used in *defrutum* production were made of bronze, copper, or lead. Some enterprising Romans realised that using lead pots created a sweeter end result, and after some experimentation found out that lead acetate could be used directly as a sweetener. Hence its name "sugar of lead".

More relevant to our story are the curse tablets. Those were prevalent throughout the Mediterranean region for centuries. Though other forms, such as clay, are known, lead was the best surviving medium. From Athens, we have examples of their usage in courts, where someone has requested that the opposing counsel falter, and from Bath in England we have all those wonderful examples of the common people seeking justice against those who pilfered their towels.

Naturally, in the construction of a fantasy world those curse tablets assume actual effectiveness. Similarly, the *voces mysticae* — words and symbols not related to any known language — that we find on real-world examples become magical symbols and words of power. I did try to maintain their spirit, with various daily usage and supplications to the gods as the driving force.

Gods and Religion

The curse tablets provide a segue to the other important thread of the novel, the relationship of religion and magic. In a world where wizards can call on the power of nature and rain fire on people, it is hard to argue with the existence of the gods. Not that Romans ever argued such existence. In fact, early Christians were named 'atheists' because they did not have a proper multitude of gods. For Romans, gods were to be found everywhere, controlling and influencing every aspect of life. They took a rather practical approach to their gods, though, and continually beseeched and consulted them to gain some influence over their lives.

An example is Cato the Elder's *De Agricultura*, from where I took the details of the *suovetaurilia*. It is a mixed collection of notes on anything relating to farm life — from animal husbandry to religious rites and from cooking recipes to advice on handling slaves.

Ancient religion was not the canonical, organised thing that we perceive in modern terms. It was a loose collection of temple cults and folk lore which varied greatly between people, regions, and time periods. Hence, the often seemingly conflicting multitude of gods and goddesses might perform very similar functions.

When looking at Roman religion, some of the core terms that can be used to describe it are as pervasive, performative, and contractual — gods are everywhere, with great to minor deities influencing everything, and there is an emphasis on ceremonies, some of whose origins were lost in time. Essentially, one continually bargains with gods through ceremonies, and their favour or displeasure evident *ipso facto* them granting the desired result. It is this spirit that I tried to capture in the novel.

Of the gods mentioned in the novel, one can draw the distinction between the major and minor ones. The main gods mentioned — such as Iovis Pater (the early name for Iuppiter, or Jupiter), Mars, Ianus (Janus), Fortuna, *et al* — were those that influenced the big world, the city. But as Felix describes, the divine spirits did not end there. While it is often hard to gauge exactly how the 'average citizen' would have viewed things from the fragmentary sources we have, there is enough evidence to show the pervasiveness of divinities around the home. The three gods of the doorway are mentioned by St Augustine in the Christian polemic against the 'multitude of gods,' and the list of gods involved in conception and childbirth Felix rattles off is indeed only a small fraction. It's not only we who often have only the name and some vague conjecture on role and origins — some of those were lost to the Roman themselves in later years. Religion has mutated and evolved in the thousand years from pre-Roman pastoralism to Christianity.

The household gods — or *dii familiares* — were a class of ancient deities involved in domestic affairs. These originated around ancestor or animistic worship and were concerned mostly with protection of the living 'little universe' of the home. The city itself had its version of them, public *lares* that fulfilled the same protective function for the whole.

The Romans recognised several broad classes of these: the *di penates*, or gods of the pantry; the *lares*, or guardian deities of places and many other domains; the *manes*, representing deceased ancestors; and the *genius* of the paterfamilias, the singular guardian angel (for women, the *Juno* spirit). Each family and place had their own set and when a family moved, some went with them while others were bound to the house. It was the responsibility of the paterfamilias to maintain proper worship of these gods, and in return they granted protection and success for the household. The other important deity in this regard was Vesta, goddess of the hearth. Though her public worship centred on the Vestal Virgins, the women of each household maintained their own ceremonies.

Which leads us to the female divinities mentioned in the novel — Bona Dea, Maia, and Magna Mater. Maia is an archaic Latin goddess of growth. She was later conflated with the Greek Pleiad of the same name, with Terra (Earth), and with the Bona Dea. The Bona Dea — good goddess — herself is a bit of a mystery as well. Possibly imported to Rome during the early republic, she was at times identified with Maia, Cybele, or other female divinities such as Ops and Ceres. Cybele, whom the Romans named Magna Mater — great mother — was an import during the Punic wars, which would make it a relatively recent event in Egretian history. Originating in the east, her statue — made from meteorite stone — was brought to Rome due to an ancient prophesy in the Sibylline Scrolls. It must have worked, as Rome came out victorious of the Punic Wars.

All this leads to an obvious confusion to the modern reader, with their expectation of well-defined gods and domains. Mythology was a living thing, evolving over the centuries. People often worshipped in local temple cults, that were only thinly collected into pantheons. I have chosen a simplified, better-delineated definition of these goddesses to highlight the public attitudes to divine beings and worship. Religion was as much a thing of politics as of piety in Rome and Egretia.

A similar evolution and confusion exists with the chthonic gods — Dis Pater, Hades, Orcus, Dea Tacitia, Trivia, Proserpina, etc. Again, I have chosen a simplified version and froze it in time for Egretia. In other cases, such as the Arval Brethren mentioned by Aemilia, I have taken obscure organisations and co-opted them into service of the *magia*.

Other Obscure References

Following are a few pieces of trivia (unrelated to the goddess Trivia, though that's where the word originated), in no particular order.

Fans of Felix will recognise his old mentors, Gordius et Falconius, as my homage to two of the greatest fictional Roman detectives: Steven Saylor's Gordianus the Finder and Lindsey Davis' Marcus Didius Falco. A third detective makes a guest appearance in this book. The medicus Felix relies on to fix his broken leg is none other than the Egretian version of Ruth Downie's Gaius Petreius Ruso. Both he and Tilla are older than in the charming Medicus Roman Mysteries books, trying for a while to build a practice in Egretia before retiring back to the country. Their appearance here is with Ms. Downie's permission and approval.

After Felix breaks his leg and decides to earn some cash by casting horoscopes for sailors, he's relying on the works of Thrasyllus. The real Thrasyllus of Mendes was a friend of the emperor Tiberius and acted as his court astrologer. His son later was astrologer for Claudius, Nero, and Vespasian. It is said that when Tiberius was in exile, Thrasyllus predicted he would later become emperor. Tiberius was about to throw him off a cliff when Thrasyllus pointed at a ship coming into the harbour — a ship that happened to carry the recall of Tiberius to Rome. His astrological text *Pinax* influenced generations of astrologers, though it did not survive.

When Felix meets Aemilia, he tells her the story of Athenodorus and the ghost in chains. This tale of Athenodorus Cananites is mentioned in a letter by Pliny the Younger towards the end of the first century CE. This is one of the oldest known 'real' haunted-house stories. Plautus, another favourite of Felix, uses it as a comedic ploy in *Mostellaria*, and there are earlier Greek plays around this concept. This reference, and the one above on Thrasyllus as well as Cicero's mention of murdered boys, were graciously pointed out to me by Philip Matyszak, whose books on Roman history I cannot recommend enough.

The statue of the boxer at Cornelia's garden, the one later coming to life, is known as *Boxer at Rest*, or *Boxer of the Quirinal* after the location in Rome where it was found. It is of Greek origin and dates to the mid-to-late Republican era. It was carefully buried a few centuries later, which accounts for its amazing preservation. Bronze statues of antiquity were often later melted to reuse the material. As well as its historical significance, the craftsmanship of *Boxer at Rest* is astounding. Pictures of it are available through Wikipedia or the Metropolitan Museum, where it was on display a few years ago.

When Felix passes through the purgamenta, or city dumps, in search of Araxus, he makes a comment regarding "A veritable hill made of shards of discarded amphorae." This is the Monte Testaccio in Rome, containing the estimated broken remains of around 53 million amphorae from the imperial era.

The one at Egretia isn't quite as large yet, but is there to illustrate the demands of a city of a million people — both in consumption and in waste disposal.

Iamblichus, in whose writing Felix finds clues about the 'true' curse tablets, was a late-3rd to early 4th century Syrian mystic, mathematician, and philosopher. He was a Neoplatonian, though followed mainly the Pythagorean mysticism. He was influential on generations of later philosophers.

The dice game Aemilia and Felix play against Crassitius is known as *tali*. Since the 'dice' were made from actual sheep's knuckles, they had uneven sides. The number value was therefore not evenly distributed, which accounts for the different value of throws. Several variations are known or conjectured about the exact rules. This game is well-known all across the Mediterranean and evidence for it can be found in anywhere from crude graffiti to fine marble statues.

The two greybeards in the Forum who provide us with running commentary about the trial — Statilius and Valdrius — are based on the Muppets' Statler and Waldorf. After 'Animal' they were my favourite Muppets. They capture well the public-performance nature of Roman trials.

Though he has no spoken lines in this work, the charioteer that Numicius buys for the Red faction — Gaius Appuleius Diocles — is important to show Felix that perhaps he and Numicius share some things in common. The original Diocles was a second century, Lusitania-born charioteer (modern Portugal), who has gone to earn over 35 million sesterces by winning 1,462 of the 4,257 *quadriga* (4-horse chariot) races he participated in. Translated into modern terms, that would make him the highest paid race driver, and probably athlete in general, of all time.

Some of the ceremonies Felix uses to combat the evil

spirits — clanging black beans, smearing a fish head with tar and calling on Tacita — are taken from Ovid. The juniper smoke to ward off bees is courtesy of Nikki "Bee" Williams — a friend, bee keeper, and fellow horror author. The psilocybe mushrooms are more commonly known as 'magic mushrooms', and their effects as hallucinogens has been known throughout the ages.

One might note that Numicius' ship was rowed by slaves, where the galley owned by Quinctius in Murder In Absentia was rowed by marines. That is a common distinction in the ancient world — navy craft were rowed by free men and citizens, while merchants might employ slaves. The conditions and life expectancy of the two groups varied wildly, as can be imagined.

Lastly, when Felix is relaxing at home — or trying to — with poetry, he is reading the latest of Catullus poems. Those of you familiar with the real-world's poet's work might recall that he wrote them to one Claudia Metelli, born of the Claudia Pulchra clan. Whether this bears any relation to Valerius' wife, is yet to be revealed.

More of Felix
Felix and the others will return in the next novel in the series, *In Victrix*. Please visit http://egretia.com for more information, including short stories, news, an expanded glossary and high-resolution maps.

IN NUMINA

GLOSSARY

Aedile one of the civil servant posts in the Senate (as opposed to the *collegia*). Aediles were responsible for maintenance of public buildings, regulation of public festivals, and enforcing public order.

Amasiuncula loved one, darling.

AUC or Ab Urbe Condita literally "from the founding of the city." This is the counting of years in Egretia.

Auctoritas a measure of personal public standing and influence. While it's the basis of the English word 'authority,' the *auctoritas* of a person stems rather from the respect of his colleagues and his clout and ability to influence others to his opinion, rather than out of any official role. Compare with *dignitas* below.

Aqua an aqueduct (literally, water).

Aqua Sextiae the main aqueduct of Egretia, bringing fresh water from six sacred springs in the foothills on the mountains to the south-west, and cascading them throughout the city.

Augur an *incantator* specialising in augury, the branch of *magia* concerned with divination, prognostication, and clairvoyance.

Aureus a gold coin, worth 25 *denarii*.

Avia grandmother.

Avrilis the second month of the Egretian year — our April.

Bireme a war galley with two banks of oars.

Bona Dea the Good Goddess. Concerned with chastity and fertility amongst women and the health and protection of the city's citizenry at large.

Cack shit. Not proper Latin (which would be *cacat*), but I like the four-letter expletive nature of the word.

Campus (pl. *Campi)* a flat expanse of ground.

Cara darling, a term of endearment. Literally precious or expensive.

Century the base unit in the legions, 80 fighting men and 20 non-combatants. Six centuries make a cohort, and ten cohorts make a legion. Each group of eight soldiers in a century tent and mess together and have a mule cart and non-combatants assigned to them.

Centurion the commander of a century (see above). The most senior and able soldier. Their ranks do not correspond to the modern non-commissioned officers. Rather, centurions were the effective field commanders, while the general with his legates and tribunes were the strategic and administrative leadership. There were some 60 *centoriones* in a legion, ranked by seniority within each cohort and across the legion.

Cestus a gladiator trained to use his fists. In fights they usually wore spiked brass gloves.

Circus the arena where games and races were held.

Citocacia stink-weed, a mild insult.

Client in the Egretian social order, a client pledged himself to a patron. His oath (which varied in formality across the ages — in Egretia it was more formal) was to serve the interests and wishes of his patron and in return was granted favours and assistance. As examples, the obligations could be to vote according to the patron's wishes or fulfil other tasks, and the favours could be money or assistance in being elected to public office. As people's standing rose, they acquired more clients — even though they might still be clients of patrons further up the social order.

Clivus (pl. *Clivii)* a slope of a hill or mountain. Often used as part of a street name, for streets on a steep incline.

Cloaca (pl. *Cloacae*) sewer drains. The Cloaca Maxima are the main sewage lines that run under Egretia.

Cloacina the divinity of the sewers, and also the protector of sexual intercourse in marriage. Her shrine was next to the Forum, close to an intersection of the major sewage lines.

Cognomen the third name of a person, often a nickname but also inherited to distinguish branched of the same *gens* (see below). For example, Spurius Vulpius Felix, the *cognomen Felix* means lucky, and was given to him; with Lucius Valerius Flaccus, the Flaccus *cognomen* is inherited from father to son in the ancient *gens Valeria* and their branch would be known (in plural) as the *Valerii Flaccii*.

Cohort the main tactical unit of legion. Composed of six centuries, or about 480 fighting men and 120 non-combatants at full strength.

Collegium (pl. *Collegia*) a college, an association. In Latin that would have been a loose association of artisans, a sodality rather than a medieval guild. In Egretia, however, I have chosen to mix in elements of the Greek / Alexandrian 'museon' — to also become an institute of knowledge, learning, and teaching, as well as administration.

Collegium Incantatorum college of sorcerers.

Collegium Mercatorum college of merchants.

Collegium Militum college of soldiers.

Compitalia the annual festival in honour of the *lares*, those of the home, of the crossroads and the public *lares* of Egretia.

Cunnus (pl. *Cunni*) cunt.

Consul the highest-ranking elected public official. They were the executives of the senate. Two consuls were elected yearly and served from one Martius to the next.

Contio an assembly, often of a political nature.

Convivium a banquet or feast.

Corculum darling, sweetheart.

Curia an assembly hall, usually in reference to the senate.

Cursus Honorum the "course of offices", a sequential order of public offices held by aspiring politicians. In Egretia, it includes public offices within the senate and within the colleges. One could be a *quaestor* in a particular college and use it as an admission for the Senate, rather than stand election as a public *quaestor*, however that was not common due to the restrictions on senators.

Curule (Latin: *curulis*) relating to the imperium-holding magistrates of Rome. The curule chair (*sella curulis*) was a symbol of that power.

Decury in the senate and other organisations, a division of ten men. Interestingly, the cavalry used it as well, but not the legions (where men tented and messed in groups on eight).

Deliciae meae my darling.

Denarius (pl. *Denarii*). A silver coin, worth four *sestertii*. One of the most common denominations. Accounting was done in *sestertii*, but since they were heavy bronze coins most people preferred to carry the smaller, silver *denarii*.

Dignitas a measure of personal public standing. More than just dignity, it is the person's worth in the public's eyes, a measure of his reputation for moral fibre. It was the most important aspect for any one in public life, such as senators and other on the cursus honorum. Compare with *auctoritas* above.

Dis god of the underworld, both richness of soil and minerals and of the dead. Also, the name of the place where the shades of the dead go.

Dominus master. Female: *domina*. When addressing a person, the case *'domine'* is used.

Domus a private house or home, usually in the city. Country houses are usually referred to as villas.

Elementor an *incantator* who specialised in manipulating the six elements of *magia*.

Endotercissus a day "cut in half," where sacrifices were prepared in the morning and offered at night, but business was permitted around midday.

Ephemezica a large city-state in Hellica. Refer to the maps in the beginning on the book or online.

Fascinum the embodiment of the divine phallus. Charms made in the image of a winged penis and testicles were used to ward off the 'evil eye'.

Fellator one who performs oral sex; used as verbal abuse. Felix's favourite curse, *fellator asini*, is one who performs oral sex on donkeys.

Felix lucky.

Forum a public open space. Most *fora* (plural) would have had many public structures associated with them — from small buildings to large temples on the edges, with altars, fountains and plinths for statues in their midst.

Forum Bovarium the meat markets.

Forum Egretium the heart of Egretia, where the main buildings and administrative centres lie, and where the population gathers to hear and discuss the news.

Forum Frumentarium the grain markets. In Egretia it also doubles as the Forum Holitorium — the vegetable and oil markets. This is where the public grain was stored; private merchants might have had other stores and shops throughout the city.

Forum Piscarium the fish markets of Egretia. Considering the maritime nature of the Egretian culture, fish and fish products (like *garum*) were a significant staple.

Garum fermented fish sauce. In Rome, this was done with fish meat and guts fermented with salt. The addition of cuttlefish and the distinction of grades based on it is a purely Egretian thing. (There were undoubtedly different grades in Roman times, but the terms I used were more likely in use during different historical periods rather than relating to quality.)

Gens (pl. *Gentes*) a family or clan, all the members sharing the same *nomen gentilucum* (second name). For example, Lucius Valerius Flaccus belongs to the *gens Valeria*.

Gladiator a combatant that fought for the entertainment of the crowds. Mostly men (though there were women gladiatrices and other curiosities), mostly slaves or criminals given this as a choice to exile or death. Because of the high training costs, gladiators had to want to become one, and fights were rarely to the death. Traditionally gladiatorial games were part of funeral rites, but in recent years as their popularity grew any excuse would do to display a good match.

Some gladiators achieved celebrity status, particularly

later in the republic and into the empire period, and were used for more private entertainment. Those that survived five years, or thirty matches, were usually given their freedom, though they suffered from social stigmas (as well as any other debilitating injuries they may have sustained).

Gladius the short straight sword favoured by the Egretians.

Haruspicy the art of reading fortunes in animal entrails. The person practising it is called a haruspex.

Hellica a region to the East of Egretia known for its high art, philosophical predilections, and almost constant warring between its city-states. Named after the river Helios and the largest city-state of the region. Corresponds to our ancient Greece.

Heraclion a large city-state in Hellica, sitting on a promontory on the eastern gate to the Bay of Euxis. It is the on the border between the primarily Egretian regions to the west and Hellican regions to the east.

Ides the middle of the month, either the 13th or the 15th depending on the number of days in the month. See notes.

Imago (pl. *Imagines*) a wax mask of dead relatives, mounted with a wig and painted to look lifelike. Only those who have achieved public *nobilitas* — i.e. attaining high office in the senate or priesthoods — were allowed to have their likeness made into an imago. Copies were kept by the man's descendants and paraded in funerals and special occasions. Needless to say, women were almost never granted the *ius imagines* — rights to have an *imago* made for them. They were part of the ancestor veneration that was pervasive in Roman and Egretian cultures.

Imperium the power to command. This was the province of the senior magistrates during their year as elected officials, and when on extended commissions.

Insula (pl. *Insulae*) literally an island, it was used for the large tenement houses. These houses were a single structure occupying a full block, with streets lanes all around them separating them from other buildings. Hence "an island."

Irrumator the receiver of oral sex. Used as verbal abuse less offensive than 'Fellator' (q.v.).

Intercalaris the period between the last month of the year, December, and the first month of the new year, Martius. It was of variable length, 60 or 61 days.

Kalends the first day of the month.

Lanista the operator of the gladiator school. Not necessarily the owner or trainer of the gladiators, but often so. This position attracted a social stigma.

Lar (pl. *Lares*) guardian deities. Their origin is uncertain; they may have been hero-ancestors, guardians of the hearth, fields, boundaries or fruitfulness, or an amalgamation of these. Houses, families, fields, crossroads and even Egretia itself have their own *lares*.

Latifundium (pl. *Latifundia*) a very extensive parcel of privately owned or leased land, used for large-scale farming (grain, olives or wines) or for grazing.

Legion the smallest independent army unit that can wage a war. Made up of 10 cohorts, or about 4,800 fighting men and 1,200 non-combatants.

Libitina the Egretian Goddess of funeral and burial. Her temple was outside the city walls in a sacred grove. Undertakers had their offices there (or in the street of the embalmers) and were known as *libitinarii*. Her temple held records of all deaths in the city.

Loggia a covered exterior gallery or corridor usually on an upper level, with the outer wall open to the elements and the roof supported by a series of columns.

Ludi games or festivals. Traditionally games included chariot races and wrestling or boxing matches — but not gladiatorial games. The gladiatorial games were reserved for funeral rites, but in recent years they have started to make it into general games under the flimsiest of excuses, as a way for politicians to attract the crowds.

Ludi Egretani the "Egretian Games," occurring yearly on September 12 to 14, similar to the early *Ludi Romani*. Chariot races were the crowd's favourite part of the entertainment, with competing factions based on colours (red, white, green, and blue).

Ludi Florae known also as the Floralia, these games are dedicated to the goddess Flora. The festival had a licentious, pleasure-seeking atmosphere and featured many theatrical performances

Ludi Megalenses see *Megalenses Ludi*.

Magia the magical energy that permeates the world of Egretia. Its nature is a topic much debated amongst the philosophers.

Magia Elementi elemental magic, according to the classification of the Collegium Incantatorum. There were six recognised elements.

Magia Inanitas magic of the empty spaces, the void. The most mind-bending of all branches.

Magia Vita life magic, pertaining to living things.

Magia Vita Terminalis magic of the end of life, a proscribed branch of the *magia vita*.

Magister (pl. *Magistri)* expert.

Magistri Carneum literally "masters of the flesh" — doctors and healers, but with education in *magia vita*.

Magna Mater the Great Mother. A goddess that was not native to Egretia but imported after some conquests in the east. Her original name was Cybele and she was initially identified with the Bona Dea, but later grew a cult of her own amongst the high class women of the city.

Maior greater; when applied to siblings it means the elder.

Martius the first month of the Egretian year. Begins on the first new moon before the spring equinox. Named after Mars, the god of war and an agricultural guardian, for the beginning of the agricultural and military campaign year.

Mater mother.

Megalenses Ludi the Megalensian games, dedicated to the great mother. These were not the usual circus games, but contained many theatre plays and much dining and carousing in good nature. The great mother herself was an import to Egretian culture from the East. Her priests were eunuchs and her main worshippers were women.

Mentula (pl. *Mentulae*) the primary word for a penis. Used as an insult would translate to prick, dick.

Mentulam caco a common form of verbal abuse. Literally "I shit on your dick".

Meum mel darling, a term of endearment. Literally "my honey".

Minor lesser; when applied to siblings it means the younger.

Moecha a slut.

Mons a tall hill or a mountain.

Montes a mountain range.

Mos Maiorum the unwritten code. How things are done, from private life to public office. Literally, the established custom (*mos*) of the ancestors (*maiores*).

Mulsum wine sweetened with honey; often spiced as well.

Myrmillo (pl. *Myrmillones*) a heavily armed gladiator bearing a large square shield in the left hand and a metal sleeve and *gladius* (short sword) in their right, and a metal greave on their left leg. Their biggest distinction was the heavy helmet stylised as a fish head.

Nefas religiously forbidden, against divine law.

Nefastum scientiam forbidden or dangerous knowledge.

Nobilitas "the known," those people and families who have achieved a public standing. Even though this is the root for English 'nobility' the term is not quite the same and does not equate with modern perception of aristocracy. A family would be considered part of the *nobilitas* when a member achieved fame, became a *nobilis*. Usually this meant by attaining a consulship, although other cases are known. Contrast to *Novus Homo* below.

Nones the fifth or seventh of the month. See notes.

Novus Homo (pl. *Homines Novi*) a "new man". The first of a family to be elected into the senate and attain a high position (properly a consul, but generally also applies to *praetors* and *rhones*).

Nundinae (singular *nundinum*, but not commonly used) an eight-day interval between market days. The Egretian equivalent of a week. Due the Egretian way of inclusive counting, seven regular days plus one market day make a *novemdinae* — literally, nine days.

Officius the first (lowest) grade of public official within the colleges. It was not part of the *cursus honorum*.

Pater father.

Paterfamilias father of the family, the head of the household. The *paterfamilias* had absolute rule over his family. He could order what each would do and could — in theory, at least — execute them without punishment. While some of the more extreme measures were socially frowned upon, the status of the man as the absolute head of the household was deeply protected by law.

Patina technically a large, shallow pan, it often refers to any dish of eggs and toppings cooked in such a pan. Etymologically the source of the modern Spanish *paella*. The egg dish itself is somewhat between an omelette and a custard, and toppings ranged from nuts and berries, to jellyfish, to sausages and brains.

Pharos a lighthouse. Usually referring to the great lighthouse of Egretia.

Pons a bridge.

Porta a gate in the walls.

Praenomen the first name of a person, e.g. Gaius, Marcus etc. Note that women did not have a praenomen but were named after the *gens* (family name). There were only about 30 odd names, of which about half were archaic and not in regular use. Three names — Lucius, Gaius, and Marcus — accounted for almost two-thirds of the population.

In this book I went with the later spelling of G in Gaius, Gnaeus etc., rather than C (Caius, Cnaeus), and Caeso instead of Kaeso, as the old forms were falling out of favour around the Mid-Republic era, and they are less familiar for modern readers. I did use 'I' instead of 'J' for Iunius (Junius), Iovis (Jove) etc. The sound the letter makes is a consonantal I and using J for the /dz/ sound came much later in English.

Praetor a high-ranking public official, second to the consuls. There were normally six praetors in a year.

Priapus a rustic fertility god, protector of gardens, livestock, and male genitalia. Usually depicted with an erect phallus.

Princeps Senatus the first senator, the leader of the house.

Perduellio high treason, punishable by death.

Pyxis (pl. *Pyxidae*) a small box with a close-fitting lid, often used to store women's cosmetics or other creams and unguents.

Quadran a minor copper coin, worth 1/40th of a *denarius* (or 1/10 of a *sestertius*).

Quaestor a low ranking official. The first rung in the *cursus honorum*.

Quirite the language of the people of Egretia.

Quirites (plural) the citizens of Egretia. Based on the old word for spear (*quiris*), it was used in Rome as well to refer to citizens.

Res magiae literally, "a thing of magic".

Retiarius a gladiator trained to fight with a weighted net and a trident. Their only armour was a padded greave on their left arm. They were highly mobile warriors, and thus often pitted against the heavily armed but slower gladiators. At first it may seem like they were under-classed, but the development of the *secutor* shows that they needed to be better balanced

Rhone a made-up word. In Egretian, *rhonus*. Equivalent to a Roman *aedile*, with the senior rhone of each collegium — the *primus rhonus* — equal to a praetor in terms of social rank, if not civil authority.

Discerning readers will note that this word has a more Greek feel to it than Latin — a reminder of the Alexandrian elements mixed into Egretian culture. The rhones would be a position within the collegia, which in turn are again based on the Alexandrian museon (of which the Great Library was just a part). I mixed the two traditions here, and gave it a fantasy name and spin.

Saltatrix tonsa a "shaved dancing girl" or drag queen.

Secutor a variation of the *myrmillo*, this gladiator was developed specifically to fight against *retiarii*. Wearing essentially the same armour and weapons, their helmets were smooth to prevent the net from catching on them and had only two round holes for the eyes to counter the prongs of the trident.

Semi a bronze coin, worth half a *sestertius* (or 1/8th of a *denarius*).

Sestertius (pl. *Sestertii*) a bronze coin. One quarter of a *denarius*. The price of a good meal.

Sopio a caricature with an abnormally large penis. Priapus is often depicted as such.

Stadium (pl. *Stadia*) 600 feet, or about 180 meters.

Stercus shit.

Sterculius or **Sterquilinus** the god of faeces. Originally an agricultural god of manure, he was later adapted to city life.

Stigma originally (in Latin) a hot mark tattooed (branded) on runaway slaves. In Egretia, it means tattoos of magical power.

Strigil a curved tool, often made of metal, used to scrape dirt and sweat off the body during Egretian baths. A person would have his body rubbed with oil, and then scraped with the strigil to remove the oil and the dirt. Only then would they move to the hot baths to soak.

Stola the female equivalent of the toga, it was the traditional garment for women. Made from linen.

Stultus stupid, idiot.

Sui iuris under her own right. Refers to women who managed to have legal rights for independent living by themselves, without being required to have a male relative act as their paterfamilias.

Tablinum the office of the master of the house. Usually connecting the atrium and the peristyle garden at the back.

Talent a measurement based on how much a man can carry, roughly 30 kg (66 lbs). Often used to measure large sums of money or bullion. A talent of silver *denarii* contains 6,250 coins (equivalent to 25,000 *sestertii*) and would be enough to pay for a cohort of soldiers for a month.

Triclinium a formal dining room, with three long couches arranged in a U shape. The men reclined, while women sat on chairs facing them. Long low tables in front of each couch were set to hold the food and drinks. In recent times and with looser company, women started to recline together with the men as well.

Veneficitor an *incantator* who specialises in the *Veneficium* branch of the Collegium Incantatorum.

Veneficium the study of herbs and poisons, the properties and methods thereof. Part of the classification of magic according to the *Collegium Incantatorum*.

Verpa another insult based on a word for penis, referring to its erect form.

Via a main road.

Vicus a main street.

Vigiles the watchmen in Egretia, tasked mainly with fire-fighting and keeping the public order as a side-job.

Visus verum true sight.

Voces mysticae words not recognisable in any human language. In the context of Egretian magic, there are the words and sounds of power that *incantatores* use to direct the *magia*.

Vomitorium *(pl. Vomitoria)* the hallways leading out of the circuses, getting their names from how people are spewing forth from inside. Not, as some Internet memes claim, a room to vomit in.

BONUS MATERIAL

When I write the stories and novels, I make a point that the antagonists be more than just villains. They are people, with their own lives, desires, agendas — which just happen to be at odds with our protagonist. They have their own stories. And one of the best ways to get to know people, is to let them tell their stories in their own words.

So, without further ado here is what Numicius told me, roughly at the time the novel starts.

***

I am Gaius Numicius. My family is the plebeian branch of the Numicii, not related to the patrician Numicii Prisci. Our family originated in Tusculum, though we have lived in Egretia for several generations. My father was a praetor, and I intend to reach the consulship.

My mother passed away this spring, during *Martius*. A more noble Egretian matron you could not find anywhere.

Devoted to the gods and to my late father, never a trace of scandal associated with her.

I wish to build a shrine in her memory, dedicated to the Bona Dea. She believed in our old Egretian gods, saw their *numina* everywhere. She objected to the rise of foreign goddesses like the *Magna Mater*.

For this I need a sizable plot of land. I wanted to buy a crumbling *insula* somewhere on the outer slopes of the Meridionali, raze it, and build the shrine there as a beacon against the tide of foreign gods seeping through the quarters of the poor. Giving those people access to our old gods, showing them the right way, integrating them into the Egretian life by accepting it rather than diluting it. A worthy legacy for my mother, keeping her shade safe in the underworld.

At the same time, I was trying to get the senate to vote funds for extending the Egretian road from Helva to Arbarica, following my return from my year of praetorship in Arbarica last year. Valerius Flaccus has opposed this motion, notionally on the grounds that public contracts are the purview of the censors, but also attacking me personally, besmirching my good name. While true that I would gain from the improved trade routes that might pass through my rural holdings in the Montes Arborii, the language and accusations he used were altogether too personal. Him, a cynical and impious man, a hypocrite with his own rural estates benefiting from spurious legislation of his cronies, a traitor to his Egretian ancestry, dared call me a *lupae filius* and worse, and bring my mother into his.

I spent the year away in the service of our city, came back to find my mother on her death-bed, and was keeping up with my senatorial duties. Political rivalries aside, insulting a man's dying mother is a step too far for anyone.

It was then that my man Ambustus offered me a way to kill two birds in one stone. His suggestion gave me means to force some public humiliation upon Valerius and his idiotic insistence on rental-properties-only for senators. I shall bring down the wrath of the gods upon his holdings, cause him to appear as a negligent landlord, embarrass him, and also get one of his insulae on the cheap. What better way of getting back at that supporter of foreign gods, than erect a monument to our true divinities on grounds he failed to protect?

Now this G. Hirtuleius Ambustus is a bit of a loathsome character, but if anyone could get Valerius tenants to abandon him quickly and in screams, he's the man. I admit I didn't care to look too closely at his methods — his word that he will make it appear as if the gods intervened against Valerius was all I wanted to know.

This just leaves getting my hands on said *insula* without Valerius knowing. A bit of help from my bankers, a few willing intermediaries, and an agent to approach him at just the right moment. He will be more than happy to sell — not knowing that in so doing he is leaving himself open to public embarrassment. On the one hand, my family's tenets of piety to our original deities would prevail and my mother's memory will be honoured, and on the other Valerius will appear as both blasphemous and inept in the execution of his duties.

All will be revealed to Valerius when I decide it so. I shall give a speech in the senate like never before and will make his humiliation public and complete.

IN NUMINA

Printed in Great Britain
by Amazon

18647506R00212